DATE DUE

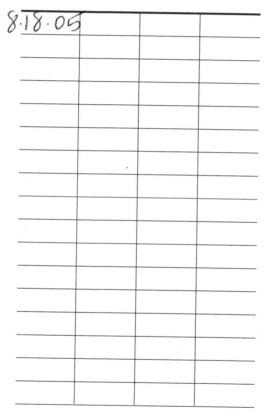

8.18.05			

Demco

The Garden of Reading

The Garden of Reading

An Anthology of Twentieth-Century Short Fiction about Gardens and Gardeners

edited by
MICHELE SLUNG

OVERLOOK DUCKWORTH
New York · Woodstock · London

First published in the United States in 2005 by
The Overlook Press, Peter Mayer Publishers, Inc.
Woodstock & New York

WOODSTOCK:
One Overlook Drive
Woodstock, NY 12498
www.overlookpress.com
[for individual orders, bulk and special sales, contact our Woodstock office]

NEW YORK:
141 Wooster Street
New York, NY 10012

LONDON:
Gerald Duckworth & Co. Ltd.
Greenhill House
90-93 Cowcross Street
London EC1M 6BF

∞ The paper used in this book meets the requirements for paper
permanence as described in the ANSI Z39.48-1992 standard.

Cataloging-in-Publication Data is available from the Library of Congress

Book design and type formatting by Bernard Schleifer
Printed in the United States of America
ISBN 1-58567-508-3
ISBN 0-7156-3263-9 (UK)
FIRST EDITION
3 5 7 9 8 6 4 2

for Lorraine
who cultivates many gardens

Contents

Blue Poppies

"'Who is that person over there digging in that flowerbed?' asked Mother, looking towards the Duchess."

The Occasional Garden

"The one consoling point about our garden is that it's not visible from the drawing-room or the smoking room, so unless people are dining or lunching with us they can't spy out the nakedness of the land."

Flavors of Exile

"Yet there I sat all day, watching the tiny ants at their work, letting them run over my legs, waiting for the pomegranate fruit to ripen."

The Secret Garden

"He grew our humble native plants first of all in order to draw them, and in drawing them he created a new sort of gardening which would affect the taste of a generation."

See No Weevil

"Literally hundreds of flowers and weeds have been named for their discoverers: forsythia for Forsythe, zinnia for Zinn, dahlia for Dahl, fuchsia for Fuchs and so on."

Christmas Roses

"In the autumn she not only raked all the leaves, but she got down on her knees and picked every stray fallen leaf out of the flower beds where they tended to lodge under rose bushes."

The Garden of the Villa Mollini

"He wanted in the design of this garden, to express a simple and optimistic philosophy. He believed that his life was a journey of discovery, revelation and surprise and that it led forward perpetually, never back."

Preface

The very first story was about a garden. Yet granting that primacy, why, then, have there been so few others in the post-Eden eons? For some of us, the odd novel may come to mind—for example, Frances Hodgson Burnett's *The Secret Garden*, Elizabeth von Arnim's *Elizabeth and Her German Garden*, Giorgio Bassani's *The Garden of the Finzi-Continis*—but when it comes to such once notorious but now almost forgotten titles as *The Garden of Allah* by Robert Hichens or Sir Richard Burton's translation of the Arabic classic *The Perfumed Garden*, well, they never had much to do with mulch, anyway.

But, of course, that's not the point. And, in the larger sense, all gardens and all stories do have something important in common: they require an act of imagination

The genesis of this collection can be traced to a pair of splendidly imagined tales by two celebrated English men of letters: "Earth to Earth" by Robert Graves and "The Fig Tree" by V. S. Pritchett. I happened across both of these quite a while ago, but since one's mind always forges links—and since my own prefers its links to take the form of lists, it was when I read the Pritchett that I remembered the Graves and then I began both to pay attention to, and eventually seek out—at first only for my own interest—stories in which gardens or plants or flowers or trees figured.

The list kept getting longer.

What I was always on the lookout for were stories that made use of gardens or, really, the *idea* of gardens. (Of course, every garden created is a story all its own, or actually, a vast collection of stories, the editing of which is never done.) I wanted stories that would illuminate the way these spaces—these echoes of Eden all around us—possess existences running parallel to the emotions of the human who made them, or how gardens and what grow there are perpetually offering up mystery and meaning, secrets and surprises, grief and glory.

The origin of the word "anthology," in fact, relates to gardens. Its coinage lies in the notion of a garland—-from the Greek *anthologia*, which itself comes from the roots *anthos* (flower) and *legein* (to gather)—and the earliest printed collections of stories and poems reflected this. Thus, my garland is in a long tradition, and at the same time fresh: these stories by writers as diverse as Barbara Pym and Stephen King, James Thurber and Sandra Cisneros, Eudora Welty and J.G. Ballard, Rosamunde Pilcher and Garrison Keillor have never been set together before, and yet they fit remarkably well.

Not tidily, I think, for that's not the right word. But well in the sense that the disparate elements of any garden begin, under the oversight of its gardener, to grow harmoniously together and yet always has the potential to display something unexpected, to engage our eye in a new way, to ring a change in our spirit as we observe it.

John Evelyn, the seventeenth-century English diarist, once wrote "The principal Art of a Gardiner consists in pruning." And that an anthologist has to do, as well: after I became launched and once the stories I found began to have some heft as a pile, it was soon obvious that a number of them were not going to make the final cut. "Click of the shears, harsh chatter of hard-billed birds!" That memorable aural evocation of the act of pruning itself came from a discarded story, "Bygone Spring," by that always lyrical garden lover Colette, but it was left behind, with regret, after I decided in favor of an even more sensuous selection from her, "Grape Harvest," with its perfect celebration of ripeness.

L. P. Hartley's "Up the Garden Path" was another reluctantly discarded, along with Virgina Woolf's "Kew Gardens." Reading the parts of the intended whole again and again is what the diligent purveyor of stories does. Myself, each time, I look to measure the strengths and weaknesses of the various pieces, juggling the styles, themes and voices for maximum effect. One wants nothing too common, and so in this way I also found myself weeding out the too frequently reprinted "Rappaccini's Daughter" by Nathaniel Hawthorne, despite having long thrilled to the tragic fate of the beautiful, innocent Beatrice, herself impervious to but as deadly as any noxious plant. Cruelly experimented upon by her father, whose passion is rare botanical poisons, she has been kept away from the world until a young student spies her from a next-door window and is entranced.

But here's a cutting, just to give a taste of its gothic horticultural excesses: "Yet Giovanni's fancy must have grown morbid while he looked down into the garden; for the impression the fair stranger made upon him was as if here were another flower, the human sister of those vegetable ones, as beautiful as they, more beautiful than the richest of them, but still to be touched only with a glove, to be approached without a mask. As Beatrice came down the garden path, it was observable that she handled and inhaled the odor of several of the plants which her father had most assiduously avoided."

(Confession: when it comes to botanical fantasy, John Collier's "Green Thoughts," which you'll find here, is hardly rare—but still, because of this writer's sui generis talent, a far from ordinary perennial.)

And though it's wholly indulgent to mention it—since few are ever likely to come across it or track it down—I disciplined myself to leave out "Hornby Mills Garden" (1872) by the rather bad nineteenth-century novelist Henry Kingsley (brother of Charles, of *Water Babies* fame), much as its sheer eccentricity pleased me. I discovered it by accident, while searching for something else—the very definition of serendipity, of course. However, its leisurely discourse about the changing fashions in mid-Victorian gardens—presented as a philosophical conversation between two gentlemen traveling to Cambridge by train—was in the end a little rambling, and somewhat precious.

It would have sat amid its fellows in these pages like an too-ornate birdbath, I'm afraid.

Not really for the kind of gardeners who crave only hard-core practical texts, this collection's for any sort of reader. In short, you don't need to know your way around a seed catalogue to appreciate, for example, the unexpectedness of Lisa St. Aubin de Terán's "The Lady Gardener" or the tender affirmations of Anne Rosner's "Prize Tomatoes" or the poignant sense of loss conveyed by David Guterson's "The Flower Garden."

As the English writer H.E. Bates once described them, "Gardens . . . should be like lovely, well-shaped girls: all curves, secret corners, unexpected deviations, seductive surprises and then still more curves."

I couldn't have said it better.

The garden is a ground plot for the mind.

—THOMAS HILL
The Gardener's Labyrinth, 1577

The Flower Garden

DAVID GUTERSON

WHEN I WAS YOUNG—seventeen—I had a paper route which I remember as a meandering through early summer, a ritual pilgrimage along old broad streets beneath maples just shooting out a soft haze of fresh buds. With my papers in their drapesack striking off my back and belly, and with a thick load of rubber bands coiled over my knuckles, I'd hike alone across the east side of town, rolling my papers tightly in thirds as I went and tossing them high in delicate arcs to land lightly in doorway's and on porch steps. My route took me where the homes were large and venerable and still, where the lawns were broad and insistently manicured beneath the new-budding maples. Wherever I went, timeworn and meditative old men stood by and watched me behind the glitter of sprinklers, or pulled weeds mutely with a bland concentration, and plump-armed women in cotton dresses and tough black shoes hovered busily under clotheslines, dropping white sheets into deep wicker baskets. From eyes made large and watery by spectacles they watched me half-amused, half-sad and sentimentally, the women with wooden clothespins in their mouths, the men clutching garden spades and weeding forks or lawn rakes. As I walked I would catch the hot fruit sugar fragrance of the pies that baked in their kitchens, or the powdered soap smell of the drying sheets, or the mint-and-tinder scent of lawns mowed too often, and I would hear the lazy clinking of occasional wind chimes. Hummingbirds and blue jays gathered at feeders and a gold light fell out of a blue sky, intensifying, somehow, the stillness in everything.

When the drapesack was empty I flew home, knocked the dust from my cleats, rubbed neat's-foot oil into the soft heart of my glove—checking to see that its webbing was cinched tightly—and then I pulled my cap down low and ran up to Adams Field, where the Cardinals worked out though the late afternoon, where I stretched and warmed up and threw batting practice while the infield dust drifted low across the bleachers and the clean white chalklines were erased by the base runners. The catcher in his shinguards and facemask and chestpad sent me signals from under his well-worn glove. I learned to throw a breaking ball hard that summer; I got my slider down, privately dreaming of a shot at the majors, and followed Whitey Ford, Warren Spahn and Don Drysdale in the boxes. The sun flooded richly over the backstop and diamond, and when I turned to watch the high flies crest in the outfield a halo of pink light engulfed the spinning ball. I saw little else but what could be seen from the pitcher's mound at Adams Field. The view from there was of the game whirling magically around me, holding me delicately in its order and process and symmetry and motion, a fragile web of rule and action— myself at its center—that fended the world off perfectly, thwarted it completely, muted its terror with something as simple as a drag bunt laid neatly out across the infield.

In July new houses were added to my route, and Anna Lewis—who had black ringlets of hair at the nape of her neck, and a pair of dark moles at the base of one cheek, and blue eyes that could not be disturbed by commotion—lived in one of them: a three-story white clapboard colonial near one end of Tullis Street, a tall shuttered house set back behind hedges. Sitting cross-legged on a bench made of cool gray stone beside a sundial on a tapering pedestal she read *War and Peace* and *Persuasion* and *Dead Souls* in its flower gardens which bloomed from May until the end of September with at least sixty species of perennials.

That first day on Tullis Street I trudged up the flagstones beyond the clasped gate in the perfect hedge, wedging a paper together as I went and smelling the honeysuckle, and then in a bend in the garden path I came on Anna, who frowned gravely up at me from out of the pages of the book she cradled in both palms, thumbs weighing the pages down, blue eyes casting me in the mold of intruder, her face tanned a clear sharp brown and the black tangled gloss of her hair framed in yellow sunlight. All around her, in a half-moon surrounding the stone bench and sundial, were flowers in sloped beds that rose to a high picket fence; beach stones lined the garden paths, and shade trees grew where the paths converged, in the midst of the garden at a raised gazebo beside a miniature fountain. With Anna behind me I tossed my paper, lofted it onto the high, broad porch, then turned again and passed her on the flagstones. As I did she glanced up at me, and a smile of amusement formed beneath the frown; her face seemed strong and brown, broad from ear to ear and gleaming as she held her book shut, marking her place with a forefinger. While I watched her black hair seemed to ripple in the sunlight and her wary eyes moved to the book once more. She shook her head once, briskly, not lifting her eyes, and the mane of her hair spilled over her forehead like a woven shield, iridescent and beautiful.

I was struck there and then I know now—the point of something sharp seemed lodged against my breastbone—not so much by beauty or romance but by my need and a nudging dread of it: dread of everything I would have to say and do against my will and yet precisely as my will wished. I knew about war from the baseball diamond—the private, intimate war of pitcher and batter in which subtleties of action are either gratifying or horrible—but not of the inner battle in which, even at seventeen, we recognize within desire the necessity of suffering. That comprehension of possible loss—of compromise, perhaps—and Anna's beauty filled me as I stood there, though Anna was not exactly beautiful—the bones in her face were too large somehow, and the chin a bit too narrow—her beauty had no being unless you were me and the time twenty-one years ago.

"Looks like a nice spot to read," I pointed out, mostly because I was no master of words and yet words seemed necessary.

"It is nice," she said. "It's very nice."

There was that odd frown again, that sobriety and calm. I fell charmed by two traits: good posture and courteousness. They did me in as they had done in boys before me who in time had become husbands.

"What are you looking at?"

"This? *Madame Bovary.*"

She'd said it this way: *Ma-dahm Boo-vah-ree.* I only nodded, though. "I haven't read it," I admitted.

"It's worth reading," said Anna. "I love it."

"That's good," I answered and, because I'd lost the vaguest connection to my natural brand of thought, because my disorientation in her presence felt so horribly complete, I changed the subject instantly. "These flowers are something. They're everywhere."

She looked at me with an astonishment so subtle I noted it only as a refraction of light in her eyes, a drawing inward of the corners of her lips. She looked at me and let her forefinger slide from where all along it had been marking her place in *Madame Bovary.* Anna rose and loosed upon me a grace such as 1 had never witnessed, becoming as she emerged from her seated posture an extension of my pathetic and absurd delusions. All of that hair. The exactitude, the coolness of her back's repose. I noticed, too, the length of her fingers. She was a girl composed of striking odd details. Take them as a whole and nothing matched precisely.

"You like them?" she said.

"Sure. How can I help myself?"

"You do?"

"Of course." But I didn't, not especially. I was lost in a conversation that impelled itself beyond the boundaries of my true thoughts. 1 was merely talking, saying things that did not necessarily reflect what was in my heart, because I wanted to be speaking with her; I knew that much.

"They've been a job," said Anna. "Constant work. But if everyone helps, and you do a bit each day, and don't get behind or let them get ahead of you, you don't notice it. Let things go and it becomes a miserable chore."

"Like a lot of things," I said.

"Everything," Anna insisted. "So many things are like that." She smiled, somewhat sage, and then both of us lowered our eyes.

I can tell you how I left there: light-footed and ecstatic and sick to my stomach all at once, rolling my papers too tightly and conjuring up futures in which Anna and flowers figured prominently. Within that madness I began to run, leaping up stairways and crashing over lawns, flipping my papers at porches breathlessly while the old stony men in their yards looked on in silence, mystified, betrayed by memories that no longer reached back into boyhood.

This is how it went: I would find Anna in the garden almost daily, reading or culling bouquets or pinching the tops of the annuals off between her fingers, and on the days she was not there I felt strongly the weight of time, which seemed to languish between our encounters, and eventually she taught me the names of all the flowers and how to identify them in bloom—gaillardia, sedum, loosestrife, feverfew: one by one I came to know them separately, according to the shapes and colors of their petals, leaves and stems. It was the sort of esoterica I had never had an interest in but which now composed a whole world. We would linger at the stone bench, I would pull my drapesack of papers off, and Anna would put her book down and quiz me on the flowers I had memorized. We worked our way around the paths, kneeling at the beds beside the blooms, and there was something perfect and athletic, rolling, natural, in the way Anna's arms and hands moved through the plants and bushes, pushing stems back or cupping petals while the bees flew in and out among the stalks and leaves. The more carefully I noted her gentleness and the ease of her knowledge the more agitated I became, and I would eye her as I eyed the flowers, secretly. When I found her pulling weeds—balanced on the balls of her feet, crouching and leaning into the flower beds—she looked up at me with pinpricks of sweat along her hairline, where the skin was whiter, and the black tendrils at the base of her neck seemed slick and oily. She rose smoothly and brushed the dirt out of her summer dress—she wore one every day, and they were all many sizes too large—and then she clapped the dust from her hands and stood with her fingertips poised against her hips, looking out over the flower garden. She wore sandals bound behind the ankle and over the flank of the foot with flimsy straps, and her calves shone in the sun and her brown shoulders and neck shone, and she might scratch her throat or cheek thoughtfully, leaving a smudge of dirt behind, and then she moved down the path in that fluid yet controlled way of hers, smooth and long-boned and utterly at home among the flowers. And all of that made me sentimental, which I knew was a weakness but couldn't help.

Occasionally I saw Anna's mother—who was thin and narrow in the face, wore a gardening apron everywhere and parted her hair severely down the middle—moving along the flagstone paths and dragging a hose behind her, or darting about with a can full of fish fertilizer, and whenever our eyes met she smiled faintly and cryptically, but hardly ever said a word to me directly. Anna's father, Doctor Herbert Franklin Lewis, was thick and ruddy and wore coarse suits. On Saturday afternoons he worked in his garden, or sat in the gazebo with his heavy legs crossed and smoked a cigar meditatively, clutching a glass of iced tea between his hairy fingers and whistling unrecognizable tunes. He paid his bill for the newspaper promptly and tipped me twenty-five cents magnanimously, flicking his bow tie and caressing the great red wattles of skin that fell over his throat in separate flaps. He was a large, difficult and serious man who spoke to me often of the vagaries of baseball, wiping his face all around with a handkerchief and exuding a domestic, comfortable confidence. I often think of him now as one of a dying breed of men, who want, really, nothing for themselves, who have effaced their innermost desires without self-flagellation, and—in order to avoid the desperations of solitude—have given themselves over completely to their wives and to their children, and ultimately to their children's children, and done it with a magnificent serenity.

Mostly, though, Anna and I were alone in the garden, and I began to linger there, late for practice. Eventually we lay in the grass that fronted the gazebo, where one day I pressed myself over her at last, locked my forearms against her cheeks and curled my hands through her hair. She was pensive, uncertain, her face paled slightly and silence overtook her; she seemed to be studying my face, searching its features for a truth that stubbornly remained hidden, and her hands only rested below my shoulder blades, waiting and plaintive and still. In time, though, I saw that her eyes were no longer wary, and when I pressed myself over her I felt her back arch and her hips swell to meet mine. It was a form of paradise and I knew it even then: the depth of the sunlight as it glowed through the garden, the bitter, private, fleshy taste of Anna's lips and mouth, the warm abrasiveness of grass against my arms and legs, and the choking scent of flowers everywhere, all around us, shutting the world out forever.

Yet at times, at the core of bliss, I would feel a dread I'd never felt before; I would dream through my ears the clack of a bat, resonant and crystalline, but when I lifted my head up to listen for it, it ceased to exist altogether. My chest tightened, seized up in knots, and Anna peered into my eyes suspiciously: I got up suddenly and hurried away from there with my eyebrows knit and my jaw jutting, saying I was late for baseball practice. And, in hurrying away, alone and loping along the streets effortlessly, I felt a transformation taking place; the further I got from the flower garden and the closer to Adams Field, the more ecstatic I became, until before long Anna seemed like a dream, beautiful and tranquil and surrounded by flowers, but far from the stuff of which my real life was made. By the time I reached the pitcher's mound I felt no dread anymore, could not remember dread at all, and I would throw batting practice with a soaring heart, at the hub of the wheel of the baseball field.

That summer season came and went, the Pittsburgh Pirates won the World Series, the flowers knit themselves up against winter, and everywhere I took my papers that fall maple leaves rattled drily in the windy streets, curled like fists and skating in hordes along the asphalt. With school again—my last year of it—I brought the papers around at three; Anna was no longer in the garden (the air had turned too sharp and cold) but in the evenings I walked up and we sat by the fire with the television on softly and our schoolbooks open. Doctor Lewis hunkered down beside us in his thick padded armchair and eventually slept peacefully with a cold cigar between his fingers, and Mrs. Lewis seemed always to be padding back and forth stealthily behind us in her slippers and awkward chenille bathrobe. The wall clock ticked like thunder and the fire popped and fizzled and Doctor Lewis wheezed through one nostril and exhaled his breath like a clogged bellows, and Anna and I leaned together in the calm purple wash of the television's light, not asleep and not awake, in a trance of sorts until the clock belled eleven and the late-night news came on. With the news Doctor Lewis stuffed and perked up, lit his cigar again and watched in a daze with his arms folded across his belly. "Sports report," he said to me. "Let's all be quiet now."

Irrelevant football scores perhaps, or meaningless trades in distant cities, or the retirement of a gladiator no longer filled with the requisite bravado, the requisite innocence and awe. "He was a superb ath-alete," Doctor Lewis commented on the occasion of some obscure player's slide from the fields of glory. "Absolutely superb. A whiz."

On another occasion, as we sat through a round of advertisements, he waxed candidly prophetic. "Don't be frightened by failure, son," he warned me out of nowhere, from no source—just sudden words spoken boldly. "The world is filled with men who dream of their own importance. No, don't be fooled by the prospect of failure. You've a fine, fine arm. A fine arm. Who knows? The true loss would be in not trying a 'tall, with one so young as you are. . . ." But I don't think he knew how to finish, or even quite what he meant to say. Doctor Lewis was a lost and sentimental man; he went off to bed when the news was done without any further advice. I had the sense that the confusion and mystery he'd left me with were purposeful.

"What was he talking about?" I asked his too-lovely and too-quiet daughter.

"Baseball." Just one word. Then: "You."

We talked for some time, with great seriousness, and about matters better left untouched by children. At last, because she'd implied for so long that the words were really necessary, I told Anna that I loved her. I said it with my head hung and my eyes averted. I remember there were icicles hanging from the eaves; it was just before Thanksgiving and the killing-frost had come and gone—she cupped my face in her hands as we sat side by side on her mother's sofa and—with eyes that were stern, wet and scared, eyes that were serious even about themselves—Anna said she loved me too, plainly and boldly and with too much painstakingly con-cocted drama for me not to feel ill about everything. She waited for me to fill the empty space that followed, to ladle emotion into it—staring at me, and me sick about it, sweating. I felt her breath on my face and smelled her clean flesh and just-washed hair—something like a tremor went through me which I suppressed and concealed while I made a comic face, a parody of lovesickness, a mask as reply, an image of what I kept myself from being or becoming—she didn't laugh and I flicked out the light behind us and kissed her with a force that I wished could obliterate the need for words but which failed to do so; I didn't know what I felt, not really, not well enough to articulate it anyway, and within my excesses of ecstasy and dread there was only turmoil and uncertainty about Anna. I knew that, suddenly, too well.

Later, walking home in the cold through streets that were dark but for the blurred glow of streetlamps, I felt relief at having a bed of my own to return to. At home I stared hard at the ceiling of my room, knowing what I felt and knowing it was a betrayal of feelings I had felt to be true until then: I squeezed my eyes shut until a thousand helixes of light shot forth inside them, and told myself I loved Anna a hundred times until somehow, in the silent utterance, it seemed to have become true and I could finally sleep.

A wave, though, had been set in motion. That winter I waited, mostly, for baseball season; I threw some, indoors, and I gave up my paper route to concentrate on pitching. When spring came my arm was already strong, and I had added a sweeping knuckleball to my repertoire. The ground thawed in a sudden rush of heat, the grass turned green in the field again and the team turned out in the afternoon beneath skies that were turquoise and empty of clouds. In the evenings I often showed up at the Lewises' and met Anna in the garden—reading, as always, at the stone bench—and it was then, in April, that we began to plant a slope of the yard with a few perennial flowers of our own.

I don't remember where the idea came from anymore, but no doubt it was Anna's: she was obsessed with gardening, with gardens and books about people who never lived by people who were no longer living. One evening, simply, I found myself busy with a hoe and rake, rooting up strips of lawn behind the gazebo. We plowed a long crescent of soil to a depth of twelve inches, and shoveled the earth through an angled rock screen, and then we tilled in four twenty-pound bags of steer manure and raked a clean contour into the bed. I spread a thin layer of vermiculite one Saturday and we sat down at the stone bench and made out our garden plan meticulously. We sketched in, along the edge of the lawn, Jacob's-coat, heliotrope, zinnias, astilbe, bearded iris, alyssum, baptisia, forget-me-nots and evening primroses. Behind these we added white regal lilies and pink phlox—late summer flowers—backed by a line of delicate snake-root. Lastly, we filled in with gas plant and butterfly weed and a few day lilies—long-suffering flowers that will bloom even where there is no nurturing and little sustenance.

The sun fell behind the house while we planned and measured, and it became too dark to see our sketch easily. I went home, but all the next week, evenings, we planted with nursery sets and fragile garden cuttings, and raked over a layer of leaf mulch, shredded, in order to keep the weeds from taking root in the dark loose soil. By the middle of April—baseball season—

Anna and I had a flower garden of our own to care for, and sometimes, as I waited to throw from the home dugout at Adams Field, I would wonder suddenly when the first blooms would begin to appear, and I wanted to be there when the buds began to open in the sun below the white gazebo.

That was a surprising, golden season—my last good season, really, in baseball (there is something, though, to be said to the good for my seasons as a spectator since then, too). My arm had hardened over the winter and I'd found my throwing strength at last; I learned to concentrate on the mound, to expurgate the unnecessary clutter of the world at game time, and when I got behind on a batter or had men on base I still kept my focus on the strike zone. I'd come to insist that the enclosed world of baseball protect me altogether finally, and as love became more difficult I probed the intricacies of pitching more deeply and perhaps more desperately, too. As long as the game lasted I was safe, hidden, but when it ended—when the season ended, I feared—I would come to myself in a shudder of self-knowledge and absorb the turmoil of love once more. It was a strategy of disciplined withdrawal, yes—how many athletes are driven by the confusions of their lives to do well at games?—but within it my numbers led the High School League: nine and one, sixty-five strikeouts, a two-point-three-one e.r.a. I pitched eight complete games—two of them three-hitters, three of them shutouts—and *The Clarion*—the newspaper I'd delivered on the east side once—wrote me up in June as a bona fide major league prospect.

Two days after graduation the Kansas City Athletics called. They wanted me in their farm system, at Chambers, upstate, for two-seventy-five a month plus per diem and bus fare and a chance to step right into the rotation or, if that didn't work out, a guaranteed spot in the bullpen. I told them yes immediately, that I would report in three days, and then I went over to see Anna Lewis, figuring in my head as I walked the time it would take before I was pitching in the big leagues.

It was a drowsy hot June afternoon, moist and sweltering and windless. At the stone bench in the flower garden you could smell the thick spice of clove pinks; behind the sundial you could see the red heads of bee balm thrusting up toward the heat of the sun. Anna's book—*Mansfield Park* this time—lay on its spine with the pages open; it seemed absurd and tiresome and petty in light of the Kansas City Athletics. I wound along the flagstones to the gazebo. From there I could see Anna kneeling at the border of our garden, dressed in her mother's dirt-stained gardening apron and with her hair crimped into a loose bun full of black tendrils. Black sprigs of hair fell away from her ears and her neck as she worked with a weeding spade along the sliver of astilbe we had planted, tossing the uprooted weeds behind her with a minute turn of the wrist. They lay limply behind her in a long broken row at the edge of the lawn slope, each with its own root-crust of earth crumbling into the green grass and drying to a listless gray hue in the heavy swelter.

Perennials—even nursery starts—come into their own only gradually, and seldom make much of a show before their second season. Our garden was too new and tender and therefore scarcely in flower; the best we could hope for was a few forget-me-nots and, perhaps late in summer, some pink phlox and a smatter of snakeroot. The astilbe, though, had miraculously bloomed—it was the middle of June already and nearing the solstice; the days had been long and hot and at dawn all month the sudden rains had come—and now they showed their feathery spires in a halo around Anna. I went down the lawn slope and began to gather up the pulled weeds. Sliding along with one knee in the grass and a clutter of weeds dangling from one fist I told Anna about Kansas City and Chambers and the two-seventy-five a month the Athletics would pay me to play baseball. My memory of this moment is clear—my life, in retrospect, seems to have turned on it—Anna rose and dusted off her apron, smacked the dirt from her hands and reached into the pocket of her summer dress. She held the envelope out to me; I let fall the tangle of weeds in my hand and sat back on the lawn to read what it contained.

A school in Pennsylvania—Saint Alphonse College—had offered Anna a full scholarship to study literature: now I knew what all her books fed into. I read the letter twice; halfway through the third reading I knew that she would go, that when the season ended in Chambers and I came home she would be gone, that when she returned the next summer I would be pitching somewhere else again and wanted to, and that this would go on endlessly and we would see each other almost never, until at last we were entirely strangers. I didn't know whether or not this was what I wanted, whether dread or ecstasy ought finally to be the state of things; I loved her as long as it was simple—as it was in the flower garden—but now the sticky web of the larger world was swiftly settling over us. And so I slowly forced the letter back inside its envelope and laid it on the lawn, and found I couldn't bring myself to say anything. I knew that it had never been right; she was solemn and cerebral and bound for college and I was a baseball player. Suddenly in Anna I saw the prospect of a future that might not include baseball, if I so chose; baseball, really, meant leaving her, even without the hindrances of logistics and Pennsylvania and time. What had come to pass was not a problem but a looking glass, a mirror in which the truth emerged as solid as a diamond. Love was too hard; it argued I could not be my own center alone, that there were others on the planet with me—love was impossible and too much to ask of a boy. We sat on the lawn in the white light of the sun and Anna insisted that distance was no object; I agreed with that, but already I had moved farther off than she could ever realize.

"It'll work out," I told her. "It won't change anything."

But of course she knew that I lied. It was as obvious as my shame. "I'm not going to change," she said. The words trembled, the voice came softly. "I swear to it. I swear to it by these flowers, right now."

She'd read too many books, but I didn't say that. "Swearing isn't any good," I said. "We'll just have to try to work it out."

"But how?"

"I don't know."

"What about keeping the flowers going?"

"What about it? I'd try."

"Swear to it."

"I can't swear."

"I didn't think you could," she revealed at last. "I kind of suspected— I felt it right here." She placed her hand over her heart and held it there for a moment. "Right here. Right *here*!"

I couldn't look at her though. "Leave me alone," I said. "Okay?"

"Did I hear you correctly?" asked Anna.

"Don't talk to me," I heard myself say. "I don't love you. It doesn't have anything to do with your college or anything else. I just don't love you."

I was marveling at the blades of grass in the lawn as I spoke these words. Each molecule of each blade had taken on an unsettling, perfect clarity of being; each appeared shot through with a quiet green inner light. It seemed to me I couldn't fix myself on anything else at that moment, nothing but the texture of the lawn seemed real, and when I brought my head up at last I realized the silence had lasted too long, that Anna was no longer beside me. Something like panic overtook me in a flood and I jumped to my feet, disoriented, crazed, with just time to see her recede toward the house, recede through the flowers and then run up the porch steps, black hair streaming toward me as she turned through the door—and then Anna completely disappeared.

Chambers turned out to be a grim and dusty town, a long, narrow street of slatternly storefronts surrounded by blocks of austere and weather-beaten homes. A kind of stasis, disquieting and ever-present, seemed to oppress the very buildings along Main Street, and nothing moved but the occasional, slow-eyed dogs who stalked their tails in the lonely shadows, stirring the dust up and eyeing everything sadly. The searing summer wind carried the aroma of sulfur from the nearby mill, and the air smelled of insecticide in the early evenings. The townspeople, like figures in a dream, moved slowly and aimlessly when they moved at all, but came to the baseball games suddenly transformed (the games were like prayer meetings or old-time revivals) and sat fanning themselves and wiping their faces on their shirtsleeves in the bleachers, yapping in ecstasy at every base hit, swooning at every home run.

Chambers played in the Northern League, a Double A circuit that took in Saradon and Vicksburg, Oxacala and Merton, Larabee and Burris and Minapee City. The team bus rambled over roads as straight as ramrods, over pavement that sweated from a distant vantage but was only full of pockmarks and holes when you passed over it to wherever you were going. We were a team, mostly, of journeymen minor leaguers, men who had played baseball everywhere and were no longer surprised when they were traded or sold—men who played baseball for a living mechanically, with only a faint trace left of the hope they had once held inside. Some of them had had their day in the majors, of which they never spoke, and had followed a downward trajectory ever since, as though it were somehow their duty to see things through to their proper, inevitable ends. We played in dust and heat, slept on buses and in sweltering hotels, endured, with a consensual stoicism, our undeniable anonymity. I won my first start on bluster and optimism, but then I lost four badly and fell out of the rotation. Chambers used me in long relief rarely; the rest of the time I chewed gum in the bullpen, watching and wondering where I'd gone wrong.

I suppose you could say that the dream fell away then; the shell broke around me and I felt no protection in the game any longer, but only the little-known reality of it. In my room over the auto parts store on the main street of Chambers I began to have nightmares, hideous dreams in which the void of my future expressed itself as a chasm, dark and impossible to avoid. From my vantage in the bullpen the actual game seemed far away and I would daydream through whole innings, sitting forward with my elbows on my knees and my face in my hands, staring at the dusty ground. More and more I thought of the flower garden, wondered what bloomed there and what sort of birds had come to the feeders. By the time the season ended it seemed quite important—the possibility that our pink phlox had blossomed, that the candelabralike flowers of snakeroot had opened up, that perhaps the alyssum or Jacob's-coat would surprise us—the image of that lost world of color and light seemed always before me now, a salve of sorts for the wound the game had turned into.

Kansas City did not renew my contract, and I came home with baseball behind me, as if seeing the world for the first time. In my hometown the hard light of summer had softened and annealed; winds slightly cooler than summer winds blew, and in the mornings the sky appeared a heavy shade of mottled gray. I wandered a lot; at Adams Field a crowd of younger boys had come to dominate the baseball diamond, and sometimes I would sit against the chain-link fence behind the elementary school, watching their games from the hilltop. More often I would ponder the lost Eden of the flower garden, and once or twice, when night came, I passed by the hedge at the Lewis home. Beyond the clasped gate there was only darkness and the shadowy flickerings of the television in the front window, where Doctor Lewis, I knew without a doubt, looked at the late news and chewed on his cigar in the easy chair. It seemed to me that all across town the streets themselves had changed; they were narrower, the quiet in them had become a sad thing—they seemed desolate, and I saw now, improbably, that there were intricate lives in every home. *A job*, I began to say to myself, seeing how most men came out of their houses in the morning—but I couldn't bring myself, yet, to look for one. I spoke only when spoken to, and I am sure that people spoke of me as one who had failed at his dream. Yet everywhere I went I thought of our flower garden and not of baseball; perhaps, I said to myself, the day lilies have come out, or the evening primroses, or the clump of zinnias has bloomed. By the time September ended I had led myself to believe in the elusive perfection of that place, and stubbornly felt the urge to go there, to stand among the flowers one more time.

A night came in October when I awoke at two A.M. and knew the killing-frost had come. The sharp air of winter flooded at the window, and outside, illuminated by the glitter of the full moon, the leaves on the cottonwood in the yard had bound themselves up and dropped to the lawn. It dawned on me then that the flowers in our garden would close against winter now, and I got up and dressed quickly, shivering all up and down my neck and back and arms. I went out hurriedly into the street and ran toward Anna's in the cold moonlight, barreling up the old broad avenues of my paper route. When I turned into Tullis I stopped and waited while the steam of my breath died down. Moonlight bronzed everything—the leaves in the rigid maples, the clean, silent porches, the frost on the lawns and the gables and trellises—and the windowpanes all up and down the street shimmered like deep pools of water. The frost had hardened to a crust that fractured readily underfoot, and the night dew, silver in color, lay in drops the size of small pearls on the blade tips. The flowers, I thought: they will have folded up already where the frost is this thick, and I noticed uneasily a disturbance in the air then, and a steady drumming in the pit of my stomach, and my spine tightened as I walked and the tips of my ears felt furious with cold. I unclasped the gate I'd unclasped hundreds of times; inside the trimmed hedge each flagstone appeared as a ragged square of impeccable light; the three-story house rose hugely against the blue-black of the night sky, luminous, familiar, melancholy and silent—an impenetrable fortress of silver-white clapboard, with long eaves glistening beneath the moon.

Perhaps, I told myself one more time, everything will be in blossom— and then I stepped carefully along the lit flagstones. I went through the bend in the garden path; I came on the stone bench; on the low knoll to my left and before me I saw the outline of the white gazebo. I wound through the paths and down the shadowed lawn slope, but the garden Anna and I had planted was only a dark mass of stems now, everything cut back to a foot in height and mulched with several inches of raked leaves from the rest of the yard.

Everything else was as it should be, as it had been, but I had no place in it anymore. I'd trespassed in order to be there at all, and suddenly I felt more alone than I ever had, more desolate, more burdened by my own soul and by who I was, however ineluctably, and it began to seem as if my presence in that place at night beneath the moon marked the last moment ever in which I could really be young. Years have passed, but still today—on buses going downtown, in restaurants booming with noise, on airplanes as they lift off, at weddings and at movies and at baseball games when those moments arrive and the field disappears and I find myself burrowing backward in time, lost in myself as the game goes on—I have felt in my heart that same widening aloneness that buried me then: the loneliness that boys feel who are forever afraid of death and of becoming men.

The Tree

ROSAMUNDE PILCHER

A T FIVE O'CLOCK on a sultry, sizzling London afternoon in July, Jill Armitage, pushing the baby buggy that contained her small son Robbie, emerged through the gates of the park and started to walk the mile of pavements that led to home.

It was a small park and not a very spectacular one. The grass was trodden, the paths fouled by other people's dogs, the flower beds filled with things like lobelia and hot red geraniums and strange plants with beetroot-colored leaves, but at least there was a children's corner, and a shady tree or two, and some swings and a see-saw.

She had packed a basket with some toys and a token picnic for the two of them, and this was now slung on the handles of the buggy. All that could be seen of her child was the top of his cotton sun hat and his red canvas sneakers. He wore a skimpy pair of shorts and his arms and shoulders were the color of apricots. She hoped that he had not caught the sun. His thumb was in his mouth, he hummed to himself, *meh, meh, meh*, a sound he made when he was sleepy.

They came to the main road and stood, waiting to cross. Traffic, two lanes deep, poured in front of them. Sunlight flashed on windscreens, drivers were in shirt sleeves, the air was heavy with the smell of exhaust and petrol fumes.

The lights changed, brakes screeched, and traffic halted. Jill pushed the buggy across the road. On the far side was the greengrocer's shop, and Jill thought about supper that evening, and went in to buy a lettuce and a pound of tomatoes. The man who served her was an old friend—living in this run-down corner of London was a little like living in a village—and he called Robbie "My love" and gave him, free, a peach for his supper.

Jill thanked the greengrocer and trudged on. Before long she turned into her own street, where the Georgian houses had once been quite grand, and the pavements were wide and flagged with stone. Since getting married and coming to live in the neighborhood, she had learned to take for granted the decrepitude of everything, the dingy paint, the broken railings, the sinister basements with their grubby drawn curtains and damp stone steps sprouting ferns. But over the last two years, hopeful signs of improvement had begun to show in the street. Here, a house changed hands intact, scaffolding went up, great Council skips stood at the road's edge and were filled with all sorts of interesting rubbish. There, a basement flat sported a new coat of white paint, and a honeysuckle was planted in a tub, and in no time at all had reached the railings, twisting and twining with branches laden with blossom. Gradually, windows were being replaced, lintels repaired, front doors painted shiny black or cornflower blue, brass handles and letter boxes polished to a shine. A new and expensive breed of car stood at the pavement's edge and a whole new and expensive breed of mothers walked their offspring to the corner shop, or brought them home from parties, carrying balloons and wearing false noses and paper hats.

Ian said that the district was going up in the world, but really, it was just that people could no longer afford to buy property in Fulham or Kensington, and had started to try their luck further afield.

Ian and Jill had bought their house when they were married, three years ago, but still they had the dead weight of a mortgage hanging around their necks, and since Robbie was born and Jill had stopped working, their financial problems were even more acute. And now, to make matters worse, there was another baby on the way. They had wanted another baby; they had planned for another baby, but perhaps not quite so soon.

"Never mind," Ian had said when he got over the shock. "We'll have it all over and done with in one fell swoop, and just think what fun the children will be for each other, only two years apart."

"I just feel we can't afford it."

"It doesn't cost anything to have a baby."

"No, but it costs a lot to bring them up. And buy them shoes. Do you know what it costs to buy Robbie a pair of sandals?"

Ian said that he didn't know and he didn't want to. They would manage somehow. He was an eternal optimist and the best thing about his optimism was that it was catching. He gave his wife a kiss and went out to the off-license around the corner and bought a bottle of wine which they drank that evening, with their supper of sausage and mash.

"At least we've got a roof over our heads," he told her, "even if most of it belongs to the Building Society."

And so they had, but even their best friends had to admit that it was an odd house. For the street, at its end, turned in a sharp curve, and Number 23, where Jill and Ian lived, was tall and thin, wedge-shaped in order to accommodate the angle of the bend. It was its very oddness that had attracted them in the first place, as well as its price; for it had been allowed to reach a sad state of dilapidation and needed much done to it. Its very oddness was part of its charm, but charm didn't help much when they had run out of the time, energy, and means to attend to the outside painting, or apply a coat of Snow-cem to its narrow frontage.

Only the basement, paradoxically, sparkled. This was where Delphine, their lodger, lived. Delphine's rent helped to pay the mortgage. She was a painter who had turned, with some success, to commercial art, and she used the basement as a London pied-a-terre, commuting between this and a cottage in Wiltshire, where a decrepit barn had been converted into a studio, and an overgrown garden sloped down to the reedy banks of a small river. Every so often, Jill and Ian and Robbie were invited to this enchanting place for a weekend, and these visits were always the greatest treat—a feast of ill-assorted guests, enormous meals, quantities of wine, and endless discussions on esoteric subjects usually quite beyond Jill's comprehension. They made, as Ian was wont to point out when they returned to humdrum old London, a nice change.

Delphine, enormously fat in her flowing caftan, was sitting now out-side her own front door, basking in the shaft of sunlight which, at this time of the day, penetrated her domain. Jill lifted Robbie out of the buggy, and Robbie stuck his head through the railings and stared down at Delphine, who put down her newspaper and stared back at him from behind round, black sunglasses.

"Hello, there," she said. "Where have you been?"

"To the park," Jill told her.

"In this heat?"

"There's nowhere else to go."

"You should do something about the garden."

Delphine had been saying this, at intervals, over the last two years, until Ian told her that if she said it once more, he, personally, would stran-gle her. "Cut down that horrible tree."

"Don't start on that," Jill pleaded. "It's all too difficult."

"Well, at least you could get rid of the cats. I could hardly sleep last night for the yowling."

"What can we do?"

"Anything. Get a gun and shoot them."

"Ian hasn't got a gun. And even if he had, the police would think we were murdering someone if we started blasting off at the cats."

"What a loyal little wife you are. Well, if you won't shoot the cats, how about coming down to the cottage this weekend? I'll drive the lot of you in my car."

"Oh, Delphine." It was the best thing that had happened all day. "Do you really mean it?"

"Of course." Jill thought of the cool country garden, the smell of elderflowers; of letting Robbie paddle his feet in the shallow pebbly waters of the river.

"I can't think of anything more heavenly . . . but I'll have to see what Ian says. He might be playing cricket."

"Come down after dinner and I'll give you both a glass of wine. We'll discuss it then."

By six o'clock, Robbie was bathed, fed—on the juicy peach—and asleep in his cot. Jill took a shower, put on the coolest garment she owned, which was a cotton dressing gown, and went down to the kitchen to do something about supper.

The kitchen and the dining room, divided only by the narrow staircase, took up the entire ground floor of the house, but still were not large. The front door led straight into this, so that there never seemed to be anywhere to hang coats or park a pram. At the dining-room end, the window faced out onto the street; but the kitchen had enormous French windows of glass, which seemed to indicate that once there had been a balcony beyond, with perhaps a flight of steps leading down into the garden. The balcony and the steps had long since disintegrated, been demolished, perhaps—disappeared and the French windows opened onto nothing but a twenty-foot drop to the yard beneath. Before Robbie was born they used to let the windows stand open in warm weather, but after his arrival, Ian, for safety, nailed them shut, and so they had stayed.

The scrubbed pine table stood against these windows. Jill sat at it and sliced tomatoes for the salad in a preoccupied sort of way, gazing down at the horrible garden. Encased as it was by high, crumbling brick walls, it was a little like looking down into the bottom of a well. Near the house there was the brick yard, and then a patch of straggling grass, and then desolation, trodden earth, old paper bags that kept blowing in, and the tree.

Jill had been born and brought up in the country and found it hard to believe that she could actually dislike a garden. So much so that even if there had been any form of access, she would not hang her washing out, let alone allow her child to play there.

And as for the tree—she positively hated the tree. It was a sycamore, but light-years away from the friendly sycamores she remembered from her childhood, good for climbing, shady in summer, scattering winged seed-pods in the autumn. This one should never have grown at all; should never have been planted, should never have reached such a height, such density, such somber, depressing size. It shut out the sky, and its gloom discouraged all life except the cats, who prowled, howling, along the tops of the walls and used the sparse earth as their lavatories. In the autumn, when the leaves fell from the tree and Ian braved the cats' messes to go out and build a bonfire, the resultant smoke was black and stinking, as though the leaves had absorbed, during the summer months, everything in the air that was dirty, repellent, or poisonous.

Their marriage was a happy one, and most of the time Jill wanted nothing to be different. But the tree brought out the worst in her, made her long to be rich, so that she could damn the expense and get rid of it.

Sometimes she said this, aloud, to Ian. "I wish I had an enormous private income of my own. Or that I had a marvelously wealthy relation. Then I could get the tree cut down. Why hasn't one of us got a fairy godmother? Haven't you got one hidden away?"

"You know I only have Edwin Makepeace, and he's about as much good as a wet weekend in November."

Edwin Makepeace was a family joke, and how Ian's parents had ever been impelled to make him godfather to their son was an enigma that Jill had never got around to solving. He was some sort of a distant cousin, and had always had a reputation for being humorless, demanding, and paranoically mean with his money. The passing years had done nothing to remedy any of these traits. He had been married, for a number of years, to a dull lady called Gladys. They had had no children, simply lived together in a small house in Woking renowned for its gloom, but at least Gladys had looked after him, and when she died and he was left alone, the problem of Edwin became a constant niggle on the edge of the family's conscience.

Poor old chap, they would say, and hope that somebody else would ask him for Christmas. The somebody else who did so was usually Ian's mother, who was a truly kind-hearted lady, and it took some determination on her part not to allow Edwin's depressing presence to totally dampen the family festivities. The fact that he gave her nothing more than a box of hankies, which she never used, did nothing to endear him to the rest of the party. It wasn't, as they pointed out, that Edwin didn't have any money. It was just that he didn't like parting with it.

"Perhaps we could cut down the tree ourselves."

"Darling, it's much too big. We'd either kill ourselves or knock the whole house down."

"We could get a professional. A tree surgeon."

"And what would we do with the bones when the surgeon had done his job?"

"A bonfire?"

"A bonfire. That size? The whole terrace would go up in smoke,"

"We could take it out into the street, bit by bit."

"Through Delphine's flat?"

"At least we could *ask* somebody. We could get an estimate."

"My love, I can give you an estimate. It would cost a bomb. And we haven't got a bomb."

"A garden. It would be like having another room. Space for Robbie to play. And I could put the new baby out in a pram."

"How? Lower it from the kitchen window on a rope?"

They had had this conversation, with varying degrees of acrimony, too many times.

I'm not going to mention it again, Jill promised herself, but . . . She stopped slicing the tomato, sat with the knife in one hand and her chin resting on the other hand, and gazed out through the grimy window that couldn't be cleaned because there was no way of getting at it.

The tree. Her imagination removed it; but then what did one do with what remained? What would ever grow in that bitter scrap of earth? How could they keep the cats away? She was still mulling over these insuperable problems when there came the sound of her husband's latchkey in the lock. She jumped, as though she had been caught doing something indecent, and quickly started slicing the tomato again. The door banged shut and she looked up over her shoulder to smile at him.

"Hello, darling."

He dumped his briefcase, came to kiss her. He said, "God, what a furnace of a day. I'm filthy, and I smell. I'm going to have a shower, and then I shall come and be charming to you .

"There's a can of lager in the fridge."

"Riches indeed." He kissed her again. "You, on the other hand, smell delicious. Of freesias." He began to pull his tie loose.

"It's the soap."

He made for the stairs, undressing himself as he went. "Let's hope it does the same for me."

Five minutes later he was down again, bare-footed, wearing an old pair of faded jeans and a short-sleeved shirt he had bought for his honeymoon.

"Robbie's asleep," he told her. "I just looked in." He opened the fridge, took out the can of lager and poured it into two glasses, then brought them over to the table and collapsed into a chair beside her. "What did you do today?"

She told him about going to the park, about the free peach, about Delphine's invitation for the weekend. "She said she'd drive us down in her car."

"She is an angel. What a marvelous thought."

"She's asked us down for a glass of wine after dinner. She said we could talk about it.

"A little party, in fact."

"Oh, well, it makes a nice change."

They looked at each other, smiling. He put out a hand and laid it on her flat and slender stomach. He said, "For a pregnant lady, you look very toothsome." He ate a piece of tomato. "Is this dinner, or are we defrosting the fridge?"

"It's dinner. With some cold ham and potato salad."

"I'm starving. Let's eat it and then go and beat Delphine up. You did say she was going to open a bottle of wine?"

"That's what she said."

He yawned. "Better if it was two."

The next day was Thursday and as hot as ever, but somehow now it didn't matter, because there was the weekend to look forward to.

"We're going to Wiltshire," Jill told Robbie, flinging a load of clothes into the washing machine. "You'll be able to paddle in the river and pick flowers. Do you remember Wiltshire? Do you remember Delphine's cottage? Do you remember the tractor in the field?"

Robbie said "Tractor." He didn't have many words, but this was one of them. He smiled as he said it.

"That's right. We're going to the country." She began to pack, because although the trip was a day away, it made the weekend seem nearer. She ironed her best sun-dress, she even ironed Ian's oldest T-shirt. "We're going to stay with Delphine." She was extravagant and bought a cold chicken for supper and a little punnet of strawberries. There would be strawberries growing in Delphine's wild garden. She thought of going out to pick them, the sun hot on her back, the rosy fruits fragrant beneath their sheltering leaves.

The day drew to a close. She bathed Robbie and read to him and put him in his cot. As she left him, his eyes already drooping, she heard Ian's key in the latch and ran downstairs to welcome him.

"Darling."

He put down his briefcase and shut the door. His expression was bleak. She kissed him quickly and said, "What's wrong?"

"I'm afraid something rotten has come up. Would you mind most dreadfully if we didn't go to Delphine's?"

"Not go?" Disappointment made her feel weak and emptied as though all her happiness were being drained out of her. She could not keep the dismay out of her face. "But—oh, Ian, why not?"

"My mother rang me at the office." He pulled off his jacket and slung it over the end of the banister. He began to loosen his tie. "It's Edwin."

"Edwin?" Jill's legs shook. She sat on the stairs. "He's not *dead*?"

"No, he's not, but apparently, he's not been too well lately. He's been told by the doctor to take things easy. But now his best friend has what Edwin calls 'passed on,' and the funeral's on Saturday and Edwin insists on coming to London to be there. My mother tried to talk him out of it, but he won't budge. He's booked himself in for the night at some grotty, cheap hotel and Ma's convinced he's going to have a heart attack and die too. But the nub of the matter is that he's got it into his head that he'd like to come and have dinner with us. I told her that it was just because he'd rather have a free meal than one he has to pay for, but she swears it's not that at all. He kept saying he never sees anything of you and me, he's never seen our house, he wants to get to know Robbie . . . you know the sort of thing . . ."

When Ian was upset, he always talked too much. After a little Jill said, "Do we *have* to? I wanted so much to go to the country."

"I know. But if I explain to Delphine, I know she'll understand, give us a rain check."

"It's just that . . ." She was near to tears. "It's just that nothing nice or exciting ever happens to us nowadays. And when it does, we can't do it because of somebody like Edwin. Why should it be us? Why can't somebody else look after him?"

"I suppose it's because he doesn't have that number of friends."

Jill looked up at him, and saw her own disappointment and indecision mirrored in his face.

She said, knowing what the outcome would inevitably be, "Do you want him to come?"

Ian shrugged, miserably. "He's my godfather."

"It would be bad enough if he was a jolly old man, but he's so gloomy."

"He's old. And lonely."

"He's dull."

"He's sad. His best friend's just died."

"Did you tell your mother we were meant to be going to Wiltshire?"

"Yes. And she said that we had to talk it over. I said I'd ring Edwin this evening."

"We can't tell him *not* to come."

"That's what I thought you'd say." They gazed at each other, knowing that the decision was made; behind them. No country weekend. No strawberries to be picked. No garden for Robbie. Just Edwin.

She said, "I wish it wasn't so hard to do good deeds. I wish they just happened, without one having to do anything about them."

"They wouldn't be good deeds if they happened that way. But you know something? I do love you. More, all the time, if possible." He stooped and kissed her. "Well . . ." He turned and opened the door again. "I'd better go down and tell Delphine."

"There's cold chicken for supper."

"In that case I'll see if I can rustle up enough loose change for a bottle of wine. We both need cheering up."

Once the dreadful disappointment had been conquered, Jill decided to follow her own mother's philosophy—if a thing is worth doing, it's worth doing well. So what, if it was only dreary old Edwin Makepeace, fresh from a funeral; it was still a dinner party. She made a cassoulet of chicken and herbs, scrubbed new potatoes, concocted a sauce for the broccoli. For dessert there was fresh fruit salad, and then a creamy wedge of Brie.

She polished the gate-leg table in the dining room, laid it with the best mats, arranged flowers (bought late yesterday from the stall in the market), plumped up the patchwork cushions in the first-floor sitting room.

Ian had gone to fetch Edwin. He had said, his voice sounding shaky over the telephone, that he would take a taxi, but Ian knew that it would cost him ten pounds or more and had insisted on making the journey himself. Jill bathed Robbie and dressed him in his new pajamas, and then changed herself into the freshly ironed sundress that had been intended for Wiltshire. (She put out of her mind the image of Delphine, setting off in her car with no one for company but her easel and her weekend bags. The sun would go on shining; the heatwave would continue. They would be invited again, for another weekend.)

Now, all was ready. Jill and Robbie knelt on the sofa that stood in the living-room bay window, and watched for Edwin's arrival. When the car drew up, she gathered Robbie into her arms and went downstairs to open the door. Edwin was coming up the steps from the street, with Ian behind him. Jill had not seen him since last Christmas and thought that he had aged considerably. She did not remember that he had had to walk with a cane. He wore a black tie and a relentless dark suit. He carried no small gift, no flowers, no bottle of wine. He looked like an undertaker.

"Edwin."

"Well, my dear, here we are. This is very good of you."

He came into the house, and she gave him a kiss. His old skin felt rough and dry and he smelt, vaguely, of disinfectant, like an old-fashioned doctor. He was a very thin man; his eyes, which had once been a cold blue, were now faded and rheumy. There was high color on his cheekbones, but otherwise he looked bloodless, monochrome. His stiff collar seemed a good size too large, and his neck was stringy as a turkey's.

"I was so sorry to hear about your friend." She felt that it was important to get this said at once.

"Oh, well, it comes to all of us, yerknow. Three score years and ten, that's our allotted span, and Edgar was seventy-three. I'm seventy-one. Now, where shall I put my stick?"

There wasn't anywhere, so she took it from him and hung it on the end of the banister.

He looked about him. He had probably never before seen an openplan house.

"Well, look at this. And this"—he leaned forward, his beak of a nose pointing straight into Robbie's face— "is your son."

Jill wondered if Robbie would let her down and burst into tears of fright. He did not, however, simply stared back into Edwin's face with unblinking eyes.

"I . . . I kept him up. I thought you'd like to meet each other. But he's rather sleepy." Ian now came through the door and shut it behind him. "Would you like to come upstairs?"

She led the way, and he followed her, a step at a time, and she heard his labored breathing. In the sitting room she set the little boy down, and pulled up a chair for Edwin. "Why don't you sit here?"

He sat, cautiously. Ian offered him a glass of sherry, and Jill left them, and took Robbie upstairs to put him into his cot.

He said, just before he put his thumb into his mouth, "Nose," and she was filled with love for him for making her want to laugh.

"I know," she whispered. "He *has* got a big nose, hasn't he?"

He smiled back, his eyes drooped. She put up the side of the cot and went downstairs. Edwin was still on about his old friend. "We were in the Army together during the war. Army Pay Corps. After the war, he went back to Insurance, but we always kept in touch. Went on holiday once together, Gladys and Edgar and myself. He never married. Went to Budleigh Salterton." He eyed Ian over his sherry glass. "Ever been to Budleigh Salterton?"

Ian said that no, he had never been to Budleigh Salterton.

"Pretty place. Good golf course. Of course, Edgar was never much of a man for golf. Tennis when we were younger, and then he took up bowls. Ever played bowls, Ian?"

Ian said that no, he had never played bowls.

"No," said Edwin. "You wouldn't have. Cricket's yer game, isn't it?"

"When I can get the chance."

"Yer probably pretty busy."

"Yes, pretty busy."

"Play at weekends, I expect."

"Sometimes."

"I watched the Test Match on my television set." He took another cautious sip at his Tio Pepe, his lips puckered. "Didn't think much of the Pakistanis."

Jill, discreetly, got to her feet and went downstairs to the kitchen. When she called to them that dinner was ready, Edwin was still talking about cricket, recalling some match in 1956 that he had particularly enjoyed. The drone of this long story was stilled by her interruption. Presently the two men came down the stairs. Jill was at the table, lighting the candles.

"Never been in a house like this," observed Edwin, sitting down and unfolding his napkin. "How much did yer pay for it?"

Ian, after a tiny hesitation, told him.

"When did yer buy it?"

"When we were married. Three years ago."

"Yer didn't do too badly."

"It was in rotten shape. It's still not great shakes, but we'll get it straight in time."

Jill found Edwin's disconcerting stare directed at herself. "Yer mother-in-law tells me yer having another baby."

"Oh. Well . . . yes, I am."

"Not meant to be a secret, is it?"

"No. No, of course not." She picked up the cassoulet in oven-gloved hands and pushed it at him. "It's chicken."

"Always fond of chicken. We used to have chicken in India during the war . . ." He was off again. "Funny thing, how good the Indians were at cooking chicken. Suppose they had a lot of practice. Yer weren't allowed to eat the cows. Sacred, you see .

Ian opened the wine, and after that things got a little easier. Edwin refused the fruit salad, but ate most of the Brie. And all the time he talked, seeming to need no sort of response, merely a nod of the head or an attentive smile. He talked about India, about a friend he had made in Bombay; about a tennis match he had once played in Camberley; about Gladys's aunt, who had taken up loom-weaving and had won a prize at the County Show.

The long, hot evening wore on. The sun slid out of the hazed city sky, and left it stained with pink. Edwin was now complaining of his daily help's inability to fry eggs properly, and all at once Ian excused himself, got to his feet, and took himself off to the kitchen to make coffee.

Edwin, interrupted in his free flow, watched him go. "That yer kitchen?" he asked.

"Yes."

"Let's have a look at it." And before she could stop him, he had hauled himself to his feet and was headed after Ian. She followed him, but he would not be diverted upstairs.

"Not much room, have you?"

"It's all right," said Ian. Edwin went to the French windows and peered out through the grimy glass.

"What's this?"

"It's . . ." Jill joined him, gazing in an agonized fashion at the familiar horror below. "It's the garden. Only we don't use it because it's rather nasty. The cats come and make messes. And anyway, we can't get to it. As you can see," she finished tamely.

"What about the basement?"

"The basement's let. To a friend. Called Delphine."

"Doesn't she mind living cheek-by-jowl with a tip like that?"

"She's—she's not here very often. She's usually in the country."

"Hmm." There was a long, disconcerting silence. Edwin looked at the tree, his eyes travelling from its grubby roots to the topmost branches. His nose was like a pointer and all the sinews in his neck stood out like ropes.

"Why don't yer cut the tree down?"

Jill sent an agonized glance in Ian's direction. Behind Edwin's back, he threw his eyes to heaven, but he said, reasonably enough, "It would be rather difficult. As you can see, it's very large."

"Horrible, having a tree like that in yer garden."

"Yes," agreed Jill. "It's not very convenient."

"Why don't yer do something about it?"

Ian said quickly, "Coffee's ready. Let's go upstairs.

Edwin turned on him. "I said, why don't yer do something about it?"

"I will," said Ian. "One day."

"No good waiting for one day. One day yer'll be as old as me and the tree will still be there."

"Coffee?" said Ian.

"And the cats are unhealthy. Unhealthy when children are about the place."

"I don't let Robbie out in the garden," Jill told him. "I couldn't even if I wanted to, because there is no way we can get to it. I think there used to be a balcony and steps down to the garden, but they'd gone before we bought the house, and somehow . . . well, we've never got around to doing anything about replacing them." She was determined that she would not make it sound as though she and Ian were penniless and pathetic. "I mean, there's been so much else to do."

Edwin said "Hmm" again. He stood, his hands in his pockets, gazing through the window, and after a bit Jill wondered if he was drifting off into some sort of a coma. But then he became brisk, took his hands out of his pockets, turned to Ian and said, testily, "I thought you were making us coffee, Ian. How long do we have to wait for it?"

He stayed for another hour, and his endless flow of deadly anecdote never ceased. At last the clock from a neighboring church began to chime eleven o'clock, and Edwin set down his coffee cup, glanced at his own watch, and announced that it was time for Ian to drive him back to his hotel. They all went downstairs. Ian found his car keys and opened the door. Jill gave Edwin his stick.

"Been a pleasant evening. Liked seeing yer house."

She kissed him again. He went out and down the steps and crossed the pavement. Ian, trying not to look too eager, stood with the door of the car open. The old man cautiously got in, stowed his legs and his stick. Ian shut the door and went around to the driving seat. Jill, smiling still, waved them off. When the car disappeared around the corner at the end of the street, and not before, she let the smile drop, and went inside, exhausted, to start in on the washing up.

In bed that night, "He wasn't too bad," said Jill.

"I suppose not. But he takes everything so for granted, as though we all owed him something. He could at least have brought you a single red rose, or a bar of chocolate."

"He's just not that sort of a person."

"And his stories! Poor old Edwin, I think he was born a bore. He's so terribly good at it. He probably Bored for his school, and went on to Bore for England. Probably captained the team."

"At least we didn't have to think of things to say."

"It was a delicious dinner, and you were sweet to him." He yawned enormously and heaved himself over, longing for sleep. "Anyway, we did it. That's the last of it.

But in that Ian was wrong. That was not the last of it, although two weeks passed by before anything happened. A Friday again, and as usual Jill was in the kitchen, getting supper ready, when Ian returned home from the office.

"Hello, darling."

He shut the door, dumped his briefcase, came to kiss her. He pulled out a chair and sat down, and they faced each other across the table. He said, "The most extraordinary thing has happened."

Jill was instantly apprehensive. "Nice extraordinary or horrid extraordinary?"

He grinned, put his hand in his pocket, and pulled out a letter. He tossed it across to her. "Read that."

Mystified, Jill picked it up and unfolded it. It was a long letter and typewritten. It was from Edwin.

My dear Ian

This is to thank you for the pleasant evening with you both, and the excellent dinner, and to say how much I appreciated your motoring me to and fro. I must say that it goes against the grain, being forced to pay exorbitant taxi fares. I much enjoyed meeting your child and seeing your house. You have, however, an obvious problem with your garden, and I have given the matter some thought.

Your first priority is obviously to get rid of the tree. On no account must you tackle it yourself. There are a number of professional firms in London who are qualified to deal with such work, and I have taken the liberty of instructing three of them to call on you, at your convenience, and give you estimates. Once the tree has gone, you will have more idea of the possibilities of your plot, but in the meantime I would suggest the following:

The letter continued, by now reading like a builder's specification. Existing walls made good, repointed, and painted white. A trellis fence, for privacy, erected along the top of these walls. The ground cleared and leveled, and laid with flags—a drain to be discreetly incorporated in one corner for easy cleaning. Outside the kitchen window a wooden deck— preferably teak—to be erected, supported by steel joists, and with an open wooden staircase giving access to the garden below.

I think [Edwin continued] this more or less covers the structural necessities. You may want to construct a raised flower bed along one of the walls, or make a small rockery around the stump of the removed tree, but this is obviously up to yourselves.

Which leave us with the problem of the cats. Again, I have made some enquiries and discovered that there is an excellent repellent which is safe to use where there are children about. A squirt or two of this should do the trick, and once the soil and grass have been covered by flags, I see no reason why the cats should return for any function, natural or otherwise.

This is obviously going to cost quite a lot of money. I realize that, with inflation and the rising cost of living, it is not always easy for a young couple, however hard they work, to make ends meet. And I should like to help. I have, in fact, made provision for you in my Will, but it occurs to me that it would be much more in keeping to hand the money over to you now. Then you will be able to deal with your garden, and I shall have the pleasure of seeing it completed, hopefully before I, too, follow my good friend Edgar, and pass on.

Finally, your mother indicated to me that you had given up a pleasurable weekend in order to cheer me up on the evening of Edgar's funeral. Your kindness equals her own, and I am fortunate to be in a financial position when I am able, at last, to repay my debts.

With best wishes,

Yours

Edwin

Edwin. She could hardly see his spiky signature because her eyes were full of tears. She imagined him, sitting in his dark little house in Woking, absorbed in their problems, working them all out; taking time to look up suitable firms, probably making endless telephone calls, doing little sums, forgetting no tiny detail, taking trouble.

"Well?" said Ian, gently.

The tears had started to slide down her cheeks. She put up a hand and tried to wipe them away.

"I never thought. I never thought he'd do anything like *this*. Oh, Ian, and we've been so horrible about him."

"You were never horrible. You wouldn't know how to be horrible about anybody."

"I . . . I never imagined he had any money at all."

"I don't think any of us did. Not that sort of money."

"How can we ever thank him?"

"By doing what he says. By doing just exactly what he's told us to do, and then asking him around to the garden-warming. We'll throw a little party." He grinned. "It'll make a nice change."

She looked out of the window, through the grimy glass. A paper bag had found its way into the garden from some neighboring dustbin, and the nastiest of the tom cats, the one with the torn ear, was sitting on top of the wall, eyeing her.

She met his cold green stare with equanimity. She said, "I'll be able to hang out my washing. I shall get some tubs, and plant bulbs for the spring, and pink ivy-leafed geranium in the summer. And Robbie can play there and we'll have a sandpit. And if the deck is big enough, I can even put the baby out there, in the pram. Oh, Ian, isn't it going to be *wonderful?* I won't ever have to go to the park again. Just think."

"You know what I think?" said Ian. "I think it would be a good idea to go and give old Edwin a ring."

So they went together to the telephone and dialed Edwin's number, and stood very close, with their arms around each other, waiting for the old gentleman to answer their call.

Prize Tomatoes

ANNE ROSNER

ALL RIGHT, EVERYONE at attention. There's been ample time since watering for revival. Beans! Pick up those bottom leaves. New tomato plants, stand up! That's it. Erect stems, leaves perpendicular. Remember, I have plans to enter tomatoes in the county fair this year. So you must work very hard. You all look beautiful. I'm proud of the effort you've all put forth this evening. Thank you and good night.

I'm lingering. Going into the house seems an undeserved sentence. I glance around the familiar landscape. New townhouses loom, a smug wall, to the east. The lights of a new shopping center reflect in the darkening sky. Turning westward, I can see a large field stretching away into a line of trees. When I face this way, the neighborhood of large homes retains its air of remoteness that I loved when our house was first built.

The twilit sky holds me, and I, standing in the purity of the sun's last rays, could be only another briefly drawn streak, like the evening clouds.

A door slams at the house. I know without turning that my daughter, Barbara, will be standing on the porch looking worriedly toward the garden. "Dad." Her voice is carried on the soft air.

I wave, smiling a smile she can't see from the porch. But this casual smile prepares me to walk to the house. Light, light step. Easy, loose gait. The picture of a man returning from engaging in a modest interest. She'll wait, my sentinel daughter, until she sees that I'm going into the house.

Barbara, her husband, Dick, and their two children had been contemplating a move when I went into the hospital three years ago. It was decided that it would work out well for everyone if she and her family moved into my house when I came home from the hospital. Shaky and acutely mindful of the emptiness of the big house, I had not resisted, had indeed been grateful for the arrangement.

I approach the porch. Barbara says, "It's getting dark. I was afraid you might get chilled."

"Yes," I agree, "I think I will get a sweater."

An anxious flash across her eyes. "You're going to come back from your room, aren't you, Dad?" she asks. "There's a very good play on television tonight. I thought we could all watch it."

Dr. Hooper, the psychiatrist, has told her that I'm not to spend too much time alone.

"That sounds great," I say. "I'll just get the sweater and be back out." Barbara retreats to the living room. I enter my bedroom, sighing in resignation because I'll have to postpone looking through the new seed catalogue that came in the mail today until everyone is in bed. Although Dr. Hooper has released me from his care, he and his advice hang about the house like iron-willed specters.

The children are both out for the evening. Dick, Barbara, and I settle into our tacitly appointed places before the television. The play proves to be avant-garde, hard to follow. My mind wanders. I think about the cabbage. Just the under-leaves seem a bit ragged. I remind myself to question Mr. Miggs about a possible culprit. Not cabbage worms, I know, because those are easy to see. Maybe—.

"Dad, did you notice the way these sets have been designed for the scene changes? Isn't that clever?"

I start. No need to panic. Calm, cool. Maybe just a nod will do. I nod. She buys it. I try again to concentrate on the show. Lucky Dick has fallen asleep, unnoticed. God, I'm weary of Barbara's concern.

She's tired tonight. Dark smudges have appeared under her eyes. She's relaxed and forgets to hold her chin up. The telltale sag in her jawline touches me.

She was more frightened than my other two children, I think, when I went to the hospital. She's more frightened still by the changes in the man who came home from the hospital.

I've overheard her on the phone, explaining to her friends, explaining to herself what happened. "It was Mother's death. It simply undid him. You know how devoted they were."

It's true what she says. Peg's death had much to do with it, but not in any way she might imagine. It wasn't as if we were young. Peg was sixty-three and I was sixty-five. That was four years ago last winter.

The devotion? Well, I'll concede a mutual respect. If there was devotion, it was the formal and dutiful devotion of habit—until the end, that is.

Peg died of a peculiar slow-growing form of cancer. We knew she had it for five years. She bore it with the serenity of people who have been forced to acknowledge their own deaths. I bore it, barely believing in its existence.

Almost precisely a year before she died, Peg told me one evening, in nothing more than a conversational tone, "Walter, there's something that's bothered me for more than thirty years. I think I'd feel better if you knew."

"What is it?"

"I had an affair when we were living in Shreveport." Then she laughed very girlishly and shrugged.

"With whom?" I asked.

"You didn't know him."

"For how long?"

"Two years.

I said, "Peg, I can't believe this. Then you were in love with him."

"I thought I was at the time," she said. Then she reached out and touched my arm. "Walter, I've never had any regrets about being married to you. Can you understand that?"

I jumped up and strode about the room, slamming the fist of one hand into the palm of the other. I wonder if I harbored some notion of beating up my wife's lover. I don't remember. All I remember is the gesture. I said, "I'll have to think about this."

For several days, I sorted through the feeling her confession had raised in me. There was an odd quality to my sense of betrayal in that it seemed to have so little to do with the other man. He seemed only a part, but certainly not the cause, of my agitation.

No, the element in it that ached with the persistence of a stubborn thorn was that I would have been absolutely certain that Peg was incapable of having the affair in the first place. It was a breach of trust, to be sure, but that seemed too small to describe the abyss that opened between us.

In those days after her confession, I had no reason to doubt her ability to have carried the secret for thirty years without my slightest suspicion. If I had been the sort of man then who doubted his own perceptions, I might have thought she had never told me, so unchanged was her customary equanimity. Freshly wounded, I saw her calm dignity as an added treachery.

The incident might have slipped silently below the surface of our lives, like so many things in the past, had I not pinpointed the source of my pain.

We were sitting at a late supper one night. Peg said, "Do you think Charlotte would like to come away with us this summer?"

I glanced up from my plate. Her face, lit by the one lamp in the room, was suddenly vivid, like a blurry photo coming into sharp focus. With a stupefying panic I realized that I didn't know this woman who had borne my three children, who had slept beside me for most of my life, who had been the one constancy in my life. And now she was dying.

I blurted, "I've had a couple of affairs myself." That lay flatly over us a moment. What a foolish thing to say. I tried again.

"What I mean is, it doesn't matter—your affair. I want—. I want—."

"You want what, Walter?"

I couldn't put my mouth around the enormity of what I wanted. "I want to talk" was the best I could do.

We lay awake most of the night, uncertain where to begin: haphazardly evoking memories, questioning each other. Toward morning, I held her, already so thin from the voraciousness of her illness. Her fragility was terrifying in its awful mortality. Peg, Peg. Peg o' my heart, did I sing to you as a young man?

Each time together then brought surprises: the joy of discovering each other without the expectancy of first love, deepened by the chill breath of Peg's measured time.

I loved her for the first time, was bound to her in parts of myself I had never known. Later, when she lay in the hospital, her skin tugged firmly, quite youthfully over her face by the rapacious disease, when tears were no longer strange to me, I cried, "Peg, all the years we wasted together. That loss is unbearable to me."

She said, "We couldn't have done this at any other time. We were far too much the sort of people that we were."

She offered it as comfort, I know, but it resounded down the empty well of my soul and continued to echo long after she died.

So Barbara was right in thinking that her mother's death had caused the eventual darkness that descended over my life. With Peg gone, I became the only one who heard those echoes.

The show ends. Barbara stirs in her chair, nudges Dick awake. I'm free to go now. We've all done our duty.

She rises. I sit quietly, not to appear too eager. "Well, Dad, I'll see you in the morning. Are you going to watch more television?"

"No, I don't think so," I say with a well-placed yawn. "I'm going to go to bed."

Good night. Good night.

In my room, I quickly search out the new seed catalog and position the lamp for the best light.

Fruit trees, shrubs. I'm idly flipping the pages. Flowers require slightly more attention. Maybe next year I'll try some flowers.

I linger for a moment over the red grapes. I've considered an arbor—not so much from any particular fondness for grapes but because of memories of sitting in the opulent shade of my grandmother's arbor as a boy. Yes, grapes might be interesting.

The vegetable section begins. I glance at the clock and listen for sounds in the house. The children when they come home will see my light, but fortunately they are teenagers—an age when whatever I do holds so little interest as to be invisible.

I pore over each picture, read the printed section underneath. I'm convinced that the people who compose the written information are rabid gardeners, too. Who but a gardener could describe rhubarb in such terms: "blushing red, clear through to the heart," "full shapely leaves?"

I'm captured by the catalog, entranced by the possibilities presented in the glossy pictures of potatoes, corn, and

The doorknob has turned so softly that I don't know Barbara is there until she speaks. "Dad, it's three o'clock."

I shove the catalog guiltily into a shelf in the night table. Easy, easy. "I'm just going to bed, Barbara," I say. "You could have knocked." That, as Dr. Hooper would say, is a reasonable demand.

"I'm sorry," she says. "I thought you had fallen asleep with your light on."

She remains in the doorway in uncomfortable silence. Then says, "I don't like to check up on you." She's pleading because she really doesn't like it. "But you know Dr. Hooper spoke to us very specifically about your getting enough rest."

"I'm old enough to decide when to go to bed."

"Dad," she says, "I know I annoy you, but I don't know what else to do to get you to take care of yourself."

I wonder if she means she annoys me in general. During the bleak time right before I went to the hospital, Barbara confronted me tearfully, "You have always loved Charlotte better than me," and I—too raw, too naked in my despair to lie to her—said nothing. She remembers, I know.

"I'm fine," I say.

She hesitates, then says in a rush, "The garden scares me. It reminds me of the CB."

"It wasn't a CB," I say and turn from her.

"O.K., Dad, O.K. Will you promise you'll go to bed?"

"Yes," I say, and climb obediently into bed after she leaves.

The earth smell blowing through the window makes me anxious to be in the garden in the morning. I'm only slightly sleepy. Old men don't need much sleep.

I think of the radio. It wasn't a CB. It was a ham outfit. I built it myself from a kit. At first my son, John, and Barbara had been quite happy about my interest. Good therapy, Dr. Hooper had pronounced.

Barbara, uneasy as my keeper, was grateful for the time I spent with the radio, I suppose.

It was a wonderful radio. I could send signals nearly anywhere in the world, and because night is the best time for reception and transmission, I was many times bent over my set, headphones over my ears, when the sun came up. I slept most of the day, saw Dr. Hooper once a week, and operated my radio at night.

I should have seen it coming—the end of my radio. Dr. Hooper was very insistent that I talk about something besides the radio when I saw him. That made the sessions all the more arduous, as I thought of little else.

Especially after Cecelia. I contacted her in the Philippines. The signal was amazingly clear. Her voice held all the lush mystery of her home. Its cadence described a tropical fragrance around my room. Her English was quite good, and I began to call her every night.

She was twenty, a student of philosophy at the University of Manila. For her I played the experienced older man, seasoned and unsurprised by life. "How wise you are, Walter," she said many times, and I would chuckle comfortably. The distance between us secured the fraud.

Because she loved Aristotle particularly, I studied him, searching for ideas to intrigue her. I must have done enough because she spent a great deal of time with me nearly every night.

The evenings with the family seemed interminable. I paced. I checked my watch, sat restlessly watching television—waiting for the time to pass.

There were times when it was difficult to reach her, but with the patience of love I turned the dials for as long as it took, straining to hear her voice, however faint.

I don't know what happened. She was young, after all. Perhaps she simply lost interest. Perhaps her radio had been damaged in some way, but weeks went by and I couldn't reach her. I did everything I knew to do. I checked with the shop where I had bought the kit, but nothing helped.

My agitation became apparent. I was aware of low-voiced telephone conversations. Barbara was alerting the rest of the family. Even sensing their growing concern, I couldn't control the panic of my loss.

One early morning, after a night of frantic searching for Cecelia, I rose to the window and began to shout in desperation, "Cecelia, Cecelia. Oh please, Cecelia."

Barbara and Dick crashed into the room—Barbara shaking visibly at the sight of my tear-stained face, Dick circling me warily.

Dr. Hooper was called, medication secured. I began to see him three times a week.

I disliked going to see Dr. Hooper. In fact, I probably dislike Dr. Hooper. He has a sharp nose that points downward, seeming always to be calling attention to his shoes. He is a hard-faced man who makes much of small things. As though seeing him three times a week weren't punishment enough for alarming my family, he neatly disposed of my radio as well.

"Walter, you must see what this radio has meant to you," he said. Your need for communication was served without your having to risk any real intimacy. That is why it became such an obsession. Because you need the communication.

"I think, and I have told the family the same thing, that it's fine for you to enjoy the radio, but you must put it into balance with the rest of your life."

But I didn't enjoy the radio any more. I had seen the radio as a great benevolent spider spinning a shining web over the world at the touch of my fingers. After Dr. Hooper, it became only a perverse instrument of a crazy old man. It gathered dust in my room until my grandson dismantled it for parts.

At last, I'm sleepy. Ah, Cecelia, why did you leave me?

Barbara and Dick are off to work, the children still sleeping. In the garden the lettuce holds the dew in its fluted depths. Last year tiny black insects riddled the leaves with holes. Mr. Miggs suggested planting raddishes in their rows "to draw them devils off the lettuce." This year the leaves are unblemished and the little bugs reside, apparently oblivious to the lettuce, on the tough, useless radish leaves.

I kneel, carefully sliding my fingers along the stem of a weed that has grown hidden within the lettuce leaves, then shoved its imprudent head above them. It grows there among the cultivated plants. I place my fingers as close to the ground as possible. Otherwise the stem will break off from the root and the weed will put out another shoot within days. Broken off at the ground, weeds enlarge in the root to return tougher than ever. I must pull up the entire root.

I give a light tug. It remains fixed. I exert more pressure. The root begins to give. Rolling my wrist, I give it a final yank. Too hard. It comes out, the stem broken. You son of a bitch, I'll get you. I thrust my hand into the lettuce, gently pushing the leaves aside, and see the end of the weed. It has broken right at the ground. I dig with my fingers around the shaft, losing a lettuce leaf in the process. All right, now I'm angry. I'm going to get you if I have to stay out here all day. With only my fingertips,

I get a sturdy hold and pull. Hah! there you are. That's the end of you.

Inspection, inspection everybody. Corn, you have a goal—knee-high by the Fourth of July. Kale, recovering nicely from an insect attack. And my beauties, the tomatoes, are in flower, yellow blossoms dotting the dark green vines. I have such plans for you at the fair this year.

"Dad?"

I turn. My younger daughter, Charlotte, stands at the edge of the garden. She is the baby and the rebel of the family. I smile in welcome.

"You look so peaceful out here," she says.

Her remark makes me love her very much.

"Hello, dear." I embrace her.

She has been dieting again. Her face is gaunt beneath a deep tan.

"Come on," I say, "I'll get you a cup of coffee."

"No, no, you go on with what you've been doing."

She teases me—the only one of the three who dares to do that. "So what are you doing today, Farmer Brinkman?"

"I'm pea picking. I'm going to freeze them."

She seldom visits when Barbara is here. Their views of the world have been irreconcilable since childhood.

She sees where I'm going to work and sits down at the end of the row. Because the sun has risen in the sky, I roll my shirtsleeves up. The harsh sunlight shines on my arms; the scars on the inside of my wrists are as bright as lightning. Charlotte sees. She winces with an almost imperceptible shudder.

I'm told that Charlotte was the one who found me, lying on the blood-soaked bed. So much blood, they all agreed, and yet I didn't die.

I wanted to die. There was no fear when I slid the razor painlessly across my wrists—just a relief as though it made no difference whether that red flow emptied onto the crisp white sheets or remained encased in my veins.

I pull my gloves from my pocket, slip them on, adjust them over my wrists. Charlotte and I are relieved.

She talks of a recent trip to Bermuda she has made. I haven't been there in a long time and don't care to go. The pea pods strike the pail with hollow thuds.

Later, in the kitchen, the blancher sends up great clouds of steam. I'm proud to have my daughter know that I'm efficient about the business of preserving food.

Charlotte shells peas, admires their sweet odor, and we make each other laugh. It's a wonderful day.

The grandchildren, Carrie and Mike, straggle sleepily into the kitchen and stay. They too love Charlotte. She makes us all laugh with a story of a drunken man on a plane trying to pick her up. She uses words which make me flinch, and that makes me laugh all the more.

Carrying several plastic bags for her freezer, Charlotte kisses us all and leaves.

At dinner that evening my son, John, drops by. I know Barbara has told him she is worried about me. She and her family are silent as John and I talk.

"So, how're you doing, Dad?" he asks.

"Fine, John. How are you?"

"Oh, I'm fine," he says, with an "of course" just barely unspoken. "Barbara tells me you're getting pretty hung up on this garden of yours."

"I enjoy it. I wouldn't say I was hung up on it," I answer evenly. "Hey, you know what I think?" he says as though the idea has just occurred to him. "It would be good for you to get back to work. That's what you need. Will you consider it?" John and I have had this conversation many times.

"No, I will not."

"For God's sake, why not? You're wasting away with nothing to do." Mike, still warmed, I suppose, by the camaraderie of the morning in the kitchen, says, "Maybe he's tired of being a corporate robber." "Michael," Dick and Barbara admonish in unison. Mike looks to me for affirmation. I can't meet his eye, nor can I claim his romantic motive. I can't explain to John why I won't return to work—John who loves the family business with all the devotion I imbued in him, loves it just as I did, building from the sturdy foundation my father had laid.

I have no words to tell him how that which had been central to my life had moved so irretrievably to the periphery, how the finely honed heavy machinery parts manufactured there no longer seem to have much to do with me.

John runs the business with a competence I don't question, and I am satisfied.

No, John, no. He leaves defeated by an old man's stubbornness.

Barbara and I are alone at the table. She regards me sharply. "Dad, will you at least think about what John said?"

"I have thought about it. A lot. I'm not going back to work."

"Why not?" Her voice rises.

"Because I don't want to.

"Dad—"

"I don't want to discuss it." I rise from the table and pick up a light jacket.

"I'm going out now," I say, walking toward the door.

"Where?" she demands.

"To visit a friend," I reply shortly, slamming the door behind me.

I walk down the long driveway and turn left toward the shopping center.

If I hurry, I can catch the nine-thirty bus. Mr. Miggs will be riding home from work now. I quicken my pace and am soon at the shopping center. I can see a bus in the distance. It pulls to the curb and picks up the large crowd of people there. My bus comes into view several minutes later. I reach the corner as it stops, step aboard, and drop my money into the coin box as the doors close behind me with a pneumatic sigh.

I look expectantly toward the back of the bus. Mr. Miggs is there. He doesn't sit in the back because he is black, he has assured me, but because that's the best vantage point for watching the other passengers. "You can see everybody without turning your head," he explains. "People don't like it if they think you're watching them."

Mr. Miggs waves and smiles. He is tall and reedlike. He is missing half his upper teeth. The remaining teeth are strong and large. The even division of the missing and existing teeth gives his dignified face a comic aspect. Despite his children's embarrassment he refuses to wear the dentures they have bought for him.

I place my hand on the back of each seat to keep my balance. I sit down next to Mr. Miggs, who welcomes me as always: "Good evening, Mr. Brinkman. How are you tonight?"

Our friendship is contained within the bus. He rides the bus home from work each evening and I catch it at nine-thirty at my stop, riding to the end of the line in the city where he gets off. Then the bus turns around, and I ride home alone. I don't know where Mr. Miggs lives.

Tonight as we ride through the night into the city, we talk of our dead wives. When I leave the bus, I'm pleasantly lost in memories of my college days and meeting Peg.

I met Mr. Miggs two years ago, shortly after the demise of my radio. I was buoyed in my loss by the drug Dr. Hooper prescribed for me. It was a comfortless tranquility. The mild summer evenings hung heavily without the radio and I began to take long walks.

I discovered the new shopping center to be a place of constant activity. I enjoyed strolling there or sitting on a bench watching the crowds.

One night, feeling particularly aimless, I was attracted by the self-contained mobility of the passing buses. I boarded a bus to the city on impulse.

Almost immediately, I regretted it. As I stepped aboard, I was hit by a wave of heavy, still, hot air. The driver intoned in a weary voice, "Air conditioning's broke. Got fans but no cooling."

Unable to think of a graceful retreat, I paid and sat down. There were few people on the bus. Two young boys jostled each other and made faces out the windows. A young woman cradled a small child, tired and irritable in the heat. I was touched by her patience as he squirmed and whined smudging the window with his restless hands. In the rear seat, an elderly black man sat nearly immobile, his eyelids lowered. I might have thought he was dozing off except that the eyes visible below the lids were as alert and sagacious as the hawks' that occasionally perch atop our fence. He divided his attention among the passengers with a judicious liveliness.

I was not, however, too interested in my fellow passengers because the bouncing of the bus and the closeness of the air seemed to collect inside my head. We passed several empty stops. I felt dizzy and nauseous. I leaned forward, resting my head on the back of the next seat. A fuzzy panic grew as I felt more and more faint.

Disoriented and weak, I was only vaguely aware of a hand on my shoulder. "You all right?" The black man's face was blurry as he leaned over me. The nausea had reached my throat. Afraid to speak, I shook my head.

"Driver, driver, open a window. You got a sick man back here," the black man called with authority.

The bus lurched and the driver called irritably, "Windows don't open no more. Goddamned bus is supposed to be air conditioned."

"Well, it ain't. So stop the bus."

The bus came to a halt and the doors swung open. With the first rush of air into the bus, I began to feel better.

"Can you walk?" he asked.

"I think so."

He supported my elbows. I was conscious of the tautness of the muscles in his thin arms.

"We get you out in the air, you perk right up," he said, guiding me toward the door.

The driver shouted, "I can't wait for you. You hear me, you two?"

"Don't worry about us," my new friend called.

"Please," I said, much revived, "I don't want you to miss your bus."

"That's all right. I catch another one. Us old mens has got to stick together."

We found a bench at the nearest bus stop and sat down. We were in a rundown, black neighborhood at the very outskirts of the city.

"I'm very grateful to you," I said, "but I'm fine now. Please take the next bus."

He studied my face with the same keenness I had noticed on the bus. "You better let me call your family come and get you. You awful pale. I don't know if you be all right." We both glanced around the shabby neighborhood surrounding us, and began to laugh.

"You awful pale. You awful pale. Oh my," he chortled.

Serious again, he repeated, "You let me call your family. I wait 'til they come."

The thought of Barbara swooping down in all her frantic concern was chilling.

"Oh no, I can't do that. I can't call my children. They don't even know where I am tonight. They'll just—" I stopped, hearing how foolishly fearful of my children I must sound.

"Yes, children," he said, "can sure be vexatious when you get old. I think they don't ever forget all them times you made them mad when they was little ones. They just been waiting for us to get old and weak. Then they got the upper hand. It funny how it go like that."

"It is funny, isn't it?" I said, delighted by his understanding. "My name is Walter Brinkman," I said, extending my hand.

"Good evening, Mr. Brinkman. I'm Mason Miggs."

And for all of our friendship we have retained this formality. We decided that I should take a cab. With an air of abashment, Mr. Miggs went to a phone booth to call the son with whom he lived, to explain his lateness. "They worry, you know," he said, shrugging. "Then they make a racket." I knew he would lie about his lateness to his son, just as I would lie to Barbara.

As Mr. Miggs and I waited, he mentioned that he rode the same bus every evening. The next night, wishing only to thank him again, I boarded the nine-thirty bus. It surprised me to find that Mr. Miggs and I seemed to have so many things to talk about. His wry humor and enthusiasm were compelling. After that first evening, I have found myself more and more often riding the bus simply to visit with Mr. Miggs. He seemed unconcerned that I ride the bus with no particular destination

Now, two years later, my family still knows nothing of Mr. Miggs. I tell them I visit Stan Garrity, an old friend whose face I barely remember.

Good, the cabbage is heading. The middle leaves turn inward and press against each other to form the concise heads. How do you know to perform this way? Why not turn outward to create leafy branches like the kale?

I'm going to learn to make sauerkraut this year. There's always more cabbage than we can possibly eat fresh.

The tomatoes cling to the vines like small, green fists. The fruit is well formed, the skin smooth. They are Chesapeake variety, well suited to this soil. It seems as though one plant is producing particularly well. I reach down into the wire hoops that support them to trim the yellow leaves.

It's time for a pep talk, tomatoes. You will represent all of us assembled here at the county fair! You will compete for ribbons. I fully expect to see a blue ribbon laid across the best of you. It's something you should be striving for, going to the fair. Enough said. I have confidence in you.

Last year at the fair, laid on the long tables in the produce exhibits, were squash, green beans heaped on white paper plates, fiery red peppers and waxy green ones, potatoes, pumpkins, pungent onions, precisely rowed ears of corn, fat red tomatoes, and so many more. Some could only boast of size, ostentatious and grotesque. Oh, but the serious competitors —perfection of their kind. This year mine will be there, too.

Yes, I'll start with one entry but in a prestige event: tomatoes, the crown of any garden.

I pace the garden, smiling, snapping my fingers in anticipation. "Dad?" Barbara so soon? I check my watch. It's early. Puzzled, I go into the house.

"Hi, you're home early," I say.

Barbara purses her lips in exasperation. "Oh Dad, did you forget? The party is tonight."

Uh oh. A weak chuckle. "I'm sorry. It did slip my mind."

"Did you at least check the liquor when it came, as I asked you?"

"Yes, yes, I did do that. All accounted for." I resist an urge to salute. Barbara wouldn't laugh.

"Thanks," she says, kissing me on the cheek. "I'm sorry I barked at you. I feel a little overwhelmed right now."

"Sure. Well, look, let me help."

"Would you? I could really use it."

Barbara organizes well. We work together smoothly with little conversation.

I'm glad to help her, comfortable in her company until she begins to tidy the living room.

She takes a copy of a news magazine and lays it atop a carefully arranged stack of magazines on the coffee table. The magazine is six years old. Inside, there is an article on my business with a picture of me interposed in the column.

I reread it not long ago. It describes me as "dynamic, inexhaustible." It goes on to say that, "at sixty-three, there is no sign of the energetic Walter Brinkman releasing the reins of absolute power he holds at *Brinkman International.*"

Barbara has several copies of these magazines. She continues to display them for reasons I refuse to dwell upon.

She often tells Dick when she thinks I don't hear her, "He's just lost his confidence, that's all. In no time at all he'll be wise, wonderful Dad again." She tells him as though Dick needed the reassurance.

Every time she says it, I want to shout at her, just as I want to shout at her now: "That man is dead. What's more, I don't mourn him. He crept out in the blood that stained the bed. There was so little of him left by then. Indeed, he had unraveled to a sad, gray tatter, that man, and left me behind to pay his debts."

But I'm not brave enough to tell my children this late in their lives that I was wrong about so many things; that, as sincere as my certainty was, it served me so poorly when I needed it.

I had wanted to protect them, to arm them, as any parent does. As Peg observed, I was too much the sort of person that I was to have done any differently. Nevertheless, I'm frightened for their vulnerability, frightened that they have shaped their lives around the wisdom of a man who thought the only vanity he need be forgiven was his pleasure in looking well in a dinner jacket.

Barbara starts out of the room, saying over her shoulder, "I invited the Garveys. I thought you'd enjoy seeing them." I wouldn't, but say nothing.

When she is gone, I take the magazine and slip it out of sight. Later at the party, the magazine has reappeared on the table. I sit, with a smile I'm hoping is friendly and relaxed. My dinner jacket, it seems to me, drapes unevenly across my chest.

Frank Garvey is pushing a conversation along with the rugged determination of loyalty to an old friendship.

"So, when are you going back to work?" he asks.

"I'm not going back."

"Ho well, you've got something going. I know you, Walter. You're the man who said he'd never retire." He is jovial and pokes me in the chest. Without a trace of compassion, I say, "You're right. No retirement for me, Frank. I've taken up gardening, in fact."

He recovers quickly, "No kidding? You'll be interested in this then. We're having our place landscaped."

Then he pins me to the chair with a lengthy story of the laying of the piping to a new fountain he and his wife have had sent from Italy.

Despite his best efforts, long silences fall. Finally, I allow my chin to drop gradually onto my chest; a reasonable picture of a man caught in a doze. I peer through slitted lids as Frank's back recedes. He's no less relieved than I, I'm sure, to be done with the conversation.

"Dad." Barbara touches my shoulder.

"Oh, I'm sorry." I shake my head. "I must have dropped off." "Are you tired?"

"Yes. If you don't mind, Barbara, I'll go to bed now. The party can probably get along without me. Everyone seems to be having a good time.

Barbara isn't pleased. "Well, if you feel you simply can't stay awake, go ahead."

I pretend I don't hear the pique in her voice. "Thanks, dear. I'll see you in the morning."

I walk straight through the house and out of the back door.

The air is pleasant. I walk toward the closing shopping center. I look at my watch—nine-twenty I can catch the bus.

The bus and I arrive at the corner at the same moment. I board and approach Mr. Miggs at the back of the bus. He gestures toward my dinner jacket. "You going to a dance?"

I laugh, unembarrassed. I know Mr. Miggs will relish my escape from the party as much as I do.

"My daughter was giving a party. She insisted I put in an appearance. There didn't seem to be much to say to anyone.

Mr. Miggs nods, smiling. "Yes, yes," he says, "they put you out for looks, just like the cookies.

"Before I had my heart attack, they'd let me drink at their parties. When I used to get to dancing, and they all stand around and say, 'Ain't that something, that old man do them funny dances?' but back of that, they saying, 'That old man a fool. He too old for all of that.'"

"Then if you don't get up and dance, they say, 'Ain't that sad and he used to be so lively.'" We laugh.

"They don't want you to be old, they just want you to act old," he says, "or leastways how they see old before they get there. That's because they don't know about being old."

"No, they don't."

"But that's all right," he says slyly, "because they don't know the bad of it but they don't know the good of it either. Like how you get to loving little things you wouldn't have thought much about when you was a young man.

"Little things like my garden," I add.

"And like my job," he says. "Anyway, getting old going to take them by surprise just like it did you and me."

Mr. Miggs works, although his children don't want him to. They don't like his working because of his heart condition, but they more especially don't like his job. Yet every weekday afternoon he rides out of the city into the suburbs to a house where he was a gardener until the heart attack made him unable to handle the heavy work. Mr. Miggs often speaks of his illness. I never speak of mine.

On his job now, he stays in the kitchen, drinking coffee and reading the paper, until nine, when the man who has hired him comes home from work. The man's wife is afraid to be alone in the house, and she can't find a man who will stay past five. Mr. Miggs says she will call through the kitchen door, "Mason, Mason, what is that noise?" He has only to call back, "That's the dog" or "Only the wind, and she is comforted.

His children, all professionals whom he worked to educate, are ashamed of his job.

It's the having somewhere to go every day that's important enough for him to resist all his children's threats and cajolery. He explains, "The days, they don't just run together, all the same, no more. You know how they can do.

"And as for the children, I give in a lot of times because I'm plain too tired to fight. But everybody know when enough is enough. Then you can't give no ground."

Because the bus is more crowded than usual tonight, Mr. Miggs and I must share the rear seat with three teen-aged girls who comb their hair and giggle. We lower our voices. He asks after the garden as one might inquire after relatives.

Everything is doing well, I tell him, but I'm worried about late blight in the tomatoes. I hate to think of the disfigurement the disease could cause so close to the fair.

He consoles me, "You don't get that unless you got a real wet summer. We ain't had that. They be fine. You listen to me because I know."

He shakes a long finger at me. "You got a good garden. All them things you bring me taste just fine. I don't get no flavor from the things in the grocery stores. Back home when I was a child, my mama always had a garden. When she'd start canning and line all them jars up in the cupboard, why, we thought we was rich." His eyes have a faraway look. "Yes, I always did love a garden and yours is a fine one. I can tell."

"It is, Mr. Miggs," I say. "I wish you could see it. Perhaps you could . . ."

I stop. Buoyed by his compliments, I have nearly invited Mr. Miggs to my house. I shudder, picturing Barbara at the sight of him. He would hear as well as I the warning bells behind her politely impassive face.

I feel a sharp twist of anguish at having hurt my friend. But he says without rancor, "Mr. Brinkman, it might surprise you, but it wouldn't be easy for me to take you home either. You see, they'd all start, 'What that white man want with you?' because they'd never think you and me could be friends. And when you look at it, it is peculiar. So it's all right because I know how it is."

A heaviness settles in me that lingers after we say goodbye. Mr. Miggs forgives what I cannot.

The fair is two weeks away. The garden pulses with a common breath in its full-blown extravagance. The plants enfold the nighttime dampness in their dense depths, releasing it in steady clouds when the morning sun lies in shadowless lengths along the rows. The cabbage heads are tight-skinned and shiny, like bald men. The stems of the string beans stagger beneath the weight of the pods. The cucumber vines greedily creep over every available inch of soil. The cornstalks tower above the rest of the garden, shaking their long, thin leaves like nervous fingers. I've decided to have a greenhouse built this fall. The winter won't press so heavily this year.

A greenhouse! I have plans that I've copied from a library book: glass for the life-giving sunlight, water, and heat. With cold frames outside, I can plant well into December.

In the fall, I'll have a greenhouse. After the fair, when I'm not so busy, I'll call a builder.

The tomatoes are tinged a faint red. They're round, their pulp pressing evenly against the skin. They're prize tomatoes, for certain. Their pungent odor rises in the heat. In untangling several vines, my hand is yellow to the wrist from the fine powder under the leaves. Prize tomatoes, going to the fair.

I make excuses to go out in the evenings. Barbara is anxious. I tell her I visit Stan Garrity. Instead, Mr. Miggs and I ride the bus—he with a protective arm encircling a large bag of canned vegetables I have brought for him, and I exuberant and talkative about the fair.

Barbara is attentive to me. I see the mental picture she does when she regards me. "Out again tonight, Dad?" she asks, her eyes fixed to draw an answer larger than her casual question demands.

I'm careless, too excited by the fair to conceal it. I hear my laugh—a loud, sharp bark that makes her jump. I walk to my garden, rubbing my hands, thinking of the fair. I leave the house without explanation to meet Mr. Miggs, sometimes in defiance, sometimes only because I've forgotten the danger in alarming Barbara.

The sun slants low in the sky. Tomorrow is the fair, and this evening I select the tomatoes I will take.

I stoop in the garden, poking a sure hand through the wide wire hoops around the tomato plants. I carefully pull six from the vine. I chose these six, weeks ago, while they were still green. None is a disappointment. My eye was that sure! How beautiful you are, your symmetry, your uniform color. Six glossy, red globes, the pick of the vines. The jewels of my garden.

I lay them in a small basket beside me, delicately and gently, so as not to bruise them. They're perfect. They're . . .

"Dad." Barbara stands by the garden, her arms folded ominously.

"I ran into Stan Garrity in the supermarket today," she says. "He said he hasn't seen you in years."

"Oh, really? It doesn't seem that long. Old age showing up, I guess."

"Where are you going in the evenings?" she demands.

I stand, staked by the resolution of her stare. "I don't think that at my age I should have to account for my whereabouts," I say in a voice braver than I feel.

"I would agree with you, except for the-the-the trouble you've had. I'm responsible for you and I think you owe me this much just to put my mind at ease."

"Good God, Barbara, I'm not running a diamond-smuggling operation or patronizing the local ladies of the evening."

"You're not going to tell me, are you?" she says and the idea that she expects that I will not tell her crystallizes a decision I hadn't made.

"No."

"I'm sorry to hear that," she says, starting for the house. I feel a pang of fear at the genuine regret in her voice.

That fear pricks at me as I lift the basket. I worry that leaving tonight will antagonize her further, but Mr. Miggs must see the tomatoes that will go to fair. Cradling the basket tenderly under one arm, I walk toward the shopping center to meet the bus.

On the bus, Mr. Miggs examines each tomato with meticulous scrutiny. He pronounces them all as fine as any he's seen. I'm ready for the fair.

I'm awake before first light this morning. I don't rise until I hear the rest of the family. Sleeplessness is a bad sign, Dr. Hooper has told us all.

In the clarity of the early morning, I see the threat of Barbara's anxiety. With the fair nearly here, I'm afraid I've waited too long to mollify her. I lay my plans. The tomatoes wait atop my dresser.

"What are you going to do today?" Barbara asks at breakfast. "I'd planned to go out for a while. Might play a little golf. I'm rather tired of the garden just now.

Bingo! Right on target. Barbara leans over to kiss me. "Oh, that sounds wonderful. Have a good time.

"I will," I say, chiding myself for considering Barbara so formidable. Later, I walk the rows of the garden, touching a leaf here and there, and thinking of the fair. I took the tomatoes there this morning to enter them into exhibit for tonight's judging. I placed them in a basket and covered them with a small towel. I've seen people carrying their pets in just such a way. Traveling in the opposite direction that I take with Mr. Miggs, I took a bus ride to the fairgrounds in the next town.

What a place, the fair! So early in the morning and already a large cow was being coaxed and pushed into a stall by two children who barely rose above her flank. A nanny goat bleated in an alarming human wail when her kid was taken from the truck before her. Pigs grunted as they slammed their ponderous bodies against the slats of their pens. Roosters crowed, people shouted, the horses in the vans moved restlessly in the excitement. The rides on the midway sat hunched and silent, great metallic beasts. A wondrous place, the fair.

Although I stayed as long as I dared, I couldn't wait long enough to see the tomatoes put into exhibit. It would be late in the day, I was told, and I've promised myself that Barbara shall have nothing to fault in my behavior. Just as I have my plan, so I know does she: to be sprung into action at the first sign of what she deems craziness.

When she comes home from work, she will find me in the house, reddened from the sun and speaking of a pleasant golf game.

I stay home in the evening and play canasta with Dick and Barbara.

She says several times, "Isn't this nice, Dad? Isn't this fun?" I heartily agree each time.

I'm badly beaten in the game because although I didn't see the tomatoes put into exhibit, I know how they must look. The exhibits are all displayed on the starkness of white paper plates. Perhaps the tomatoes reflect a pinkness on the plate from the lights overhead. People walk by the tables, and how the tomatoes must shine. Of the ones I saw brought in, surely none were better than mine.

I don't dwell on the image as I can't appear distracted to Barbara. I'm very tired when I go to bed.

The next day I run some errands for the family. This takes longer than I expect. There is not time to go to the fair without risking being late for dinner. Even with so much to do, time passes with the perversity I remember from waiting for Christmas as a child. By dinner time, the anticipation has compressed into a solid warmth in my chest.

The judging begins at six-thirty. If I leave right after dinner, I'll arrive just in time. The children aren't home for dinner. An extra burden of conversation falls on me. I'm holding my own and Barbara seems relaxed.

Slowly, deliberately, fork to mouth and back to plate; again fork to mouth and back to plate until the plate is empty. I thank Barbara for the meal, then say offhandedly, "I think I'll take a little walk." It's a quarter to six.

Barbara's head snaps up, "Where are you going?" There's a hard edge to her voice that warns me to be very cautious. Dick looks away. This is it.

"I'm going to the shopping center," I say, starting for the door. "I have a few things I want to pick up.

"I'll drive you up.

"I'd rather walk, Barbara."

"No." Her eyes never leave my face.

The bubble of excitement explodes into anger. "You can't keep me here," I shout.

Dick rises and comes toward me. "Now, take it easy, Walter. We think it's best if you stay around the house for awhile, until you get yourself. calmed down."

"I was perfectly calm until my daughter began treating me like a ten-year-old."

I take a step toward the door. Dick catches my arm firmly. "Come on, Walter." He is pleading.

"Dad," Barbara says, "you haven't fooled me for one minute in the last few days. This garden has been exactly like the CB."

"It wasn't a CB, goddamnit!" I shout.

"Whatever. I want you to see Dr. Hooper again. In the meantime, I want you to stay home where the people who love you can protect you.

"Protect me from what?" Dick still grips my arms.

"From yourself, for right now. I'm not going to stand by and allow you to slide into—into what we had before."

"This isn't the same thing, I swear to you." I'm seized by desperation at the implacability of her expression.

"Dad, people who have your—problem often don't recognize it themselves."

"I simply won't stand for this," I say. "I'm leaving." The pressure of Dick's hand on my arm increases. He guides me to a chair and presses my shoulder until I sit down.

"Who are you, Dick, Barbara's goon?" My cheeks are hot with humiliation. Dick is embarrassed. "I'm sorry, Walter. I wish it were different."

"Dad, listen please." Barbara sits opposite to me at the table. "I'm going to stay home from work tomorrow. Then you and I will go to see Dr. Hooper. He's told me that we could have an appointment at a moment's notice."

I'm defeated, too uncertain that what they say is untrue. "All right." I rise. "I'm going to my room now, if that's permitted these days."

"Of course, Dad. Listen—" I go to my room.

I sit on the edge of my bed, blank, drained, a crazy, old man, not to be trusted out alone. My eyes scan the room and come to rest on the basket that carried the tomatoes to the fair.

No, by God, they're not going to do this. Mr. Miggs is right. Everybody knows when enough is enough. I pace around the room, hot with rage. Then I hurriedly pick up the phone and dial. It rings so many times. At last, "Hello?"

"Charlotte, Charlotte," I say, "you must help.me,"

Charlotte laughs in confusion. "Dad, slow down. What is it?"

"I made plans to go out tonight for something very important, and Barbara has refused to allow me out, if you can imagine anything so absurd. She even has Dick acting like some sort of henchman. He was actually muscling me around."

Charlotte is wary. "I can hardly believe that. Why?"

"You know how Barbara is. Because I haven't been to the country club and don't socialize with people she considers acceptable, she thinks I'm off the track again. Once her mind's set, well, you know how she is." I feel only a faint pang of shame for exploiting my daughters' rivalry.

"What do you want me to do?" she asks.

"Come plead my case for me.

"Be right there." She hangs up.

I stand by the window, watching the road in front of the house. Car after car goes by. Charlotte doesn't live far away but it's a long time until she pulls into the driveway. It's seven-thirty.

I leave my room and let her in the back door. "Thanks for coming, honey," I say. Barbara enters the room behind me.

Charlotte is brisk. "What's going on here, Barbara? Dad says you've refused to let him go out. Who in the hell gave you that right?"

Barbara's face reddens. "How dare you come marching in here, telling me what to do about Dad? You see him only when it suits you. You've refused to even listen to anything I've tried to tell you about him. You know nothing about what's been going on around here. If you were here, you'd know he's—he's having trouble again.

"And you're a psychiatrist, I suppose," Charlotte says. "What wild, strange things is he doing?"

Dick appears behind Barbara as she says, "He's obsessed with that garden, Charlotte. He disappears at night until all hours, and won't tell me where he's going."

"I'm home by eleven every night," I say, quietly.

Charlotte laughs. "He gardens and he stays out until eleven. Yes, indeed, Barbara, that's certainly bizarre behavior. I think you're the one that's crazy."

Barbara's voice chokes with rage. "I don't expect you to understand. You weren't even in the country when we had the CB incident a couple of years ago.

"It wasn't a CB," I say, almost to myself.

Charlotte clicks her tongue in disgust, and turns to me. "Come on, Dad. I'll take you where you want to go.

"Oh no, you don't," Barbara screams. "Dick."

"Just let them go," Dick says. "This is ridiculous."

Barbara wheels on him. She is utterly betrayed. "Dick, do something. Call the police."

Dick starts toward us, reluctantly. "Charlotte, come on, now. Leave Dad here with us. We'll take care of him."

Charlotte's feet are planted in a combative stance. Her eyes gleam with the joy of the contest. "Stop right there, fucker," she says.

Dick stops as though she has pointed a gun at him. He sputters, "There's no need for that sort of language."

"Oh," shrieks Barbara.

Charlotte turns again to me. "Where do you want to go, Dad?"

"To the fair. To the fair, James," I crow.

She takes my hand and we hurry out to her car. It's a small sports car. The top is down. As we speed up the road, the wind catches our hair and waves it like banners around our heads. I laugh in great hiccoughs of exhilaration. Charlotte is perhaps now a little doubtful, but she drives me to the fairgrounds. She stops at the gate, saying, "I can't stay. Can you get home?" I assure her I can.

"O.K.," she says. "Take care of yourself, will you, or Barbara will have my head on a platter."

"I'm fine, honey."

I walk through the fairgrounds. The sun is setting. Throngs of people walk between the buildings housing the livestock. The animals are quiet here at the end of the day. They have given over the activity to the people. The aroma around the pens, however, attests to their presence.

The rides on the midway scream and thunder, streaking into the darkening sky in garish bolts, then plummeting again toward the ground.

I push through the crowds toward the produce display building. I'm caught again in the celebration of the fair. I think the excitement I feel is a premonition that I won't miss the tomato judging.

Closer, closer. I can see the wide doors propped open and a flow of people issuing through them. It's not over. It can't be. I glance again at my watch. It's 8:35.

I hurry toward the door. I question a man I've seen descend the ramp of the building. "Is the produce judging over?"

"Yes," he says, "they just finished."

Feeling hot tears pressing my eyelids, I retreat into the shadow of the building. These tears are ludicrous, of course. Here I am hiding in the shadows from a crowd of strangers, and weeping. Over what? Six tomatoes!

The tomatoes. The way they looked lying in the basket in the garden; round and perfect. Yes, perfect. I wasn't there for the judging, but then I didn't need to be. The judges saw the tomatoes, turned them over, looked with knowing eyes.

I walk slowly toward the door. I'm afraid now to know, afraid of being wrong in my judgment of the tomatoes. I reach the door and, squaring my shoulders, walk into the vast, harshly lit room. The tomato exhibits are set on a central table. I can see them from the door. There are ribbons laid across some of them. Some are blue ribbons. One in each class of tomato.

When I reach the table, I walk alongside as I imagine a disinterested observer might. I turn over several ribbons in other classes, read the names of the exhibitors: "Tomato-Rutgers—Henry Ames." Henry has taken a second place. "Tomato-Hybrid Red—Lucille Banks." Lucille has taken a blue ribbon.

The Chesapeakes—my class—are set near the end of the table. I hesitate, then turn over the white ribbon, third place. My name isn't there. I turn over the red ribbon, second place, thinking, "Second would be nothing to be ashamed of." My name isn't there.

I inspect the losers. Some I know aren't mine. Their flaws are too obvious. My hand trembles as I reach for the blue ribbon. I turn it over and read, "Tomato-Chesapeake—Walter Brinkman."

Prize tomatoes! My tomatoes! Blue-ribbon tomatoes!

I lay the ribbon down on the plate and touch the tomatoes gently. I feel light, as though my body were no more than air. I smile. I want to laugh out loud, to clap my hands, point out the tomatoes to who ever passes by. Mr. Miggs, I wish that you were here.

Mr. Miggs. I check my watch. I'm only a stop or two above his stop. There's plenty of time to catch his bus. I take a last look at the tomatoes, the ribbon. Tomorrow I'll come with a camera. Goodbye, my beauties.

I walk slowly. I consider going home, but Barbara's enraged face is far too vivid. I stop, stand gazing into the trees at the edge of the fairgrounds. The sun has sunk below the horizon. The sky behind the trees, still softly lit in gold, casts a long shadow behind me.

A strange peace settles over me as the sky fades into gray. I feel whole again, for the first time since Peg's death—not the same, to be sure, but no less than I was before. A man who has raised prize tomatoes must know something, something of great value perhaps. Surely I have something yet to teach my children. I, still with much to learn from the pain that disassembled and rearranged me, am different but not lost.

Oddly, Barbara's anger has lost its threat. The worst she can do is to send me back to Dr. Hooper, and he, after all, doesn't know everything. He wouldn't know a prize tomato if he saw one.

I begin to walk toward the gate. Ah, Barbara, I do love you. With effort, we could be friends, you and I. I believe I have the courage now to try to explain to you some of what has happened to me. I was quite a persuasive man at one time; perhaps I still am. Who knows? You may find you can love me just as well now as before. Ours are primal ties that go far beyond appearances. We'll test those ties, Barbara, I promise.

Yes, I'll ride the bus home, talk to Barbara tonight. But first I have one more thing to do.

My strides feel long and strong. The bus stop is an easy distance away. The bus pulls up just as I reach the curb. I climb aboard and take the seat at the back.

Mr. Miggs will be surprised to see me already on the bus. So much has happened and we have so little time to talk.

The familiar jostling of the bus seems to heighten my exhilaration. I watch the lights glide over the windows as we near Mr. Migg's stop.

Through the window I see him rise from the bench, his back erect. Boarding the bus, he blinks in the glare. As he turns toward the back, he spots me. His half-and-half grin splits his face.

Unable to wait until he sits down, I say as he approaches, "Mr. Miggs, next Saturday you must come to see my garden and stay to dinner afterward. I won't take 'no' for an answer."

He halts, his hand clutching the back of a seat in the rocking aisle of the bus. "Well, I'll be," he says, "then I guess you better call me Mason."

The Garden of Time

J. G. BALLARD

TOWARDS EVENING, when the great shadow of the Palladian villa filled the terrace, Count Axel left his library and walked down the wide rococo steps among the time flowers. A tall, imperious figure in a black velvet jacket, a gold tie-pin glinting below his George V beard, cane held stiffly in a white-gloved hand, he surveyed the exquisite crystal flowers without emotion, listening to the sounds of his wife's harpsichord, as she played a Mozart rondo in the music room, echo and vibrate through the translucent petals.

The garden of the villa extended for some two hundred yards below the terrace, sloping down to a miniature lake spanned by a white bridge, a slender pavilion on the opposite bank. Axel rarely ventured as far as the lake; most of the time flowers grew in a small grove just below the terrace, sheltered by the high wall which encircled the estate. From the terrace he could see over the wall to the plain beyond, a continuous expanse of open ground that rolled in great swells to the horizon, where it rose slightly before finally dipping from sight. The plain surrounded the house on all sides, its drab emptiness emphasizing the seclusion and mellowed magnificence of the villa. Here, in the garden, the air seemed brighter, the sun warmer, while the plain was always dull and remote.

As was his custom before beginning his evening stroll, Count Axel looked out across the plain to the final rise, where the horizon was illuminated like a distant stage by the fading sun. As the Mozart chimed delicately around him, flowing from his wife's grace hands, he saw that the advance column of an enormous army was moving slowly over the horizon. At first glance, the long ranks seemed to be progressing in orderly lines, but on closer inspection, it was apparent that, like the obscured detail of a Goya landscape, the army was composed of a vast throng of people, men and women, interspersed with a few soldiers in uniforms, pressing forward in a disorganized tide.

Some labored under heavy loads suspended from crude yokes around their necks, others struggled with cumbersome wooden carts, their hands wrenching at the wheel spokes, a few trudged on alone, but all moved on at the same pace, bowed backs illuminated in the fleeting sun.

The advancing throng was almost too far away to be visible but even as Axel watched, his expression aloof yet observant, it came perceptibly nearer, the vanguard of an immense rabble appearing from below the horizon. At last, as the daylight began to fade, the front edge of the throng reached the crest of the first swell below the horizon, and Axel turned from the terrace and walked down among the time flowers.

The flowers grew to a height of about six feet, their slender stems, like rods of glass, bearing a dozen leaves, the once transparent fronds frosted by the fossilized veins. At the peak of each stem was the time flower, the size of a goblet, the opaque outer petals enclosing the crystal heart. Their diamond brilliance contained a thousand faces, the crystal seeming to drain the air of its light and motion. As the flowers swayed slightly in the evening air, they glowed like flame-tipped spears.

Many of the stems no longer bore flowers, and Axel examined them all carefully, a note of hope now and then crossing his eyes as he searched for any further buds. Finally he selected a large flower on the stem nearest the wall, removed his gloves and with his strong fingers snapped it off.

As he carried the flower back on to the terrace, it began to sparkle and deliquesce, the light trapped within the core at last released Gradually the crystal dissolved, only the outer petals remaining intact, and the air around Axel became bright and vivid, charged with slanting rays that flared away into the waning sunlight. Strange shifts momentarily transformed the evening, subtly altering its dimensions of time and space. The darkened the portico of the house, its patina of age stripped away, loomed with a curious spectral whiteness as if suddenly remembered in a dream.

Raising his head, Axel peered over the wall again. Only the farthest rim of the horizon was lit by the sun, and the great throng, which before had stretched almost a quarter of the way across the plain, had now receded to the horizon, the entire concourse abruptly flung back in a reversal of time, and appeared to be stationary.

The flower in Axel's hand had shrunk to the size of a glass thimble, the petals contracting around the vanishing core. A faint sparkle flickered from the center and extinguished itself, and Axel felt the flower melt like an ice-cold bead of dew in his hand.

Dusk closed across the house, sweeping its long shadows over the plain, the horizon merging into the sky. The harpsichord was silent, and the time flowers, no longer reflecting its music, stood motionlessly, like an embalmed forest.

For a few minutes Axel looked down at them, counting the flowers which remained, then greeted his wife as she crossed the terrace, her brocade evening dress rustling over the ornamental tiles.

"What a beautiful evening, Axel." She spoke feelingly, as if she were thanking her husband personally for the great ornate shadow across the lawn and the dark brilliant air. Her face was serene and intelligent, her hair, swept back behind her head into a jeweled clasp, touched with silver. She wore her dress low across her breast, revealing a long slender neck and high chin. Axel surveyed her with fond pride. He gave her his arm and they walked down the steps into the garden.

"One of the longest evenings his summer," Axel confirmed, adding: "I picked a perfect flower, my dear, a jewel. With luck it should last us for several days." A frown touched his brow, and he glanced involuntarily at the wall. "Each time now they seem to come nearer."

His wife smiled at him encouragingly and held his arm more tightly.

Both of them knew that the time garden was dying.

Three evenings later, as he had estimated (though sooner than he secretly hoped), Count Axel plucked another flower from the time garden.

When he first looked over the wall the approaching rabble filled the distant half of the plain, stretching across the horizon in an unbroken mass. He thought he could hear the low, fragmentary sounds of voices carried across the empty air, a sullen murmur punctuated by cries and shouts, but quickly told himself that he had imagined them. Luckily, his wife was at the harpsichord, and the rich contrapuntal patterns of a Bach fugue cascaded lightly across the terrace, masking any other noises.

Between the house and the horizon the plain was divided into four huge swells, the crest of each one clearly visible in the slanting light. Axel had promised himself that he would never count them, but the number was too small to remain unobserved, particularly when it so obviously marked the progress of the advancing army. By now the forward line had passed the first crest and was well on its way to the second; the main bulk of the throng pressed behind it, hiding the crest and the even vaster concourse spreading from the horizon. Looking to left and right of the central body, Axel could see the apparently limitless extent of the army. What had seemed at first to be the central mass was no more than a minor advance guard, one of many similar arms reaching across the plain. The true center had not yet emerged, but from the rate of extension Axel estimated that when it finally reached the plain it would completely cover every foot of ground.

Axel searched for any large vehicles or machines, but all was amorphous and uncoordinated as ever. There were no banner or flags, no mascots or pike-bearers. Heads bowed, the multitude pressed on, unaware of the sky.

Suddenly, just before Axel turned away, the forward edge of the throng appeared on top of the second crest, and swarmed down across the plain. What astounded Axel was the incredible distance it had covered while out of sight. The figures were now twice the size, each one clearly within sight.

Quickly, Axel stepped from the terrace, selected a time flower from the garden and tore it from the stem. As it released its compacted light, he returned to the terrace. When the flower had shrunk to a frozen pearl in his palm he looked out at the plain, with relief saw that the army had retreated to the horizon again.

Then he realized that the horizon was much nearer than previously, and that what he assumed to be the horizon was the first crest.

When he joined the Countess on their evening walk he told her nothing of this, but she could see behind his casual unconcern and did what she could to dispel his worry.

Walking down the steps, she pointed to the time garden. "What a wonderful display, Axel. There are so many flowers still."

Axel nodded, smiling to himself at his wife's attempt to reassure him. Her use of "still" had revealed her own unconscious anticipation of the end. In fact a mere dozen flowers remained of the many hundred that had grown in the garden, and several of these were little more than buds—only three or four were fully grown. As they walked down to the lake, the Countess's dress rustling across the cool turf, he tried to decide whether to pick the larger flowers first or leave them to the end. Strictly, it would be better to give the smaller flowers additional time to grow and mature, and this advantage would be lost if he retained the larger flowers to the end, as he wished to do, for the final repulse. However, he realized that it mattered little either way; the garden would soon die and the smaller flowers required far longer than he could give them to accumulate their compressed cores of time. During his entire lifetime he had failed to notice a single evidence of growth among the flowers. The larger blooms had always been mature, and none of the buds had shown the slightest development.

Crossing the lake, he and his wife looked down at their reflections in the still black water. Shielded by the pavilion on one side and the high garden wall on the other, the villa in the distance, Axel felt composed and secure, the plain with its encroaching multitude a nightmare from which he had safely awakened. He put one arm around his wife's smooth waist and pressed her affectionately to his shoulder, realizing that he had not embraced her for several years, though their lives together had been timeless and he could remember as if yesterday when he first brought her to live in the villa.

"Axel," his wife asked with sudden seriousness, "before the garden dies . . . may I pick the last flower?"

Understanding her request, he nodded slowly.

One by one over the succeeding evenings, he picked the remaining flowers, leaving a single small bud which grew just below the terrace for his wife. He took the flowers at random, refusing to count or ration them, plucking two or three of the smaller buds at the same time when necessary. The approaching horde had now reached the second and third crests, a vast concourse of laboring humanity that blotted out the horizon. From the terrace Axel could see clearly the shuffling, straining ranks moving down into the hollow towards the final crest, and occasionally the sounds of their voices carried across to him, interspersed with cries of anger and the cracking of whips. The wooden carts lurched from side to side on tilting wheels, their drivers struggling to control them. As far as Axel could tell, not a single member of the throng was aware of its overall direction. Rather, each one blindly moved forward across the ground directly below the heels of the person in front of him, and the only unity was that of the cumulative compass. Pointlessly, Axel hoped that the true center; far below the horizon, might be moving in a different direction, and that gradually the multitude would alter course, swing away from the villa and recede from the plain like a turning tide.

On the last evening but one, as he plucked the time flower, the forward edge of the rabble had reached the third crest, and was swarming past it. While he waited for the Countess, Axel looked at the two flowers left, both small buds which would carry them back through only a few minutes of the next evening. The glass stems of the dead flowers reared up stiffly into the air, but the whole garden had lost its bloom.

Axel passed the next morning quietly in his library, sealing the rarer of his manuscripts into the glass-topped cases between the galleries. He walked slowly down the portrait corridor, polishing each of the pictures carefully, then tidied his desk and locked the door behind him. During the afternoon he busied himself in the drawing-rooms, unobtrusively assisting his wife as she cleaned their ornaments and straightened the vases and busts.

By evening, as the sun fell behind the house, they were both tired and dusty, and neither had spoken to the other all day. When his wife moved towards the music-room, Axel called her back.

"Tonight we'll pick the flowers together, my dear," he said to her evenly. "One for each of us."

He peered only briefly over the wall. They could hear, less than half a mile away, the great dull roar of the ragged army, the ring of iron and lash, pressing on towards the house.

Quickly, Axel plucked his flower, a bud no bigger than a sapphire. As it flickered softly, the tumult outside momentarily receded, then began to gather again.

Shutting his ears to the clamor, Axel looked around at the villa, counting the six columns in the portico, then gazed out across the lawn at the silver disc of the lake, its bowl reflecting the last evening light, and at the shadows moving between the tall trees, lengthening across the crisp turf. He lingered over the bridge where he and his wife had stood arm in arm for so many summers—

"Axel!"

The tumult outside roared into the air, a thousand voices bellowed only twenty or thirty yards away. A stone flew over the wall and landed among the time flowers, snapping several of the brittle stems. The Countess ran towards him as a further barrage rattled along the wall. Then a heavy tile whirled through the air over their heads and crashed into one of the conservatory windows.

"Axel!" He put his arms around her, straightening his silk cravat when her shoulder brushed it between his lapels.

"Quickly, my dear, the last flower!" He led her down the steps and through the garden. Taking the stem between her jeweled fingers, she snapped it cleanly, then cradled it within her palms.

For a moment the tumult lessened slightly and Axel collected himself. In the vivid light sparkling from the flower he saw his wife's white, frightened eyes. "Hold it as long as you can, my dear, until the last grain dies."

Together they stood on the terrace, the Countess clasping the brilliant dying jewel, the air closing in upon them as the voices outside mounted again. The mob was battering at the heavy iron gates, and the whole villa shook with the impact.

While the final glimmer of light sped away, the Countess raised her palms to the air, as if releasing an invisible bird, then in a final access of courage put her hands in her husband's, her smile as radiant as the vanished flower.

"Oh, Axel!" she cried.

Like a sword, the darkness swooped down across them.

Heaving and swearing, the outer edges of the mob reached the knee-high remains of the wall enclosing the ruined estate, hauled their carts over it and along the dry ruts of what once had been an ornate drive. The ruin, formerly a spacious villa, barely interrupted the ceaseless tide of humanity. The lake was empty, fallen trees rotting at its bottom, an old bridge rusting into it. Weeds flourished among the long grass in the lawn, overrunning the ornamental pathways and carved stone screens.

Much of the terrace had crumbled, and the main section of the mob cut straight across the lawn, by-passing the gutted villa, but one or two of the more curious climbed up and searched among the shell. The doors had rotted from their hinges and the floors had fallen through. In the music-room an ancient harpsichord had been chopped into firewood, but a few keys still lay among the dust. All the books had been toppled from the shelves in the library, the canvases had been slashed, and gilt frames littered the floor.

As the main body of the mob reached the house, it began to cross the wall at all points along its length. Jostled together, the people stumbled into the dry lake, swarmed over the terrace and pressed through the house towards the open doors on the north side.

One area alone withstood the endless wave. Just below the terrace, between the wrecked balcony and the wall, was a dense, six-foot-height growth of heavy thorn-bushes. The barbed foliage formed an impenetrable mass, and the people passing stepped around it carefully, noticing the belladonna entwined among the branches. Most of them were too busy finding their footing among the upturned flagstones to look up into the center of the thorn-bushes, where two stone statues stood side by side, gazing out over the grounds from their protected vantage point. The larger of the figures was the effigy of a bearded man in a high-collared jacket, a cane under one arm. Beside him was a woman in an elaborate full-skirted dress, her slim, serene face unmarked by the wind and rain. In her left hand she lightly clasped a single rose, the delicately formed petals so thin as to be almost transparent.

As the sun died away behind the house a single ray of light glanced through a shattered cornice and struck the rose, reflected off the whorl of petals on to the statues, lighting up the gray stone so that for a fleeting moment it was indistinguishable from the long-vanished flesh of the statues' originals.

How the Crab Apple Grew

GARRISON KEILLOR

IT HAS BEEN A quiet week in Lake Wobegon. It was warm and sunny on Sunday, and on Monday the flowering crab in the Dieners' backyard burst into blossom. Suddenly, in the morning, when everyone turned their backs for a minute, the tree threw off its bathrobe and stood trembling, purple, naked, revealing all its innermost flowers. When you saw it standing where weeks before had been a bare stick stuck in the dirt, you had to stop, it made your head spin.

Becky Diener sat upstairs in her bedroom and looked at the tree. She was stuck on an assignment from Miss Melrose for English, a 750-word personal essay, "Describe your backyard as if you were seeing it for the first time." After an hour she had thirty-nine words, which she figured would mean she'd finish at 1:45 P.M. Tuesday, four hours late, and therefore would get an F even if the essay was great, which it certainly wasn't.

How can you describe your backyard as if you'd never seen it? If you'd never seen it, you'd have grown up someplace else, and wouldn't be yourself, you'd be someone else entirely, and how are you supposed to know what that person would think?

She imagined seeing the backyard in 1996, returning home from Hollywood. "Welcome Becky!" said the big white banner across McKinley Street as the pink convertible drove slowly along, everyone clapping and cheering as she cruised by, Becky Belafonte the movie star, and got off at her old house. "Here," she said to the reporters, "is where I sat as a child and dreamed my dreams, under this beautiful flowering crab. I dreamed I was a Chinese princess." Then a reporter asked, "Which of your teachers was the most important to you, encouraging you and inspiring you?" And just then she saw an old woman's face in the crowd, Miss Melrose pleading, whispering, "Say me, oh please, say me," and Becky looked straight at her as she said, "Oh, there were so many, I couldn't pick out one, they were all about the same, you know. But perhaps Miss—Miss—Oh, I can't remember her name—she taught English, I think—Miss Milross? She was one of them. But there were so many."

She looked at her essay. "In my backyard is a tree that has always been extremely important to me since I was six years old when my dad came home one evening with this bag in the trunk and he said, 'Come here and help me plant this'—"

She crumpled the sheet of paper and started again.

"One evening when I was six years old, my father arrived home as he customarily did around 5:30 or 6:00 P.M. except this evening he had a wonderful surprise for me, he said, as he led me toward the car.

"My father is not the sort of person who does surprising things very often so naturally I was excited that evening when he said he had something for me in the car, having just come home from work where he had been. I was six years old at the time."

She took out a fresh sheet. "Six years old was a very special age for me and one thing that made it special was when my dad and I planted a tree together in our backyard. Now it is grown and every spring it gives off large purple blossoms. . . ."

The tree was planted by her dad, Harold, in 1976, ten years after he married her mother, Marlys. They grew up on Taft Street, across from each other, a block from the ballfield. They liked each other tremendously and then they were in love, as much as you can be when you're so young. Thirteen and fourteen years old and sixteen and seventeen: they looked at each other a lot. She came and sat in his backyard to talk with his mother and help her shell peas but really to look at Harold as he mowed the lawn, and then he disappeared into the house and she sat waiting for him, and of course he was in the kitchen looking out at her. It's how we all began, when our parents looked at each other, as we say, "when you were just a gleam in your father's eye," or your mother's, depending on who saw who first.

Marlys was long-legged, lanky, had short black hair and sharp eyes that didn't miss anything. She came over to visit the Dieners every chance she got. Her father was a lost cause, like the Confederacy, like the search for the Northwest Passage. He'd been prayed for and suffered for and fought for and spoken for, by people who loved him dearly, and when all was said and done he just reached for the gin bottle and said, "I don't know what you're talking. about," and he didn't. He was a sore embarrassment to Marlys, a clown, a joke, and she watched Harold for evidence that he wasn't similar. One night she dropped in at the Dieners' and came upon a party where Harold, now nineteen, and his friends were drinking beer by the pail. Harold flopped down on his back and put his legs in the air and a pal put a lit match up to Harold's rear end and blue flame came out like a blowtorch, and Marlys went home disgusted and didn't speak to him for two years.

Harold went crazy. She graduated from high school and started attending dances with a geography teacher named Stu Jasperson, who was tall and dark-haired, a subscriber to *Time* magazine, educated at Saint Cloud Normal School, and who flew a red Piper Cub airplane. Lake Wobegon had no airstrip except for Tollerud's pasture, so Stu kept his plane in Saint Cloud. When he was en route to and from the plane was almost the only time Harold got to see Marlys and try to talk sense into her. But she was crazy about Stu the aviator, not Harold the hardware clerk, and in an hour Stu came buzzing overhead doing loops and dives and dipping his wings. Harold prayed for him to crash. Marlys thought Stu was the sun and the moon; all Harold could do was sit and watch her, in the backyard, staring up, her hand shielding her eyes, saying, "Oh, isn't he marvelous?" as Stu performed aerial feats and then shut off the throttle and glided overhead singing "Vaya con Dios" to her. "Yes, he is marvelous," said Harold, thinking, "DIE DIE DIE."

That spring, Marlys was in charge of the Sweethearts Banquet at the Lutheran church. Irene Holm had put on a fancy winter Sweethearts Banquet with roast lamb, and Marlys wanted to top her and serve roast beef with morel mushrooms, a first for a church supper in Lake Wobegon. Once Irene had referred to Marlys's dad as a lush.

Morel mushrooms are a great delicacy. They are found in the wild by people who walk fifteen miles through the woods to get ten of them and then never tell the location to a soul, not even on their deathbeds to a priest. So Marlys's serving them at the banquet would be like putting out emeralds for party favors. It would blow Irene Holm out of the water and show people that even if Marlys's dad was a lush, she was still someone to be reckoned with.

Two men felt the call to go and search for morels: Harold put on his Red Wing boots and knapsack and headed out one evening with a flashlight. He was in the woods all night. Morels are found near the base of the trunk of a dead elm that's been dead three years, which you can see by the way moonlight doesn't shine on it, and he thought he knew where some were, but around midnight he spotted a bunch of flashlights behind him, a posse of morelists bobbing along on his trail, so he veered off and hiked five miles in the wrong direction to confuse them, and by then the sun was coming up so he went home to sleep. He woke at 2:00P.M., hearing Stu flying overhead, and in an instant he knew. Dead elms! Of course! Stu could spot them from the air, send his ground crew to collect them for Marlys, and the Sweethearts Banquet would be their engagement dinner.

Stu might have done just that, but he wanted to put on a show and land the Cub in Lake Wobegon. He circled around and around, and came in low to the west of town, disappearing behind the trees. "He's going to crash!" cried Marlys, and they all jumped in their cars and tore out, expecting to find the young hero lying bloody and torn in the dewy grass, with a dying poem on his lips. But there he was standing tall beside the craft, having landed successfully in a field of spring wheat. They all mobbed around him and he told how he was going up to find the morels and bring them back for Marlys.

There were about forty people there. They seemed to enjoy it, so he drew out his speech, talking about the lure of aviation and his boyhood and various things so serious that he didn't notice Harold behind him by the plane or notice the people who noticed what Harold was doing and laughed. Stu was too inspired to pay attention to the laughter. He talked about how he once wanted to fly to see the world but once you get up in the air you can see that Lake Wobegon is the most beautiful place of all, a lot of warm horse manure like that, and then he gave them a big manly smile and donned his flying cap and scarf and favored them with a second and third smile and a wave and he turned and there was Harold to help him into the cockpit.

"Well, thanks," said Stu, "mighty kind, mighty kind." Harold jumped to the propeller and threw it once and twice, and the third time the engine fired and Stu adjusted the throttle, checked the gauges, flapped the flaps, fit his goggles, and never noticed the ground was wet and his wheels were sunk in. He'd parked in a wet spot, and then during his address someone had gone around and made it wetter, so when Stu pulled back on the throttle the Cub just sat, and he gave it more juice and she creaked a little, and he gave it more and the plane stood on its head with its tail in the air and dug in.

It pitched forward like the *Titanic*, and the propeller in the mud sounded like he'd eaten too many green apples. The door opened and Stu climbed out, trying to look dignified and studious as he tilted eastward and spun, and Harold said, "Stu, we didn't say we wanted those mushrooms sliced."

Harold went out that afternoon and collected five hundred morel mushrooms around one dead elm tree. Marlys made her mark at the Sweethearts dinner, amazing Irene Holm, who had thought Marlys was common. Harold also brought out of the woods a bouquet of flowering crab apple and asked her to marry him, and eventually she decided to.

The tree in the backyard caine about a few years afterward. They'd been married awhile, had two kids, and some of the gloss had worn off their life, and one afternoon, Harold, trying to impress his kids and make his wife laugh, jumped off the garage roof, pretending he could fly, and landed wrong, twisting his ankle. He lay in pain, his eyes full of tears, and his kids said, "Oh poor Daddy, poor Daddy," and Marlys said, "You're not funny, you're ridiculous."

He got up on his bum ankle and went in the woods and got her a pint of morels and a branch from the flowering crab apple. He cut a root from another crab apple and planted the root in the ground. "Look, kids," he said. He sharpened the branch with his hatchet and split the root open and stuck the branch in and wrapped a cloth around it and said, "Now, there, that will be a tree." They said, "Daddy, will that really be a tree?" He said, "Yes." Marlys said, "Don't be ridiculous."

He watered it and tended it and, more than that, he came out late at night and bent down and said, "GROW. GROW. GROW." The graft held, it grew, and one year it was interesting and the next it was impressive and then wonderful and finally it was magnificent. It's the most magnificent thing in the Dieners' backyard. Becky finished writing 750 words late that night and lay down to sleep. A backyard is a novel about us, and when we sit there on a summer day, we hear the dialogue and see the characters.

The Nosegay

Sylvia Townsend Warner

"So you're doing a bit of mountaineering," said the voice from over the hedge.

Mary Matlask, standing on a kitchen chair in the middle of her garden path, cast a look of contained hate at her neighbor. A worse neighbor no woman who loved a garden could have. Her hens came through the hedge, her thistledown floated over it; she kept a rolling tomcat and three children who played at ball.

"My roses grow so high," said Mary Matlask, "that I can't reach them from the ground."

She was an old woman, so bleached and brittle that it seemed as though the rays of the sun, beating down on her, might snap her in two. The kitchen chair rocked on the uneven path. Its seat was slippery, it was not easy for her to keep her footing, and to stand so, with her arms stretched above her head, turned her giddy. But there she must stay, impaled on Mrs. Colley's ravening gaze. Pride would not let her descend without her flower; malice delayed the gathering of it, for she knew full well that Mrs. Colley only waited to see which of the few blossoms she would pick; and so she remained, uneasily poised, snipping off the withered blooms.

At last, yielding to a continuous yelling from her cottage, Mrs. Colley withdrew. Smiling disdainfully, Mary Matlask ceased snipping off the withered heads, and watched her go. Then once more she raised her arms, swiftly, excitedly, her uneasy balance forgotten. Her expression had changed. With a look of awed delight she reached for a pink rose-bud, and cut it carefully from the branch.

It was the last bud the tree would put forth that summer. It had only opened that morning, it was still faultlessly virginal and brilliant. She eyed it with solemn satisfaction. It was exactly what she needed, the .perfect center for her nosegay.

All her life Mary Matlask had made nosegays, constructing each after the same pattern—with a central flower, a boss, and round it concentric bands of other flowers, and the whole finished off with a rim of leaves or fern. The materials of the bouquet varied with the season, but the manner was always the same. In spring there might be a center of blue violets, rimmed with tightly packed primroses, or the first double daffodil ramparted with wallflowers; in the autumn the center swelled to a massive dahlia with asters and marigolds encircling it, their colors clashing resolutely but their formation strictly preserved. But the best nosegays were the summer nosegays, whose centre could be a rose.

Proud of her art, sure of her mastery, Mary Matlask went on composing nosegays as stubbornly as Cezanne went on painting apples. She gave them to children, to brides, to the bed-ridden, to the dead. She gave them to her landlord when she paid her rent. She gave them to Mr. Trudge, who lived in a dusty bungalow writing books on economics, and who never remembered to put them in water. She gave them to Mrs. Daniels at the Manor, who lived only for hunting, and to Mrs. Cullibere, the rector's wife, who worked on a handloom and felt sure that flowers should look natural. She gave them to the postman, to the baker, to visitors who paused outside her cottage to say it was the prettiest in the village; and during June and July, when the plentifulness of her garden drove her to a frenzy of artistic expression, she gave them to Mrs. Colley.

But this nosegay was a different pair of shoes. It had been commissioned, it was, at last, a recognition of her art. This very morning she had received a letter from Mrs. Chichester, whose nurse, so long ago, she had been—a letter saying:

> "It is ages since I saw you, but I still remember the posies you used to make. Do you still make them? And could you make one tomorrow? For Miss Ursula—my baby daughter—you remember her, but now she is almost grown-up—wants one for a dance. She will drive over tomorrow, with a friend of hers, some time early in the afternoon, on the chance that you can manage to give her one. If you have a rose left in the garden, please put a rose in the middle."

It was a pity that they had not been able to give her longer notice; she would have liked to meditate the work of art for a previous day or two. And it was a pity that the request had not come earlier in the summer, when the pinks were blooming, and white flowers more plentiful. A nosegay for a young lady should contain a good deal of white, to be suitable. But she had the essential, the rose, the year's last and loveliest. There was a song about that, thought Mary Matlask. *"All its lovely companions are faded and gone."* And carrying the rose indoors, where it should repose in a basin until the moment of assembling the nosegay arrived, she began to sing, till the thought that Mrs. Colley might be listening checked her shrill staggering voice.

This would be one in the eye for Mrs. Colley. A car driving up to the door, two young ladies, both in the height of fashion, stepping out, the chauffeur attending on them; and all to carry away a nosegay made by Mary Matlask. Pray God the woman would be at home! Were she not, she would hear about it; such things do not happen in a village without bruit; but seeing would be better than believing.

All that morning, under the scorching sun, Mary Matlask walked up and down her garden, prospecting and pillaging. It was not to be lightly undertaken, this masterpiece. Her most exquisite taste must be invoked. Marigolds, for instance, would never do; their smell could not be permitted in a ballroom. But there were the everlasting peas, pink and white, elegant on their short stalks. There were the montbretias, whose orange sprays would make a delicate sprigged border to the built-up composition. There were the white asters to ring the central rose, and the mauve asters to surround the white; and by picking all she had, and by careful spacing, a further ring of alternate crimson and yellow carnations could be contrived. Carnations were very genteel flowers. Gentlemen wore them in their button-holes, and who knew but that, this very night, some fine young gentleman might not beg one of Mary Matlask's clove carnations from Miss Ursula's nosegay?

The picture of the nosegay became so clear in her mind's eye that when, the materials gathered, she came to build it up, it seemed to her that never had the work of assemblage been so easy, never had she worked so deftly nor so infallibly. But when the completed masterpiece had been firmly bound with wool, and put in a bucket under a damp cloth to stand on the watered cold stone of the outhouse, Mary Matlask was shaking from head to foot and ravaged by such a headache that a cup of tea was all she felt equal to for her lunch.

The clock ticked so loudly that it seemed as though its vibrations would shake down the house. Its pale face stared at her. "I must go upstairs," she thought, "put on my best dress and smarten myself." Her shaking hands drove the pin of her brooch into her flesh. She dropped the comb and broke it, she spilled the little flask of lavender water.

Downstairs the clock was louder than ever. She began to set the table for tea; for it would only be proper to offer a cup of tea, whether they condescended to it or no. Ladies drank China tea, she knew, and China tea was not to be bought at the local shop; but by making the Indian tea very weak she might be able to offer a cup without offense. Earlier in that long arduous morning she had polished the tea-things and baked scones and rock-cakes. Now it only remained to cut the bread and butter and the lettuce sandwiches. But if the young ladies were coming in the car they might be hungry, they might like a boiled egg with their tea. Mary kept no hens; she dared not go as far as the farm in case the car arrived; for fresh eggs, stooping her pride, she must inquire at Mrs. Colley's.

To Mrs. Colley's she went, carrying a formal basket, holding up her skirts lest the slops of that threshold should sully them.

"I am expecting visitors," she said. "Two young ladies who will come in a car."

"Haven't they enough to eat at home?" asked Mrs. Colley. But in her haughty fat face her eyes sparkled with curiosity, darting in and out like two earwigs in a turnip.

The kettle was set to boil, and the saucepan for the eggs. Delayed by her errand next door, Mary Matlask was in a panic lest the water should not boil before the two young ladies came; and she raked and fed the range till it blazed. Kettle and saucepan had been twice emptied and twice renewed before the car drew up at the gate. There was no chauffeur to spring out and hold open the door. It was a tiny car, open, little larger than the coffin of a motor-bicycle. Only the suddenness of its arrival and the imperious loudness of its horn could uphold it in the watching eyes of Mrs. Colley.

But the young ladies, for all they were so queerly dressed, Miss Ursula's friend even in trousers, were grand enough and condescending enough to quell a regiment of Colleys, choosing that moment to hang out their disgracing underclothes on the line, staring for all they were worth. "Darling old Mat!" cried Miss Ursula, "of course we should love an egg to our tea. How sweet of you to think of it!" And in the middle of the garden she flung her arms round Mary Matlask and kissed her.

Torn between pride and anguish Mary attended their praising progress round her denuded garden, knowing that Mrs. Colley behind the hedge was overhearing every gracious word, knowing that in another minute the eggs (why had she not got four, got six?) would be hardboiled. Hard-boiled they were. Miss Ursula's friend ate barely more than the top of hers; but for all that the tea-party went with a swing, wave on wave of pride and excitement surging through Mary Matlask as passionately as the waves of her headache crashed each after each to its climax under her neatly combed parting. Such affable young ladies. And the window being open, and their voices so clear, Mrs. Colley would certainly overhear every word they spoke.

Now from its stone-floored cloister and its damp veil emerged the nosegay. This should have been the crowning moment, and if admiration could make it so it would have been. But suddenly conscious of a fault in hospitality Mary Matlask realized that the other young lady should have a nosegay too. Not so fine as Miss Ursula's, of course; but still, a nosegay. Trembling, stiffened against the waves of her headache and her fears of doing amiss, of not seeming respectful enough, she heard herself speak the decisive words. "Oh, Miss Ursula, if you could spare another five minutes, I should so like to gather a few flowers for the other young lady. That is, if she'd accept them."

"Why, Mat, of course. Another nosegay! How sweet of you. She'd love one. Wouldn't you, Nonny?"

"Adore one," replied the young lady in trousers. All together they walked into the garden, still raked by Mrs. Colley's attention, Miss Ursula most recklessly brandishing her nosegay in the sun. For a while they followed her round, asking the name of this flower and that; then they drew apart, talking to each other, seeking the shade of the elder-tree in the hedge. Eavesdropping Mrs. Colley crept nearer. "She will hear every word," thought Mary Matlask. "She will know now how grand they are, even if she didn't know before. For they will certainly be talking of the ball."

Without their assistance the selection of a second nosegay became easier. At first it had seemed to her that there was not a flower left in the garden; but released into creative solitude she soon became carried away, and it appeared that the second nosegay might almost equal the first, though, alas! for its centre there was no rose, only a begonia.

Absorbed in her art she hurried about the garden, tearing at the fuchsia, gathering and discarding. Now for the final flourish of asparagus fern. It grew near where they were standing, a dense thicket. But they were deep in conversation, they would not mind her coming near. They had no notion, disregarding beings from a higher world, that Mrs. Colley, pressed against the hedge, was gulping down their every word.

"Isn't she an old pet?" said Miss Ursula. The gentry spoke like that, tossing away words as they tossed away shillings and half-crowns.

"Enchanting," answered the friend, "and makes the sweetest lettuce sandwiches. But, my dear, what will you do with that vegetation? You don't propose to wear it, do you, all chewed up with greenfly, and crawling with earwigs?"

"My God, no! But I wanted a specimen of the genuine Victorian article, for Wallers to copy in proper flowers. I shall drop it with them on the way back. There will be plenty of time."

"I see," said the friend. "Quite a good . . . Hush! Here she comes. Look what she's got for me!"

August

JANE SMILEY

D URING THE FIRST PART of the interview, when we are sitting on the porch looking down the valley, I try for exactitude more than anything—$343.67. She is impressed, which pleases me, makes me impressed with myself, and then ashamed, so I say, "And seventy-four cents of that I found, so I really made only $342.93. I suppose there might be a few more pennies somewhere, in a pocket or something." She writes it down with a kind of self-conscious flourish of her pen—a Bic "round stic," ten for ninety-nine cents, plus tax, if you buy them at the beginning of the school year—and I can see that momentary pause while she inventories all the things about her that she couldn't have if her income for last year were, like mine, $343.67. The view at the far end of the valley, the scattered houses of Moreton against the west face of Snowy Top, clears suddenly of August haze, and a minute later I feel a strong southwesterly breeze. Rain by mid-afternoon.

The other subjects in her book, some Seed-Save people, a tree-fruits fanatic, a raised-bed specialist, a guy who's breeding field corn back to its prehistoric varieties, all of them are going to be included for innovative gardening. Me I don't think she would have used if I'd had an outside job, or if Liz, my wife, had a job. We are no more up-to-date than Rodale, and she, that is, Tina, the interviewer, will know my methods from looking at the beds. But the money. That gets her. I say, "Before Tommy was born, our income usually hovered around a hundred and fifty dollars a year. But you simply can't raise a kid on a hundred and fifty dollars a year." A kid likes to have nice school supplies, for example. In September I expect to go to K-Mart and spend six dollars or so on school supplies. Tommy likes the trip. He chooses very carefully.

The gardens lie around the house in a giant horseshoe, five ranges, forty-five separate beds of plants, some neat, some shaggy, all productive. There is nothing to brag about, to her, she knows her stuff, and anyway, this time of year everyone looks like a terrific gardener. The plants are thick and hung with fruit, but not unusual. She fingers the leaves, pulls some soil out from under the mulch, looks for pests. There are a few, but not many. I rely on companion planting, crop rotation, garden sanitation. It works, but she doesn't ask about it. The praise she has to offer is in the sensuality and pleasure of her gestures, the way she lingers over each bed.

This is better. I didn't like the way the focus was so clearly on the money before. Money is the precise thing Liz and I don't focus on, which is why we earn so little. As soon as you bring up the money, I notice, conversation gets sociological, then political, then moral. I would rather talk about food, or swimming, or turkey hunting, or building furniture. The thing to do would be to get Liz to say, "Oh, Bob can make anything," in that factual way she has, explanatory rather than boastful, but Liz is offended by the whole interview process, by the light it shines on our lives and the way it makes a story of us. My promise to her was that Tina wouldn't ask her any questions and that she and Tommy wouldn't have to appear in any photographs.

The fact is, I should like this unaccustomed view of the Miller family, Robert, Elizabeth, and Thomas, on their small but remarkably productive acreage just outside Moreton, Pennsylvania. The fact is that years ago, when I had first bought the land and was building the big compost heaps behind the chicken shed, I used to imagine some interviewer just like Tina passing through, showing just her degree of dignity, respectability, and knowledgeable interest. I used to plan how I would guide her around the beds, then undug, show her through the house, then unbuilt, seat her in the chairs, feed her off the table, entertain her on the porch, and through imagining her, I saw all the details she might like. I imagined I would tell her, as I did during the interview, that imagination itself was the key— once I knew what it was specifically that I wanted, then either I would build it or it would turn up. And here she is, though I stopped looking for her long ago, right on schedule, reacting as she was destined to react. The pleasure of that is a private one, not one Liz would share, but not one I am inclined to give up, either.

It's true that I even foresaw that she would focus on the money. That's what I focused on myself then, how I had bought this great piece of land at an estate sale for only thirty-three hundred dollars, that was about sixty dollars an acre, as if all the acres were interchangeable. The bargain was precious, a good omen, a substitute for knowing what I was doing. Now the land has a personality, is without dollar value, and each acre is simply more or less useful or beautiful or ripe for improvement. The money embarrasses me. I should have been less exact. I should have said, "We made some. Enough. I don't know how much." But there is false humility in that, too, since I do know how much, since I do pay property taxes and buy school supplies and Tommy's yearly ticket on the school bus. Tina stands up and stares down the valley, then takes a deep breath. As we turn toward my workshop, she says, 'This spot is paradise, isn't it?"

On my grandfather's farm in Ohio, the shop was neater than the kitchen, the tools shone more brightly than the silverware. For me, still, my workshop is apart from everything else. We try to cultivate orderly habits, but I don't mind the ebb and flow of schoolbooks, projects, articles of clothing, or toys through the house. Piles accumulate, are disposed of. Here nothing accumulates. When I am not working, the place looks like a museum exhibit—galleries of narrow shelves holding planes, chisels, knives, joiner's saws, files, hammers, mallets, rulers, gouging tools, sandpaper. Light pours through the open skylight and the window above the workbench. Each space is neatly labeled identifying the resident tool, calling out for any absent one. The floor is swept (Liz made the broom one year, didn't like it in the house, and sent it out here). In a way this workshop IS money, since it contains an irreplaceable treasury of tools, but other than the sandpaper, every item came to me as a gift, an inheritance, or a castoff. The planes, for example, with their thick beechwood stocks and blue steel blades, have been outmoded by table saws and routers, and auctioneers at farm sales used to thank me for taking them away by the basketful. I refinished the stocks and reseated the hardware. Now I am told people ransack antique stores for old planes to give their living rooms that "country" look. I could not afford to replace these. Tina glances around politely, and says, "Lovely," before stepping back outside and staring at the gardens again. When I join her, she remarks, "The best carrot germination I ever got was fifty percent, and that was the time I nicked each seed with a file." I cough. Carrot seed is about the size of beach sand.

Liz waves to me from the porch. Lunch is ready. Although she disapproves of the interview, she wants to please the visitor. She has asked me every day about the menu for lunch, about whether she should bake the sourdough bread from whole wheat or white flour (our biggest expense after property taxes), whether I think any melons will be ready, what the chances are that Tina will be repelled by the wild foods—purslane, blackberries, angelica—that we eat routinely and enjoy. I, on the other hand, have been wanting to impress. "I built that chest from a black walnut Liz and I chopped down ourselves. I found the axle and the wheels for that wagon in the junkyard. I built the box myself. We caught these trout this morning. We gave up row planting before any books came out about it." My own bragging voice followed me around to every job for days. It cannot be done, this task I give myself, the task of communicating the pleasures of our life in this valley, even to an ear that longs to hear of them.

I would begin with the weight and cottony fragrance of the quilts we've made, an "All Hands Around" on the bed, a big log cabin in rainbow colors against black on the wall. In sixteen years we've made twelve quilts, used up one, burned a hole in another. In the winter we use two or three for warmth, and the first thing I see in the morning, in the white light of our whitewashed bedroom, is the clashing colors of the quilts spilling away from me over the bed. Then, under my feet, I feel the smooth-painted floorboards. The windows are uncurtained and unshaded, usually fiat gray with morning fog. All of this is familiar and comforting.

Or I could begin with something even more inexpressible, which would be the stiffness of muscles worked the day before and sensed afresh a moment after waking. I think my consciousness must rouse before my senses, because there is always, always, a pain-free moment, and then the ache flows in. I like the ache. It tells me what I did yesterday, suggests what I might do today, even how I might do it. Farm work doesn't have to be backbreaking. It can be as aerobically sound and healthfully taxing as any other sort of exercise. Liz calls this "spading-as-sport" my private obsession, but another early morning pleasure is her sleepy, admiring rake of fingertips over my pectorals and abdominals.

Or there's Tommy's room, when I pass his doorway first thing in the morning, when Tommy is thoroughly asleep. He seems afloat in his bed, under his quilt, a green, orange, and yellow "Rail Fence." On the shelves I built are the toys we made him. He sleeps in a shirt Liz wove (I built the loom) on a straw tick the three of us stuffed. Across the room he has known since birth is the rocking cradle I copied, in local butternut, from a picture in a book I got out of the library. The headboard and footboard trim is carved with a twist, to look like a piece of rope, then the twist is repeated in the four braces that hold up the cradle. The lambskin lying across the mattress Liz made came from one of our lambs. The lamb's wool of the baby blankets was spun from some of the others. Liz's mother taught me to crochet, and I used to crochet while Liz knitted. When I look into my son's room, my pleasure is the knowledge that I have brought all of my being to bear here—not just hands and brain, but seed, too, and not just seed, but hands and brain, too. If he were really afloat, his bed would bump against the window, and he could look upon the orchard I planted, then bump against the shelves I built, where he could snatch down tops and cars and blocks and tools and dolls we've made him, this is a lovely sea, I think, tiny, enclosed, friendly, all his, and his alone.

Lunch doesn't look too weird—a plate of sliced tomatoes and green peppers, a couple of trout, cold boiled potatoes, beet greens, blackberries. Tommy follows his mother back and forth between the range and the table in a way I find annoying, and so I say, "Son, sit down!" He tenses, smiles, sits down. He is a good boy. Tina sits beside him and he offers her the pitcher of cold springwater, as he should. She looks around the room.

I can't help it. I lean back in my chair and say, "You know, it's remarkable what I've gleaned for free over the years. We have fishing rods and ponies and bicycles, a canoe, plenty of tools, sheep, two goats, lots of chickens. We tried a couple of turkeys a few years ago, and a cow, but she gave too much milk. This house has double-hung windows, figured brass doorknobs, a front door with a big pearly oval of etched glass. An old man in State College gave me that kitchen range. It's from the twenties. He found it in his barn. A guy I know in Moreton hauled it for me, in exchange for three lambs. It cooks our food and keeps the entire house warm. The first five years I lived here I spent getting to know people and offering things, then asking for things they were about to discard. Now, when people for miles around want to get rid of something, they send me a card. Incoming mail is free. Every so often I jerk loose and buy a couple of dollars' worth of stamped postcards for replies." I smile. "Compared to scrounging in Vietnam, which I did, this is no big deal."

We begin helping ourselves to the food. Tina asks, "What do you do for transportation?" Her manner is mild. I was the one looking forward to this, so I'm not sure why it puts me on edge. I say, "We think about it."

Liz doesn't like my brusqueness. She smiles and says, "He means that we plan ahead. Most days nobody goes anywhere except Tommy to school on the school bus, anyway."

"If I have a job or am trading something, part of the bargain is that they come here and pick me or it up. Besides, it's only three miles to town. We can walk or ski. Tommy can ride the pony." The tomatoes are delicious, sweet and firm and juicy. I never plant hybrids, only old fashioned varieties like Rutgers and Marglobe and Roma. I save the seed from the best plants and best fruits, selecting for hardiness and flavor. It works. The thing is, going away should be something you contemplate, not something you do automatically."

"Could you live this way farther back in the mountains?"

"You mean, where it's colder, harder to get places, and rockier?"

"Yeah."

"You really mean, if not this extreme, then why not more extreme, as extreme as possible? Why not Alaska or the Australian outback?"

"I didn't mean that, but why not?"

"Why not really live off the land. Grubs and ants and spearing fish with a sharpened stick."

"Bob, come on," Liz says, then she turns to Tina. 'We went through that about five years ago. Bob kept looking at brochures about land in Montana and British Columbia."

"We didn't ever send in the business reply cards, though. I was joking then, I'm joking now. My purposes aren't extreme, or political. My aim wasn't to choose the hardest path and prove I could do it. It was the same as everyone else's claim. It was to prosper. You don't prosper on hilly, rocky soil. It's more expensive to live outside of town. We're self-contained, not isolated and hostile."

Tommy relishes everything on his plate, not preferring the sweet to the savory, the cooked to the fresh, the domestic to the wild. He is a model eater, would devour grubs and ants and roots if they were on the table. Can Tina see what a miraculous child he is, how enthusiastic and open and receptive to guidance? Before he was born, I used to imagine a child-raising program that was purely example-setting. I would go about my work and he would accompany me, gradually assuming responsibility for the tasks that he was strong enough and smart enough for. There would be a lot of informative conversation, I thought—me explicating techniques and him asking intelligent questions. The reality is better than that. He tags along as eagerly as anyone could hope for, but he does all the talking. A lot of it is questions, but much of it is observations, remarks, little stories, bits of songs that are going through his head. There is a large category of stray sounds that simply escape his lips, from grunts to hisses to yells that I hope he has the sense to contain when he is at school but that I like for their animal quality, for their way of saying, "This organism is alive."

Which is not to say that example-setting is sufficient. I find that he does need a lot of molding and guidance, but that is another task we plan for, Liz and I.

After lunch there is a routine of work—bringing the animals into the barn out of the sun, checking water buckets, looking for eggs—that I think Tina should accompany me on, but when we sit back in our seats, Liz speaks up and says, "Tina and I will clear this up. Why don't you and Tommy come back in an hour for a swim?"

Considering that, when I asked her what she thought about this interview a couple of weeks ago, she said that she would rather chase pigs in a snowstorm, I am a little surprised. But it is a relief. Tommy runs out ahead of me, knowing that after chores he can ride the pony for half an hour before his rest time. He doesn't notice the view, but I do, every time the screen door slaps shut behind me, I pause and stare down the valley meadow toward Moreton, Snowy Top, and the dusky receding folds of the mountains beyond. My land is laid out rather deceptively—the smallest part is open field, valley floor, but all of these acres are visible from the house, and all of them are flat. The slope from the foot of the valley to the house is only three degrees, which is unusual around these parts. There has always been a farm on this site, and the barn remains, though the original house burned down in 1904—it was a big house and a big fire that the volunteer fire department could see from town but couldn't get to, because over a mile of the road was drifted in. One of the children ran burning from the house, but they rolled him in the snow and saved his life. The article took up half the front page of the Moreton *Record*. The family moved in with relatives in town, and their descendants farmed from there— keeping this land in pasture for seventy years, and running sheep and heifers and horses on it. When I bought it, the soil was so well fertilized that all I had to do the first year was turn under the turf and dig the beds. The other outbuildings were pretty up-to-date, too: the lean-to workshop beside the barn, a well-ventilated root cellar ten feet from the foundation of the old house (when I scraped dirt and caked mud off the old door, I found its surface scorched black from the fire, but the shelves inside that once held bins of vegetables were only dusty).

Most of the land I own runs up the hillsides in a bowl shape, to either side and behind the house, and that woodlot hadn't been touched or exploited in seventy, or even a hundred years. It took me three years just to drag the deadfall out, and I heated my house for seven and a half years on that. If I'd had the stone masonry built around the range that I have now, it would have lasted twice that long. What we do is build our first fire in mid-September, then make sure a small fire is in the stove every minute thereafter. All that masonry will have heated up by about mid-October, and after that we only have to keep it warm. It works. I use a lot less wood than the woodlot produces, and it's all hardwood. We even burn black walnut and cherry, wood the cabinetmaking companies would pay me for if they knew I had it. That's my luxury, my conspicuous consumption—I burn black walnut for heat.

From the house, everything is perfect. The natural landscape offers enclosed, familiar, pleasing curves, softened with August haze and prolific vegetation—sugar maple, black cherry, hickory, butternut, walnut, beech, yellow birch, and white oak are some of what I can see from here—and I respond, unfailingly, with love ("regard" and "inspiration," looking and inhaling). From everywhere else on the property, I must view my own mistake, the house. I built it—yes, I built it~mostly from brick torn out of the streets of State College, Pennsylvania, and pine pallets that I ripped the nails out of one by one. Recognizing my accomplishment doesn't mean I've ever been satisfied with it. I resent its lack of grandeur more than its lack of size. What I meant to keep simple I made humble, and I made a mistake siting it, because I thought it would be easier to use the old foundation than lay another one. If we were to add on now, we would have to add outward, creating an ungainly, flat building. If I'd built farther back—into the hillside as I first intended—it would have been easy to add on upward, just to tear off the roof and build another small house on top of the old one. And we would have been closer to the springhouse. Sometimes I can see the structure I might have built so clearly that the frustration of what I've done is explosive. Here we live, here we will always live. No gardens, barns, sheds will ever mitigate the permanence of this mistake.

Chores completed, I return. The women are sitting at the table, still, talking about home schooling. Tina looks skeptical, which makes Liz speak more assertively, expressing none of the doubts she has expressed to me. Home schooling is my idea, and her arguments are ones I've made to her. "Actually," she is saying, "studies show that they get along better with the other kids once they get to college, because they have a real sense of themselves and a sense of their own abilities."

"But don't they miss the other kids?"

"I don't know if Tom would. We sent him to kindergarten, because we felt guilty about keeping him so isolated. He gets along okay, but until you've really considered home schooling, I don't think you realize what a compromise school is, how regimented it is, and how the others expect you to act so you'll fit in. And around here there's nothing to do, so most of the high-school kids gather at one of the big ponds and drink, then drive around endangering themselves and everyone else. It's not like a big suburban school, where they might be, only might be, exposed to something new."

"Well, social life has meant a lot to Libby since she's been in kindergarten—"

Libby must be a daughter. They have covered a lot of ground in my absence, and I am sort of shocked by the name, "Libby," rather idle-rich-sounding, as if this project of Tina's is a whimsy after all, not committed or serious as it would be if she had no children, or her daughter's name was, say, Susie.

"But she's a girl. Bob was a loner in school. I wasn't. I think I missed more than he did. I just had the same experiences everyone else had. I don't feel like my life had any integrity until I came here."

"It's lovely—"

"And you know at first I hated it. I didn't have any inner resources at all. I thought I would die of loneliness, even on days when Bob would talk to me." She smiles slyly at me. "This was not how I intended to spend my life."

"I just think it takes a lot of fortitude to have your child at home, to be responsible for everything that goes into his head. What does Tommy think?"

Now I speak up. "He likes the idea, but we promised him one more year in the grammar school before we make up our minds."

Liz glances at me. I make the truthful emendation. "Well, he doesn't always like it. But his schooling is my decision to make. He understands that. Anyway, we're a closely knit family, and there's so much going on around here all the time that he doesn't want to miss anything. And as for taking responsibility for what goes into his head, that ATTRACTS me."

Tina sits back. She says, "Your lives are so completely of a piece. I admire—"

"You know, I always think I'm going to love being admired, but then I get nervous when it happens, I think because you shouldn't be admired for doing something you needed to do. I mean, until I moved here, I was so filled with frustrated yearning that it was this or suicide. When I was Tommy's age, I thought it was yearning to be on my own. When I was a teenager, I thought it was lust. When I was in the army, and in Vietnam, I thought it was the desire to go home. But it was none of those things. I never figured out what it was, but it ceased. Tommy doesn't have it. He's enthusiastic about the farm and the animals and fishing and helping us cook and grow things, everything we do here that we couldn't do if we lived in town." Just now the rain begins, steady and warm, lifting the scent of the grass, of the valley's whole morning, through the screen door—wildflowers, tomato plants, walnut leaves, pony and sheep manure, the rainwater itself. It is a smell so thick and various that I can nearly see it, and I inhale sharply. Liz laughs and leans toward Tina. "Put this in your book. Bob pretends to have opinions, but the real truth about him is that his senses are about three times sharper than normal. He's really just a farm animal scratching his back in the dust."

"Not true!" I say. "What I really am is a body attached to a pair of hands that can't stop making things. Inclination precedes conviction. I want to make, therefore I decided making is valuable. The more I want to make, the more valuable making is."

"Very nice, sweetie," says Liz, standing up and kissing the top of my head. "But running your hand down the board precedes making."

Tommy appears on the porch, dripping, but doesn't come in. He calls, "Hey, Daddy, I got the pony and the foal in before the rain started! They didn't get wet at all!"

"Did you wipe off the bridle?"

"Yes, Daddy."

"Even the corners of the bit?"

"Yes, Daddy."

Liz hands him a towel and he dries off in the doorway. He has what we call "the look." His face is too bright, his eyes too eager, a kind of rigidity seems to grip him when he is still, but when he moves, the movements are quick and broad. Liz recognizes it, too, and says, patiently, "Sweetie, time to settle down for your rest. You want some milk before you go up? Sit by Daddy, and I'll pour you some.

He might sit. He might run into the other room. He might knock over this chair. I must have had the look, too, when I was his age, because I remember the feeling perfectly, a feeling of imminent eruption, fearsome, alluring, uncontrollable. It was like standing in a dim, warm, small room and having an astonishing bright light switched on every so often, and when the light was on I couldn't remember what it was like for the light to be off. From the ages of about nine to about twelve, I worked steadily to lighten the room molecule by molecule, until the bright light no longer shocked me, and the room glowed comfortably. What I actually did I can't remember, but I remember the sensations of light, the feeling of having labored, and my father remarking that I had gotten to be a good boy after all, no longer "all over the place like a crazy person." My first real feeling of accomplishment, the first time I knew that I could master myself.

Perhaps because of Tina, Tommy sits quietly, drinks his milk, and doesn't knock over his chair until he stands up. Liz picks it up with ostentatious care and I say, 'Time for your rest, son. When you come down, I want you to show me the chapter you've read."

"How many pages?'"

"A whole chapter."

"Even if it's ten pages?"

"A whole chapter."

He contains himself and marches off. All of these things happen every day, and yet they seem so peculiar with Tina at the table, making notes in her head. I am tempted to apologize, but I don't know for what, so I hold my tongue.

When we are undressing that night for bed, I admit it, that the interview was a bad idea. "I mean, I hate feeling this detached from everything. Look at my foot going under the covers. Look at my hands pulling the blankets up, aren't these lovely quilts, look at my wife, 'Liz' she's called, blowing out the lamp."

Liz laughs, reaches under the covers to tickle me lightly. "She thought you were a genius."

"What?"

"You heard me."

"When did she say that?"

"After lunch, then again before she left. She said, 'Everything he touches he transforms into something beautiful and useful.'"

"What did you say?"

"I said that I agreed."

"You did?"

She runs her hand over my face in the darkness, a gesture that is tender and proprietary at the same time. She says, "I told her I hoped she put that in the book, because that's what's true about you."

After we make love, when I am nearly asleep, I feel her ease out of bed, then I feel her turn, kneel beside the bed, and begin to pray. I hear that murmuring all night, even after I know in my sleep that her solid weight is unconscious beside me.

The next day is Saturday. At breakfast, Liz says, 'You remember about the church meeting this afternoon?"

"I remember."

"I'll be home about six, unless someone gives me a ride to the end of the road. I might be home by five-twenty or so."

"Fine."

"Really?"

"Liz, you don't have to ask. It's fine."

"Good. I'm looking forward to it."

About a year ago, Liz started shopping around for a church to attend. There are ten churches in Moreton and she went to every one, judging them more on ambience than on doctrine. The two Quaker congregations, having within living memory been one, were hyper-aware of each other, she said, the Episcopalians enjoyed themselves too much, the

Presbyterians were engaged in easing out their minister, and on down the line, until she decided upon the "Bright Light Fellowship," a Pentecostal sect whose prophet resides in Gambier, Ohio. I was frankly astonished that my wife, a graduate of the University of Pennsylvania and a voracious reader, could feel at ease in this collection of the rural poor, the badly educated, and the nakedly enthusiastic, but that is exactly what she feels there, she says. Privately, I think she feels humbled, which is a feeling she is in favor of as a way of life. She began participating in January, and attended every Sunday. If it snowed, she went on skis, if it rained, she wore rubber boots and a poncho. She asks me if I mind. I do, but I would rather not, and I certainly don't want to influence her. Nevertheless, it has become one of those marital topics of conversation, a rift that we consciously avoid making an argument of. My own religious views are deistic, you might say. I notice that days when she goes to church, for whatever reason, are special days, obstructing the smooth flow of time that I like. She assumes that this is my main objection. I also notice that, however else she arranges and varies her time with, and communication with, Tommy and me, she never fails to kneel at bedtime and make a lengthy prayer. That, both the unfailing regularity of it, and the awkwardness of its insertion into our nightly routine, is the real bone of contention. I have been married to Liz for a long time—twelve years—and I intend to be married to her forever, so I am cautious about drawing any conclusion as to whether this issue is a passing one, one that can be resolved through compromise, or simply a large, heavy object that sits in the living room, obstructing traffic, grudgingly accommodated, year after year.

Of course I have forgotten about the church meeting, so my response, because there has to be one, is to hold a little aloof—to go out in the workshop and dive into a project of my own rather than to do something more friendly, like sort iris corms on the front porch. What I do is remind myself that I am a genius, and, when I step into the workshop, that lends even these kitchen chairs I am making the glow of loveliness. They are made from ash saplings, with woven rush seats, and my tools are, basically, my draw knife and a bucket of water. There are chairs like them in every antique store—rounded stiles, ladder-backs, four stretchers below the seat—but mine are the only comfortable ones I've ever sat in. The seat is roomier, for one thing, and I soak the stiles and angle them backward so that you don't feel like you're about to be strapped in and electrocuted. I soak all the mortise joints, too, before I put everything together, and they dry and shrink around the tenon so tightly that the whole chair might have been carved from a single piece of wood. These are almost finished. All I have left is a carving of leaves and vines into the top rung of the ladder-back.

Well, it is a pleasant day. I sit on one of the chairs I've made and decorate another one. The chestnut tree above me is alive with light and shade, the weather is warm and breezy, my wife and son go about their business with evident satisfaction. The valley that is our home is soothingly beautiful, safe, and self-contained. We eat a lunch that we have provided for ourselves, and afterward I am so involved with my carving that I forget Liz is gone until I see her come walking down the road, and then, no matter who she's been with, all I want to do is to meet her, kiss her, and walk her to the house.

"Guess what?" she says.

"I'm a genius?"

"Yeah. You know how I can tell?"

"How?"

"You forgot that school starts Tuesday."

"This Tuesday? I thought that wasn't till after Labor Day this year."

"Monday is Labor Day. It's been September for four days now."

"Tina was supposed to come on the fifteenth of August."

"Well, she was two weeks late and we didn't even notice. She ought to put that in her book."

"You went to church last Sunday. Didn't you realize what day it was?"

"It didn't come up. It's not like when you're a Catholic and you're always counting backwards or forwards to some major holiday."

"Well, I guess that shows that the prophet is a man of his time. He figures everybody knows what day it is."

"If you really want to know, what he figures is that every day might as well be the last."

We haven't talked about specifics of dogma very much, but I let it drop. Anyway, Tommy comes out of the barn where he has been haying and watering the ponies for the night, and greets his mother as if she has been gone since Christmas. She swings him up into her arms, and continues walking, his arms around her neck and his legs around her waist. The voice of my father tells me that he is too old for this, but my own' voice disagrees, says that boys are isolated too soon, that as long as he seeks our bodies he should find them. And there is also this reassuring shiver of jealousy, a light touch raising the hairs on the nape of my neck, that reminds me how the pleasure of marriage and the pleasure of fatherhood take their piquancy from watching, left out, as they nuzzle and giggle and tease. He never tries to impress her, she never tries to mollify him.

We haven't used birth control since our marriage and she only got pregnant once. Most of the time I forget that it could happen again. Secretly, I have only ever managed to imagine one boy child. Maybe imagination is the key there, too. "Lovely sunset," says Liz, and Tommy says, "We fried green tomatoes with basil for dinner."

"Mmm," says his mommy. "I just love that."

We stroll up the road toward the house, toward the dinner laid on the table, and this is what we expect: to eat and be satisfied, to find comfort in each other's company, to relinquish the day and receive the night, to make an orderly retreat from each boundary that contains us—the valley, the house, the room, the covers, wakefulness—in perfect serenity. Well, of course I am thankful, arid of course a prayer lifts off me, but there is nothing human about it, no generalizations, nor even words, only the rightness of every thing that is present expressing itself through my appreciation.

Grape Harvest

Colette

I HAD WRITTEN TO my friend Valentine: "Come, they'll be harvesting the grapes." She came, wearing flat-heeled canvas shoes and an autumn-colored skirt; one bright-green sweater, and another pink one; one hat made of twill and another made of velvet, and both, as she said, "invertebrate." If she hadn't called a slug a snail, and asked if bats were the female of the screech owl, she wouldn't have been taken for "someone from Paris."

"Harvesting the grapes?" she asked, astonished. "Really? Despite the war?"

And I understood that deep down she was finding fault with all that the pretty phrase "harvesting the grapes" seems to promise and call forth of rather licentious freedom, singing and dancing, risqué intentions, and overindulgence. Don't people traditionally refer to it as "the festival of the grape"?

"Despite the war, Valentine," I confessed. "What can you do? They haven't found a way of gathering the grapes without harvesting them. There are a lot of grapes. With the full-flavored grapes we'll make several casks of the wine that's drunk young and doesn't gain anything from aging, the wine that's as rough on the mouth as a swear word, and which the peasants celebrate the way people praise a boxer: 'Damn strong stuff,' being unable to find any other virtues in it."

The weather was so beautiful the day of the harvest, it was so enjoyable to dally along the way, that we didn't reach the hillside until around ten o'clock, the time when the low hedges and the shady meadows are still drenched in the blue and the cold of dripping dew, while the busy Limousin sun is already stinging your cheeks and the back of your neck, warming the late peaches under their cottony plush, the firmly hanging pears, and the apples, too heavy this year, which are picked off by a gust of wind. My friend Valentine stopped at the blackberries, the fuzzy teasel, even at the forgotten ears of maize whose dry husks she forced back and whose kernels she gobbled down like a little hen.

Like the guide, in the desert, walking ahead and promising the lagging traveler the oasis and the spring, I cried out to her from a distance, Come on, hurry up, the grapes are better, and you'll drink the first juice from the vat, you'll have bacon and chicken in the pot!"

Our entry into the vineyard caused no commotion. The work pressed on, and moreover, our attire warranted neither curiosity nor even consideration. My friend had agreed, in order to sacrifice herself to the blood of the grape, that I lend her an old checked skirt, which since 1914 had seen many other such sacrifices, and my personal adornments didn't go beyond an apron-smock made of polka-dot sateen. A few weather-beaten heads were raised above the cordons of vines, hands held out two empty baskets toward us, and we set to work.

Since my friend Valentine was thinning her bunches of grapes like an embroideress, with delicate snips of her scissors, it pleased a jovial and mute old faun, popping up opposite her, to give her something of a fright, and then silently show her how the clusters of grapes come off the stock and drop into the basket, if one knows how to pinch a secret suspension point, revealed to the fingers by a little abscess, a swelling where the stem breaks like glass. A moment later, Valentine was gathering the grapes, sans scissors, as quickly as her instructor the faun, and I didn't want her doing better or more than I, so the eleven o'clock sun wasted no time in moistening our skin and parching our tongues.

Whoever said grapes quench one's thirst? These Limousin grapes, grafted from American stock, so ripe they had split, so sweet they were peppery, staining our skirts, and being crushed in our baskets, inflamed us with thirst and intoxicated the wasps. Was my friend Valentine searching, when she straightened up to rest from time to time, was she searching the hillside, amid the well-regulated comings and goings of the empty and full baskets, for the child cupbearer who might bring an earthen jar filled with cool water? But the children carried only bunch after bunch of grapes, and the men—three old caryatids with muscles bared—transported only purple-stained tubs toward the gaping storeroom of the farm at the bottom of the hill.

The exuberance of the pure morning had gone away. Noon, the austere hour when the birds are silent, when the shortened shadow crouches at the foot of the tree. A cope of heavy light crushed down on the slate roofs, flattened out the hillside, smoothed out the shady fold of the valley. I watched the sluggishness and melancholy of midday descend over my energetic friend. Was she looking around her, among the silent workers, for a gaiety she might find fault in perhaps? Some relief—which she didn't wait for long.

A village clock was answered by a joyful murmuring, the sound of clogs on the hardened paths, and a distant cry:

"Soup's on! soup's on! soup's on!"

Soup? Much more and much better than soup, in the shelter of a tent made of reed thatch draped with ecru sheets, pinned up by twigs with green acorns, blue convolvulus, and pumpkin flowers. Soup and all its vegetables, yes, but boiled chicken too, and short ribs of beef, and bacon as pink and white as a breast, and veal in its own juices. When the aroma of this feast reached my friend's nose, she smiled that unconscious, expansive smile one sees on nurslings who have had their fill of milk and women who have had their fill of pleasure.

She sat down like a queen, in the place of honor, folded her purple-stained skirt under her, rolled back her sleeves, and cavalierly held out her glass to her neighbor to the right, for him to fill, with a saucy laugh. I saw by the look on her face that she was about to call him "my good man" . . . but she looked at him, kept quiet, and turned toward her neighbor to the left, then toward me as though in need of help and advice . . . As it was, country protocol had seated her between two harvesters who between them carried, slightly bent under such a weight, a hundred and sixty-six years. One was thin, dried up, pellucid, with bluish eyes and impalpable hair, who lived in the silence of an aged sprite. The other, still a giant, with bones fit for making clubs, singlehandedly cultivated a piece of land, boasting ahead of time, in defiance of death, about the asparagus he'd get out of it "in four or five years!"

I saw the moment when Valentine, between her two old men, began losing her cheerfulness, and I had a liter of cider taken to her by a page who was just the sort to distract her, one of those beaming boys a little ungainly for their sixteen years—with a submissive and deceitful forehead, brown eyes, and a nose like an Arab—and every bit as handsome as the hundred-times-praised shepherds of Italy. She smiled at him, without paying him much attention, for she was in the grip of a statistical preoccupation. She asked the wispy old man, then the powerful octogenarian, their ages. She leaned forward to learn that of another frizzy-haired and wrinkled laborer who only admitted to seventy-three years. She gathered still other figures known to all from the far ends of the table—sixty-eight and seventy-one—began muttering to herself, adding up lustra and centuries, and was laughed at by a strapping young wench five times a mother, who shouted to her from where she sat: "Say, then, you like 'em like wine, huh, with cobwebs on the cork!"— provoking cracked laughter and young laughter, remarks in dialect and in very clear French as well, which made my friend blush and renewed her appetite. She wanted some more bacon, and cut into the peasant bread, made of pure wheat, brown but succulent, and demanded from the gnarled giant an account of the war of 1870. It was brief.

"What's to say? it wasn't a very pretty sight . . . I remember everybody falling all around me and dying in their own blood. Me, nothin' . . . not a bullet, not a bayonet. I was left standing, and them on the ground . . . who knows why?"

He fell into an indifferent silence, and the faces of the women around us darkened. Until then, no mother deprived of her sons, no sister accustomed to double work without her brother, had spoken of the war or those missing, or groaned under the weariness of three years . . . The farmer's wife, tight-lipped busied herself by setting out thick glasses for the coffee, but she said nothing of her son, the artilleryman. One gray-haired farmer, very tired, his stomach cinched up with a truss, said nothing about his four sons: one was eating roots in Germany, two were fighting, the fourth was sleeping beneath a machine-gunned bit of earth . . .

From a very old woman, seated not far from the table on a bundle of straw, came this remark: "All this war, it's the barons' fault . . ."

"The barons?" inquired Valentine with great interest. "What barons?"

"The barons of France," said the cracked voice. "And them of Germany! All the wars are the fault of the barons."

"How's that?"

My friend gazed at her avidly, as if hoping that the black rags would fall, and that the woman would rise up, a hennin on her head, her body in vair, croaking, "I, I am the fourteenth century!" But nothing of the kind happened, the old woman merely shook her head, and all that could be heard were the drunken and confident wasps, the puffing of a little train off in the distance, and the mawing gums of the pellucid old man . . .

Meantime, I had broken the maize *galette* with my hands, and the tepid coffee stood in the glasses, which the harvesters were already turning away from, back toward the blazing hillside . . .

"What," said Valentine, astonished, "no siesta?"

"Yes, of course! But only for you and me. Come over under the hazelnut trees, we can let ourselves melt away, ever so gently, with heat and sleep. The grape harvest isn't allowed the siesta that goes with the wheat harvest. There they are already back at work, look . . .

But it wasn't true, for the ascending column of men and women had just halted, attentive . . .

"What are they looking at?"

"Someone's coming through the field . . . two ladies. They're waving to the harvesters . . . They know them. Did you invite any of your country neighbors?"

"None. Wait, I think I know that blue dress. Why . . . Why . . . it's . . ."

"They're . . . Why, yes, certainly!"

Unhurried, coquettish, one beneath a straw hat, the other beneath a white parasol, our two maids moved toward us. Mine was swinging, above two little khaki-colored kid shoes, a blue serge skirt which set off the saffron-colored lawn of her blouse. My friend's soubrette, all in mauve, was showing her bare arms through her openwork sleeves, and her belt, made of white suede like her shoes, gripped a waist which fashion might perhaps have preferred less frail.

From our hideaway in the shade, we saw ten men run up to them, and twenty hands hail them on the steep slope, while envious little girls carried their parasols for them. The aged giant, suddenly animated, sat one of the maids down on an empty tub and hoisted the whole thing onto his shoulder; a handsome, suntanned adolescent smelled the handkerchief he had snatched from one of the two young women. The heavy air seemed light to them, now that two women's laughter, affected, deliberately prolonged, had set it in motion . . .

"They've gone to considerable expense, heavens!" murmured my friend Valentine. "That's my mauve Dinard dress from three years ago. She's redone the front of the bodice . . ."

"Really?" I said in a low voice. "Louise has on my serge skirt from two years ago. I would never have believed it could look so fresh. You could still find magnificent serge back then . . . The devil if I know why I ever gave her my yellow blouse! I could use it on Sundays this year."

I glanced involuntarily at my polka-dot apron-smock, and I saw that Valentine was holding, between two contemptuous fingers, my old checked skirt, covered with purple stains. Above us, on the roasting hillside, the mauve young woman and the yellow one were walking amid flattering laughter and happy exclamations. The elegance, the Parisian touch, the chatelaine's dignity, of which we had deprived the grape harvest, were no longer missing, thanks to them, and the rough workers once again became gallant, youthful, audacious, for them . . .

A hand, that of a man kneeling, invisible, between the vine stocks, raised a branch laden with blue grapes up to our maids, and both of them, rather than fill any basket, plucked off what pleased them . . .

Then they sat down on their unfolded handkerchiefs on the edge of a slope, parasols open, to watch the harvesting of the grapes, and each harvester rivaled the other in ardor before their benevolent idleness.

Our silence had lasted a long time, when my friend Valentine broke it with these words, unworthy, to be sure, of the great thought they expressed: "What I say is . . . bring back feudalism!"

Earth to Earth

ROBERT GRAVES

Y ES, YES AND YES! Don't get me wrong, for goodness' sake. I am heart
and soul with you. I agree that Man is wickedly defrauding the
Earth-Mother of her ancient dues by not putting back into the soil as
much nourishment as he takes out. And that modem plumbing is, if you
like, a running sore in the body politic. And that municipal incinerators
are genocidal rather than germicidal.

And that cremation should be made a capital crime. And that dust
bowls created by the greedy plough . . .

. . . Yes, yes and yes again. *But!*

Elsie and Roland Hedge—she a book-illustrator, he an architect with suspect lungs—had been warned against Dr. Eugen Steinpilz. "He'll bring
you no luck," I told them. "My little finger says so decisively."

"You too?" asked Elsie indignantly. (This was at Brixham, South
Devon, in March 1940.) "I suppose you think that because of his foreign
accent and his beard he must be a spy?"

"No," I said coldly, "that point hadn't occurred to me. But I won't con-
tradict you."

The very next day Elsie deliberately picked a friendship—I don't like
the phrase, but that's what she did—with the Doctor, an Alsatian with an
American passport, who described himself as a *Naturphilosoph;* and both
she and Roland were soon immersed in Steinpilzerei up to the nostrils. It
began when be invited them to lunch and gave them cold meat and two
rival sets of vegetable dishes—potatoes (baked), carrots (creamed),
bought from the local fruiterer; and potatoes (baked) and carrots
(creamed), grown on compost in his own garden.

The superiority of the latter over the former in appearance, size and especially flavor came as an eye-opener to Elsie and Roland. Yes, and yes, I know just how they felt. Why shouldn't I? When I visit the market here in Palma, I always refuse La Torre potatoes, because they are raised for the early English market and therefore reek of imported chemical fertilizer. Instead I buy Son Sardina potatoes, which taste as good as the ones we used to get in England fifty years ago. The reason is that the Son Sardina farmers manure their fields with Palma kitchen-refuse, still available by the cart-load—this being too backward a city to afford effective modem methods of destroying it.

Thus Dr. Steinpilz converted the childless and devoted couple to the Steinpilz method of composting. It did not, as a matter of fact, vary greatly from the methods you read about in the *Gardening Notes* of your favorite national newspaper, except that it was far more violent. Dr.. Steinpilz had invented a formula for producing extremely fierce bacteria, capable (Roland claimed) of breaking down an old boot or the family Bible or a torn woolen vest into beautiful black humus almost as you watched. The formula could not be bought, however, and might be communicated under oath of secrecy only to members of the Eugen Steinpilz Fellowship—which I refused to join. I won't pretend therefore to know the formula myself, but one night I overheard Elsie and Roland arguing in their garden as to whether the planetary influences were favorable; and they also mentioned a ram's horn in which, it seems, a complicated mixture of triturated animal and vegetable products—technically called "the Mother"—was to be cooked up. I gather also that a bull's foot and a goats pancreas were part of the works, because Mr. Pook the butcher afterwards told me that he had been puzzled by Roland's request for these unusual cuts. Milkwort and penny-royal and bee-orchid and vetch certainly figured among the Mother's herbal ingredients; I recognized these one day in a gardening basket Elsie had left at the post office.

The Hedges soon had their first compost heap cooking away in the garden, which was about the size of a tennis court and consisted mostly of well-kept lawn. Dr. Steinpilz, who supervised, now began to haunt the cottage like the smell of drains; I had to give up calling on them. Then, after the Fall of France, Brixham became a war-zone whence everyone but we British and our Free French or Free Belgians allies were extruded. Consequently Dr. Steinpilz had to leave; which he did with very bad grace, and was killed in a Liverpool air-raid the day before he should have sailed back to New York. But that was far from closing the ledger. I think Elsie must have been in love with the Doctor, and certainly Roland had a hero-worship for him. They treasured a signed collection of all his esoteric books, each called after a different semi-precious stone, and used to read them out aloud to each other at meals, in turns. Then to show that this was a practical philosophy, not just a random assemblage of beautiful thoughts about Nature, they began composting in a deeper and even more religious way than before. The lawn had come up, of course; but they used the sods to sandwich layers of kitchen waste, which they mixed with the scrapings from an abandoned pigsty, two barrowfuls of sodden poplar leaves from the recreation ground, and a sack of rotten turnips. Looking over the hedge, I caught the fanatic gleam in Elsie's eye as she turned the hungry bacteria loose on the heap, and could not repress a premonitory shudder.

So far, not too bad, perhaps. But when serious bombing started and food became so scarce that housewives were fined for not making over their swill to the national pigs, Elsie and Roland grew worried. Having already abandoned their ordinary sanitary system and built an earth-closet in the garden, they now tried to convince neighbors of their duty to do the same, even at the risk of catching cold and getting spiders down the neck. Elsie also sent Roland after the slow-moving Red Devon cows as they lurched home along the lane at dusk, to rescue the precious drop-pings with a kitchen shovel; while she visited the local ash-dump with a packing case mounted on wheels, and collected whatever she found there of an organic nature—dead cats, old rags, withered flowers, cabbage stalks and such household waste as even a national wartime pig would have coughed at. She also saved every drop of their bath-water for sprin-kling the heaps; because it contained, she said, valuable animal salts.

The test of a good compost heap, as every illuminate knows, is whether a certain revolting-looking, if beneficial, fungus sprouts from it. Elsie's heaps were grey with this crop, and so hot inside that they could be used for haybox cookery; which must have saved her a deal of fuel. I call them "Elsie's heaps," because she now considered herself Dr. Steinpilz's earthly delegate; and loyal Roland did not dispute this claim.

A critical stage in the story came during the Blitz. It will be re-membered that trainloads of Londoners, who had been evacuated to South Devon when war broke out, thereafter de-evacuated and re-evacu-ated and re-de-evacuated themselves, from time to time, in a most disor-ganized fashion. Elsie and Roland, as it happened, escaped having evac-uees billeted on them, because they had no spare bedroom; but one night an old naval pensioner came knocking at their door and demanded lodg-ing for the night. Having been burned out of Plymouth, where everything was chaos, he had found himself walking away and blundering along in a daze until he fetched up here, hungry and dead-beat. They gave him a meal and bedded him on the sofa but when Elsie came down in the morning to fork over the heaps, she found him dead of heart-failure.

Roland broke a long silence by coming, in some embarrassment, to ask my advice. Elsie, he said, had decided that it would be wrong to trouble the police about the case; because the police were so busy these days, and the poor old fellow had claimed to possess neither kith nor kin. So they'd read the burial service over him and, after removing his belt-buckle, trouser buttons, metal spectacle-case and a bunch of keys, which were irreducible, had laid him reverently in the new compost heap. Its other contents, he added, were a cartload of waste from the cider-factory, salvaged cow-dung, and several basketfuls of hedge clippings. Had they done wrong?

"If you mean 'will I report you to the Civil Authorities?' the answer is no," I assured him. "I wasn't looking over the hedge at the relevant hour, and what you tell me is only hearsay." Roland shambled off satisfied.

The War went on. Not only did the Hedges convert the whole garden into serried rows of Eugen Steinpilz memorial heaps, leaving no room for planting the potatoes or carrots to which the compost had been prospectively devoted, but they scavenged the offal from the Brixham fish-market and salvaged the contents of the bin outside the surgical ward—at the Cottage Hospital. Every spring, I remember, Elsie used to pick big bunches of primroses and put them straight on the compost, without even a last wistful sniff; virgin primroses were supposed to be particularly relished by the fierce bacteria.

Here the story becomes a little painful for members, say, of a family reading circle; I will soften it as much as possible. One morning a policeman called on the Hedges with a summons, and I happened to see Roland peep anxiously out of the bedroom window, but quickly pull his head in again. The policeman rang and knocked and waited, then tried the back door; and presently went away. The summons was for a blackout offense, but apparently the Hedges did not know this. Next morning he called again, and when nobody answered, forced the lock of the back door. They were found dead in bed together, having taken an overdose of sleeping tablets. A note on the coverlet ran simply:

Please lay our bodies on the heap nearest the pigsty. Flowers by request. Strew some on the bodies, mixed with a little kitchen waste, and then fork the earth lightly over.

E.H.; R.H.

George Irks, the new tenant, proposed to grow potatoes and dig for victory. He hired a cart and began throwing the compost into the River Dart, "not liking the look of them toadstools," as he subsequently explained. The five beautifully clean human skeletons which George unearthed in the process were still awaiting identification when the War ended.

The Monkey Garden

SANDRA CISNEROS

THE MONKEY DOESN'T LIVE there anymore. The monkey moved—to Kentucky—and took his people with him. And I was glad because I couldn't listen anymore to his wild screaming at night, the twangy yakkety-yak of the people who owned him. The green metal cage, the porcelain table top, the family that spoke like guitars. Monkey, family, table. All gone.

And it was then we took over the garden we had been afraid to go into when the monkey screamed and showed its yellow teeth.

There were sunflowers big as flowers on Mars and thick cockscombs bleeding the deep red fringe of theater curtains. There were dizzy bees and bow-tied fruit flies turning somersaults and humming in the air. Sweet sweet peach trees. Thorn roses and thistle and pears. Weeds like so many squinty-eyed stars and brush that made your ankles itch and itch until you washed with soap and water. There were big green apples hard as knees. And everywhere the sleepy smell of rotting wood, damp earth and dusty hollyhocks thick and perfumy like the blue-blond hair of the dead.

Yellow spiders ran when we turned rocks over and pale worms blind and afraid of light rolled over in their sleep. Poke a stick in the sandy soil and a few blue-skinned beetles would appear, an avenue of ants, so many crusty lady bugs. This was a garden, a wonderful thing to look at in the spring. But bit by bit, after the monkey left, the garden began to take over itself. Flowers stopped obeying the little bricks that kept them from growing beyond their paths. Weeds mixed in. Dead cars appeared overnight like mushrooms. First one and then another and then a pale blue pickup with the front windshield missing. Before you knew it, the monkey garden became filled with sleepy cars.

Things had a way of disappearing in the garden, as if the garden itself ate them, or, as if with its old-man memory, it put them away and forgot them. Nenny found a dollar and a dead mouse between two rocks in the stone wall where the morning glories climbed, and once when we were playing hide-and-seek, Eddie Vargas laid his head beneath a hibiscus tree and fell asleep there like a Rip Van Winkle until somebody remembered he was in the game and went back to look for him.

This, I suppose, was the reason why we went there. Far away from where our mothers could find us. We and a few old dogs who lived inside the empty cars. We made a clubhouse once on the back of that old blue pickup. And besides, we liked to jump from the roof of one car to another and pretend they were giant mushrooms.

Somebody started the lie that the monkey garden had been there before anything. We liked to think the garden could hide things for a thousand years. There beneath the roots of soggy flowers were the bones of murdered pirates and dinosaurs, the eye of a unicorn turned to coal.

This is where I wanted to die and where I tried one day but not even the monkey garden would have me. It was the last day I would go there.

Who was it that said I was getting too old to play the games? Who was it I didn't listen to? I only remember that when the others ran, I wanted to run too, up and down and through the monkey garden, fast as the boys, not like Sally who screamed if she got her stockings muddy.

I said, Sally, come on, but she wouldn't. She stayed by the curb talking to Tito and his friends. Play with the kids if you want, she said, I'm staying here. She could be stuck-up like that if she wanted to, so I just left.

It was her own fault too. When I got back Sally was pretending to be mad . . . something about the boys having stolen her keys. Please give them back to me, she said punching the nearest one with a soft fist. They were laughing. She was too. It was a joke I didn't get.

I wanted to go back with the other kids who were still jumping on cars, still chasing each other through the garden, but Sally had her own game.

One of the boys invented the rules. One of Tito's friends said you can't get the keys back unless you kiss us and Sally pretended to be mad at first but she said yes. It was that simple.

I don't know why, but something inside me wanted to throw a stick. Something wanted to say no when I watched Sally going into the garden with Tito's buddies all grinning, it was just a kiss, that's all. A kiss for each one. So what, she said.

Only how come I felt angry inside. Like something wasn't right. Sally went behind that old blue pickup to kiss the boys and get her keys back, and I ran up three flights of stairs to where Tito lived. His mother was ironing shirts. She was sprinkling water on them from an empty pop bottle and smoking a cigarette.

Your son and his friends stole Sally's keys and now they won't give them back unless she kisses them and right now they're making her kiss them, I said all out of breath from the three flights of stairs.

Those kids, she said, not looking up from her ironing.

That's all?

What do you want me to do, she said, call the cops? And kept on ironing.

I looked at her a long time, but couldn't think of anything to say, and ran back down the three flights to the garden where Sally needed to be saved. I took three big sticks and a brick and figured this was enough.

But when I got there Sally said go home. Those boys said leave us alone. I felt stupid with my brick. They all looked at me as if *I* was the one that was crazy and made me feel ashamed.

And then I don't know why but I had to run away. I had to hide myself at the other end of the garden in the jungle part, under a tree that wouldn't mind if I lay down and cried a long time. I closed my eyes like tight stars so that I wouldn't, but I did. My face felt hot. Everything inside hiccuped.

I read somewhere in India there are priests who can will their heart to stop beating. I wanted to will my blood to stop, my heart to quit its pumping. I wanted to be dead, to turn into the rain, my eyes melt into the ground like two black snails. I wished and wished. I closed my eyes and willed it, but when I got up my dress was green and I had a headache.

I looked at my feet in their white socks and ugly round shoes. They seemed far away. They didn't seem to be my feet anymore. And the garden that had been such a good place to play didn't seem mine either.

The Lawnmower Man

STEPHEN KING

I N PREVIOUS YEARS, Harold Parkette had always taken pride In his lawn. He had owned a large silver Lawnboy and paid the boy down the block five dollars per cutting to push it. In those days Harold Parkette had followed the Boston Red Sox on the radio with a beer in his hand and the knowledge that God was in his heaven and all was right with the world, including his lawn. But last year, In mid-October, fate had played Harold Parkette a nasty trick. While the boy was mowing the grass for the last time of the season, the Castonmeyers' dog had chased the Smiths' cat under the mower.

Harold's daughter had thrown up half a quart of cherry Kool-Aid into the lap of her new jumper, and his wife had nightmares for a week afterward. Although she had arrived after the fact, she *had* arrived in time to see Harold and the green-faced boy cleaning the blades. Their daughter and Mrs. Smith stood over them, weeping, although Alicia had taken time enough to change her jumper for a pair of blue jeans and one of those disgusting skimpy sweaters. She had a crush on the boy who mowed the lawn.

After a week of listening to his wife moan and gobble in the next bed, Harold decided to get rid of the mower. He didn't really *need* a mower anyway, he supposed. He had hired a boy this year; next year he would just hire a boy *and* a mower. And maybe Carla would stop moaning in her sleep. He might even get laid again.

So he took the silver Lawnboy down to Phil's Sunoco, and he and Phil dickered over it. Harold came away with a brand-new Kelly blackwall tire and a tankful of hi-test, and Phil put the silver Lawnboy out on one of the pump islands with a hand-lettered FOR SALE sign on it.

And this year, Harold just kept putting off the necessary hiring. When he finally got around to calling last year's boy. his mother told him Frank had gone to the state university. Harold shook his head in wonder and went to the refrigerator to get a beer. Time certainly flew, didn't it? My God, yes.

He put off hiring a new boy as first May and then June slipped past him and the Red Sox continued to wallow in fourth place. He sat on the back porch on the weekends and watched glumly as a never ending progression of young boys he had never seen before popped out to mutter a quick hello before taking his buxom daughter off to the local passion pit. And the grass thrived and grew in a marvelous way. It was a good summer for grass; three days of shine followed by one of gentle rain, almost like clockwork.

By mid-July, the lawn looked more like a meadow than a suburbanite's backyard, and Jack Castonmeyer had begun to make all sorts of extremely unfunny jokes, most of which concerned the price of hay and alfalfa. And Don Smith's four-year-old daughter Jenny had taken to hiding in it when there was oatmeal for breakfast or spinach for supper.

One day in late July, Harold went out on the patio during the seventh-inning stretch and saw a woodchuck sitting perkily on the overgrown back walk. The time had come, he decided. He flicked off the radio, picked up the paper, and turned to the classifieds. And half way down the Part Time column, he found this: *Lawns mowed. Reasonable.* 776-2390.

Harold called the number, expecting a vacuuming housewife who would yell outside for her son. Instead, a briskly professional voice said, "Pastoral Greenery and Outdoor Services . . . how may we help you?"

Cautiously. Harold told the voice how Pastoral Greenery could help him. Had it come to this, then? Were lawncutters starting their own businesses and hiring office help? He asked the voice about rates, and the voice quoted him a reasonable figure.

Harold hung up with a lingering feeling of unease and went back to the porch. He sat down, turned on the radio, and stared out over his glandular lawn at the Saturday clouds moving slowly across the Saturday sky. Carla and Alicia were at his mother-in-law's and the house was his. It would be a pleasant surprise for them if the boy who was coming to cut the lawn finished before they came back.

He cracked a beer and sighed as Dick Drago was touched for a double and then hit a batter. A little breeze shuffled across the screened-in porch. Crickets hummed softly in the long grass. Harold grunted something unkind about Dick Drago and then dozed off.

He was jarred awake a half hour later by the doorbell. He knocked over his beer getting up to answer it.

A man in grass-stained denim overalls stood on the front stoop, chewing a toothpick. He was fat. The curve of his belly pushed his faded blue overalls out to a point where Harold half suspected he had swallowed a basketball.

"Yes?" Harold Parkette asked, still half asleep.

The man grinned, rolled his toothpick from one corner of his mouth to the other, tugged at the seat of his overalls, and then pushed his green baseball cap up a notch on his forehead. There was a smear of fresh engine oil on the bill of his cap. And there he was, smelling of grass, earth, and oil, grinning at Harold Parkette.

"Pastoral sent me, buddy," he said jovially, scratching his crotch. "You called, right? Right, buddy?" He grinned on endlessly.

"Oh. The lawn. You?" Harold stared stupidly.

"Yep, me." The lawnmower man bellowed fresh laughter into Harold's sleep-puffy face.

Harold stood helplessly aside and the lawnmower man tromped ahead of him down the hall, through the living room and kitchen, and onto the back porch. Now Harold had placed the man and everything was all right. He had seen the type before, working for the sanitation department and the highway repair crews out on the turnpike. Always with a spare minute to lean on their shovels and smoke Lucky Strikes or Camels, looking at you as if they were the salt of the earth, able to hit you for five or sleep with your wife anytime they wanted to. Harold had always been slightly afraid of men like this; they were always tanned dark brown, there were always nets of wrinkles around their eyes, and they always knew what to do.

"The back lawn's the real chore," he told the man, unconsciously deepening his voice. "It's square and there are no obstructions, but it's pretty well grown up." His voice faltered back into its normal register and he found himself apologizing: "I'm afraid I've let it go."

"No sweat, buddy. No strain. Great-great-great." The lawnmower man grinned at him with a thousand traveling-salesman jokes in his eyes. 'The taller, the better. Healthy soil, that's what you got there, by Circe. That's what I always say."

By Circe?

The lawnmower man cocked his head at the radio. Yastrzemski had just struck out "Red Sox fan? I'm a Yankees man, myself." He clumped back into the house and down the front hall. Harold watched him bitterly.

He sat back down and looked accusingly for a moment at the puddle of beer under the table with the overturned Coors can in the middle of it.

He thought of getting the mop from the kitchen and decided it would keep.

No sweat. No strain.

He opened his paper to the financial section and cast a judicious eye at the closing stock quotations. As a good Republican, he considered the Wall Street executives behind the columned type to be at least minor demigods—

(By Circe??)

—and he had wished many times that he could better understand the Word, as handed down from the mount not on stone tablets but in such enigmatic abbreviations as pct. and Kdk and 3.28 up 2/3. He had once bought a judicious three shares in a company called Midwest Bisonburgers, Inc., that had gone broke in 1968. He had lost his entire seventy-five-dollar investment. Now, he understood, bisonburgers were quite the coming thing. The wave of the future. He had discussed this often with Sonny, the bartender down at the Goldfish Bowl. Sonny told Harold his trouble was that he was five years ahead of his time, and he should . . .

A sudden racketing roar startled him out of the new doze he had just been slipping into.

Harold jumped to his feet, knocking his chair over and staring around wildly.

"That's a lawnmower?" Harold Parkette asked -the kitchen. "My God, *that's* a lawnmower?'

He rushed through the house and stared out the front door. There was nothing out there but a battered green van with the words PASTORAL GREENERY, INC. painted on the side. The roaring sound was in back now. Harold rushed through his house again, burst onto the back porch, and stood frozen.

It was obscene.

It was a travesty.

The aged red power mower the fat man had brought in his van was running on its own. No one was pushing it; in fact, no one was within five feet of it. It was running at a fever pitch, tearing through the unfortunate grass of Harold Parkette's back lawn like an avenging red devil straight from hell. It screamed and bellowed and farted oily blue smoke in a crazed kind of mechanical madness that made Harold feel ill with terror. The overripe smell of cut grass hung in the air like sour wine.

But the lawnmower man was the true obscenity.

The lawnmower man had removed his clothes—every stitch. They were folded neatly in the empty birdbath that was at the center of the back lawn. Naked and grass-stained, he was crawling along about five feet behind the mower, eating the cut grass. Green juice ran down his chin and dripped onto his pendulous belly. And every time the lawnmower whirled around a corner, he rose and did an odd, skipping jump before prostrating himself again.

"*Stop!*" Harold Parkette screamed. "*Stop that!*"

But the lawnmower man took no notice, and his screaming scarlet familiar never slowed. If anything, it seemed to speed up. Its nicked steel grill seemed to grin sweatily at Harold as it raved by.

Then Harold saw the mole. It must have been hiding in stunned terror just ahead of the mower, in the swath of grass about to be slaughtered. It bolted across the cut band of lawn toward safety under the porch, a panicky brown streak.

The lawnmower swerved.

Blatting and howling, it roared over the mole and spat it out in a string of fur and entrails that reminded Harold of the Smiths' cat. The mole destroyed, the lawnmower rushed back to the main job.

The lawnmower man crawled rapidly by, eating grass. Harold stood paralyzed with horror, stocks, bonds, and bisonburgers completely forgotten. He could actually see that huge, pendulous belly expanding. *The lawnmower man swerved and ate the mole.*

That was when Harold Parkette leaned out the screen door and vomited into the zinnias. The world went gray, and suddenly he realized he was fainting, *had* fainted. He collapsed backward onto the porch and closed his eyes. . . .

Someone was shaking him. Carla was shaking him. He hadn't done the dishes or emptied the garbage and Carla was going to be very angry but that was all right. As long as she was waking him up, taking him out of the horrible dream he had been having, back into the normal world, nice normal Carla with her Playtex Living Girdle and her buck teeth—

Buck teeth, yes. But not Carla's buck teeth. Carla had weak-looking chipmunk buck teeth. But these teeth were—

Hairy.

Green hair was growing on these buck teeth. It almost looked like—

Grass?

"Oh my God," Harold said.

"You fainted, buddy, right, huh?" The lawnmower man was bending over him, grinning with his hairy teeth. His lips and chin were hairy, too. Everything was hairy. And green. The yard stank of grass and gas and too sudden silence.

Harold bolted up to a sitting position and stared at the dead mower. All the grass had been neatly cut. And there would be no need to rake this job, Harold observed sickly. If the lawnmower man had missed a single cut blade, he couldn't see it. He squinted obliquely at the lawnmower man and winced. He was still naked, still fat, still terrifying. Green trickles ran from the corner of his mouth.

"What is this?" Harold begged.

The man waved an arm benignly at the lawn. "This? Well, it's a new thing the boss has been trying. It works out real good. Real good, buddy. We're killing two birds with one stone. We keep getting along toward the final stage, and we're making money to support our other operations to boot. See what I mean? Of course every now and then we run into a customer who doesn't understand—some people got no respect for efficiency, right?—but the boss is always agreeable to a sacrifice. Sort of keeps the wheels greased, if you catch me."

Harold said nothing One word knelled over and over in his mind, and that word was "sacrifice." In his mind's eye he saw the mole spewing out from under the battered red mower.

He got up slowly, like a palsied old man. "Of course," he said and could only come up with a line from one of Alicia's folk-rock records. "God bless the grass."

The lawnmower man slapped one summer-apple-colored thigh. "That's pretty good, buddy. In fact, that's damned good. I can see you got the right spirit. Okay if I write that down when I get back to the office? Might mean a promotion."

"Certainly," Harold said, retreating toward the back door and striving to keep his melting smile in place. "You go right ahead and finish. I think I'll take a little nap—"

"Sure, buddy," the lawnmower man said, getting ponderously to his feet. Harold noticed the unusually deep split between the first and second toes, almost as if the feet were . . . well, cloven.

"It hits everybody kinda hard at first," the lawnmower man said. "You'll get used to it." He eyed Harold's portly figure shrewdly. "In fact, you might even want to give it a whirl yourself. The boss has always got an eye out for new talent."

"The boss," Harold repeated faintly.

The lawnmower man paused at the bottom of the steps and gazed tolerantly up at Harold Parkette. "Well, say, buddy. I figured you must have guessed . . . God bless the grass and all."

Harold shook his head carefully and the lawnmower man laughed.

"Pan. Pan's the boss." And he did a half hop, half shuffle In the newly cut grass and the lawnmower screamed into life and began to trundle around the house.

'The neighbors—" Harold began, but the lawnmower man only waved cheerily and disappeared.

Out front the lawnmower blatted and howled. Harold Parkette refused to look, as if by refusing he could deny the grotesque spectacle that the Castonmeyers and Smiths— wretched Democrats both—were probably drinking in with horrified but no doubt righteously I-told-you-so eyes.

Instead of looking, Harold went to the telephone, snatched it up, and dialed police headquarters from the emergency do-cal pasted on the phone's handset.

"Sergeant Hall," the voice at the other end said.

Harold stuck a finger In his free ear and said, "My name is Harold Parkette. My address is 1421 East Endicott Street. I'd like to report . . ." What? What would he like to report? A man is in the process of raping and murdering my lawn and he works for a fellow named Pan and has cloven feet?

"Yes, Mr. Parkette?"

Inspiration struck. "I'd like to report a case of indecent exposure."

"Indecent exposure," Sergeant Hall repeated.

"Yes. There's a man mowing my lawn. He's in the, uh, altogether."

"You mean he's naked?" Sergeant Hall asked, politely incredulous.

"Naked!" Harold agreed, holding tightly to the frayed ends of his sanity. "Nude. Unclothed. Bare-assed. On my front lawn. Now will you get somebody the hell over here?"

'That address was 1421 West Endicott?" Sergeant Hall asked bemusedly.

"East!" Harold yelled. "For God's sake—"

"And you say he's definitely naked? You are able to observe his, uh, genitals and so on?"

Harold tried to speak and could only gargle. The sound of the insane lawnmower seemed to be growing louder and louder, drowning out everything in the universe. He felt his gorge rise.

"Can you speak up?" Sergeant Hall buzzed. "There's an awfully noisy connection there at your end—"

The front door crashed open.

Harold looked around and saw the lawnmower man's mechanized familiar advancing though the door. Behind it came the lawnmower man himself, still quite naked. With something approaching true insanity, Harold saw the man's pubic hair was a rich fertile green. He was twirling his baseball cap on one finger.

"That was a mistake, buddy," the lawnmower man said reproachfully. "You shoulda stuck with God bless the grass."

"Hello? Hello, Mr. Parkette—"

The telephone dropped from Harold's nerveless fingers as the lawnmower began to advance on him, cutting through the nap of Carla's new Mohawk rug and spitting out brown hunks of fiber as it came.

Harold stared at it with a kind of bird-and-snake fascination until it reached the coffee table. When the mower shunted it aside, shearing one leg into sawdust and splinters as it did so, he climbed over the back of his chair and began to retreat toward the kitchen, dragging the chair in front of him.

"That won't do any good, buddy," the lawnmower man said kindly. "Apt to be messy, too. Now if you was just to show me where you keep your sharpest butcher knife, we could get this sacrifice business out of the way real painless . . . I think the birdbath would do . . . and then—"

Harold shoved the chair at the lawnmower, which had been craftily flanking him while the naked man drew his attention, and bolted through the doorway. The lawnmower roared around the chair, jetting out exhaust, and as Harold smashed open the porch screen door and leaped down the steps, he heard it—smelled it, felt it—right at his heels.

The lawnmower roared off the top step like a skier going off a jump. Harold sprinted across his newly cut back lawn. but there had been too many beers, too many afternoon naps.

He could sense it nearing him, then on his heels, and then he looked over his shoulder and tripped over his own feet.

The last thing Harold Parkette saw was the grinning grill of the charging lawnmower, rocking back to reveal its flashing, greenstained blades, and above it the fat face of the lawnmower man, shaking his head in good-natured reproof.

"Hell of a thing," Lieutenant Goodwin said as the last of the photographs were taken. He nodded to the two men in white, and they trundled their basket across the lawn. "He reported some guy on his lawn not two hours ago."

"Is that so?" Patrolman Cooley asked.

"Yeah. One of the neighbors called in, too. Guy named Castonmeyer. He thought it was Parkette himself. Maybe it was, Cooley. Maybe it was."

"Sir?"

"Crazy with the heat," Lieutenant Goodwin said gravely, and tapped his temple. "Schizo-fucking-phrenia."

"Yes sir," Cooley said respectfully.

"Where's the rest of him?" one of the white-coats asked.

"The birdbath," Goodwin said. He looked profoundly up at the sky.

"Did you say the birdbath?" the white-coat asked.

"Indeed I did," Lieutenant Goodwin agreed. Patrolman Cooley looked at the birdbath and suddenly lost most of his tan.

"Sex maniac," Lieutenant Goodwin said, "Must have been."

"Prints?" Cooley asked thickly.

"You might as well ask for footprints," Goodwin said. He gestured at the newly cut grass.

Patrolman Cooley made a strangled noise in his throat.

Lieutenant Goodwin stuffed his hands Into his pockets and rocked back on his heels. "The world," he said gravely, "is full of nuts. Never forget that, Cooley. Schizos. Lab boys say somebody chased Parkette through his own living room with a lawnmower. Can you imagine that?"

"No sir," Cooley said.

Goodwin looked out over Harold Parkette's neatly manicured lawn. "Well, like the man said when he saw the black-haired Swede, it surely is a Norse of a different color."

Goodwin strolled around the house and Cooley followed him. Behind them, the scent of newly mown grass hung pleasantly in the air.

A Curtain of Green

Eudora Welty

E VERY DAY ONE SUMMER in Larkin's Hill, it rained a little. The rain was a regular thing, and would come about two o'clock in the afternoon.

One day, almost as late as five o'clock, the sun was still shining. It seemed almost to spin in a tiny groove in the polished sky, and down below, in the trees along the street and in the rows of flower gardens in the town, every leaf reflected the sun from a hardness like a mirror surface. Nearly all the women sat in the windows of their houses, fanning and sighing, waiting for the rain.

Mrs. Larkin's garden was a large, densely grown plot running downhill behind the small white house where she lived alone now, since the death of her husband. The sun and the rain that beat down so heavily that summer had not kept her from working there daily. Now the intense light like a tweezers picked out her clumsy, small figure in its old pair of men's overalls rolled up at the sleeves and trousers, separated it from the thick leaves, and made it look strange and yellow as she worked with a hoe— over-vigorous, disreputable, and heedless.

Within its border of hedge, high like a wall, and visible only from the upstairs windows of the neighbors, this slanting, tangled garden, more and more over-abundant and confusing, must have become so familiar to Mrs. Larkin that quite possibly by now she was unable to conceive of any other place. Since the accident in which her husband was killed, she had never once been seen anywhere else. Every morning she might be observed walking slowly, almost timidly, Out of the white house, wearing a pair of the untidy overalls, often with her hair streaming and tangled where she had neglected to comb it. She would wander about for a little while at first, uncertainly, deep among the plants and wet with their dew, and yet not quite putting out her hand to touch anything. And then a sort of sturdiness would possess her—stabilize her; she would stand still for a moment, as if a blindfold were being removed; and then she would kneel in the flowers and begin to work.

She worked without stopping, almost invisibly, submerged all day among the thick, irregular, sloping beds of plants. The servant would call her at dinnertime, and she would obey; but it was not until it was completely dark that she would truthfully give up her labor and with a drooping, submissive walk appear at the house, slowly opening the small low door at the back. Even the rain would bring only a pause to her. She would move to the shelter of the pear tree, which in mid-April hung heavily almost to the ground in brilliant full leaf, in the center of the garden.

It might seem that the extreme fertility of her garden formed at once a preoccupation and a challenge to Mrs. Larkin. Only by ceaseless activity could she cope with the rich blackness of this soil. Only by cutting, separating, thinning and tying back in the clumps of flowers and bushes and vines could she have kept them from overreaching their boundaries and multiplying out of all reason. The daily summer rains could only increase her vigilance and her already excessive energy. And yet, Mrs. Larkin rarely cut, separated, tied back. . . . To a certain extent, she seemed not to seek for order, but to allow an over-flowering, as if she consciously ventured forever a little farther, a little deeper, into her life in the garden.

She planted every kind of flower that she could find or order from a catalogue—planted thickly and hastily, without stopping to think, without any regard for the ideas that her neighbors might elect in their club as to what constituted an appropriate vista, or an effect of restfulness, or even harmony of color. Just to what end Mrs. Larkin worked so strenuously in her garden, her neighbors could not see. She certainly never sent a single one of her fine flowers to any of them. They might get sick and die, and she would never send a flower. And if she thought of *beauty* at all (they regarded her stained overalls, now almost of a color with the leaves), she certainly did not strive for it in her garden. It was impossible to enjoy looking at such a place. To the neighbors gazing down from their upstairs windows it had the appearance of a sort of jungle, in which the slight, heedless form of its owner daily lost itself.

At first, after the death of Mr. Larkin—for whose father, after all, the town had been named—they had called upon the widow with decent frequency. But she had not appreciated it, they said to one another. Now, occasionally, they looked down from their bedroom windows as they brushed studiously at their hair in the morning; they found her place in the garden, as they might have run their fingers toward a city on a map of a foreign country, located her from their distance almost in curiosity, and then forgot her.

Early that morning they had heard whistling in the Larkin garden. They had recognized Jamey's tune, and had seen him kneeling in the flowers at Mrs. Larkin's side. He was only the colored boy who worked in the neighborhood by the day. Even Jamey, it was said, Mrs. Larkin would tolerate only now and then. . . .

Throughout the afternoon she had raised her head at intervals to see how fast he was getting along in his transplanting. She had to make him finish before it began to rain. She was busy with the hoe, clearing one of the last patches of uncultivated ground for some new shrubs. She bent under the sunlight, chopping in blunt, rapid, tireless strokes. Once she raised her head far back to stare at the flashing sky. Her eyes were dull and puckered, as if from long impatience or bewilderment. Her mouth was a sharp line. People said she never spoke.

But memory tightened about her easily, without any prelude of warning or even despair. She would see promptly, as if a curtain had been jerked quite unceremoniously away from a little scene, the front porch of the white house, the shady street in front, and the blue automobile in which her husband approached, driving home from work. It was a summer day, a day from the summer before. In the freedom of gaily turning her head, a motion she was now forced by memory to repeat as she hoed the ground, she could see again the tree that was going to fall. There had been no warning. But there was the enormous tree, the fragrant chinaberry tree, suddenly tilting, dark and slow like a cloud, leaning down to her husband. From her place on the front porch she had spoken in a soft voice to him, never so intimate as at that moment, "You can't be hurt." But the tree had fallen, had struck the car exactly so as to crush him to death. She had waited there on the porch for a time afterward, not moving at all—in a sort of recollection—as if to reach under and bring out from obliteration her protective words and to try them once again . . . so as to change the whole happening. It was accident that was incredible, when her love for her husband was keeping him safe.

She continued to hoe the breaking ground, to beat down the juicy weeds. Presently she became aware that hers was the only motion to continue in the whole slackened place. There was no wind at all now. The cries of the birds had hushed. The sun seemed clamped to the side of the sky. Everything had stopped once again, the stillness had mesmerized the stems of the plants, and all the leaves went suddenly into thickness. The shadow of the pear tree in the center of the garden lay callous on the ground. Across the yard, Jamey knelt, motionless.

"Jamey!" she called angrily.

But her voice hardly carried in the dense garden. She felt all at once terrified, as though her loneliness had been pointed out by some outside force whose finger parted the hedge. She drew her hand for an instant to her breast. An obscure fluttering there frightened her, as though the force babbled to her, The bird that flies within your heart could not divide this cloudy air. . . . She stared without expression at the garden. She was clinging to the hoe, and she stared across the green leaves toward Jamey.

A look of docility in the Negro's back as he knelt in the plants began to infuriate her. She started to walk toward him, dragging the hoe vaguely through the flowers behind her. She forced herself to look at him, and noticed him closely for the first time—the way he looked like a child. As he turned his head a little to one side and negligently stirred the dirt with his yellow finger, she saw, with a sort of helpless suspicion and hunger, a soft, rather deprecating smile on his face; he was lost in some impossible dream of his own while he was transplanting the little shoots. He was not even whistling; even that sound was gone.

She walked nearer to him—he must have been deaf —almost stealthily bearing down upon his laxity and his absorption, as if that glimpse of the side of his face, that turned-away smile, were a teasing, innocent, flickering and beautiful vision—some mirage to her strained and wandering eyes.

Yet a feeling of stricture, of a responding hopelessness almost approaching ferocity, grew with alarming quickness about her. When she was directly behind him she stood quite still for a moment, in the queer sheathed manner she had before beginning her gardening in the morning. Then she raised the hoe above her head; the clumsy sleeves both fell back, exposing the thin, unsunburned whiteness of her arms, the shocking fact of their youth.

She gripped the handle tightly, tightly, as though convinced that the wood of the handle could feel, and that all her strength could indent its surface with pain. The head of Jamey, bent there below her, seemed witless, terrifying, wonderful, almost inaccessible to her, and yet in its explicit nearness meant surely for destruction, with its clustered hot woolly hair, its intricate, glistening ears, its small brown branching streams of sweat, the bowed head holding so obviously and so fatally its ridiculous dream.

Such a head she could strike off, intentionally, so deeply did she know, from the effect of a man's danger and death, its cause in oblivion;

and so helpless was she, too helpless to defy the workings of accident, of life and death, of unaccountability. . . . Life and death, she thought, gripping the heavy hoe, life and death, which now meant nothing to her but which she was compelled continually to wield with both her hands, ceaselessly asking, Was it not possible to compensate? to punish? to protest? Pale darkness turned for a moment through the sunlight, like a narrow leaf blown through the garden in a wind.

In that moment, the rain came. The first drop touched her upraised arm. Small, close sounds and coolness touched her.

Sighing, Mrs. Larkin lowered the hoe to the ground and laid it carefully among the growing plants. She stood still where she was, close to Jamey, and listened to the rain falling. It was so gentle. It was so full—the sound of the end of waiting.

In the light from the rain, different from sunlight, everything appeared to gleam unreflecting from within itself in its quiet arcade of identity. The green of the small zinnia shoots was very pure, almost burning. One by one, as the rain reached them, all the individual little plants shone out, and then the branching vines. The pear tree gave a soft rushing noise, like the wings of a bird alighting. She could sense behind her, as if a lamp were lighted in the night, the signal-like whiteness of the house. Then Jamey, as if in the shock of realizing the rain had come, turned his full face toward her, questions and delight intensifying his smile, gathering up his aroused, stretching body. He stammered some disconnected words, shyly.

She did not answer Jamey or move at all. She would not feel anything now except the rain falling. She listened for its scattered soft drops between Jamey's words, its quiet touching of the spears of the iris leaves, and a clear sound like a bell as it began to fall into a pitcher the cook had set on the doorstep.

Finally, Jamey stood there quietly, as if waiting for his money, with his hand trying to brush his confusion away from before his face. The rain fell steadily. A wind of deep wet fragrance beat against her.

Then as if it had swelled and broken over a daily levee, tenderness tore and spun through her sagging body.

It has come, she thought senselessly, her head lifting and her eyes looking without understanding at the sky which had begun to move, to fold nearer in softening, dissolving clouds. It was almost dark. Soon the loud and gentle night of rain would come. It would pound upon the steep roof of the white house. Within, she would lie in her bed and hear the rain. On and on it would fall, beat and fall. The day's work would be over in the garden. She would lie in bed, her arms tired at her sides and in motionless peace: against that which was inexhaustible, there was no defense.

Then Mrs. Larkin sank in one motion down into the flowers and lay there, fainting and streaked with rain. Her face was fully upturned, down among the plants, with the hair beaten away from her forehead and her open eyes closing at once when the rain touched them. Slowly her lips began to part. She seemed to move slightly, in the sad adjustment of a sleeper.

Jamey ran jumping and crouching about her, drawing in his breath alternately at the flowers breaking under his feet and at the shapeless, passive figure on the ground. Then he became quiet, and stood back at a little distance and looked in awe at the unknowing face, white and rested under its bombardment. He remembered how something had filled him with stillness when he felt her standing there behind him looking down at him, and he would not have turned around at that moment for anything in the world. He remembered all the while the oblivious crash of the windows next door being shut when the rain started. . . . But now, in this unseen place, it was he who stood looking at poor Mrs. Larkin.

He bent down and in a horrified, piteous, beseeching voice he began to call her name until she stirred.

"Miss Lark'! Miss Lark'!"

Then he jumped nimbly to his feet and ran out of the garden.

Blue Poppies

JANE GARDAM

M Y MOTHER DIED with her hand in the hand of the Duchess. We were at Clere in late summer. It was a Monday. Clere opens on Mondays and Tuesdays only. It is not a great house and the Duke likes silence. It offers only itself. "No teas, no toilets!" I once heard a woman say on one of the few coaches that ever found its way there. "It's not much, is it?" Clere stands blotchy and molding and its doves look very white against its peeling portico. Grass in the cobbles. If you listen hard you can still hear a stable clock thinly strike the quarters.

Mother had been staying with me for a month, sometimes knowing me, sometimes looking interestedly in my direction as if she ought to. Paddling here, paddling there. Looking out of windows, saying brightly, "Bored? Of course I'm not bored." Once or twice when I took her breakfast in bed she thought I was a nurse. Once after tea she asked if she could play in the garden and then looked frightened.

Today was showery. She watched the rain and the clouds blowing.

"Would you like to go to Clere?"

"Now what is that?"

"You know. You've been there before. It's the place with the blue poppies."

"Blue poppies?"

"You saw them last time."

"*Meconopsi?*" she asked. "I really ought to write letters."

My mother was ninety-one and she wrote letters every day. She had done so since she was a girl. She wrote at last to a very short list of people. Her address book looked like a tycoon's diary. Negotiations completed. Whole pages crossed our. The more recent crossings-off were wavery.

We set out for the blue poppies and she wore a hat and gloves and surveyed the rainy world through the car window. Every now and then she opened her handbag to look at her pills or wondered aloud where her walking stick had gone.

"Back seat."

"No," she said, "I like the front seat in a car. It was always manners to offer the front seat. It's the best seat, the front seat."

"But the stick is on the back seat."

"What stick is that?'

At Clere the rain had stopped, leaving the grass slippery and a silvery dampness hanging in the air. The Duchess was on the door, taking tickets. That is to say she was at the other side of a rickety trestle table working in a flower border. She was digging. On the table a black tin box stood open for small change and a few spotted postcards of the house were arranged beside some very poor specimens of plants for sale at exorbitant prices. The Duchess's corduroy behind rose beyond them. She straightened up and half turned to us, great gloved hands swinging, caked in earth.

The Duchess is no beauty. She has a beak of ivory and deep-sunken, hard blue eyes. Her hair is scant and colorless. There are ropes in her throat. Her face is weather—beaten and her haunches strong, for she has created the gardens at Clere almost alone. When she speaks, the voice of the razorbill is heard in the land.

The Duke. Oh, the poor Duke! We could see him under the portico seated alone at another rough table eating bread. There was a slab of processed cheese beside the bread and a small bottle of beer. He wore a shawl and his face was long and rueful. His near-side shoulder was raised at a defensive angle to the Duchess, as if to ward off blows. I saw the Duchess see me pity the neglected Duke as she said to us, "Could you hold on? Just a moment?" and turning back to the flowerbed she began to tug at a great, leaden root.

My mother opened her bag and began to scrabble in it. "Now, this is my treat."

"There!" cried the Duchess, heaving the root aloft, shaking off soil, tossing it down. "Two, is it?"

"*Choisia ternata*," said my mother. "One and a half."

A pause.

"For the house, is it? Are you going round the house as well as the garden?"

"We really came just for the poppies," I said, "and it's two, please."

"Oh, I should like to see the house," said my mother. "I saw the poppies when I stayed with Lilian last year."

I blinked.

"Lilian thinks I can't remember," my mother said to the Duchess. "This time I should like to see the house. And I shall pay."

"Two," I signalled to the Duchess, smiling what I hoped would be a collaborative smile above my mother's head. I saw the Duchess think, "A bully."

"One and a half," said my mother.

"Mother, I am over fifty. It is children who are half-price."

"And senior citizens," said my mother. "And I am one of those as I'm sure Her Grace will believe. I can prove it if I can only find my card."

"I'll trust you," said the Duchess. Her eyes gleamed on my mother. Then her icicle-wax face cracked into a smile drawing the thin skin taut over her nose. "I'm a Lilian, too," she said and gave a little cackle that told me she thought me fortunate.

We walked about the ground floor of the house, though many corridors were barred, and small ivory labels hung on hooks on many doors. They said "PRIVATE" in beautifully painted copperplate. In the drawing room, where my mother felt a little dizzy—nothing to speak of—there was nowhere to sir down. All the sofas and chairs were roped off, even the ones with torn silk or stuffing sprouting out. We were the only visitors and there seemed to be nobody in attendance to see that we didn't steal the ornaments.

"Meissen, I'd think, dear," said my mother, picking up a little porcelain box from a table. "Darling, oughtn't we to get this valued?" On other tables stood photographs in silver frames. On walls hung portraits in carved and gilded frames. Here and there across the centuries shone out the Duchess's nose.

"Such a disadvantage," said my mother, "poor dear. That photograph is a Lenare. He's made her very hazy. That was his secret, you know. The haze. He could make anybody look romantic. All the fat young lilies. It will be her engagement portrait."

"I'm surprised her mother let her have it done."

"Oh, she would have had to. It was very much the thing. Like getting confirmed. Well, with these people, more usual really than getting confirmed. She looks as though she'd have no truck with it. I agree. I think she seems a splendid woman, don't you?"

We walked out side by side and stood on the semicircular marble floor of the porch, among the flaking columns. The Duke had gone. The small brown beer-bottle was on its side. Robins were pecking about among the crumbs of bread. The Duchess could be seen, still toiling in the shrubs. Mother watched her as I considered the wet and broken steps down from the portico and up again towards the gardens, and my fury at my mother's pleasure in the Duchess. I wondered if we might take the steps one by one, arm in arm, with the stick and a prayer. "Who is that person over there digging in that flower-bed?" asked Mother, looking towards the Duchess. "A gardener, I suppose. They often get women now. You know—I should like to have done that."

Down and up the steps we went and over the swell of the grass slope. There was a flint arch into a rose garden and a long white seat under a *gloire de Dijon* rose. "I think I'll sit," said my mother.

"The seat's wet."

"Never mind."

"It's sopping."

She sat and the wind blew and the rose shook drops and petals on her. "I'll just put up my umbrella."

"You haven't an umbrella"

"Don't be silly, dear, I have a beautiful umbrella It was Margaret's. I've had it for years. It's in the hall-stand."

"Well, I can't go all the way home for it."

"It's not in your home, dear. You haven't got a hall-stand. It's in *my* home. I'm glad to say I still have a home of my own."

"Well, I'm not going there. It's a hundred miles. I'm not going a hundred miles for your umbrella."

"But of course not. I didn't bring an umbrella to *you*, Lilian. Not on holiday. I told you when you collected me: 'There's no need for me to bring an umbrella because I can always use one of yours.' Lilian, this seat is very wet."

"For heaven's sake then— Come with me to see the blue poppies."

The Duchess's face suddenly peered round the flint arch and disappeared again.

"Lilian, such a very strange woman just looked into this garden. Like a hawk."

"Mother. I'm going to see the poppies. Are you coming?"

"I saw them once before. I'm sure I did. They're very nice, but I think I'll just sit."

"Nice!"

"Yes, *nice*, dear. *Nice*. You know I can't enthuse like you can. I'm not very imaginative I never have been."

"That is true."

"They always remind me of Cadbury's chocolates, but I can never remember why."

I thought, "senile." I must have said it.

I did say it.

"Well, yes. I dare say I am. Who is this woman approaching with a cushion? How very kind. Yes, I would like a cushion. My daughter forgot the umbrella. How thoughtful. She's *clever,* you see. She went to a university. Very clever, and *imaginative,* too. She insisted on coming all this way —such a wet day and, of course, most of your garden is over—because of the blue of the poppies. Children are so funny, aren't they?"

"I never quite see why everybody gets so worked up about the blue," said the Duchess.

"*Meconopsis Baileyii,*" said my mother.

"Yes."

"*Benicifolia.*"

"Give me *Campanula carpatica,*" said the Duchess.

"Ah! Or *Gentiana verna angulosa,*" said my mother. "We sound as if we're saying our prayers."

The two of them looked at me. My mother regarded me with kindly attention, as if I were a pleasant acquaintance she would like to think well of. "You go off," said the Duchess. "I'll stay here. Take your time."

As I went I heard my mother say, "She's just like her father of course. You have to understand her; she hasn't much time for old people. And, of course, she is *no* gardener."

When I came back—and they were: they were just like Cadbury's chocolate papers crumpled up under the tall black trees in a sweep, the exact color, lying about among their pale hairy leaves in the muddy earth, raindrops scattering them with a papery noise—when I came back, the Duchess was holding my mother's hand and looking closely at her face. She said, "Quick. You must telephone. In the study. Left of the portico. Says 'Private'" on a disc. *Run!*" She let go the hand, which fell loose. Loose and finished. The Duchess seemed to be smiling. A smile that stretched the narrow face and stretched the lines sharper round her eyes. It was more a sneer than a smile. I saw she was sneering with pain. I said, "My mother is dead." She said, "Quick. Run. Be quick."

I ran. Ran down the slope, over the porch, and into the study, where the telephone was old and black and lumpen and the dial flopped and rattled. All done, I ran out again and stood at the top of the steps looking up the grassy slope. We were clamped in time. Round the corner of the house came the Duke in a wheelchair pushed by a woman in a dark-blue dress. She had bottle legs. The two of them looked at me with suspicion. The Duke said, "Phyllis?" to the woman and continued to stare. "Yes?" asked the woman. "Yes? What is it? Do you want something?" I thought, "I want this last day again."

I walked up the slope to the rose garden, where the Duchess sat looking over the view. She said, "Now she has died."

She seemed to be grieving. I knew though that my mother had not been dead when I ran for the telephone, and if it had been the Duchess who had run for the telephone I would have been with my mother when she died. So then I hated the Duchess and all her works.

It was two years later that I came face to face with her again, at a luncheon party given in aid of the preservation of trees, and quite the other side of the country. There were the usual people—some eccentrics, some gushers, some hard-grained, valiant fund-raisers. No village people. The rich. All elderly. All, even the younger ones, belonging to what my children called "the old world." They had something of the ways of my mother's generation. But none of them was my mother.

The Duchess was over in a corner, standing by herself and eating hugely, her plate up near her mouth, her fork working away, her eyes swivelling frostily about. She saw me at once and went on staring as she ate. I knew she meant that I should go across to her.

I had written a letter of thanks of course and she had not only replied adequately—an old thick cream card inside a thick cream envelope and an indecipherable signature—but she had sent flowers to the funeral. And that had ended it.

I watched with interest as the Duchess cut herself a good half-pound of cheese and put it in her pocket. Going to a side-table she opened her handbag and began to sweep fruit into it. Three apples and two bananas disappeared, and the people around her looked away. As she reached the door she looked across at me. She did not exactly hesitate, but there was something. Then she left the house.

But in the car park, there she was in a filthy car, eating one of the bananas. Still staring ahead, she wound down a window and I went towards her.

She said, "Perhaps I ought to have told you. Your mother said to me, 'Goodbye, Lilian dear.'"

"Your name is Lilian," I said. "She was quite capable of calling *you* Lilian. She had taken a liking to you. Which she never did to me."

"No, no. She meant you," said the Duchess. "She said, 'I'm sorry, darling, not to have gone with you to the poppies.'"

The Occasional Garden

SAKI

"DON'T TALK TO ME about town gardens," said Elinor Rapsley; "which means, of course, that I want you to listen to me for an hour or so while I talk about nothing else. 'What a nice-sized garden you've got,' people said to us when we first moved here. What I suppose they meant to say was what a nice-sized site for a garden we'd got. As a matter of fact, the size is all against it; it's too large to be ignored altogether and treated as a yard, and it's too small to keep giraffes in. You see, if we could keep giraffes or reindeer or some other species of browsing animal there we could explain the general absence of vegetation by a reference to the fauna of the garden: 'You can't have wapiti *and* Darwin tulips, you know, so we didn't put down any bulbs last year.' As it is, we haven't got the Wapiti, and the Darwin tulips haven't survived the fact that most of the cats of the neighborhood hold a parliament in the center of the tulip bed; that rather forlorn-looking strip that we intended to be a border of alternating geranium and spiræa has been utilized by the cat-parliament as a division lobby. Snap divisions seem to have been rather frequent of late, far more frequent than the geranium blooms are likely to be. I shouldn't object so much to ordinary cats, but I do complain of having a congress of vegetarian cats in my garden; they must be vegetarians, my dear, because, whatever ravages they may commit among the sweet-pea seedlings, they never seem to touch the sparrows; there are always just as many adult sparrows in the garden on Saturday as there were on Monday, not to mention newly fledged additions. There seems to have been an irreconcilable difference of opinion between sparrows and Providence since the beginning of time as to whether a crocus looks best standing upright with its roots in the earth or in a recumbent posture with its stem neatly severed; the sparrows always have the last word in the matter, at least in our garden they do. I fancy that Providence must have originally intended to bring in an amending Act, or whatever it's called, providing either for a less destructive sparrow or a more indestructible crocus. The one consoling point about our garden is that it's not visible from the drawing room or the smoking-room, so unless people are dining or lunching with us they can't spy out the nakedness of the land. That is why I am so furious with Gwenda Pottingdon, who has practically forced herself on me for lunch on Wednesday next; she heard me offer the Paulcote girl lunch if she was up shopping on that day, and, of course, she asked if she might come too. She is only coming to gloat over my bedraggled and flowerless borders and to sing the praises of her own detestably over-cultivated garden. I'm sick of being told that it's the envy of the neighborhood; it's like everything else that belongs to her—her car, her dinner parties, even her headaches, they are all superlative; no one else ever had anything like them. When her eldest child was confirmed it was such a sensational event, according to her account of it, that one almost expected questions to be asked about it in the House of Commons, and now she's coming on purpose to stare at my few miserable pansies and the gaps in my sweet-pea border, and to give me a glowing, full-length description of the rare and sumptuous blooms in her rose-garden."

"My dear Elinor," said the Baroness, "you would save yourself all this heart-burning and a lot of gardener's bills, not to mention sparrow anxieties, simply by paying an annual subscription to the O.O.S.A."

"Never heard of it," said Elinor; "what is it?"

"The Occasional-Oasis Supply Association," said the Baroness; "it exists to meet cases exactly like yours, cases of backyards that are of no practical use for gardening purposes, but are required to blossom into decorative scenic backgrounds at stated intervals, when a luncheon or dinner-party is contemplated. Supposing, for instance, you have people coming to lunch at one-thirty; you just ring up the Association at about ten o'clock the same morning, and say, 'Lunch garden.' That is all the trouble you have to take. By twelve forty-five your yard is carpeted with a strip of velvety turf, with a hedge of lilac or red may, or whatever happens to be in season, as a background, one or two cherry trees in blossom, and clumps of heavily flowered rhododendrons filling in the odd corners; in the foreground you have a blaze of carnations or Shirley poppies, or tiger lilies in full bloom. As soon as the lunch is over and your guests have departed the garden departs also, and all the cats in Christendom can sit in council in your yard without causing you a moment's anxiety. If you have a bishop or an antiquary or something of that sort coming to lunch you just mention the fact when you are ordering the, garden, and you get an old-world pleasaunce, with clipped yew hedges and a sun-dial and hollyhocks, and perhaps a mulberry, tree and borders of sweet-williams and Canterbury bells, and an old-fashioned beehive or two tucked away in a corner. Those are the ordinary lines of supply that the Oasis Association undertakes, but by paying a few guineas a year extra you are entitled to its emergency E.O.N. service."

"What on earth is an E.O.N. service?"

"It's just like a conventional signal to indicate special cases like the incursion of Gwenda Pottingdon. It means you've got some one coming to lunch or dinner whose garden is alleged to be 'the envy of the neighborhood.'"

"Yes," exclaimed Elinor, with some excitement, "and what happens then?"

"Something that sounds like a miracle out of the Arabian Nights. Your backyard becomes voluptuous with pomegranate and almond trees, lemon groves, and hedges of flowering cactus, dazzling banks of azaleas, marble-basined fountains, in which chestnut-and-white pond-herons step daintily amid exotic water-lilies, while golden pheasants strut about on alabaster terraces. The whole effect rather suggests the idea that Providence and Norman Wilkinson have dropped mutual jealousies and collaborated to produce a background for an open-air Russian Ballet; in point of fact, it is merely the background to your luncheon party. If there is any kick left in Gwenda Pottingdon, or whoever your E.O.N. guest of the moment may be, just mention carelessly that your climbing putella is the only one in England, since the one at Chatsworth died last winter. There isn't such a thing as a climbing putella, but Gwenda Pottingdon and her kind don't usually know one flower from another without prompting."

"Quick," said Elinor, "the address of the Association.

Gwenda Pottingdon did not enjoy her lunch. It was a simple yet elegant meal, excellently cooked and daintily served, but the piquant sauce of her own conversation was notably lacking. She had prepared a long succession of eulogistic comments on the wonders of her town garden, with its unrivaled effects of horticultural magnificence, and, behold, her theme was shut in on every side by the luxuriant hedge of Siberian berberis that formed a glowing background to Elinor's bewildering fragment of fairyland. The pomegranate and lemon trees, the terraced fountain, where golden carp slithered and wriggled amid the roots of gorgeous—hued irises, the banked masses of exotic blooms, the pagoda-like enclosure, where Japanese sand-badgers disported themselves, all these contributed to take away Gwenda's appetite and moderate her desire to talk about gardening matters.

"I can't say I admire the climbing putella," she observed shortly, "and anyway it's not the only one of its kind in England; I happen to know of one in Hampshire. How gardening is going out of fashion. I suppose people haven't the time for it nowadays."

Altogether it was quite one of Elinor's most successful luncheon parties.

It was distinctly an unforeseen catastrophe that Gwenda should have burst in on the household four days later at lunchtime and made her way unbidden into the dining-room.

"I thought I must tell you that my Elaine has had a watercolor sketch accepted by the Latent Talent Art Guild; it's to be exhibited at their summer exhibition at the Hackney Gallery. It will be the sensation of the moment in the art world— Hullo, what on earth has happened to your garden? It's not there!"

"Suffragettes," said Elinor promptly; "didn't you hear about it? They broke in and made hay of the whole thing in about ten minutes. I was so heartbroken at the havoc that I had the whole place cleared out; I shall have it laid out again on rather more elaborate lines.

"That," she said to the Baroness afterwards, "is what I call having an emergency brain."

Flavors of Exile

Doris Lessing

A T THE FOOT OF the hill near the well, was the vegetable garden, an acre fenced off from the Big Field whose earth was so rich that mealies grew there year after year ten feet tall. Nursed from that fabulous soil, carrots, lettuces, beets, tasting as I have never found vegetables taste since, loaded our table and the tables of our neighbors. Sometimes, if the garden boy was late with the supply for lunch, I would run down the steep pebbly path through the trees at the back of the hill, and along the red dust of the wagon road until I could see the windlass under its shed of thatch. There I stopped. The smell of manure, of sun on foliage, of evaporating water, rose to my head: two steps farther, and I could look down into the vegetable garden enclosed within its tall pale of reeds, rich chocolate earth studded emerald green, frothed with the white of cauliflowers, jeweled with the purple globes of eggplant and the scarlet wealth of tomatoes. Around the fence grew lemons, paw-paws, bananas, shapes of gold and yellow in their patterns of green.

In another five minutes I would be dragging from the earth carrots ten inches long, and so succulent they snapped between two fingers. I ate my allowance of these before the cook could boil them and drown them in the white flour sauce without which—and unless they were served in the large china vegetable dishes brought from that old house in London—they were not carrots to my mother.

For her, that garden represented a defeat.

When the family first came to the farm, she built vegetable beds on the kopje near the house. She had in her mind, perhaps, a vision of the farmhouse surrounded by outbuildings and gardens like a hen sheltering its chicks.

The kopje was all stone. As soon as the grass was cleared off its crown where the house stood, the fierce rains beat the soil away. Those first vegetable beds were thin sifted earth walled by pebbles. The water was brought up from the well in the water-cart.

"Water is gold," grumbled my father, eating peas which he reckoned must cost a shilling a mouthful. "Water is gold!" he came to shout at last, as my mother toiled and bent over those reluctant beds. But she got more pleasure from them than she ever did from the exhaustless plenty of the garden under the hill.

At last, the spaces in the bush where the old beds had been were seeded by wild or vagrant plants, and we children played there.

Someone must have thrown away gooseberries, for soon the low-spreading bushes covered the earth. We used to creep under them, William MacGregor and I, lie flat on our backs, and look through the leaves at the brilliant sky, reaching around us for the tiny sharp-sweet yellow fruits in their jackets of papery white. The smell of the leaves was spicy. It intoxicated us. We would laugh and shout, then quarrel; and William, to make up, shelled a double handful of the fruit and poured it into my skirt, and we ate together, pressing the biggest berries on each other. When we could eat no more, we filled baskets and took them to the kitchen to be made into that rich jam which—if allowed to burn just the right amount on the pan—is the best jam in the world, clear sweet amber, with lumps of sticky sharpness in it, as if the stings of bees were preserved in honey.

But my mother did not like it. "Cape gooseberries!" she said bitterly. "They aren't gooseberries at all. Oh, if I could let you taste a pie made of real English gooseberries."

In due course, the marvels of civilization made this possible; she found a tin of gooseberries in the Greek store at the station, and made us a pie.

My parents and William's ate the pie with a truly religious emotion.

It was this experience with the gooseberries that made me cautious when it came to brussels sprouts. Year after year my mother yearned for brussels sprouts, whose name came to represent to me something exotic and for ever unattainable When at last she managed to grow half a dozen spikes of this plant, in one cold winter which offered us sufficient frost, she of course sent a note to the MacGregors, so that they might share the treat. They came from Glasgow, they came from Home, and they could share the language of nostalgia. At the table the four grown-ups ate the bitter little cabbages, and agreed that the soil of Africa was unable to grow food that had any taste at all. I said scornfully that I couldn't see what all the fuss was about. But William, three years older than myself, passed his plate up and said he found them delicious. It was like a betrayal; and afterwards I demanded how he could like such flavorless stuff. He smiled at me and said it cost us nothing to pretend, did it?

That smile, so gentle, a little whimsical was a lesson to me and I remembered it when it came to the affair of the cherries. She found a tin of cherries at the store, we ate them with cream; and while she sighed over memories of barrows loaded with cherries in the streets of London, I sighed with her, ate fervently, and was careful not to meet her eyes.

And when she said: "The pomegranates will be fruiting soon," I would offer to run down and see how they progressed and returned from the examination saying: "It won't be long now, really it won't—perhaps next year."

The truth was, my emotion over the pomegranates was not entirely due to the beautiful lesson in courtesy given me by William. Brussels sprouts, cherries, English gooseberries—they were my mother's; they recurred in her talk as often as "a real London peasouper," or "chestnuts by the fire," or "cherry blossom at Kew." I no longer grudged these to her; I listened and was careful not to show that my thoughts were on my own inheritance of veldt and sun. But pomegranates were an exotic for my mother; and therefore more easily shared with her. She had been in Persia, where, one understood pomegranate juice ran in rivers. The wife of a minor official, she had lived in a vast stone house cooled by water tricking down a thousand stone channels from the mountains; she had lived among roses and jasmine, walnut trees and pomegranates. But, unfortunately, for too short a time.

Why not pomegranates here, in Africa? Why not?

The four trees had been planted at the same time as the first vegetable beds; and almost at once two of them died. A third lingered on for a couple of seasons and then succumbed to the white ants. The fourth stood lonely among the Cape gooseberry bushes, bore no fruit, and at last was forgotten.

Then one day my mother was showing Mrs.MacGregor her chickens and as they returned through tangles of grass and weed, their skirts lifted high in both hands, my mother exclaimed: "Why, I do believe the pomegranate is fruiting at last. Look, look, it is!" She called to us, the children, and we went running, and stood around a small thorny tree, and looked at a rusty-red fruit the size of a child's fist. "It's ripe," said my mother, and pulled it off.

Inside the house we were each given a dozen small seeds on saucers. They were bitter, but we did not like to ask for sugar. Mrs.MacGregor said gently: "It's wonderful. How you must miss all that!"

"The roses!" said my mother. "And sacks of walnuts . . . and we used to drink pomegranate juice with the melted snow water . . . nothing here tastes like that. The soil is no good."

I looked at William, sitting opposite to me. He turned his head and smiled. I fell in love.

He was then fifteen, home for the holidays. He was a silent boy, thoughtful; and the quietness in his deep grey eyes seemed to me like a promise of warmth and understanding I had never known. There was a tightness in my chest, because it hurt to be shut out from the world of simple kindness he lived in. I sat there, opposite to him, and said to myself that I had known him all my life and yet until this moment had never understood what he was. I looked at those extraordinarily clear eyes, that were like water over grey pebbles, I gazed and gazed, until he gave me a slow direct look which showed he knew I had been staring. It was like a warning, as if a door had been shut.

After the MacGregors had gone, I went through the bushes to the pomegranate tree. It was about my height, a tough, obstinate-looking thing; and there was a round yellow ball the size of a walnut hanging from a twig.

I looked at the ugly little tree and thought Pomegranates! Breasts like pomegranates and a belly like a heap of wheat! The golden pomegranates of the sun, I thought . . . pomegranates like the red of blood.

I was in a fever, more than a little mad. The space of thick grass and gooseberry, bushes between the trees was haunted by William, and his deep calm grey eyes looked at me across the pomegranates tree.

Next day I sat under the tree. It gave no shade, but the acrid sunlight was barred and splotched under it. There was hard cracked red earth beneath a covering of silvery dead grass. Under the grass I saw grains of red, and half a hard brown shell. It seemed that a fruit had ripened and burst without our knowing—yes, everywhere in the soft old grass lay the tiny crimson seeds. I tasted one; warm sweet juice flooded my tongue. I gathered them up and ate them until my mouth was full of dry seeds. I spat them out and thought that a score of pomegranate trees would grow from that mouthful.

As I watched, tiny black ants came scurrying along the roots of the grass scrambling over the fissures in the earth, to snatch away the seeds. I lay on my elbow and watched. A dozen of them era levering at a still unbroken seed. Suddenly the frail tissue split as they bumped it over a splinter, and they were caught in a sticky red ooze.

The ants would carry these seeds for hundreds of yards; there would be an orchard of pomegranates William MacGregor would come visiting with his parents, and find me among the pomegranate trees; I could hear the sound of his grave voice, mingled with the tinkle of camel bells and the splashing of falling water.

I went to the tree every day and lay under it, watching the single fellow fruit ripening on its twig. There would come a moment when it must burst and scatter crimson seeds; I must be there when did; it seemed as if my whole life was concentrated, and ripening with that single fruit.

It was very hot under the tree. My head ached. My flesh was painful with the sun. Yet there I sat all day, watching the tiny ants their work, letting them run over my legs, waiting for the pomegranate fruit to ripen. It swelled slowly; it seemed set on reaching perfection, for when it was the size that the other had been picked, it was still a bronzing yellow, and the rind was soft. It was going to be a big fruit, the size of both my fists.

Then something terrifying happened. One day I saw that the twig it hung from was splitting off the branch. The wizened, dry little tree could not sustain the weight of the fruit it had produced. I went to the house, brought down bandages from the medicine chest, and strapped the twig firm and tight to the branch, in such a way that the weight was supported. Then I wet the bandage, tenderly, and thought of William, William, William. I wet the bandage daily, and thought of him.

What I thought of William had become a world, stronger than anything around me. Yet, since I was mad, so weak, it vanished at a touch. Once, for instance, I saw him, driving with his father on the wagon along the road to the station. I remember I was ashamed that that marvelous feverish world should depend on a half-grown boy in dusty khaki, gripping a piece of grass between his teeth as he stared ahead of him. It came to this—that in order to preserve the dream, I must not see William. And it seemed he felt something of the sort himself, for in all those weeks he never came near me, whereas once he used to come every day. And yet I was convinced it must happen that William and the moment when the pomegranate split open would coincide.

I imagined it in a thousand ways, as the fruit continued to grow. Now, it was a clear bronze yellow with faint rust-colored streaks. The rind was thin, so soft that the swelling seeds within were shaping it. The fruit looked lumpy and veined, like a nursing breast. The small crown where the stem fastened on it, which had been the sheath of the flower, was still green. It began to harden and turn back into iron-grey thorns.

Soon, soon, it would be ripe. Very swiftly, the skin lost its smooth thinness. It took on a tough pored look, like the skin of an old weather-beaten countryman. It was a ruddy scarlet now, and hot to the touch. A small crack appeared, which in a day had widened so that the packed red seeds within were visible, almost bursting out. I did not dare leave the tree. I was there from six in the morning until the sun went down. I even crept down with the candle at night, although I argued it could not burst at night, not in the cool of the night, it must be the final unbearable thrust of the sun which would break it.

For three days nothing happened. The crack remained the same. Ants swarmed up the trunk, along the branches and into the fruit. The scar oozed red juice in which black ants swam and struggled. At any moment it might happen. And William did not come. I was sure he would: I watched the empty road helplessly waiting for him to come striding along, a piece of grass between his teeth, to me and the pomegranate tree. Yet he did not. In one night, the crack split another half-inch I saw a red seed push itself out of the crack and fall. Instantly it was borne off by the ants into the grass.

I went up to the house and asked my mother when the MacGregors were coming to tea.

"I don't know, dear. Why?"

"Because. I just thought . . ."

She looked at me. Her eyes were critical In one moment, she would say the name *William.* I struck first. To have William and the moment together, I must pay fee to the family gods. "There's a pomegranate nearly ripe, and you know how interested Mrs. MacGregor is . . ."

She looked sharply at me. "Pick it, and we'll make a drink of it."

"Oh no, it's not quite ready. Not altogether. . . ."

"Silly child," she said at last. She went to the telephone and said: "Mrs. MacGregor, this daughter of mine, she's got it into her head—you know how children are."

I did not care. At four that afternoon I was waiting by the pomegranate tree. Their car came thrusting up the steep road to the crown of the hill. There was Mr. MacGregor in his khaki, Mrs.Gregor in her best afternoon dress—and William. The adults shook hands, kissed. William did not turn round and look at me. It was not possible, it was monstrous, that the force of my dream should not have had the power to touch him at all, that he knew nothing of what he must do.

Then he slowly turned his head and looked down the slope to where I stood. He did not smile. It seemed he had not seen me, for his eyes traveled past me, and back to the grown-ups. He stood to one side while they exchanged their news and greetings; and then all four laughed, and turned to look at me and my tree. It seemed for a moment they were all coming. At once, however, they went into the house, William trailing after them, frowning.

In a moment he would have gone in; the space in front of the old house would be empty. I called "William!" I had not known I would call. My voice sounded small in the wide afternoon sunlight.

He went on as if he had not heard. Then he stopped, seemed to think, and came down the hill towards me while I anxiously explained his face. The low tangle of the gooseberry bushes was around his legs, and he swore sharply.

"Look at the pomegranate," I said. He came to a halt beside the tree, and looked. I was searching those clear grey eyes now for a trace of that indulgence they had shown my mother over the brussels sprouts, over that first unripe pomegranate. Now all I wanted was indulgence; I abandoned everything else.

"It's full of ants," he said at last.

"Only a little, only where it's cracked."

He stood, frowning, chewing at his piece of grass. His lips were full and thin-skinned; and I could see the blood, dull and dark around the pale groove where the grass-stem pressed.

The pomegranate hung there, swarming with ants.

"Now," I thought wildly. "Now—crack now."

There was not a sound. The sun came pouring down, hot and yellow, drawing up the smell of the grasses. There was, too, a faint sour smell from the fermenting juice of the pomegranate.

"It's bad," said William, in that uncomfortable, angry voice, "And what's that bit of dirty rag for?"

"It was breaking, the twig was breaking off—I tied it up."

"Mad," he remarked, aside, to the afternoon. "Quite mad." He was looking about him in the grass. He reached down and picked up a stick.

"No," I cried out, as he hit at the tree. The pomegranate flew into the air and exploded in a scatter of crimson seeds, fermenting juice, and black ants.

The cracked empty skin, with its white clean-looking inner skin faintly stained with juice, lay in two fragments at my feet.

He was poking sulkily with the stick at the little scarlet seeds that lay everywhere on the earth.

Then he did look at me. Those clear eyes were grave again, thoughtful, and judging. They held that warning I had seen in them before.

"That's your pomegranate," he said at last.

"Yes," I said.

He smiled. "We'd better go up, if we want any tea."

We went together up the hill to the house, and as we entered the room where the grown-ups sat over the teacups, I spoke quickly, before he could. In a bright careless voice I said: "It was bad, after all, the ants had got at it. It should have been picked before."

The Secret Garden

Victoria Rothschild

I CAN'T IMAGINE NOW a world without Edward North in it, though I suppose that early in my parents' marriage they would have known such a place. An over-worked wartime land, and, in the barren post-war, ration gardens, run-to-seed allotments, overgrown air-raid shelters and all that rubble—the place I woke up into was exhausted. Not that as a child I noticed anything like that. To me there was just countryside and sometimes we walked in it on Saturdays, and there were hills beyond which you could see the sea. Also, fields to run in and farmers farming. That was it. It was just there, the hard, drab, sleepy place, as sure as sweet rationing. And then my father discovered North. Really. True North. In some places the name has passed into the language. We know what we mean by North. To North a place—North being verb, noun, and qualifier. North is huge. North gives quality and respect. Authenticity. You set your cap at North. You take the North way. You make more North. I was about to do a North. North was my hero.

I've done my research. I know it all. And here I am on a fine clean Englishy day opening the gate which sticks slightly until I lean my weight against it and then it slides open. I now see that everything is oiled, working well. The plants had blocked it, a gaggle of lacy bright nigellas that I now tread down. Doll-size poppies are scattered in the gravel beside a neat brick herringbone path. The house is an ordinary red brick rectory on the Suffolk-Norfolk border, a house I'd seen so often in my dreams, and is almost concealed by an abundant dusty blue clematis winding through the coils of a *Wisteria Sinensis*. I'd telephoned and written with rather lengthy reasons for wanting to be there. I told them (the wife did the correspondence) about my father and how it was that he found North.

I suggested in my letter what I had come to believe that it was I and only I who should do an interview if there was to be one. It came over rather forcefully, with a passion I hadn't expected. I also suspected North's reasons for letting me in now. He must have a sense of nearing the end. It would be that. He must be old—after all, the beginnings we're talking about were forty years ago or more. I suspected too that it was the wife, Margaret, who'd decided. Margaret North, pretty and devoted, had been his secretary, then his amanuensis, then his companion and now—that sort of wife. I must have convinced them anyway, her anyway, because I was chosen to write the story. I chose myself and they chose me. We came together, my hero and my hero worship. It all came together. She, Margaret, wanted this—the personal adjunct to fame, the story of the man that would at last accompany his achievement into posterity. They were at that point in their life, she said, they were ready. And North, seduced all over again, went along with it.

Edward North was born before the Great War, in the north of England we were told, weren't we—or was that just the chiming of words? —in a place where digging didn't mean gardens at all but mines: salvaging and using up; use rather than looks and sowing and beginning. Digging into history. Pre history. Theses have now been written by scholars, mainly Americans, from the small but passionate North industry about the events in his past that started him off. Suppositions all of them—we didn't know his background. He was a person who was just unquestionably there; so much so that facts didn't stick to him, didn't need to, in that he was fully present to us in what he did and in what we followed him in. Which was why I was here. But more of that later. A grammar school boy from one of the mining towns (Barnsley? Hull? I wasn't sure. And such was the respect he commanded or such, at least, was the manner of his entry into our world that one didn't pursue, one didn't dig, one never thought it mysterious.) The grammar school boy got a scholarship to Oxford. At Oxford, studying biology, he became fascinated with the flora and fauna around him and began to make meticulous line drawings of them. Not the fancy botanical garden monsters engendered by the Oxford scientific community but grasses and sedges and willowherbs on the roadsides, the tiny unobserved wild flowers. Not orchids, nothing lush, and certainly nothing useful. Nothing which smacked of war or austerity. I suppose this was what created his appeal: he drew what he saw out there if only we'd looked. The cowslip, the primrose, goose grass, chickweed, the creeping buttercup, fat hen, the English wayside, the English garden. My job now, as a journalist, was to put it all together at last, the work and the man, to get the story out of it.

Like everyone else—all the other Northers—I had inferred that this must be how he came to gardens: his little patch in Oxford, the window box, led to the gaze out of the window, the road side, the verges, and here we were. At true North. He grew our humble native plants first of all in order to draw them, and in drawing them he created a new sort of gardening which would affect the taste of a generation. For soon we all had native English; we all tried the medieval garden made up of daisies, clove scented pinks and sweet violets, with its briar rose hedge—these were our proven ancestors, documented in ancient texts and pictures but given to us only by North. Gardens everywhere, in our part of England anyway, sprang up all on the North pattern, along the North line. As his range expanded so did ours: we planted Biblical gardens in our backyards after the description in *Paradise Lost*, drawn for us by North. We grew laurel and irises, apple trees and figs; our gardens were deep and rich with meaning. He became such a legend that when I first told my editor I was going to interview him he said, "But isn't he dead? He must be. Surely." Such was North's status.

My father had been the Stourbridge chemist, in the pharmaceutical rather than academic sense. His shop was at the end of the main street of the village but it served several other villages as well. A colored glass swizzle stick ran up the wall outside. Inside stood old jars labeled with strange abbreviations and a chest of many drawers behind the counter—there was also the distinctive, throat-catching, chemical smell that would make me cough. I went to school in Oxford by bus, and when I came home mother would make me tea and, if we were lucky, father showed for a quick bite:

"Better go and close up now."

"Milly's chest," Mother would say, as if my potential for wheezing accounted for his absence. At least to them. One afternoon at tea, I was just back from school and my mother was making toast with sandwich spread for me. I remembered this time—like the time the teacups rattled in their saucers because of the earth tremor, or the eclipse when we were all sent home from school with photographic negatives to protect our eyes. This time, the door between home and shop was flung wide open, and there stood father. He held the evening newspaper folded into a tight, thick wedge, and then wagged it suddenly, so that she flinched, in mother's face. And mine ("And, Milly, you must look too."). His eyes flared.

"What is it, whatever is it?" my mother's hand flew to cover her mouth, her eyes rounded with fear. I looked at my plate, listened. Had the cold war broken out, had the Moustache Man come back to round up the ones he'd missed? Was father going to issue one of his rare, impassioned commands—to listen, as he had at the tremor or, as at the eclipse, not to watch? Or was he just being "strong" as my mother sometimes put it, when she was at her most distressed. But it was nothing like that. Father clutched in his hand a small line drawing of a flower. It didn't mean a thing to me. I mean we didn't have gardens then: we had few flowers; the allotment had long run to seed because of exhaustion of both soil and person; and plants were what you went to see when forced outside by some school demand on Saturdays.

"Daisies," announced my father. *"Daisies*. Chrysanths—there's this chap here drawing daisies of all things. And, look, good old chrysanths— it's where they come from. Did you ever think of that? Did anyone?" he laughed incredulously. Wonderingly. "We must start at once. We must all, we must all— and then it's cowslips. Remember cowslips? Next time—" his injunction petered into helplessness as he looked at my mother's face; blank, troubled, resistant as always to his unexpected passion and unwanted demands. But this time was different. The very next day he somehow managed to get both of us outside and we started the process now known as "Northing" in our own little back garden. From then on, every few weeks in the local paper there would be a description of a flower. It would include something of its ancestry, progeny and provenance that had to be local, local meaning of Britain. They were given to us not in Latin and not in chemist's shop botanical, but in a sweet childish demotic. Shepherd's Purse. Chickweed. Chimney Sweepers. Fat Hen. Goose grass. Daisy. Daisy. The eye of the day. The sweet beginning. And all were accompanied by touchingly precise line drawings. He gave us back what we had grown up without seeing, what we'd lost in the war, and the post-war, drew it and gave it meaning, and made it new. For love of a garden. For love of the story a garden can tell.

The North garden wasn't landscaped or designed. It was made up of little squares, each discrete, each with its own meaning and style—at least in the beginning that's how it was. Later, people would do the whole back yard as, say, "Paradise Lost"—that was always the most popular, Eden holding an attraction for even the tiredest austerity gardeners. In the beginning my father buttonholed his customers and then the neighbors. He explained the importance of North, of Northing: in this world of hardship and practicalities, of looking forward only to ease and leisure, we had forgotten the specialness, the detail of a particular English past. My mother bit her lip in worry, considering it another example of his odd passion, something to be fended off, dealt with and ignored if possible. But I caught his zeal and dug the little patch designated my own, and helped with the others (we started with three, just three little squares). At the end of the first season, when nothing at all showed on the bare earth of my "Wild Garden," I sneaked into the shop and stole the Fison's Special Flowering Fertilizer. I knew from the advertisements and the picture on the packet that huge and abundant flowers would follow; and I mixed it in. It was the only time I had seen my father change in front of my eyes: color left him, he became white with anger.

"You've caught yourself out, Milly." (Because, of course, I couldn't go near the stuff without wheezing.) "You're a cheat. A cheat. You disappoint me. You cannot build the future on a lie." He looked at my mother's twisting, nervous face, permanently disappointed in her I suspect. However, I'd learnt the lesson. I cleared out every ounce of inauthentic earth (bringing on a full asthma attack that night) and started again. Three months later when the brilliant blue speedwells and trailing buttercups brightened the wilderness of my square I was delighted.

The lesson was more profound than that. Marcus Frost of *The Herald* who gave me my first job found me slow, excessively laborious. But he came to respect my own respect for the truth of each story. A kind of scrupulousness. This is not a boast at all; I knew it was just a way of seeing and I knew too that I had my father, and North, to thank for that. The lesson of North and the lesson of trying to cheat North: they shaped the way I thought. I kept a talisman to honor that secret history: a little bay tree growing out of a tangle of speedwell stood on whatever window sill, balcony, window box I had, in whatever city.

After North's second newspaper installment ("The Cowslip") and then the third (a delicate study of "A Blade of Grass") my father started pinning up the column in his chemist's shop behind the counter so that people waiting for prescriptions would read it. Word spread. The recovering gardens of the day were neat, colorful and practical. We were impressed by groundcover and labor-saving devices—electric shears, motorized mowers, Fison's of course, everything that promised to make it easy. Herbaceous borders, island beds, show. But in Stourbridge people read North's columns at the chemist, listened to my father and watched as gradually rubble gave way to squares of earth and earth became pricked out with little dots of green. "See," my father explained to the unseeing world, "they're like framed pictures. Or windows." He had started a little trend. And we were off. Northing away, with many others not far behind us.

All the front gardens around us soon showed cowslips, primrose paths led to every front door, sweet eglantine tumbled round all the windows, the chest of many drawers held brown bags of seeds lovingly collected and Fison's had been banished for ever. After that first column, during our first season, my father had written to the paper to enquire about North. He started a round robin, the first North newsletter— a sort of how's it going in the garden this week. And people responded. They really did. Everyone came out. Everyone loved to talk about the snail problem if you don't use chemicals, and how the myrtle in "Paradise Lost" was being attacked by mildew, wrongly placed perhaps.

It seemed that these changes were happening in other parts of the country too. The wife of the editor of the *Oxford Standard* dropped in for a prescription, read North's piece ("The Speedwell family") on Father's bulletin board and told her husband who immediately wrote and demanded that North switch his column to the *Standard*. The following autumn *The Daily Chronicle* itself picked it up and soon he was on his way to being a national monument. I don't know what it was that hit such a nerve but worn-out gardens all over the country were soon Northed back to life. The changes he insisted on (everything by hand, every detail attended to, insect predators picked off by insect assistants, soil fed only by last season's corpses, no Fison's) were on a small enough scale to be manageable, and were dogmatic enough to be adhered to. In the 'sixties in the States amid all the sunflowers and flower power there started a sort of groundswell of feeling for the humble plants, the less than showy, the ones that you could trace back to their—and therefore your—roots. North plants in other words. Someone in Arizona created a small business of bumper stickers and mugs calling for Daisy Power. There was even a teapot in the shape of a Michaelmas daisy: the lid its sepals, the handle a leafy stem. North's emblem. It sold out within a week.

By the 'seventies there were North societies on both sides of the Atlantic, North news letters, complete with those distinctive drawings which were his signature and his charm. North postcards, notebook covers, posters. North, with a little beautifully detailed fine-lined daisy, or sometimes merely a grass head, the stripe of a leaf; North, with his unequalled eye for difference.

To a later designer's eye, of course, the gardens didn't look particularly nice: they were more like school gardens for teaching children. They were of their time, but they were loved. In our own little squares we had the bank of wild thyme with oxlips, woodbine and a small hedge of musk rose. Here was an Eden imagined by our blind poet: laurel underplanted with acanthus, single dwarf irises, a jasmine and tiny jewel clusters of violets, crocuses and hyacinths. There were hedges no more than a meter long of rosemary and rue, and squares of different grasses in which flourished the Day's Eye and Chimney Sweepers, coming readily to dust on those warm August nights. Not much of a garden one might think, but at that time it changed us. It gave us back something and gave us something new.

My father died, my mother remarried for love and moved into the city and I seldom had time to visit, any more than she did to be visited, but I always imagined 'home' to be a place where there were tended, worked squares, windows of meaning, this garden. It was what home was to me. It was what childhood was. All the homes I'd lived in since then, on both sides of the Atlantic, were in cities far away from the green and plants—apart, that is, from my own secret garden which I held on to, the green bay tree in its pot and the bright speedwell. For my father, home had been a place of scent and freedom, a place where he expressed himself away from the chemicals of his work. And, in my memory, it was the same for me.

So it seemed right—although I'd written on all sorts of quite other things, business exposés being my speciality, and most recently the drug companies—that when I moved back after my most recent stint in the States it should be me who wrote the first major piece about North. In all these years, with all this adulation—it seems incredible now but there had still not been a profile. People had tried—I'd tried myself—and been rejected. The Northers, the newsgroups and clubs, told us that he resisted; that he took an implacably strong line, as he did over his gardening, that the work spoke for itself. Personality counted for nothing. The child-like line drawings that stood in for photographs were all any of us had on him. The standard illustration used on the annual compilation of his columns showed only a figure bending down to one of his beloved daisies as if to pluck or stroke it. At one point the stalwarts of the North Society boasted of having unearthed certain biographical details—the Hull childhood business, and the Oxford apprenticeship—but really these barest of facts merely acted as a screen through which we imagined him. Not that there was mystery attaching to him, just an impressive, unquestionable authenticity. Biography was nothing, the man nothing; the garden and its story told it all.

The little gate, wrought metal with an open, leafy design, stuck slightly. I had to push my weight against it. The short herringbone-patterned path, its perfect decorum, perfect English history, was the sort of thing we'd have done, dad would have done, if we'd had the space in our little row, or the money. The back of my throat already caught with the roughness of tears. This was a journey back, a homecoming. My spiky, difficult father reared up in my mind's eye, his grumbles, his complaints, his indifference, the sudden odd passions, his later terrible illness—brought on by his work, the chemicals, I was sure—-his North garden having provided him with too little respite much too late. I was surprised at my feelings, the strength of them, this emotion. But of course in his oblique way, it had been my father who had started me out on this path. How could I not think of him when I was finally here, at due North? I'd been a good girl. I'd come back when he was ill and been there. And I never forgot how it had all begun:

"Here, Milly, this is yours. You must do it too." The pressure and faith. A long time ago now—-as I pushed a silent bell, rapped an iron knocker shaped like a compass, waited.

Margaret North poured tea before we looked round the garden—a still pretty, beige-haired woman with a clear, quick, slightly breathless manner. North, *my* North had been a chunky, heavy sort of fellow, reddish of hair, who'd worked his way up from some root or other by honest interest and toil. No, really. I had an unmistakable face for him, as you do for people on the end of a phone. Here, the great man, my great man, on the other hand, I found a thin, birdy person perched on the edge of our little group, an almost silent presence. Was he a bit like Lawrence? Were there the remains of a bearded, lowering but delicate figure? He spoke precisely, carefully, and not often, with a slight vagueness about his r's, a slight roll to them at odds with the crispness of diction. The wife did most of the talking.

After tea, I was to see round the North garden. Ur North, North itself. He was to take me round. I could hardly believe it. Meeting my childhood legend in this banal way over a cup of tea. Just like Marcus Frost I felt that surely North must be dead by now, surely the legend can't be taking me round his own garden?

The path leading away from the house into the distance—the garden gave onto Suffolk fields—was edged by grey fragrant lavender and lad's love, santolina, wormwood, I brushed a bush with my hand. "We had this," I confided, "And we had 'Paradise Lost' and the wild garden. We had a single peony in the long grass." And myrtle which always got mildew. And oxlips, and, of course, daisies which I think my father came to love as much as North did. I felt like a foolish girl. I felt like a child about to be shown the secret garden I'd always dreamed of. I looked around expectantly. Searchingly. I couldn't think what to ask him. I had to ask him something.

"How did you cope with mildew?"

The wife laughed, and answered for him:

"Oh my dear. How ever do you think? We *sprayed*."

I stopped walking down their path. I stood still. They, the Norths, were up ahead. Had I really heard that?

"Come." He called out to me "We're showing you our greenhouse, yes?"

I stepped into the humid air amongst fleshy orchids and towering hybrid shapes. Sprays of bright plumbago cascaded into my hair, the cloying smell of stephanotis assaulted my senses; I could hardly breathe. This was not what I expected. I expected what we had grown but better, and more and going further back—I imagined our Englishness, the subtle past, our deep identity—all of us—laid out in checkerboard style. Ours only more so. But where were the daisies? Or the chimney-sweepers, the artfully abandoned lawn, all our ancestors, our family trees? Out on the concrete patio stood pots of patched and grafted hybrids, while here, in the sickening air, their monstrous progeny—lurid, fattened and prize-worthy—were rayed out ready for a show.

I stood in the midst of these gaudy shapes and breathed in, expecting, knowing that in smell, in breath, one releases the most powerful memory. And so I did. The memory of childhood, the memory that took me straight back to that first back yard, to my father's house and the chemist's shop. A smell catching at the back of my throat, which stopped me breathing, brought it all back in a fit of a kind I hadn't had since I'd left England. I fumbled for my inhaler, carried with me out of habit, never suspecting that I would have needed it here of all places. Not at home. Not at more than home. Where the fresh air had always been.

And yet and yet here was this wife handing me a soothing glass of water—and babbling at me with her pride and her greed for praise. Telling me everything. How she'd given him her first husband's, the Professor's, books—this dour, romantic, student with his no family and a facility for copying, who'd then done a tracing from an 18th century children's drawing book of a daisy. (She even thrust it at me, the little, battered and now much used book of drawings he'd claimed as his own. *They'd* claimed.) Here, too, were the late Professor's notes on botany in English literature, mixed up with bound copies of all their fan letters and volumes of news letters. And here babbled the vain, the killer wife, doing both of them in with her desire to tell all. Because how could I not say?

How could I not tell the truth, when truth had been implanted in me indelibly: "You cannot build your future on a lie," said my father, following North. Our North. And so I learned and so I did believe.

"You're a cheat," I heard my father say. You're a cheat, I thought to myself. I would be if I didn't tell the truth. Tell the lesson I had learned. Of course I hesitated: did it matter who he really was? And what he really had done? Only in that North had meant authentic, and, above all else, true. North, my North, in his borrowed plumes had borrowed everything. Been given everything by the greedy woman beside him.

"Of course we didn't know, we had no idea really that he would become quite so popular, that the notes—they started out as notes— would take off so. We didn't *expect* such attention. It was your father's fault (she said, playfully). *We* didn't know." It had started as a single, traced drawing with literary reflections stolen from the late Professor and sent to the local newspaper. They had done it for no reason, not for any love anyway. But the idea caught and who could have guessed the world of fame and reward that followed from it or that Margaret would love it so. They couldn't believe their luck or what it allowed them to do, which was *this* garden, that patio and—their pride and joy—that greenhouse. I mean, they didn't care about the *North* garden at all. I still told myself that it wasn't North's fault—that he wasn't the cause of his own undoing—but rather that it was hers, the creature he lived with who loved him. Mainly I think that North was also quite vain and desperately fearful of being found out by the authorities (he had come over to study in the 'thirties— the accent was now clearly identifiable from old war movies). And now he was being found out by one of his biggest fans.

Was that it? Is that my garden story? Of course people moved on. Those who read my account were suitably shocked but not that interested. Like me they had got something of their own out of all the Northiana. But the North societies on both sides of the Atlantic chose to ignore the story and carry on. After all, North did mean something. The word, I mean, rather than the man.

So where's the consequence of all this? North had his garden, had his wife, his life until I came along. Later I heard that she found some younger writer researching North for a book and was helping him put all that together. The next thing. And I think North must've died but I'm not sure.

I suppose this sounds to be all about style. Or merely about gardens. I mean you could wonder what's so important about that? But perhaps that's all there is. Sorry.

See No Weevil

JAMES THURBER

I PROBABLY WOULD NEVER have known about the 'Thurberia Weevil' or the Thurberia plant, either, if Clarence R. Peterson of Brooklyn hadn't sent me a report on them taken from the pages of the *Federal Register*, a publication of the U.S. Department of Agriculture that deals with American plants and the pests that threaten them. If any insect is trailing the arbutus, or creeping up on the Virginia creeper, agents of the Department photograph and fingerprint it, give it a serial number, and keep it under surveillance. Otherwise vegetation would disappear from the Republic and some enormous caterpillar would take over where Senator McCarthy left off.

The report from the *Federal Register* that Mr. Peterson sent me contains the glad tidings, for cotton growers and Thurberia weevils, that the 1926 quarantine on the *Anthonomus grandis thurberiae* Pierce has been lifted. It seems that my cousin, the weevil, has turned out to be a harmless insect, no more dangerous to the American cotton crop than the luna moth is to the Brazilian Air Force. I don't know who Pierce is, by the way, or how he happened to pop up in the name of the Thurber weevil, but it may be that he was the agent who kept Thurberia under surveillance for twenty-five years. If I had spent the best years of my life tailing a weevil, I would certainly expect some permanent recognition. I don't know who Thurber is, either. My own branch of the family has never been very good at entomology or botany. This Thurber may have been an entomologist who discovered the Thurberia plant, or wild cotton, while hunting for weevils, or he may have been a botanist who discovered the weevil while hunting for the wild cotton plant. It is a kind of ordinary weed found in hot, arid areas of the South-west, and it is not actually cotton, and it isn't terribly wild. The Thurberia weevil likes to inhabit the Thurberia plant, anyway, but twenty-five years of research have shown that the weevil is not really a pest at all. His famous cousin, the boll weevil, is a great destroyer of cotton, but Thurberia wouldn't cross the road to examine a cotton plant, let alone try to destroy it. I don't know why it took a quarter of a century to find this out, but the wheels of government move slowly.

Thurberia, to be sure, is not the only plant named after a man. Literally hundreds of flowers and weeds have been named for their discoverers: forsythia for Forsythe, zinnia for Zinn, dahlia for Dahl, fuchsia for Fuchs, and so on. There are even muehlenbeckia and puschkinia, I found in glancing through *The New Garden Encyclopedia*. This dictionary of flora, first published in 1936, contains 1,380 pages, but Thurberia, the wild cotton, isn't mentioned in it.

I don't know what Mrs.. Thurber thought or said when Thurber came home one evening and told her that he had discovered a kind of scrubby desert plant and was going to have it named after him, but if he had belonged to my branch of the family (Thurberia Columbus) the conversation would have gone something like this . . .

"If I had to do over again," said Mrs. Thurber, "I wouldn't have married a desert botanist. I don't know why you have to go in for things like mesquite and toadbush, when everybody else's husband is finding such lovely flowers—"

"Forsythe and Wistar, if you mean them, are deciduous men," Thurber cut in, "and I happen to be xerophilous. You could have done worse—you might have married Hubbard and had that squash named after you."

"Yes, but if I had married Wilson, the ornithologist, I could have had a thrush named after me."

"Supposing you had married Newton," her husband said, "then you would have had a fig cookie named after you. And how about Mrs. Comstock?"

"I don't know any Mrs. Comstock," said Mrs. Thurber. "Comstock discovered the Comstock mealy bug," the botanist said. "It infests the catalpas and is also found on the magnolias, and it—"

"I don't care if it dances on hydrangeas," snapped Mrs. Thurber. "I don't want to hear about it. I don't see why you couldn't have gone out and found a new kind of lilac or lily of the valley."

The tired botanist lit a cigarette. "Why don't *you* go out and discover a rose?" he asked her. "After all, Dorothy Perkins did."

This kind of thing, in certain branches of the Thurber family, could go on for weeks, as it must have in the. Muehlenbeck family, when Mrs. Muehlenbeck found out that muehlenbeckia is only a kind of buckwheat.

I do not like to dwell on what happened when Thurber came home one evening, with the worried look that Mrs. Thurber knew so well.

"What's the matter?" asked Mrs. Thurber apprehensively. "Have you discovered a new kind of non-flowering buzzard bush?"

He dropped into a chair. "No," he said. "Do you remember that weevil I found on the Thurberia plant?"

She sighed. "Yes," she said, "but I keep trying to forget it." Her eyes brightened. "Has it been taken suddenly extinct?" she asked hopefully.

"No, it isn't that," he said wearily. "Something else has happened to it."

"Are you going to sit there and tell me that Pierce has taken full credit for it?" she demanded. "I always knew, he would, and I told you—"

"Pierce hasn't taken credit for anything," he said irritably. "Thurberia has turned out to be innocuous. It's not even mischievous. Its quarantine has been lifted, If you have to know."

His wife sat forward in her chair. "I knew that would happen," she said. "Don't you realize that hundreds of scientists have seen that weevil during the past hundred years, and that you were the only one foolish enough to stop and classify it? Now you've got yourself stuck with a weevil that isn't even dangerous, a weevil that lives on wild cotton, the most ordinary bush in the desert. Jane Forsythe was telling just the other day that it's as common as false fleabane. When you were out hunting for ticks and cactus and fungus, Jane's husband was discovering a beautiful. golden flower—where are you going?"

Thurber had put on his hat and coat and walked to the door. With his hand on the knob, he turned and looked at his wife. "I'm going out to discover the Thurber mealy bug," he said coldly, "and when I do, I'm going to put it on the forsythia or on Jane Forsythe, I haven't decided which yet." And he went out and banged the door after him.

Mrs. Thurber lit a cigarette and sat for a while lost in thought. It suddenly dawned on her what Belle Pierce would do when she found out that the quarantine had been lifted on the "Thurberia Weevil". She would make her husband drop his name from it, leaving the Thurbers stuck with *Anthonomus grandis thurberiae*. Their name would stand there for ever, in lower case, and become the laughing stock *(casus risus)* of the entomological world.

Christmas Roses

EDNA O'BRIEN

MISS HAWKINS HAD SEEN it all. At least she told people that she had seen it all. She told her few friends about her cabaret life when she had toured all Europe and was the toast of the richest man In Baghdad. According to herself she had had lovers of all nationalities, endless proposals of marriage, champagne in every known vessel, not forgetting the slipper. Yet Miss Hawkins had always had a soft spot for gardening and in Beirut she had planted roses, hers becoming the first English rose garden in that far off spicy land. She told how she watered them at dawn as she returned accompanied, or unaccompanied, from one of her sallies.

But time passes and when Miss Hawkins was fifty-five she was no longer in gold-meshed suits dashing from one capital to the next. She taught private dancing to supplement her income and eventually she worked in a municipal garden. As time went by, the gardening was more dear to her than ever her cabaret had been. How she fretted over it, over the health of the soil, over the flowers and the plants, over the over-all design and what the residents thought of it. Her success with it became more and more engrossing. She introduced things that had not been there before and her greatest pride was that the silly old black railing was now smothered with sweet-smelling honeysuckle and other climbing things. She kept busy in all of the four seasons, busy and bright. In the autumn she not only raked all the leaves, but she got down on her knees and picked every stray fallen leaf out of the flower beds where they tended to lodge under rose bushes. She burnt them then. Indeed there was not a day throughout all of autumn when there was not a bonfire in Miss Hawkins' municipal garden. And not a month without some blooms. At Christmas was she not proud of her Christmas roses and the Mexican firebush with berries as bright as the decoration on a woman's hat.

In her spare time she visited other municipal gardens and found to her satisfaction that hers was far better, far brighter, more daring while also well-kempt and cheerful. Her pruning was better, her beds were tidier, her peat was darker, her shrubs sturdier and the very branches of her rose bushes were red with a sort of inner energy. Of course the short winter days drove Miss Hawkins into her flat and there she became churlish. She did have her little dog, Clara, but understandably Clara too preferred the outdoors. How they barked at each other and squabbled, one blaming the other for being bad-tempered, for baring teeth. The dog was white with a little crown of orange at the top of her head and Miss Hawkins favored orange too when she tinted her hair. Her hair was long and she dried it by laying it along the length of an ironing board and pressing it with a warm iron.

The flat was a nest of souvenirs, souvenirs from her dancing days—a gauze fan, several pairs of ballet shoes gloves, photographs, a magnifying glass, programs. All of these items were arranged carefully along the bureau and were reflected in the long mirror which Miss Hawkins had acquired, so that she could continue to do her exercising. Miss Hawkins danced every night for thirty minutes. That was before she had her Ovaltine. Her figure was still trim, and on the odd occasion when Miss Hawkins got into her black costume and her stiff-necked white blouse, rouged her cheeks, pointed her insteps and donned her black patent court shoes, she knew that she could pass for forty.

She dressed up when going to see the town councillor about the budget and plans for the garden, and she dressed in her lamé when one of her ex-dancing pupils invited her to a cocktail party. She dressed up no more than three times a year. But Miss Hawkins herself said that she did not need outings. She was quite content to go into her room at nightfall, heat up the previous day's dinner, or else poach eggs, get into bed, cuddle her little dog, look at television and drop off to sleep. She retired early so that she could be in her garden while the rest of London was surfacing. Her boast was that she was often up starting her day while the stars were still in the heavens and that she moved about like a spirit so as not to disturb neighbors.

It was on such a morning and at such an unearthly hour that Miss Hawkins got a terrible shock concerning her garden. She looked through her window and saw a blue tent, a triangle of utter impertinence in her terrain. She stormed out vowing to her little dog and to herself that within minutes it would be a thing of the past. In fact she found herself closing and reclosing her right fist as if squashing an egg. She was livid.

As she came up to it Miss Hawkins was expecting to find a truant schoolchild. But not at all. There was a grown boy of twenty or perhaps twenty-one on a mattress, asleep. Miss Hawkins was fuming. She noticed at once that he had soft brown hair, white angelic skin and thick sensual lips. To make matters worse he was asleep and as she wakened him he threw his hands up and remonstrated like a child. Then he blinked, and as soon as he got his bearings he smiled at her. Miss Hawkins had to tell him that he was breaking the law. He was the soul of obligingness. He said, "Oh sorry," and explained how he had come from Kenya, how he had arrived late at night, had not been able to find a hostel, had walked around London and eventually had climbed in over her railings. Miss Hawkins was unable to say the furious things that she had intended to say, indeed his good manners had made her almost speechless. He asked her what time it was. She could see that he wanted a conversation but she realized that it was out of keeping with her original mission, and so she turned away.

Miss Hawkins was beneath a tree putting some crocus bulbs in, when the young visitor left. She merely knew it by the clang of the gate. She had left the gate on its latch so that he could go out without having to be conducted by her. As she patted the earth around the little crocuses she thought, What a pity that there could not be laws for some and not for others! His smile, his enthusiasm and his good manners had stirred her. And after all what harm was he doing. Yet, thought Miss Hawkins, bylaws are bylaws and she hit the ground with her little trowel.

As with most winter days there were scarcely any visitors to the square and the time dragged. There were the few residents who brought their dogs in, there was the lady who knitted and there were the lunchtime stragglers who had keys although Miss Hawkins knew that they were not residents in the square. Interlopers. All in all she was dispirited. She even reverted to a bit of debating. What harm had he been doing? Why had she sent him away? Why had she not discussed Africa and the game preserves, and the wilds? Oh how Miss Hawkins wished she had known those legendary spaces.

That evening, as she crossed the road to her house she stood under the lamplight and looked up the street to where there was the red neon glow from the public house. She had a very definite and foolish longing to be going into the lounge bar with a young escort and demurring as to whether to have a gin and tonic, or a gin and pink. Presently she found that she had slapped herself. The rule was never to go into public houses since it was vulgar and never to drink since it was the road that led to ruin. She ran on home. Her little dog, Clara, and herself had an argument, bared their teeth at each other, turned away from each other, and flounced off. The upshot was Miss Hawkins nicked her thumb with the jagged metal of a tin she was opening, and in a moment of uncustomary self-pity rang one of her dancing pupils and launched into a tirade about hawkers, circulars, and the appalling state the of country. This was unusual for Miss Hawkins, as she had vowed never to submit to self-pity and as she had pinned to her very wall a philosophy that she had meant to adhere to. She read it but it seemed pretty irrelevant:

> I will know who I am
> I will keep my mouth shut
> I will learn from everything
> I will train every day.

She would have ripped it off except that the effort was too much. Yet as she was able to say next day, the darkest hours are before the dawn.

As she stepped out of her house in her warm trouser suit, with the brown muffler around her neck, she found herself raising her hand in an airy, almost coquettish hello. There he was. He was actually waiting for her by the garden gate and he was as solemn as a fledgling altar boy. He said that he had come to apologize, that after twenty-four hours in England he was a little more cognizant of rules and regulations and that he had come to ask her to forgive him. She said certainly. She said he could come in if he wished, and when she walked towards the tool shed, he followed and helped her out with the implements. Miss Hawkins instructed him what to do, he was to dig a patch into which she would put her summer blooms. She told him the Latin name of all these flowers, their appearance and their characteristics. He was amazed at the way she could rattle off all these items while digging or pruning or even overseeing what he was doing. And so it went on. He would work for an hour or so and then tootle off and once when it was very cold an they had to fetch watering cans of warm water to thaw out a certain flower bed, she weakened and offered him a coffee. The result was that he arrived the next day with biscuits. He said that he had been given a present of two tickets for the theater and was she by the merest tiniest chance free and would she be so kind as to come with him. Miss Hawkins hesitated but of course her heart had yielded. She frowned and said could he not ask someone younger, someone in his own age group, to which he said no. Dash it, she thought, theater was theater and her very first calling and without doubt she would go. The play was *Othello*. Oh how she loved it, understood it and was above it all! The jealous Moor, the tell-tale handkerchief confessions, counter confessions, the poor sweet wretch Desdemona. Miss Hawkins raised her hands, acted for moment and said, "The poor dear girl caught in a jealous paradox."

As an escort he was utter perfection. When she any arrived breathlessly into the foyer, he was there, beaming. He admired how she looked, he helped remove her shawl, he had already bought a box of chocolate truffles, and was discreetly steering her to the bar to have a drink. It was while she was in the bar savoring the glass of gin-and-it that Miss Hawkins conceded what a beauty he was. She called his name, and said what a pretty name it was, what an awfully pretty name. His hands caught her attention. Hands, lovely shining nails, a gleam of health on them and his face framed by the stiff white old-fashioned collar, held in place with a gold stud. His hair was like a girl's. He radiated happiness. Miss Hawkins pinched herself three times in order not to give in to any sentiment. Yet all through the play—riveted though she was—she would glance from the side of her eye at his lovely untroubled and perfect profile. In fact the socket of that eye hurt, so frequently and so lengthily did Miss Hawkins gaze. Miss Hawkins took issue with the costumes and said it should be period and who wanted to see those drab everyday brown things. She also thought poorly of Iago's enunciation. She almost made a scene, so positive was she in her criticism. But of course the play itself was divine, simply divine. At the supper afterwards they discussed jealousy, and Miss Hawkins was able to assure him that she no longer suffered from that ghastly complaint. He did. He was a positive pickle of jealousy. "Teach me not to be," he said. He almost touched her when she drew back alarmed and offended, apparently, by the indiscretion. He retrieved things by offering to pick up her plastic lighter and light her cigarette. Miss Hawkins was enjoying herself. She ate a lot, smoked a lot, drank a lot, but at no time did she lose her composure. In fact she was mirth personified, and after he had dropped her at her front door she sauntered down the steps to her basement, then waved her beaded purse at him and said as English workmen say, "Mind how you go."

But indoors Miss Hawkins dropped her mask. She waltzed about her room, using her shawl as partner, did ooh-la-las and oh-lay-lays such as she had not done since she hit the boards at twenty.

"Sweet boy, utterly sweet, utterly well bred," Miss Hawkins assured herself and Clara, who was peeved from neglect but eventually had to succumb to this carnival and had to dance and lap in accordance with Miss Hawkins' ribald humor. God knows what time they retired.

Naturally things took a turn for the better. She and he now had a topic to discuss and it was theater. It too was his ambition and he had come to

England to study theater. So, in between pruning or digging or manuring, Miss Hawkins was giving her sage opinion of things, or endeavoring to improve his projection by making him say certain key sentences. She even made him sing. She begged him to concentrate on his alto notes and to do it comfortably and in utter freedom. Miss Hawkins made "no no no" sounds when he slipped into tenor or as she put it, sank totally into his chest. He was told to pull his voice up again. "Up up up, from the chest," Miss Hawkins would say, conducting him with her thin wrist and dangling hand, and it is true that the lunchtime strollers in the garden came to the conclusion that Miss Hawkins had lost her head. No thank you very much was her unvoiced reply to those snooping people, these spinsters, these divorcees et cetera. She had not lost her head nor any other part of her anatomy either, and what is more, she was not going to. The only concession she made to him was that she rouged her cheeks since she herself admitted that her skin was a trifle yellow. All that sunshine in Baghdad long ago and the hepatitis that she had had. As time went by she did a bit of mending for him, put leather patches on his sleeves, and tried unsuccessfully to interest him in a macrobiotic diet. About this he teased her and as he dug up a worm or came across a snail in its slow dewy mysterious course he would ask Miss Hawkins if that were a yin or yang item and she would do one of her little involuntary shrugs, toss her grey hair, and say "D'you mind!" He seemed to like that and would provoke her into situations where she would have to do these little haughty tosses and ask "D'you mind!"

It was on St. Valentine's Day that he told Miss Hawkins he had to quit the flat he was lodging in.

"I'm not surprised," she said, evincing great relief and then she went a step further and muttered something about those sort of people. He was staying with some young people in Notting Hill Gate and from what Miss Hawkins could gather they hadn't got a clue! They slept all hours, they ate at all hours, they drew national assistance and spent their time—the country's time—strumming music on their various hideous tom-toms and broken guitars. Miss Hawkins had been against his staying there, from the start and indeed had fretted about their influence over him. He defended them as best, he could, said they were idealists, and that one did the crossword puzzles and the other worked in a health-juice bar but Miss Hawkins just tipped something off the end of the shovel the very same as if she were tipping them off her consciousness. She deliberated, then said he must move in with her. He was aghast with relief. He asked did she mean it. He stressed what a quiet lodger he would be, and how it would only be a matter of weeks until he found another place.

"Stay as long as you like," Miss Hawkins said, and all through this encounter she was brusque in order not to let things slide into a bath of sentiment. But inside Miss Hawkins was rippling.

That evening she went to a supermarket so as to stock up with things. She now took her rightful place alongside other housewives, alongside women who shopped and cared for their men. She would pick up a tin, muse over it, look at the price, and then drop it with a certain disdain. He would have yin and yang, he would have brown rice, and he would have curry dishes. Some confusion had entered Miss Hawkins' mind regarding this and rather than confining it to Indian cuisine she felt that all foreigners liked it. She did however choose a mild curry. The color was so pretty being ochre, that she thought it would be very becoming on the eyelids, that is if it were not stinging. Miss Hawkins was becoming more beauty conscious and plucked her eyebrows again. At the cash register she asked for free recipes and made a somewhat idiotic to-do when they said they were out of them. In fact she flounced off murmuring about people's bad manners, bad tempers, and abominable breeding.

The night Miss Hawkins got tipsy. She danced as she might dance for him one night. It was all being exquisitely planned. He was arriving on the morrow at five. It would not be quite dark but it would be dusk, and therefore dim, so that he need not be daunted by her little room. His new nest. Before he arrived she would have switched on the lamps, put a scarf over one; she would have a nice display of forsythia in the tall china jug, she would have table laid for supper and she would announce that since It was his first night they would have a bit of a celebration. She ferreted through her six cookery books (those from her married days) before deciding on the recipe she wanted. Naturally she could not afford anything too extravagant and yet she would not want it to be miserly. It must, it simply must have "bouquet." She had definitely decided on baked eggs with a sprinkling of cheese and kidneys cooked in red wine and button mushrooms. In fact the wine had been bought for the recipe and Miss Hawkins was busily chiding herself for having drunk too much of it. It was a Spanish wine and rather heady. Then after dinner as she envisaged it, she would toss a salad. There and then Miss Hawkins picked up her wooden spoon and fork and began to wave them in the air and thought how nice it was to feel jolly and thought ahead to the attention that awaited him. He would be in a comfortable room, he would be the recipient of intelligent theatrical conversation, he could loll in an armchair and think rather than be subjected to the strumming of some stupid guitar. He had suggested that he would bring some wine and she had already got out the cut glasses, washed them and shone them so that their little wedges were a sea of instant and changeable rainbows. He had not been told the sleeping arrangements but the plan was that he would sleep on a divan and that the Victorian folding screen would be placed the length of the room when either of them wished to retire. Unfortunately Miss Hawkins would have to pass through his half of the room to get to the bathroom but as she said a woman who has danced naked in Baghdad has no repression passing through a gentleman's room in her robe. She realized that there would be little debacles, perhaps misunderstandings, but the difficulties could be worked out. She had no doubt but that they would achieve a harmony. She sat at the little round supper table and passed things politely. She was practicing. Miss Hawkins had not passed an entrée dish for years. She decided to use the linen napkins and got out two of her mother's bone napkin holders. They smelt of vanilla. "Nice man coming," she would tell her little dog, as she tripped about tidying her drawers, dusting her dressing table, and debating the most subtle position for a photograph of her, from her cabaret days.

At length and without fully undressing, Miss Hawkins flopped onto her bed with her little dog beside her. Miss Hawkins had such dratted nightmares, stupid rigmaroles in which she was incarcerated, or ones in which she had to carry furniture or cater on nothing for a host of people.

Indeed an unsavory one, in which a cowpat became confused with a fried egg. Oh was she vexed! She blamed the wine and she thanked the gods that she had not touched the little plum pudding which she had bought as a surprise for the Sunday meal. Her hands trembled and she was definitely on edge.

In the garden Miss Hawkins kept looking towards her own door lest he arrive early, lest she miss him. Her heart was in a dither. She thought, Supposing he changes his mind, or supposing he brings his horrid friends, or supposing he stays out all night, and each new crop of supposing made Miss Hawkins more bad-tempered. Supposing he did not arrive. Unfortunately it brought to mind those earlier occasions in Miss Hawkins' life when she had been disappointed, nay jilted. The day when she had packed to go abroad with her diamond-smuggling lover who never came, and when somehow out of shock, she had remained fully dressed even with her lace gloves on, in her rocking chair for two days until her cleaning woman came. She also remembered that a man proposed to her, gave her an engagement ring and was in fact already married. A bigamist. But, as he had the gall to tell her, he did not feel emotionally married, and then to make matters worse took photos of his children, twins, out of his wallet. Other losses came back to her and she remembered bitterly her last tour in the provinces when people laughed and guffawed at her and even threw eggs.

By lunchtime Miss Hawkins was quite distraught, and she wished that she had had a best friend. She even wished that there was some telephone service by which she could ring up an intelligent person, preferably a woman, and tell her the whole saga and have her fears dismissed.

By three o'clock Miss Hawkins was pacing her floor. The real trouble had been admitted. She was afraid. Afraid of the obvious. She might become attached, she might fall a fraction in love, she might cross the room, or shyly, he might cross the room and a wonderful surprise embrace might ensue and Then. It was that Then that horrified her. She shuddered, she let out an involuntary "no." She could not bear to see him leave, even leave amicably. She dreaded suitcases, packing, good-byes, stoicism, chin-up, her empty hand, the whole unbearable lodestone of it. She could not have him there. Quickly she penned the note, then she got her coat, her handbag, and her little dog in its basket and flounced out.

The note was on the top step under a milk bottle. It was addressed to him. The message said:

YOU MUST NEVER EVER UNDER ANY CIRCUMSTANCES COME HERE AGAIN.

Miss Hawkins took a taxi to Victoria and thence a train to Brighton. She had an invalid friend there to whom she owed a visit. In the train, as she looked out at the sooty suburbs, Miss Hawkins was willing to concede that she had done a very stupid thing indeed, but that it had to be admitted that it was not the most stupid thing she could have done. The most stupid thing would have been to welcome him in.

The Garden of the
Villa Mollini

ROSE TREMAIN

BEFORE THE ARRIVAL of Antonio Mollini in 1877, the villa had been called, simply, the Villa Bianca, the White House. It came to be known as the Villa Mollini, not through the vanity of Antonio Mollini himself, but through the pride of the people of the village. They wanted to be able to say—to travelers who passed that way, to relations who journeyed there from Arezzo or Rapolano or Assisi—"We have in our midst the great Mollini, the world's most renowned opera singer. He knows us and even remembers the names of our children."

In fact, Antonio Mollini was seldom there. He was forty-one when he bought the villa and his voice had entered what the critics later termed its "decade of magnificence." His life was passed in the musical capitals of Europe—Milan, Paris, Vienna. He came to the Villa Mollini only to rest, to visit his wife and to plan his garden.

He wanted, in the design of this garden, to express a simple and optimistic philosophy. He believed that his life was a journey of discovery, revelation and surprise and that it led forward perpetually, never back. In it, there was not merely one goal, one destination, but many, each one leading forwards from the next. All were different. Repetition seldom, if ever, occurred. He would not allow it to occur. And even at life's close, he thought there would be new landscapes and new visions of hope. The garden he was going to create would thus be infinitely varied, intricate and above all beautiful.

It was fortunate, then, that the terrain on which he would realize the garden wasn't flat, but sloped gently upwards away from the house to a cypress grove, and then descended, equally gently, towards a river. On the other side of the river, there were clover fields and, beyond these, a forest. The far edge of the forest was the boundary of Mollini's land.

His head gardener, Paulo Pappavincente, was the illegitimate son of a priest. Pappavincente's mother had died at his birth and he'd been brought up by aged and devout grandparents unable to conceal their shame at his existence. Though Mollini explained his philosophy carefully to Pappavincente, using simple terms, baby language almost, the gardener was unable to see life as his master saw it. To him, it led, repetitively and inevitably, to dark and deep abysses of guilt. But he didn't want to bore Mollini or anger him with chatter about his own sufferings: he wanted to design the most beautiful garden in Tuscany so that one day he could say to his own legitimate grandchildren, "I made it. I made the garden of the Villa Mollini." He did suggest, however, that a well be sunk at a certain place, not far from the house, where Mollini had thought a statue of the goddess Diana would draw the eye forward. "I think a well also beckons, Sir," he said. To his surprise and also to his relief, Mollini agreed. That night, as he knelt to say his prayers, Pappavincente began to feel that good fortune was stealing into his life.

The same night, Antonio Mollini's wife, Rosa, stared by candlelight at the half-completed sketches of the box aisles and the fountains, the herbarium and the rose trellises, the steps and terraces leading up to the cypress grove and down to the river, and said aloud, "I think he must contrive a lake."

Mollini was asleep. He lay on his back, snoring, with his legs apart From his magnificent lungs came an unmelodious kind of squealing. Rosa pulled aside the curtains of the bed and leaned over him, holding her candle.

"Antonio," she whispered, "please, Antonio."

He opened his eyes. This thin white face of Rosa's on its pale neck sometimes reminded him of a sad mask on a stick.

"What, Rosa?"

"When the river leaves our land, westwards, where does it arrive, Antonio?"

"In the village."

"Then I expect we may have to move the village."

Mollini stared up. He chose his mistresses for their roundness, for their bright color. Rosa was his little ghostly possession.

"We cannot move the village, Rosa."

Tears sparkled in her eyes.

"Please, Antonio. You must make a lake."

Pappavincente was consulted. When he heard of the plan to dam up the river, he descended once more into his habitual pessimism. Politely, he informed his master of the life-sustaining properties of the village water supply. Antonio Mollini felt ashamed. He loved the village people. He'd made a list of all their names and the names of their children so that he wouldn't forget them, and now, in the night, he'd allowed his wife to suggest something that would impoverish and destroy them. "Rosa is mad," he said to Pappavincente, "but forgive her. Since the death of Pietro, her mind often wanders astray."

The death of Pietro had occurred in the same year that Mollini's fame was born. Consumption thus played a role in both events. As Mollini sang Alfredo in Verdi's *La Traviata*, his son Pietro was dying of Violetta's disease. He refused to mourn. He looked at the little coffin. He would have more sons. He would replace Pietro. He would christen all his sons "Pietro," so that if another one died, he, too, could be replaced. Rosa accused him of callousness. "No," he said, "but I will not let death win."

Rosa didn't conceive. She knew that loss, like starvation, can make a woman barren. She would be barren forever, mourning Pietro. She longed, at that time, for a garden. She thought it would make her feel more kindly towards the world if she could bury seeds in the earth and see leaves emerge, bright green. But Mollini wasn't yet rich. They lived in Milan in a narrow house on a dark courtyard. The Villa Mollini was six years away.

In those six years, Pappavincente fathered four sons, one of whom he christened Pietro.

Mollini fathered none. His fame grew. "There is no adequate epithet to describe Mollini's voice," one French critic wrote. "To say it is like honey, or like velvet, or like silver is merely to debase it. It is like no other voice we have ever heard."

On its gentle hillside, the Villa Mollini, still known as the Villa Bianca and occupied by a professor of medicine, waited for the great man's arrival.

In the week following Rosa's dreadful request for a lake, Mollini left for Milan. On his forty-second birthday, the day he began rehearsals for La Scala's new production of Wagner's *Tristan und Isolde,* he met for the first time the internationally known soprano, Verena Dusa, and fell in love with her.

La Dusa was thirty-four. Her elbows were dimpled and her belly and breasts round and firm and fat. She was the mistress of the impresario, Riccardo Levi, from whose bed Mollini quickly wooed her.

Riccardo Levi demanded a duel and was refused. He threatened to ruin La Dusa's career, but his threats were ignored. La Dusa moved her dresses and her fan collection from Levi's apartment to Mollini's town house. In despair, Riccardo Levi wrote a letter to Rosa, telling Mollini's wife that she had been betrayed.

Rosa examined the letter. She held it near to her face because her eyesight was getting bad and Riccardo Levi had small, mean handwriting. As she read the word "betrayed," she felt a pain shoot down from her knees to the soles of her feet, as if in seconds she'd become an old crone, unable to walk. She put the letter down and stood up, clinging first to the writing table, then to the wall. She went to the window. A team of surveyors had arrived. Pappavincente was describing to them an imaginary circle, the site of his well. Rosa tapped on the window, to summon Pappavincente to help her, but her tap was too feeble and he couldn't hear her. Her maid came in a while later and found her lying on the floor. She was unable to speak. Her maid called for help. Rosa was put to bed and a doctor sent for. With the arrival of the doctor, word spread to Pappavincente and the other gardeners that the Signora was ill. Retribution, thought Pappavincente.

The doctor examined Rosa. She was in shock, he told the servants. Something must have frightened her—something she'd seen from the window, perhaps? The servants shrugged their shoulders. Rosa's maid stroked her mistress's cold white forehead. Keep her warm, said the doctor and went away. Coverlets were piled on the bed, one on top of another, so that the shape of Rosa's body disappeared completely beneath them and only her small head stuck out like a tiny sprout on a desirée potato.

She lay without speaking for a week. Her maid propped her up and spooned vermicelli broth into her narrow mouth. Outside her window, she could hear men talking and tried to turn her head to listen. "Drains," her maid explained gently. "they're here to re-route the drains and lay conduits to the fountains."

The doctor returned. His own wife quite often irritated him by succumbing to illnesses he was unable to cure except by cradling her in his arms like a baby. He looked at Rosa's blank face. He refused to cradle *her* in his arms. There were dark hairs on her top lip and creases in her eyelids. "Where is Signor Mollini?" he snapped. "He must be sent for."

So the servants sent for the priest. He, too, came and stared at Rosa and placed a palm leaf cross on her coverlet mountain and then sat down, in the silence of her room, and wrote in exquisite calligraphy to Antonio Mollini, informing him that his wife appeared to be dying.

When the letter arrived in Milan, on an early morning of grey mist, Mollini's voice—that same voice that had caused thousands of Society women to weep with wonder behind their opera glasses—was whispering playful obscenities in La Dusa's ear. She squirmed and giggled and pouted and the pout of her wide lips was so delicious and irresistible that Mollini was unable to stop himself from kissing them again and murmuring through his nose, "I love you. Verena. I love you beyond everything."

His servant knocked at his door. He rolled over and covered La Dusa's breasts with the sheet. The servant excused himself and came forward to the bed and offered Mollini the priest's letter on a silver salver. It was written on fine parchment, like a communion wafer. Mollini snatched it up and told the servant not to disturb him again that morning. The servant bowed and retreated. Mollini glanced at the letter, tossed it onto the marble bedside cabinet and turned back to La Dusa who lay with her arms above her head, waiting for his embrace.

The letter was forgotten. He remembered it at last towards six o'clock that evening, as he was preparing to leave for the opera house. He opened it as he was gargling with blackcurrant cordial. When he read the word "dying," he choked on the gargle and spat it all over the bathroom floor. He wiped his mouth, read the letter again and sat down on a stool. For the first time in several months, he remembered Pietro, and at once he saw, clearly and beautifully, where fate had led and where indeed it was leading. It was leading to La Dusa. Rosa was dying because she was unable to bear him more sons. It was fitting. Rosa was dried up, barren, old before her time. But here, right here in his bed, was Verena Dusa with her succulent round hips that would accommodate his future children. All he had to do was to marry her. It was gloriously simple. It was like stepping from a dark, shaded laurel walk onto a sunny terrace and finding at your feet pots of scented jasmine.

That same evening, Rosa spoke for the first time in seven days. She asked her maid to help her into the garden. When she crept out from under the coverlets, she seemed to have shrunk. Her long white nightgown was tangled round her feet. She looked like a chrysalis.

She was wrapped up in a cloak. Her hair was brushed and pinned up. She went hesitantly down the stairs, clinging to her maid's arm.

Pappavincente was standing in the garden in the twilight, looking at the well shafts. The water table was low. The construction workers had sunk the shafts almost fifty feet. He looked up and saw Rosa totter out with her maid. "Forgive her," Mollini had said. Pappavincente left the well and started to walk towards her. Her maid sat her down on a little stone seat. She stared about her in bewilderment. Deep trenches had been dug in the terraces. Mounds of red earth and lengths of lead piping lay all around.

"Signora," said Pappavincente, bowing, "for your recovery we are making all these waterworks." But she only stared at him in bewilderment too, as if he were a lunatic, as if he were the village idiot. "I want," she said, looking at the devastation round her, "my husband back." Up above the chimneys of the house and above the garden several bats were circling. Rosa liked bats. "Pipistrelli," she'd call, "pipi, pipi . . ."

Unaware that the priest had written to Mollini, Rosa that night had the lamp lit on her writing desk and sat down with her pen. She told Mollini that she had been ill and that she had imagined she was lying in a grave with Pietro. Over her body, the earth had been piled higher and higher in a colossal mound, with only her head sticking out. She could not, she said, endure such imaginings and only his love could save her from them. She would forgive him his sin of the flesh if he would just return to her. She signed the letter *Your Wife Until Death, Rosa Mollini.* Her writing, unlike the priest's hand, was cramped and ugly and her spelling not terribly good.

Rosa's letter reached Milan four days later. Mollini and La Dusa had triumphed in *Tristan und Isolde* and had been invited each night to elegant suppers by the likes of the Duke of Milan and the Count of Piedmont and had reveled together in their glory. At one of these suppers Mollini had become tottering drunk on a surfeit of champagne and pleasure and had rested his head on La Dusa's bosom and proposed marriage to her. The other guests had gasped, remembering the small, elegant wife he used to bring to evenings such as these, but La Dusa had only laughed and stroked his burning cheek and told him she was his till she died.

When he read Rosa's letter (he had a hangover when it was brought to him and his head was throbbing) he knew that he wouldn't, *couldn't* go back to her. When he thought about his life with Rosa, he was amazed he'd been able to endure it for so many years. Because it seemed full of shadow. Only at Pietro's birth had the sun shone on it and after his death it had become colorless and ghostly.

But Mollini knew also that he couldn't abandon his plans for the garden to Rosa and Pappavincente, both of whose natures were pessimistic and depressive. So he decided he would take La Dusa back with him to the Villa Mollini. He was a great man, revered in the village. He could do as he liked. He was beyond criticism. And he wouldn't hide La Dusa away. Oh, no. He would move out of the rooms he'd shared with Rosa and into other rooms which he'd share with La Dusa. When they were invited out, both women would accompany him, wife and mistress. Tuscan society would be given the chance to exclaim upon La Dusa's gorgeous beauty. And Rosa? Rosa was a religious, reserved woman. She would behave piously, with dignity staying away from him most of the time, reading or sewing in her rooms or going to communion.

Having obtained La Dusa's willing agreement to these arrangements, Mollini wrote to tell Rosa that he was returning home, but that he was unable to live without Verena Dusa and that she would therefore be coming with him.

Five days later, they arrived at the Villa Mollini to be told by the servants that Rosa was dead. She had been found with a burned scrap of paper in her hand, which they thought might have been a letter. She had shot herself with one of Mollini's duelling pistols.

Summer was coming. The re-routing of the drains wasn't entirely successful. As Mollini and his love sat with their fingers entwined on the first of the terraces to be completed. they fancied they could smell something decidedly unsavory.

It had been a dry spring and the river was low. Verena Dusa went down and looked at the river and said, as she strolled along with her plump little hand fondling Mollini's velvet-clad buttocks, "You know what I would like here, my darling? A lake."

Pappavincente was summoned. "I am going to dam up the river," Mollini informed him. "Water will be taken to the village in metal containers. Every villager will have his rightful share."

Pappavincente went down to the village, informed the people what was happening and told them to march shoulder to shoulder up to the Villa and break down the gates and threaten to kill Signor Mollini if he went ahead with his dam. "We will!" said a few voices. "We won't let our river be taken away!" And some of the men got out their pitchforks and their scythes. But nearly all the women of the village folded their arms and shrugged their shoulders. "As long as we have water," they said, "we're really perfectly happy. Perhaps it will be less trouble to get water from the containers than from the river. And anyway, we mustn't forget how lucky we are to have Signor Mollini right here in our valley . . ."

They could see, however, that Pappavincente was in despair. They comforted him. "You're adding to the fame of this region with your wonderful garden," they told him, "and a lake will make it even better. You must put swans on it, Pappavincente and graceful boats."

So Pappavincente walked back up to the Villa with not one villager standing with him, shoulder to shoulder. He thought he would sell his cottage and take his wife and sons and leave Mollini for ever. But then he let himself into the garden by a side gate and stood and stared at one of the new fountains and at the water lilies he'd planted at its base and thought of all the work still to be done, and he knew that, if he left the garden, he'd regret it till he died. It was his one work of art.

Mollini had understood the look of agony on Pappavincente's face. He was relieved he'd thought up the idea of taking water to the villagers in containers, because he knew that if La Dusa wanted a lake, he would have to give her a lake. He was much too afraid of losing her to deny her anything. Indeed, he begged her, begged her on his knees with his arms round her thighs to ask of him whatever she wanted, no matter how costly, no matter how perverse. All he longed to do was to give, to give.

She laughed at him. He adored her laugh, It made him tremble with delight. "You can give me a wedding ring, Antonio!" she giggled.

He'd thought, after burying Rosa, that he would wait six months before marrying Verena. It seemed right to wait. But it was clear to him as the summer advanced that La Dusa would insist on being married before new opera commitments began for them both in September. Hardly a day went by now without her asking, "Will it be August, Antonio?"

So he decided he wouldn't wait six months. He set a date: August 17th. He wanted the dam completed by then and a chapel built at the lake's edge, where the wedding would take place. More builders were hired. The same priest who had written to Mollini on Rosa's behalf was now given money to consecrate the ground on which the chapel was going to stand. An order was sent to Lake Trasimeno for forty-two swans. A fat ruby, encircled with diamonds, was placed on La Dusa's finger. Invitations went out to all the important people in the opera world— patrons and practitioners, both—and rooms booked for them in every inn and hostelry for miles around.

Then in July, as the dam was finished and the river went dry and the first containers of water rolled in on carts to the village, Mollini fell ill. He started vomiting. Pain in his bowel made him curse in agony. He had a terrible fever.

The doctor came. He took off his tail coat and rolled up his shirtsleeves and gave Mollini an enema. The contents of the bowel were putrified, he noticed, greenish and foul. "Advanced colonic infection," he diagnosed and arranged for Mollini to be taken that night to a hospital in Siena.

La Dusa traveled in the carriage with him. His face, normally ruddy and healthy, looked grey. He was suffering. La Dusa wiped his forehead with a little lace handkerchief. She was petrified. Supposing he died before the wedding?

When they reached the hospital, Mollini appeared to be delirious, not knowing where he was. As they went in through a heavy, iron-studded door, La Dusa held her lace handkerchief to her nostrils. The stench of the place was appalling. Every breath she breathed seemed to her to be full of poison. And though it was night-time, it was a stupidly rowdy place. Doors slammed, nurses marched up and down the echoing corridors in stalwart shoes, patients cried out, gas lamps hissed, cleaning women in filthy aprons pushed iron slop buckets forward on the stone floors with their mops.

La Dusa felt sick. How could anyone be made well in such a place? As Mollini was carded in, they passed a flight of stairs leading downwards. TO THE MORGUE, said a sign. The sign was accompanied by a drawing of a hand with a pointing finger. La Dusa couldn't help noticing that the drawing of the hand was very fine, like a drawing by da Vinci or Michelangelo. This must be where their talents lie, she thought—in the direction of death.

Mollini was put into an iron bed in the middle of a long ward. La Dusa protested, but no one listened and they were left quite alone. All along the row, men were groaning and sighing. A nurse came in. She passed briskly down the line of groaning patients, barely glancing at any of them. La Dusa stood up. She took her handkerchief away from her nose, drew in a breath and then let out a high F Sharp with extraordinary force.

The nurse stopped in her tracks and stared at her with a look of utter incredulity. Several of the patients woke from sleep and raised their heads.

La Dusa heard herself shout at the nurse, "Do you know who this is? This is Antonio Mollini! Why has he been put here?"

"This is the Men's Ward, Signora."

"And why is there no surgeon? Is this what you do to your patients—put them in a line and forget them?"

"Of course we don't forget them."

"I want Signor Mollini moved to a quiet room and I want a surgeon called now!"

The nurse gave La Dusa a dirty look and stomped out of the ward. La Dusa returned to Mollini's bed and stared at him. His eyes were closed and his breathing shallow. She was glad in a way, that he couldn't see the terrible ward or hear or smell the sufferings of the other men. She stroked his hand. "I will fight for you, my love," she said.

After half an hour, the nurse returned. "There is no surgeon here at the moment," she said sourly. "Surgeons need rest, you know. But if you can pay, we can have Signor Mollini moved to a more secluded room."

"Pay?" said La Dusa, "Of course we can pay."

Mollini was lifted onto a stretcher and carried out of the ward. He was put into another iron bed in a tiny room, like a cell. A chair was brought to La Dusa and she sat down. They told her that one of the surgeons had woken up and would come and look at Mollini as soon as he had cleaned his teeth.

The door of the little cell was shut. Alone with Mollini's sufferings. La Dusa felt so frightened that she began to cry. Her tears were very bright and copious and the little lace handkerchief was soon saturated with them.

When the surgeon arrived, she was still weeping. The surgeon wore a silk cravat. He shook her hand, that was wet from holding the handkerchief. She gave him a scribbled note from Mollini's doctor. When he'd read it, he lifted up the covers and began to prod Mollini's belly.

The surgeon's hand on his bowel caused terrible pain. Mollini's eyes opened and rolled about and he choked in agony. The face of the surgeon became grave. La Dusa wiped her wet hand on her skirt and knelt by Mollini, holding him and kissing his face as the surgeon's fingers probed.

The surgeon replaced Mollini's covers and put his hands together in a kind of steeple under his chin. "We must open him up," he said.

He was taken away. La Dusa was told to wait in the tiny room. She lay on the bed and tried to doze, but her own anxiety and the unceasing noise of the hospital prevented sleep. The short night passed and a grey light seeped in through the tiny window.

At seven, Mollini was brought in on a stretched and put back into the bed. He was unconscious and pale as death. The surgeon, too, looked pale and there was sweat on his top lip. "I'm afraid," he said, "the decay of the large intestine was far advanced. We have done the only thing possible to save his life: we have cut the putrified section and joined the bowel together where the tissue was healthy. We believe he will survive."

La Dusa knew that Mollini's convalescence would be long. She rented a house in a nearby street, so that she could come at any hour of the day or night to visit her love.

In the days following the operation, Mollini seemed, very slowly, to be getting well and La Dusa was full of praise for the surgeon who had saved his life. But then, on the fifth day, the wound became infected. Mollini's temperature soared and pain returned. For the first time, the nurses became attentive and La Dusa thought again of the beautiful hand pointing downwards to the morgue and became convinced that Mollini was going to die.

She had dreams of her lost wedding. In them, the forty-two swans Mollini had ordered were black. She made a decision. She would not let Mollini die before they were joined in marriage. She asked for the priest to be sent. He arrived with his candle and his holy water, thinking he was needed to administer the last rites. But no, La Dusa told him, she wanted him to marry them. The priest looked at Mollini and shook his head. He couldn't marry them if the groom was too ill to speak, he told her, and went away, giving La Dusa a strange and suspicious look.

She was in despair. She sat and watched her lover's life ebb.

But Mollini didn't die. His body's own magnificent healing powers surprised even the surgeon by fighting the infection till it was finally vanquished. He sat up. He began to eat, to laugh, to hold Verena's hand in a strong grip.

They returned to the Villa Mollini. The chapel was finished. Rain had come and the lake was brimming. In September, Verena Dusa and Antonio Mollini were married. The bride wore white satin and swans' feathers in her hair.

In the years that followed, all the original plans made by Mollini and Pappavincente for the garden were implemented. Every statue, every shrub, every rockery and fountain was in place. "All we can do now, Master," said Pappavincente. "is to wait for everything to grow." But Mollini, whose fame and wealth had already grown to giant proportions, began to conceive the idea of buying land beyond the forest, of making pathways through the forest in order to extend his garden to the other side of it. He liked what had been achieved so far. He was especially proud of the winding maze that led down to the lake, but there were no surprises for him in the garden any more. As he turned each corner, he knew exactly what he was going to see.

The land on the other side of the wood was common land, used by the villagers as pasture for their animals. Pappavincente was told to go down to the village and inform the farmers that ten hectares of pastureland were going to be fenced off He refused to go. He was ageing and growing stubborn as he aged. "Very well," said Mollini, "I shall go myself."

He didn't often visit the village now. He had long ago stopped making his list of the names of the villagers children and he couldn't, in fact, remember the surnames of many of the villagers themselves. He knew, however, that the oldest man of the village, Emilio Verri, had recently died So Mollini decided to go straight to the house of his widow, allegedly to offer his condolences.

Signora Verri was an old, old woman. "I lost a husband, and you, Signor Mollini, you lost your beloved wife," she said as the great man bent over her and put his hand on her bony shoulders Mollini straightened up. He couldn't stand it when anyone mentioned Rosa's death. "That was long ago. Signora," he said. "and anyway, I have some good news to cheer you up. My wife, Verena, is expecting a child."

The old crone lifted her face.

"A child, Signor Mollini?"

"Yes. In the spring."

Signora Verri's eyes were wet. To her, a new child was still a miracle of God.

"God bless the child, Sir."

"Yes. He will be blessed, I'm sure. And I wanted to tell you something else. I am going to buy from the village—at a price that will keep you all in clover for many months—a little land, about twelve hectares north of my forest. And on this land, do you know what I'm going to make?"

"No, Signor."

"A child's garden."

"Ah. A child's garden?"

"Yes. It will be full of wonders. There will be peacocks and guinea fowl and rabbits and doves and goldfish and little houses in the trees and an aviary and a secret cave and hundreds of thousands of flowers."

Signora Verri went to the door of her house and called her sons. There were three of them. Their handshakes were hard and their teeth yellowed from pipe tobacco. They demanded at once to know what price Mollini would pay for the land, explaining that a loss of twelve hectares would mean a reduction in livestock.

"A fair price," said Mollini. "What's more, I will buy all the livestock you have to slaughter and put the carcasses in my ice house till my son is born, and then there will be a huge feast and everyone in the village will be invited."

He got away as quickly as he could. He looked back and saw the men of the village standing about in little groups, talking anxiously. But he wasn't worried. They'd get used to the idea of the loss of their pasture just as they'd got used to getting their water supply from containers and not from the river. They know, he told himself, that the only thing, apart from their children, which brings honor into their miserable lives is my fame. People of this calibre will sacrifice a lot to keep their dignity.

He was able to tell Pappavincente that the fencing of the land could begin straight away. "No, Master," said Pappavincente, "the ground is much too hard. We shall have to wait till the frosts are over."

Mollini agreed reluctantly. It was a very cold winter. Parts of the lake were frozen. Irritatingly, quite a few of the evergreens in the garden had died and the camellias were showing signs of winter damage. All of these would have to be torn out and replaced.

Mollini walked in the forest with his wife and showed her which ways the paths would go. They would zig-zag and cross each other, he explained. Then, little Pietro would be able to play games of tracking and hide-and-seek.

Although she tried not to show it, it saddened Verena that she was going to have to call her son Pietro. She liked the name Giuseppe, which was her father's name. But she was relieved to be pregnant at last. She was thirty-nine. Mollini had been nagging her for four years, ever since their first passionate year of love was over, to conceive. She'd tried very hard. She'd pampered herself with mounds of nutritious food. She'd even turned down an engagement to sing *Lucia di Lammermoor* in London, in order to follow Mollini to Vienna, so that he could make love to her at the right time of the month. She'd begun to fear that she would never conceive and she thought that if she didn't, it was possible that Mollini would leave her. My love is unquenchable, his is not, she told herself.

When her breasts began to swell and the time for her period had passed, she sent for the doctor. It was the same doctor who had given Mollini his enema and seen the slime in his bowel. He rolled up his sleeves. He inserted two icy fingers into Verena's vagina and pressed on her belly with the palm of the other hand. "Well," he said at last, as he disinfected his hands, your husband's wish has been granted.

She decked herself in fussy, voluptuous gowns. Her bosom became gargantuan and she liked to show it off with lace frills and little cheeky ribbons. She didn't mind that she was getting ridiculously fat. She reveled in it. And Mollini too, from the moment he knew she was expecting his child, seemed to fall in love with her all over again. Even in public, he often couldn't refrain from fondling her breasts and whispering deliciously dirty suggestions in her ear. She giggled and screeched. She was delirious with happiness.

Several rooms in the Villa Mollini were being prepared for the baby. Nurses were interviewed and two engaged for the end of April. In March, the weather grew warmer. The fencing off of the twelve hectares was completed. Nine bullocks were slaughtered and stored in the ice house. In the forest, trees were felled to make way for the paths, wire for the aviary was ordered from Florence and a million bulbs came by cart from Holland.

Then, on the night of April 1st, a cold, relentless wind began to blow from the north. This wind terrified Verena. She liked Nature to be quiet.

She put her head under her coverlet and encircled her unborn baby with her hands. An hour later, her waters broke.

The midwife came stumbling through the wind, holding her shawl round her chin. In the Villa Mollini, all the lamps were lit and the servants woken from sleep. Mollini stared at the midwife scuttling about with her towels and her basins and thought of all the births that had occurred in the village since he'd built his dam. Children were alive in the village who had never seen the river.

He went, feeling anxious, and sat on his own in his music room. Upstairs, Verena was behaving like a courageous rower, pushing with the tides. The seas were stormy. The pain tore at Verena's body and the wind tore at the garden, disturbing its order.

At dawn, the baby was born. It was a boy. It weighed less than two kilograms. Its first cry was feeble because, despite its magnificent parentage, its lungs were not properly formed. It gasped and gasped, like a little slithery eel, for air, and died within two hours.

Verena screamed till she was sick. The wind, blowing in the direction of the village, carried her screams to the ears of the villagers as the women made coffee and the men put on their working clothes.

It was strange. A few days after the baby died, Mollini sent for Pappavincente to tell him to redesign the child's garden, and then he changed his mind. Although there was now no son to inhabit the garden, Mollini realized that he still wanted it made, exactly as he'd planned it.

"Master,." said Pappavincente, "you will never bear to walk in it."

"Then someone else will."

"Who, Sir?"

"We shall see."

Verena, huge in the bed, her breasts full of milk, announced "I never want to sing again. I'm going to cancel all my contracts."

In May, Mollini left for Paris, where he was to sing Lensky in *Eugene Onegin*. Before leaving, he looked at his fat wife. She nourished herself, he decided, her own greedy flesh, not the baby's. She was still ridiculously gross and the baby, his poor little Pietro, was a tiny, sickly fish.

Verena didn't want Mollini to go to Paris. "This world," she said. "this world we inhabit of roles and costumes and competition and money isn't worth a thing." And she held Mollini so tightly to her that he felt himself suffocating. For the first time since he met her, he longed to be away from her, miles and miles away.

On the morning of his departure, Pappavincente came to see Mollini. He told him that wire for the aviary had arrived and asked him whether he should employ builders to start work on it. "Of course," said Mollini, "of course."

As the summer was coming, Mollini had decided to rent a house rather than an apartment in Paris. It wasn't far from the Bois de Boulogne. It had a pretty courtyard with a fountain.

In this house, a long way from Verena, he felt his sadness begin to ebb and his energy return. He gave a party on a warm June evening. A string quartet played Mozart sitting by his fountain, he saw bats circling over the city and remembered Rosa. He shuddered. He took the white wrist of his young co-star, Clara Buig, and held it to his lips. I will amuse myself he decided, by making love to Clara.

La Buig was twenty-two. She was French. Paris thought her enchanting. Her career was at its beginning. She wasn't known outside her country yet, but to be singing Tatiana to Mollini's Lensky would soon ensure her international status.

When Mollini's party was over, La Buig stayed behind. Mollini undressed her tenderly, as he would have undressed a child. She was slim and pale. "Do you like gardens, Clara?" he asked.

Mollini was now forty-eight. Clara Buig was young enough to be his daughter. When he touched her, her eyes watched him gravely.

The next morning, he woke alone. He sent a servant with a note inviting Clara to lunch. But Mademoiselle Buig was not at home, she was working with her voice coach. Mollini went early to the Opéra. When La Buig arrived, she was wearing a pale lemon-colored dress. She moved very gracefully, Mollini noted, like a dancer.

After the rehearsal, he invited her to supper. They would dine in the Bois after going for a stroll under the chestnut trees. But she refused. She was very tired, she said. To sing well, she needed a lot of rest.

Mollini went back to his house and sat by his fountain. He loved Paris. No other city satisfied the eye so agreeably. I shall stay here till autumn, he decided. It's so hot in Tuscany in the summer and here, it's cool. But he knew that if he stayed till autumn, Verena would arrive, with her trunks full of dresses and jewelery and her fan collection and her maids and her boxes of sweets. The thought of this arrival dismayed him. Hastily, he sat down and wrote to his wife. He informed her that there was a typhoid epidemic in Paris. "I implore you, do not come near the city," he wrote. "For my sake, my love."

And every time he saw Clara Buig, her sweet neck, her shy smile, her expressive hands, it was as if he was seeing a corner of his garden that he'd never noticed, never expected to be there, but which, given his care and his talents, would one day be the most beautiful place of all. As the days passed, he became more and more convinced that Clara Buig could not be absent from his future.

He waited. He had to wait patiently. His invitations to supper were, night after night. refused. "Why?" he asked eventually "Why, Clara?"

She took his hand, noticing as she did so that several of his nails were bitten. "The night of your party, I was so excited," she said, "so flattered. I just let myself go. I couldn't help it."

"And was that wrong, my adorable Clara?"

"Oh yes. But I won't let it happen again."

So only on stage did she look at him adoringly. Outside the Opéra. she refused ever to be alone with him.

Verena wrote to him almost every day. Her fortieth birthday was approaching. She was depressed. She begged Mollini to let her know the moment the typhoid epidemic was over so that she could come to Paris and be with him. She told him that the loss of their child had only deepened her love for him.

What she didn't say in her letters, because at first she didn't notice it. was that since the second week of April no rain had fallen and that the level of the lake was going down fast as the villagers pumped out more and more water for their potato crop, for their vines, for their thirsty animals.

Pappavincente was worried about all the new shrubs he'd planted in the child's garden. Water containers were driven through the new paths in the forest. He and the other gardeners spent two hours every evening going round with watering cans.

One evening, Pappavincente took a walk up the valley. He saw that the river was dangerously low and he remembered with dread the terrible drought of 1856, when all the villages along the valley began desperately trying to sink new wells and when his grandmother had wondered aloud whether Pappavincente's existence wasn't to blame for all the anxiety and suffering.

As he walked back towards the lake, he saw La Dusa standing by it holding a parasol. He bowed to her. She was dressed in grey satin with a high lace collar and, with her feet tucked into red shoes, Pappavincente thought she looked like a fat pigeon. Her once beautiful eyes were now just two dark pleats in the flesh of her face.

"I'm so sorry, Signora," said Pappavincente, "about the baby . . ."

"Yes," said La Dusa and waddled away up the path to the forest, carrying her weight, as she carried her sorrow, awkwardly.

The forest was cool. A hundred times, Verena had rehearsed in her mind the day when she would push the ornate baby carriage under the magnificent fans of oak and beech and watch the dappling of sunlight on her son, Giuseppe. Now, she was there alone. And it was her birthday. She stopped and folded her parasol and examined her hands for signs of age. Mollini's wedding ring was wedged so tightly onto her finger, she was unable, these days, to take it off. "Look at these fat hands!" she said aloud and recalled with a strange kind of fascination the beautifully drawn thin hand pointing downwards to the hospital morgue.

She'd intended to visit the child's garden. Mollini had refused to discuss with her his decision to carry on with the project and the thought of this garden being designed and planted for someone who would never see it filled her with sadness. She found, as she neared it and caught sight of the half-completed aviary that she really didn't want to go there, and anyway she was out of breath.

She returned to the house. On the first terrace she noticed that the drains were stinking again. The smell was disgusting, but she lingered near it for a moment. It reminded her of happier times.

On the opening night of *Eugene Onegin*, La Dusa arrived, uninvited, in Paris.

Mollini's house was filled with servants preparing for a party. Lanterns had been lit all round the courtyard and tables set up near the fountain.

Mollini wasn't there. La Dusa dressed herself in a white gown and put feathers in her hair. She didn't go to the Opéra, but sat in the cool garden sipping champagne and questioning the servants about the typhoid epidemic. "What typhoid epidemic?" they inquired politely.

When Mollini returned, Clara Buig was with him, holding on to his arm. La Dusa looked at them. Mollini had grown a beard, put on weight. He looked like an English king. When he saw his wife, he bowed—just as Pappavincente had bowed to her beside the lake—and led Clara Buig forward and introduced her formally. La Dusa didn't get up. She ignored Clara's outstretched hand, but reached up and pulled Mollini towards her, so that he stumbled and fell into her lap. She bit his ear. "If you lie to me again, Antonio, I shall kill you," she said.

Two weeks later, they returned together to the Villa Mollini. On the Journey, Mollini feigned illness, a return of the pain in his bowel. And it was true, he was suffering. He was now madly, dementedly, obsessively in love with Clara Buig. He couldn't look at his wife, let alone touch her. All he could remember was the one beautiful night when Clara had let him love her, a night he had so carefully planned to repeat by giving a party in her honor.

He couldn't close his eyes without dreaming of Clara. Thoughts of her never left his mind. By the time he arrived at the Villa, he felt so troubled he had to sit down and write to her straight away and in the letter he found that he was telling her that he loved her more than he'd ever loved anyone, that his love for La Dusa had been pale in comparison. *Pale?* As he wrote this word, he couldn't help remembering certain nights, certain delectable afternoons he'd spent with Verena, but of course these had been long ago and she'd been beautiful then. And things pass, he said to himself. We move. The horizon changes. We turn a corner and a new sight greets us. This is how it has to be.

And to reassure himself, he went out into the garden. He was shocked at what he saw. The earth was parched. The smell near the house was terrible. Everywhere, as he strolled from path to path, from terrace to terrace, there were gaps in the borders and beds where plants had withered. The fountains had been turned off. The water in the fountain pools was bright green and foul-smelling. Mollini stood still and stared up at the sky. It was a deep, relentless blue. The sun on his face was fierce and all he could hear and feel was the buzzing and shimmering of the heat.

At that moment, he remembered the nine bullock carcasses. His stomach turned. Sorrow for his little dead child compounded his sickness. He sat down on a stone seat and put his head in his hands. The salt sweat from his brow stung his eyes.

He prayed the nausea would pass. It seemed like the nausea of death, when the appetite for the world drains, leaving the mind filled with loathing.

To soothe himself, he thought of his music. "Mollini's voice is not simply a voice," a Paris critic had declared, "it is an instrument. I have never before heard such an astonishing sound come out of a man." And the sickness did, after a while, begin to pass. So Mollini stood up. Instead of returning to the house—to Verena's tears and entreaties which only repelled him and were utterly in vain—he walked on down to the lake. It was no longer blue, but brownish and full of silt. He skirted it and went up into the forest. Here, it was cool. In the shade of the big trees, nettles and sweet briars were green.

He followed one of the winding paths. He began to feel better. If only, he thought, I could stroll here with Clara, with her little hand tucked into my arm.

As he neared the child's garden, he feared that all the new bushes and hedges planted in the spring would have died, but the moment he left the forest and came out again into the sunlight, he saw that everything here was living and healthy, that already roses were climbing up the trellises and that purple and white clematis were growing strongly up the sides of the aviary.

Mollini smiled. It was a smile of gratitude and a smile of hope renewed. As he looked at the faithful work of Pappavincente and the other gardeners, he knew why he had made them go on with the child's garden: he would give it to Clara.

In August, Mollini told Pappavincente that water to the village would have to be rationed. The ration was so meager and insufficient that the young men led nightly raiding parties to the lake, carrying buckets and churns, but the water itself was becoming soupy and brackish and the villagers and their animals developed intestinal illnesses.

Then, the widow Verri died. Mollini attended the funeral. He sensed, for the first time, that his presence among the villagers no longer filled them with pride. As he held out his hand for them to shake, they let their fingers touch his, but wouldn't hold his hand in a firm grip. To cheer them up and win back their reverence, he invited them to come and see the child's garden and to drink wine with him on the site of the summer house he was planning to build there.

So they came one morning and stood about awkwardly. The garden was beautiful, lush and healthy. They touched the flowers. The scent of them was extraordinary. They'd forgotten how superb the world could seem. They drank the dry white wine, bottle after bottle, and staggered home in mid-afternoon to dream muddled dreams. Before they left, Mollini had embraced the men and kissed the women on the lips. "I made them happy." he told Verena.

Verena didn't move out of her room these days. She sat up in her bed and fed her sorrow with sweet wine and chocolate. Her feet began to swell and the doctor was called. Verena burst into tears. "I know what would cure me," she sobbed "if Antonio would only take me in his arms." The doctor went away, disgusted.

"My wife is suffering," Mollini wrote to Clara, "and I cannot help but feel sorry for her. But her suffering is nothing to my own: I'm in love with a woman I cannot marry."

In September, Mollini left for Vienna. He was to take on his most demanding and difficult role, in Verdi's *Otello*. He had signed the contract on one condition, that the part of Desdemona be given to Clara Buig. And in Vienna at last Clara became Mollini's mistress. She had been so moved, she said, by his letters, she knew she could no longer resist.

He was in heaven. La Buig wasn't a sensual woman like La Dusa. There were moments, even, when her grave face beneath his reminded Mollini of Rosa's face, long, long ago. "You give our love nobility and dignity," he told Clara, "you turn the past into the future."

He was determined, now, that there would be a future with Clara. He wrote to Pappavincente with new designs for the summer house. It would no longer be a summer house: it would have a sumptuous bedroom and bathroom and fires in all the rooms. It would be Clara's residence.

As rumors of the love affair of Antonio Mollini and the 23-year-old Clara Buig spread in whispers round the tearooms and the musical salons of Vienna, it began at last to rain in Tuscany. It rained for seventeen days and nights. The villagers came out of their hovels and stuck their tongues out and let the sweet rain trickle down their throats. Verena got out of bed, threw a shawl round her shoulders and walked out in the downpour to the lake side, The water had risen by several feet, Verena walked into the water, wearing her pink satin slippers. The slippers stuck in the mud, so she waded on without them, feeling her petticoats and her skirt become heavy.

She lay on her back. She expected to sink straight away, but her large body was buoyant and she found that she was floating. She stared at the grey sky and thought how astonishingly full of color her life had been. It took her three hours to die. On the brink of death, it seemed to La Dusa that the grey cloud moved away and that the hot sun was shining on her round face. And for a second, she imagined the autumn to come and the wonderful vibrant reds and umbers of the leaves.

By the time the winter came, Clara's house was finished. Mollini, however, didn't bother to have the fires lit.

"Clara will live with me in the Villa Mollini," he told Pappavincente, so the shutters were closed and the place locked.

When Clara Buig at last arrived at the Villa Mollini, however, and was led by a maid to the very room La Dusa had occupied, she refused to sleep there. The house, in fact, gave her the creeps, she said. She couldn't possibly spend a night in it.

Mollini wrapped her in her velvet coat and walked with her, arm in arm, through the garden, round the lake and up into the forest. The great trees were silent. Winter had begun to bite early this year.

The pleasure Mollini took from seeing Clara's little gloved hand on his arm was acute, too precious and fleeting to mention. They walked on in silence, descending at last down the intricate paths of the child's garden to Clara's house. Golden pheasants in the aviary squawked and pecked at the wire as they passed.

Mollini opened the shutters of the house and got on his knees and lit a fire in one of the grates.

Clara walked on her own from room to room and then went outside again and walked all round the house. It was nicely set in the child's garden, surrounded by stone terraces and ornate balustrading and small cypresses. At the back of it, however, about forty yards away, Clara could see an ugly post-and-rails fence and beyond this a boring slope of empty pastureland.

"What is that?" she asked Mollini.

Mollini had followed her outside and now looked to where she was pointing.

"Common land," said Mollini. "The village people use it to graze their cattle."

La Buig sniffed. Then she turned her stern child's face towards Mollini and said: "You know what I would like to see there instead of that?"

"No, my love."

"An English lawn. This whole garden is nothing but steps and piazzas and gazebos and mazes and borders and beds. If I'm going to live here, I really want a lawn."

Mollini sent for Pappavincente. One of his sons arrived instead and told him that Pappavincente was ill and couldn't come.

Mollini went at once to the village, not to tell the people that he was going to take away the rest of their pasture for Clara's lawn, but to see the old man and take him some of the strong red wine he knew he liked to drink.

"We believe he's dying," said Signora Pappavincente. She was holding a rag to her nose, and when Mollini went into the room where Pappavincente lay, it seemed to him that the odor of death was indeed very strong.

"Listen, old friend," he whispered to Pappavincente, "remember all that you've achieved here. Dwell on that. Feel proud of it. You've made the most beautiful garden in Tuscany, perhaps the most beautiful garden in all Italy. And it's not finished yet. It lives on. It changes and grows. It will last for ever."

Pappavincente's head rolled on the pillow and he turned his staring, angry eyes on Mollini. "I have sinned, Master," he said.

He died that night. Mollini wanted him buried in the garden, but the old man's family were stubborn and wouldn't allow it.

Mollini explained to Clara that the whole village would be in mourning for a while and that it would be impossible, just at the moment, to mention the land he was going to take for her lawn.

"I understand," said Clara, "but you will tell them in the spring?"

"Yes. In the spring."

"Because I want to push my baby's bassinet on the lawn. Like an English duchess. You see?"

"Your baby's bassinet, Clara?"

"Yes, Antonio. I'm going to have your child."

Mollini took Clara's serious little face in his hands and covered it with kisses. Three weeks later, he married her. Once again, the cream of the opera world was invited to the Villa Mollini. Among the cream was an extraordinarily beautiful English soprano called Marion Shepherd. Marion Shepherd told Mollini that she thought his garden was as unbelievable as his voice and smiled such a dazzling smile that Mollini was forced to reach out and caress her mouth with his finger.

On the wedding night, Clara Buig was very restless. The baby inside her, little Pietro, as Mollini called him, kept kicking her and her head seemed to be full of strange visions and fears.

The dawn was icy cold, but as soon as the sky was light, Clara got up and dressed herself and went out into the garden. She didn't wake Mollini. He lay snoring on his back with his legs apart.

She walked towards the Villa Mollini itself, which seemed to beckon her. On the way, she came across an old stone well with delicate arching ironwork that she'd never noticed before. I expect it's just ornamental, she thought, like everything else in this garden. But she was curious about it, so she walked to the edge of it and peered in. Much to her surprise, she found that she was looking down into darkness.

A Garden Plot

W. W. Jacobs

THE ABLE-BODIED MEN of the village were at work, the children were at school singing the multiplication-table lullaby, while the wives and mothers at home nursed the baby with one hand and did the housework with the other. At the end of the village an old man past work sat at a rough deal table under the creaking signboard of the Cauliflower, gratefully drinking from a mug of ale supplied by a chance traveler who sat opposite him.

The shade of the elms was pleasant and the ale good. The traveler filled his pipe and, glancing at the dusty hedges and the white road baking in the sun, called for the mugs to be refilled, and pushed his pouch towards his companion. After which he paid a compliment to the appearance of the village.

"It ain't what it was when I was a boy," quavered the old man, filling his pipe with trembling fingers. "I mind when the grindstone was stuck just outside the winder o' the forge instead o' being one side as it now is; and as for the shop winder—it's twice the size it was when I was a young 'un."

He lit his pipe with the scientific accuracy of a smoker of sixty years' standing, and shook his head solemnly as he regarded his altered birthplace. Then his color heightened and his dim eyes flashed.

"It's the people about 'ere 'as changed more than the place 'as," he said, with sudden fierceness; 'there's a set o' men about here nowadays as are no good to anybody; reg'lar raskels. And if you've the mind to listen *I* can tell you of one or two as couldn't be beat in London itself.

"There's Tom Adams for one, lie went and started wot 'e called a Benevolent Club. Threepence a week each we paid agin sickness or accident, and Tom was secretary. Three weeks arter the club was started he caught a chill and was laid up for a month. He got back to work a week, and then 'e sprained something in 'is leg; and arter that was well 'is inside went wrong. We didn't think much of it at first, not understanding figures; but at the end o' six months the club hadn't got a farthing, and they was in Tom's debt one pound seventeen-and-six.

"He isn't the only one o' that sort in the place, either. There was Herbert Richardson. He went to town, and came back with the idea of a Goose Club for Christmas. We paid twopence a week into that for pretty near ten months, and then Herbert went back to town again, and all we 'ear of 'im, through his sister, is that he's still there and doing well, and don't know when he'll be back.

"But the artfullest and worst man in this place—and that's saying a good deal, mind you—is Bob Pretty. Deep is no word for 'im. There's no way of being up to 'im. It's through 'im that we lost our Flower Show; and, if you'd like to 'ear the rights o' that, I don't suppose there's anybody in this place as knows as much about it as I do—barring Bob hisself that is, but 'e wouldn't tell it to you as plain as I can.

"We'd only 'ad the Flower Show one year, and little anybody thought that the next one was to be the last. The first year you might smell the place a mile off in the summer and on the day of the show people came from a long way round, and brought money to spend at the Cauliflower and other places.

"It was started just after we got our new parson, and Mrs. Pawlett, the parson's wife, 'is name being Pawlett, thought as she'd encourage men to love their 'omes and be better 'usbands by giving a prize every year for the best cottage garden. Three pounds was the prize, and a metal teapot with writing on it.

"As I said, we only 'ad it two years. The fust year the garden as got it was a picter, and Bill Chambers, 'im as won the prize, used to say as 'e was out o' pocket by it, taking 'is time and the money 'e spent on flowers. Not as we believed that, you understand, 'specially as Bill did 'is very best to get it the next year, too. 'E didn't get it, and though p'r'aps most of us was glad 'e didn't, we was all very surprised at the way it turned out in the end.

"The Flower Show was to be 'eld on the 5th o' July, just as a'most everything about here was at its best. On the 15th of June Bill Chambers's garden seemed to be leading, but Peter Smith and Joe Gubbins and Sam Jones and Henery Walker was almost as good, and it was understood that more than one of 'em had got a surprise which they'd produce at the last moment, too late for the others to copy. We used to sit up here of an evening at this Cauliflower public-house and put money on it. I put mine on Henery Walker, and the time I spent in 'is garden 'elping 'im is a sin and a shame to think of.

"Of course some of 'em used to make fun of it, and Bob Pretty was the worst of 'em all. He was always a lazy, good-for-nothing man, and 'is garden was a disgrace. He'd chuck down any rubbish in it: old bones, old tins, bits of an old bucket, anything to make it untidy. He used to larf at 'em awful about their gardens and about being took up by the parson's wife. Nobody ever see 'im do any work, real 'ard work, but the smell from 'is place at dinner-time was always nice, and I believe that he knew more about game than the parson hisself did.

"It was the day arter this one I'm speaking about, the 16th o' June, that the trouble all began, and it came about in a very eggstrordinary way. George English, a quiet man getting into years, who used when 'e was younger to foller the sea, and whose only misfortin was that 'e was a brother-in-law o' Bob Pretty's, his sister marrying Bob while 'e was at sea and knowing nothing about it, 'ad a letter come from a mate of his who 'ad gone to Australia to live. He'd 'ad letters from Australia before, as we all knew from Miss Wicks at the post office, but this one upset him altogether. He didn't seem like to know what to do about it.

"While he was wondering Bill Chambers passed. He always did pass George's house about that time in the evening, it being on 'is way 'ome, and he saw George standing at 'is gate with a letter in 'is 'and looking very puzzled.

"'Evenin', George,' ses Bill.

"'Evenin',' ses George.

"'Not bad news, I 'ope?' ses Bill, noticing 'is manner, and thinking it was strange.

"'No,' ses George. 'I've just 'ad a very eggstrordinary letter from Australia,' he ses, 'that's all.'

"Bill Chambers was always a very inquisitive sort o man, and he stayed and talked to George until George, arter fust making him swear oaths that 'e wouldn't tell a soul, took 'im inside and showed 'im the letter.

"It was more like a story-book than a letter. George's mate, John Biggs by name, wrote to say that an uncle of his who had just died, on 'is deathbed told him that thirty years ago he 'ad been in this very village, staying at this 'ere very Cauliflower, whose beer we're drinking now. In the night, when everybody was asleep, he got up and went quiet-like and buried a bag of five hundred and seventeen sovereigns and one half-sovereign in one of the cottage gardens till 'e could come for it agin. He didn't say 'ow he come by the money, and, when Bill spoke about that, George English said that, knowing the man, he was afraid 'e 'adn't come by it honest, but anyway his friend John Biggs wanted it, and, wot was more, 'ad asked 'im in the letter to get it for 'im.

"'And wot I'm to do about it, Bill,' he ses, 'I don't know. All the directions he gives is, that 'e thinks it was the tenth cottage on the right-'and side of the road, coming down from the Cauliflower. He thinks it's the tenth, but 'e's not quite sure. Do you think I'd better make it known and offer a reward of ten shillings, say, to any one who finds it?'

"'No,' ses Bill, shaking 'is 'ead. 'I should hold on a bit if I was you, and think it over. I shouldn't tell another single soul, if I was you.'

"'I b'lieve you're right,' ses George. 'John Biggs would never forgive me if I lost that money for 'im. You'll remember about it keeping secret, Bill?'

"Bill swore he wouldn't tell a soul, and 'e went off ome and 'ad his supper, and then 'e walked up the road to the Cauliflower and back, and then up and back again, thinking over what George 'ad been telling "im, and noticing, what 'e'd never taken the trouble to notice before, that 'is very house was the tenth one from the Cauliflower.

"Mrs. Chambers woke up at two o'clock next morning and told Bill to get up farther, and then found 'e wasn't there. She was rather surprised at first, but she didn't think much of it, and thought, what happened to be true, that 'e was busy in the garden, it being a light night. She turned over and went to sleep again, and at five when she woke up she could distinctly 'ear Bill working 'is 'ardest. Then she went to the winder and nearly dropped as she saw Bill in his shirt and trousers digging away like mad. A quarter of the garden was all dug up, and she shoved open the winder and screamed out to know what 'e was doing.

"Bill stood up straight and wiped 'is face with his shirt-sleeve and started digging again, and then his wife just put something on and rushed downstairs as fast as she could go.

"'What on earth are you a-doing of, Bill?' she screams.

"'Go indoors,' ses Bill, still digging.

"'Have you gone mad?' she ses, half crying.

"Bill just stopped to throw a lump of mold at her, and then went on digging till Henery Walker who also thought 'e 'ad gone mad, and didn't want to stop 'im too soon, put 'is 'ead over the 'edge and asked 'im the same thing.

"'Ask no questions and you'll 'ear no lies, and keep your ugly face your own side of the 'edge,' ses Bill. 'Take it indoors and frighten the children with,' he ses. 'I don't want it staring at me.'

"Henery walked off offended, and Bill went on with his digging. He wouldn't go to work, and 'e 'ad his breakfast in the garden, and his wife spent all the morning in the front answering the neighbor's questions and begging of 'em to go in and say something to Bill. One of 'em did go, and came back a'most directly and stood there for hours telling diff'rent people wot Bill 'ad said to 'er, and asking whether 'e couldn't be locked up for it.

"By tea-time Bill was dead-beat, and that stiff he could 'ardly raise 'is bread and butter to his mouth. Several o' the chaps looked in in the evening, but all they could get out of 'im was, that it was a new way o' cultivating 'is garden 'e 'ad just 'eard of, and that those who lived the longest would see the most. By night-time 'e'd nearly finished the job, and 'is garden was just ruined.

"Afore people 'ad done talking about Bill, I'm blest if Peter Smith didn't go and cultivate 'is garden in exactly the same way. The parson and 'is wife was away on their 'oliday, and nobody could say a word. The curate who 'ad come over to take 'is place for a time, and who took the names of people for the Flower Show, did point out to 'im that he was spoiling 'is chances, but Peter was so rude to 'im that he didn't stay long enough to say much.

"When Joe Gubbins started digging up 'is garden people began to think they were all bewitched, and I went round to see Henery Walker to tell 'im wot a fine chance 'e'd got, and to remind 'im that I'd put another ninepence on 'im the night before. All 'e said was: 'More fool you.' and went on digging a 'ole in his garden big enough to put a 'ouse in.

"In a fortnight's time there wasn't a garden worth looking at in the place, and it was quite clear there'd be no Flower Show that year, and of all. the silly, bad-tempered men in the place them as 'ad dug up their pretty gardens was the wust.

"It was just a few days before the day fixed for the Flower Show, and I was walking up the road when I see Joe and Henery Walker and one or two more leaning over Bob Pretty's fence and talking to 'im. I stopped too, to see what they were looking at and found they was watching Bob's two boys a-weeding of 'is garden. it was a disgraceful, untidy sort of place, as I said before, with a few marigolds and nasturtiums, and sich-like put in anywhere, and Bob was walking up and down smoking of 'is pipe and watching 'is wife hoe atween the plants and cut off dead marigold blooms.

"'That's a pretty garden you've got there, Bob,' ses Joe, grinning.

"'I've seen wuss,' ses Bob.

"'Going in for the Flower Show, Bob?' ses Henery, with a wink at us.

"'O' course I am,' ses Bob, 'olding 'is 'ead up; 'my marigolds ought to pull me through,' he ses.

"Henery wouldn't believe it at fust, but when he saw Bob show 'is missus 'ow to pat the path down with the back o' the spade and hold the nails for 'er while she nailed a climbing nasturtium to the fence, he went off and fetched Bill Chambers and one or two others, and they all leaned over the fence breathing their 'ardest and a-saying of all the nasty things to Bob they could think of.

" 'It's the best-kep' garden in the place,' ses Bob. 'I ain't afraid o' your new way o' cultivating flowers, Bill Chambers. Old-fashioned ways suit me best; I learnt 'ow to grow flowers from my father.'

" 'You ain't 'ad the cheek to give your name in, Bob?' ses Sam Jones, staring.

"Bob didn't answer 'im. 'Pick those bits o' grass out o' the path, old gal,' he ses to 'is wife; 'they look untidy, and untidiness I can't abear.'

"He walked up and down smoking 'is pipe and pretending not to notice Henery Walker, wot 'ad moved farther along the fence, and was staring at some drabble-tailed-looking geraniums as if 'e'd seen 'em afore but wasn't quite sure where.

" 'Admiring my geraniums, Henery?' ses Bob at last.

" 'Where'd you get 'em?' ses Henery, 'ardly able to speak.

" 'My florist's,' says Bob in a off-hand manner.

" 'Your *wot*?' asks Henery.

" 'My florist,' ses Bob.

" 'And who might 'e be when 'e's at home?' asked Henery.

" 'Tain't so likely I'm going to tell you that,' ses Bob. 'Be reasonable, Henery, and ask yourself whether it's likely I should tell you 'is name. Why, I've never seen sich fine geraniums afore. I've been nursing 'em inside all the summer, and just planted 'em out.'

" 'About two days arter I threw mine over my back fence,' ses Henery Walker, speaking very slowly.

" 'Ho,' ses Bob, surprised. 'I didn't know you 'ad any geraniums, Henery. I thought you was digging for gravel this year.'

"Henery didn't answer him. Not because 'e didn't want to, mind you, but because he couldn't.

" 'That one,' ses Bob, pointing to a broken geranium with the stem of 'is pipe, 'is a "Dook o' Wellington," and that white one there is wot I'm going to call "Pretty's Pride." That fine marigold over there, wot looks like a sunflower, is called "Golden Dreams."

" 'Come along, Henery,' ses Bill Chambers, bursting, 'come and get something to take the taste out of your mouth.'

" 'I'm sorry I can't offer you a flower for your button-'ole,' ses Bob, perlitely, 'but it's getting so near the Flower Show now I can't afford it. If you chaps only knew wot pleasure was to be 'ad sitting among your inner-cent flowers, you wouldn't want to go to the public-house so often.'

"He shook 'is 'ead at 'em, and telling his wife to give the "Dook o' Wellington" a mug of water, sat down in the chair agin and wiped the sweat off 'is brow.

"Bill Chambers did a bit o' thinking as they walked up the road, and by and by 'e turns to Joe Gubbins and 'e ses:

"'Seen anything o' George English lately, Joe?'

"'Yes,' ses Joe.

"'Seems to me we all 'ave,' ses Sam Jones.

"None of 'em liked to say wot was in their minds, 'aving all seen George English and swore pretty strong not to tell his secret, and none of 'em liking to own up that they'd been digging up their gardens to get money as 'e'd told 'em about. But presently Bill Chambers ses: 'Without telling no secrets or breaking no promises, Joe, supposing a certain 'ouse was mentioned in a certain letter from forrin parts, wot 'ouse was it?'

"'Supposing it was so,' ses Joe, careful, too; 'the second 'ouse, count-ing the Cauliflower.'

"'The ninth 'ouse, you mean,' ses Henery Walker sharply.

"'Second 'ouse in Mill Lane, you mean,' ses Sam Jones, wot lived there.

"Then they all see 'ow they'd been done, and that they wasn't, in a manner o' speaking, referring to the same letter. They came up and sat 'ere where we're sitting now, all dazed-like. It wasn't only the chance o' losing the prize that upset 'em, but they'd wasted their time and ruined their gardens and got called mad by the other folks. Henery Walker's state o' mind was dreadful for to see, and he kep' thinking of 'orrible things to say to George English, and then being afraid they wasn't strong enough.

"While they was talking who should come along but George English hisself! He came right up to the table, and they all sat back on the bench and stared at 'im fierce, and Henery Walker crinkled 'is nose at him.

"'Evening,' he ses, but none of 'em answered 'im; they all looked at Henery to see wot 'e was going to say.

"'Wot's up?' ses George in surprise.

"'Gardens,' ses Henery.

"So I've 'eard," ses George.

"He shook his 'ead and looked at them sorrowful and severe at the same time.

"'So I 'eard, and I couldn't believe my ears till I went and looked for myself,' he ses, 'and wot I want to say is this: you know wot I'm referring

to. If any man 'as found wot don't belong to him 'e knows who to give it
to. It ain't wot I should 'ave expected of men wot's lived in the same place
as *me* for years. Talk about honesty,' 'e ses, shaking 'is 'ead agin, 'I should
like to see a little of it.'

"Peter Smith opened his mouth to speak, and 'ardly knowing wot 'e
was doing took a pull at 'is beer at the same time, and if Sam Jones 'adn't
been by to thump 'im on the back I b'lieve he'd ha' died there and then.

"'Mark my words,' ses George English, speaking very slow and
solemn, 'there'll be no blessing on it. Whoever's made 'is fortune by getting up and digging 'is garden over won't get no real benefit from it. He
may wear a black coat and new trousers on Sunday, but 'e won't be 'appy.
I'll go and get my little taste 'o beer somewhere else,' 'e ses. 'I can't breathe
here.'

"He walked off before any one could say a word; Bill Chambers
dropped 'is pipe and smashed it. Henery Walker sat staring after 'im with
'is mouth wide open, and Sam Jones, who was always one to take advantage, drank 'is own beer under the firm belief that it was Joe's.

"'I shall take care that Mrs. Pawlett 'ears o' this,' ses Henery at last.

"'And be asked wot you dug your garden up for,' ses Joe, 'and 'ave to
explain that you broke your promise to George. Why, she'd talk at us for
years and years.'

"'And parson 'ud preach a sermon about it,' ses Sam; 'where's your
sense, Henery?'

"'We should be the larfing-stock for miles round,' ses Bill Chambers.
'If anybody wants to know, I dug my garden up to enrich the soil for next
year, and also to give some other chap a chance of the prize.'

"Peter Smith 'as always been a unfortunit man; he's got the name for
it. He was just 'aving another drink as Bill said that, and this time we all
thought 'e'd gorn. He did hisself.

"Mrs. Pawlett and the parson came 'ome next day, an er voice got that
squeaky with surprise it was painful to listen to her. All the chaps stuck to
the tale that they'd dug their garden up to give the others a chance, and
Henery Walker, 'e went farther and said it was owing to a sermon on
unselfishness wot the curate 'ad preached three weeks afore. He 'ad a nice
little red-covered 'ymnbook the next day with 'From a friend' wrote in it.

"All things considered, Mrs. Pawlett was for doing away with the
Flower Show that year and giving two prizes next year instead, but one or
two other chaps, encouraged by Bob's example, 'ad given in their names
too, and they said it wouldn't be fair to their wives. All the gardens but
one was worse than Bob's, the men not having started till later than wot

'e did, and not being able to get their geraniums from 'is florist. The only better garden was Ralph Thomson's, who lived next door to 'im, but two nights afore the Flower Show 'is pig got walking in its sleep. Ralph said it was a mystery to 'im 'ow the pig could ha' got out; it must ha' put its foot through a hole too small for it, and turned the button of its door, and then climbed over a four-foot fence. He told Bob 'e wished the pig could speak, but Bob said that that was sinful and unchristian of 'im, and that most likely if it could, it would only call 'im a lot o' bad names, and ask 'im why he didn't feed it properly.

"There was quite a crowd on Flower Show day following the judges. First of all, to Bill Chambers's astonishment and surprise, they went to 'is place and stood on the 'eaps in 'is garden judging 'em, while Bill peeped at 'em through the kitchen winder 'arf crazy. They went to every garden in the place, until one of the young ladies got tired of it, and asked Mrs. Pawlett whether they was there to judge cottage gardens or earthquakes.

"Everybody 'eld their breaths that evening in the schoolroom when Mrs. Pawlett got up on the platform and took a slip of paper from one of the judges. She stood a moment waiting for silence, and then 'eld up her 'and to stop what she thought was clapping at the back, but which was two or three wimmin who 'ad 'ad to take their crying babies out, trying to quiet 'em in the porch. Then Mrs. Pawlett put 'er glasses on her nose and just read out, short and sweet, that the prize of three sovereigns and a metal teapot for the best-kept cottage garden 'ad been won by Mr. Robert Pretty.

"One or two people patted Bob on the back as 'e walked up the middle to take the prize; then one or two more did, and Bill Chambers's pat was the 'eartiest of 'em all. Bob stopped and spoke to 'im about it.

"You would 'ardly think that Bob 'ud have the cheek to stand up there and make a speech, but 'e did. He said it gave 'im great pleasure to take the teapot and the money, and the more pleasure because 'e felt that 'e had earned 'em. He said that if 'e told 'em all 'e'd done to make sure o' the prize they'd be surprised. He said that 'e'd been like Ralph Thomson's pig, up early and late.

"He stood up there talking as though 'e was never going to leave off, and said that 'e hoped as 'is example would be a benefit to 'is neighbors. Some of 'em seemed to think.that digging was everything, but 'e could say with pride that 'e 'adn't put a spade to 'is garden for three years until a week ago, and then not much.

"He finished 'is remarks by saying that 'e was going to give a tea-party up at the Cauliflower to christen the teapot, where 'e'd be pleased to welcome all friends. Quite a crowd got up and followed 'im out then, instead o' waiting for the dissolving views, and came back 'arf an hour arterwards, saying that until they'd got as far as the Cauliflower they'd no idea as Bob was so pertickier who 'e mixed with.

"That was the last Flower Show we ever 'ad in Claybury, Mrs. Pawlett and the judges meeting the tea-party coming 'ome, and 'aving to get over a gate into a field, to let it pass. What with that and Mrs. Pawlett tumbling over something farther up the road, which turned out to be the teapot, smelling strongly of beer, the Flower Show was given up, and the parson preached three Sundays running on the sin of beer-drinking to children who'd never 'ad any and wimmen who couldn't get it."

The Lady Gardener

LISA ST. AUBIN DE TERÁN

Nobody at the nursing home liked to bother Gladys. She had come and gone now in a haze of pent-up rage for seven years. She knew her way around the corridors as well as any member of staff, and she could always make her way, unaccompanied, past the Macmillan and Nightingale wards, past the side room where the girl with the twisted face who was no more than a torso tucked into the top part of the bed lay unvisited, and on to the room where her own daughter Sally lay and had lain for more than half her life. It was eight years since the car had hit her, but the verdict was always the same: brain-dead, and hitched to the tubes and drips and bags and the yards of plastic that were all that Sally had now for her adolescence.

Gladys herself was soothed by these visits to her daughter. She fitted them in whenever she could. She would sit for hours behind the half-blinds silently discussing all the minor worries that had come to beset her in her early middle age. There were slugs on her borders again, and Simpson was behind with the mowing, the front brake-discs were going on the Daimler. Sally was the perfect listener.

At three o'clock exactly, Gladys rose to leave. She had a small traveling bag with her in worn red leather, and a summer coat. She was well dressed for the small Norfolk village where she lived, but not strikingly so for London, and, standing as she did at a mere five foot four, with her rather snubbed features and her dull olive skin, she made no effort to be striking. In fact, she thought, she owed half her success in her job to the very unobtrusiveness of her appearance. Pausing between the massive gate-posts of the clinic to take a last look at Sally's window, Gladys certainly didn't look anything out of the ordinary But then, as she herself had explained at her interview it isn't what you look like, it's what you feel like and how capably you work that counts, and Gladys just happened to be the best.

She caught the three-thirty train to Liverpool Street, and drifted through East Anglia, with an open book on her knee, reflecting on the sequence of events that had led her to where she was. She had become so English over the years, with her tweeds and her Burberry and her place on the flower-rota at the church, that she often forgot that she wasn't. She wasn't, actually even European, but she had married on a lie, and the lie had stuck, and with every passing year it seemed more and more pointless to enlighten her husband. Alec probably wouldn't have believed her anyway. For all his merits, he didn't have a very vivid imagination. So he thought she was born German, because she had once had German papers for a few years, and he didn't realize now, on the eve of their trip to Caracas that for Gladys this would really mean going home. She had been born there in the shanty town that spilled down the hill-slopes into the city in a wave of delinquency and ungathered debris.

Gladys had always had a distaste for the squalor of her birth. Her own mother had run away and left her to fend for herself in the one-room hut that couldn't keep out the rain, let alone rats or intruders Even then, Gladys's plainness had been like a shield. She had always been too small, and then, later, too ordinary, to bother with. She was fourteen when she ran away to join the guerrillas And by the time she was fifteen, she had earned herself the name of *La Loba*, the she-wolf. For three years she had never moved without a weapon, never slept without a gun. And then, one by one, there seemed to be fewer battles, fewer victories, fewer people and less fun, and *La Loba* decided to become Gladys again. So she made her last skirmish into Valera, and stole a knitted two-piece in lightweight cotton and a pair of stockings and some lace-up shoes. She swapped identity cards and papers with a German girl called Gladys Lorenz student, who had come to join the guerrillas; as Gladys Lorenz she set sail for Hamburg and from Hamburg took the train to Berlin.

That was where Alec came in. Alec was a financial adviser for Shell. He was thirty-eight, and at five foot ten he didn't tower too hopelessly over her. He had a good job and a small private income and he was the kindest man she had ever met. Alec was totally incompetent in the everyday running of his life, and he seemed to find, in Gladys, the perfect bride. However much his work took him away from Berlin, he would return, again and again, to the spotless flat on the Tempelhofer Ufer where Gladys lived. Within the year, they were married. They never agreed about anything, except the garden, and, either despite or maybe because of this, they were very happy together.

From Liverpool Street Gladys took the tube to Piccadilly and walked down to Fortnum's to meet Alec for tea. England was to play Scotland at

Wembley, and the crowds in the street were unusually large. Gladys became quite anonymous in a crowd. She was only someone to be reckoned with one to one. At tea she ate three different kinds of cake and then felt too full to talk.

"You'll get fat," Alec told her.

But she was already just that little bit too much overweight to be able to do anything about it without a great deal of effort, so she didn't bother. Besides which, she felt a sense of heightened excitement at the thought of returning to Caracas after so many years, even if it was only to be for the three days of their trip, and she was especially pleased at the thought of closing an option while she was there. It made her hungry.

Gladys looked out across the neighboring tables and fixed her stare on a woman with a pink floppy hat and far too much lipstick who was pinching a thin nervous boy while he ate, threatening him under her breath through clenched teeth. Gladys felt her anger rise. Alec paid and got up to go.

"We're late," he said, apologetically

Gladys gathered her bags together and followed him to the door. As she passed the pink hat, she paused to say:

"If you pinch that child again, I shall report you."

"What a woman!" Alec said with disgust as he held open the swing doors.

At Heathrow, their luggage was waiting for them. Gladys always sent it on a few hours ahead. Alec took a vast number of belongings with him wherever he went, and the more he traveled the more he seemed to want to have what was most precious near him. In this he had grown decidedly more neurotic since Sally's accident, taking endless pieces of stone and china, and great chunks of the library, packed in layers of wool and tissue. He had never been so close to Gladys as he was now, in gratitude for her efficiency. He liked her to travel with him wherever he went. Just being near to her calmed his nerves.

Gladys found flying very conducive to thought. She unclipped her seat-belt and lay back, remembering, as she did every day of her life, the accident of eight years ago. She remembered how the car had careered through their village at fifty miles an hour, and how Sally, on the pavement on her bicycle had seen it and stopped, and how even so it had swerved into her and thrown her back into their own garden like a clot - of compost. Further on, the car had stopped and a woman driver had staggered out. Not hurt, but drunk, so drunk she could hardly stand, and she had come and breathed whisky over the hedge. She had come crying for forgiveness.

Gladys remembered the long vigils at the National Hospital, four months of purgatory on the danger list, and then the long years without any hope. She remembered the trial, and the nine-month sentence and the warning. And she remembered how the woman had wept in court, and the judge had suspended the sentence, "because," he said, "the remorse was punishment enough." He had thanked God that Sally was still alive. But Sally was brain-dead, and only seven, and nearly as tall as Gladys even then, and she would lie for seven years like a dead heron around her mother's throat. Alec had aged and become more obsessive, carting his hobbies from port to port with him, while Gladys planned her revenge.

Gladys waited a year before she took action, and when the time came she took great pains to make the murder look like suicide. She was surprised to find, after ten years of coffee mornings and tombola, with what ease she could still kill. She was even more surprised to discover that beyond the vengeance, the real pleasure had come in the challenge and the act itself. She returned to her garden with her appetite for killing whetted as never before.

Four days later, she read an advertisement in one of the Sunday papers: "Palm Beach sponsor seeks lady gardeners for unusual work. Applicants must not be squeamish about killing slugs," and then there was an address in Percy Street. It was the bit about the slugs that really interested Gladys. It gave her an inkling of what they were after. But it wasn't until the interview that she fully realized what the job was to be. She was interviewed by a tall American woman called Cynthia who introduced herself as being "into pest control." She claimed to be compiling a paper on women's attitudes to extermination techniques, but gradually, during the course of that first interview, and then subsequent ones, she explained her true predicament.

"I work for these two very nice old ladies in Palm Beach," Cynthia had said, "but they have a problem."

Gladys had decided to say as little as possible until she learnt more where she stood.

"They're not happy with the way things happen," Cynthia had explained. "They think the world is losing its balance.

"They like to think of themselves as owning a garden," Cynthia continued, "and they would like to do a bit of weeding, just routine pest control."

Gladys listened, delighted by what she heard.

"I did a little research on you, Mrs. . . ."

"Gladys," Gladys interrupted.

"Gladys," Cynthia repeated in her deep, soothing psychiatrist's voice. "And I know about your little girl. Now I believe that women have a great role to play in life, and I believe that a capable woman is the most capable being there is, but sometimes," she paused, lowering her eyes with almost religious dismay, "they get away with murder."

Gladys nodded, and Cynthia concluded where she had begun, "Back in Palm Beach, they don't like it. Now I've done some recruiting in New York, and I've found myself a great secretary, but I can't find the women who can get out there and actually kill the slugs."

"I think you need me," Gladys told her.

Cynthia eyed her carefully. She decided that Gladys had hidden qualities.

"Tell me about yourself," Cynthia suggested, and Gladys unfolded a little of her past.

Ten days later she had got the job, but she insisted on one condition, that she was to be the only person to deal with the slugs.

"Well, I was really envisaging five or six," Cynthia told her.

"Then I'll work six times as hard," Gladys said firmly. And she had, for six years, traveling under Alec's wing, she worked her way through the old ladies' lists, eliminating the women who had "got away with murder." Some of them were public figures, most of them were not, but they had all caused suffering and been left untouched by the law. When Gladys had asked, "Why only women?" Cynthia had replied, with her favorite opening phrase:

"Research has shown, that nobody keeps the balance where women are concerned, so we're just going where we are needed."

The plane was landing at Madrid, just a transit-lounge affair before the long leg to Caracas. Gladys took her book and opened it somewhere in the middle. It was her flight book, Thackeray this time, read in bouts and snatches between take-offs and sleeping, worn open on her knees more as a mask to ward off conversation than for anything else. Not that Alec ever talked much when they were traveling. He was always mildly airsick and always worried that he might get worse, so he monitored his stomach, and kept himself to himself.

Gladys was thinking about the two old ladies, sitting out on their piazza in Palm Beach, Florida, or taking coffee in the Waldorf Astoria in New York, or visiting their daughters in East Hampton. One of them, Mildred, was wheelchair-bound, and propelled by a private nurse; Lilian, the other, was very deaf, and they were both watched over by a private army. They were the widows of oil magnates and they had spent their married lives listening to the latest figures in the Dow-Jones index.

Both the old ladies were immensely bored and immensely rich, and as they had come to know each other better, over the years, Gladys could see how they had gradually come to take the law into their own hands. She could imagine their satisfaction in feeling that they were coming down like the wrath of God through the instrument of herself, their lady gardener. The only drawback in the whole set-up was their zeal. Their lists were getting longer and longer, and Cynthia had had to extend her capacity to that of moderator, and censor their slugs. Mixed in with the criminals were the names of those who had done nothing worse than criticize Mildred's make-up, or whisper words that Lilian could not hear. The old ladies were growing vicious.

Gladys always did things herself anyway. It was just the way she was. She always went round the garden after Simpson, her gardener, had finished, redoing little jobs to her own satisfaction. And she always checked out the women she was to get close to; before she killed them, she made sure that they really had done what they were accused of doing. She allowed no extenuating circumstances. She didn't want to know why the woman who ran her Sally down was drunk. For Gladys, carelessness and thoughtlessness were failures, and failure was guilt. It was not her job to be fair, merely to restore a sense of balance. She would have had no more thought of putting the slugs on her herbaceous border on trial before baiting them than she would have had of trying the slugs on her lists. They were eating her delphiniums, and they had to go.

Gladys slept a little on the plane, and woke up feeling disheveled and out of sorts. She pulled her skirt straight, and made her way to the bathroom at the back of the cabin. In her toilet-bag she had a miniature tooth-mug which she filled with tap-water, disregarding the usual warnings about its undrinkable quality. She carefully prepared herself a glass of liver salts, drinking them while they were still fizzy. Gladys's stomach and liver could have been galvanized they were so strong, but she liked the taste of the salts, and always carried a tin of them in her handbag, together with an enormous jar of aspirin, her make-up, her flight book, and a minute container of Mace nerve gas made to look just like a lipstick. The Mace often came in very useful. Cynthia would probably have to get her another container after this trip, she thought.

Gladys hadn't followed an option for five and a half weeks, and it made her rather edgy. The killing had come to be what drink or cigarettes were to her friends, halfway between a pleasure and an addiction. Every three months a new list would be made up and handed to her by Cynthia, who in turn would have liaised and haggled with the old ladies to come to the names that stood. Gladys would take the whole list, like so many options, picking out slugs as she saw them and not as they wanted them. The old ladies specifically didn't want publicity, they just wanted success. Gladys had a way of making most of the deaths look like suicide, and a way of waiting. The woman she was after in Caracas had been on one of her lists for four years.

Cynthia had a fair-sized file on her. She was called Maria Perez, she was twenty-nine, beautiful, rich and spoiled. Four years ago she had been the mistress of the registrar of a children's clinic. One night when he was on duty, he had left the building to have dinner with Maria Perez, leaving her telephone number in case of an emergency. Before driving to her house in an elegant suburb of Caracas known as Valle Arriba, he had locked the children into their wards. During his absence, a fire had broken out at the clinic, and no one had been able to reach him. The evidence at the inquest had caused a scandal.

Maria Perez took the three telephone calls herself that came from the clinic, and each time she denied that the registrar was in her house.

"But there is no one in charge here," a distraught nurse had told her.

"Then you be in charge," Maria Perez had said, and hung up.

Later, the same nurse had tried again.

"The firemen haven't come, and we can't unlock the doors to get the children out."

"It's none of my business," Maria Perez had told her, "let them climb out of the windows."

But the windows were barred, and before any firemen could break through the doors and fumes, sixteen children died of asphyxiation. Two months later, the registrar shot himself, the enquiry was closed, and Maria Perez walked away from the courtroom smiling.

Gladys had a cutting from a recent society magazine. It read: "A Day in the Life of Maria Perez. Every morning, at half past ten, Maria takes her adorable chihuahua, Fifi, for a walk by her fabulous mansion in Valle Arriba . . ." That was really all Gladys needed to know. This time it would be so easy that she would have qualms about keeping her pay. Whenever this happened, she donated her wages to The Latin People's Trust for Endangered Species, a charity that was dear to her heart.

Gladys rubbed some complementary almond cream into her face and then looked at herself in the mirror. She knew that she wasn't pretty, but nobody could say that she didn't have a pleasant face. And but for Sally, she reflected, no one would say that she didn't have a pleasant life, lots of free travel and a lovely husband. The "Fasten your seat belt" sign came up, and Gladys swung her way back to her seat, feeling lucky and smiling: even her job, that was so much a part of her, didn't take her time away from Alec or the garden, or her visits to Sally or her entertaining.

The plane landed on its nose, as they so often do in South America, and then bumped and thumped to a standstill with an alarming chorus of shrieks and cries from the passengers and crew.

"Thank God it's stopped," Alec said, after they had screeched to a halt. "Are you all right, poppet?"

"Yes, I'm fine, thanks. How about you?"

"Well, I'm all right, but I'm damn glad I didn't bring any of my Tiffany this time."

Later he asked, "Where are we staying?"

"At a place called the Tamanaco. It looked a bit like something out of *Star Wars* on the brochure, but I think it'll be quite fun.

"By the way," she added, casually, "I think I'll do a bit of shopping tomorrow morning."

Alec squeezed her hand, "You and your shopping," he said indulgently, "wherever we go, you've always got a bit of shopping to do."

There was a hired car waiting for them at the desk, and they had a drive of over fifty kilometers from the airport at Maiquetía to the city itself. Gladys always did the driving, and they lurched from side to side of their hired Mustang all along the coast road, swerving and swingtailing through the thick traffic to the hotel. Alec arrived looking rather ashen, his knuckles aching from gripping the seat.

"Are you all right, darling?" Gladys asked him as she helped him from the car.

"Yes," he said, shakily, "I must say, I was rather worried about how you'd manage with those maniacs, but in the end, I was more scared about falling over the cliff."

"I wouldn't let anything happen to you, Alec," Gladys said reassuringly. "Anyway, I'm starving."

Gladys found dinner and all its trappings one of her great pleasures in life. She had second and third helpings of the guasacaca and then ploughed her way through the following courses, ending up with a sugary fudge so sweet it cloyed.

Alec said, "I don't know how you can eat that muck."

"It's rather nice, actually," Gladys told him.

He pulled a face.

"Well, you eat snails," she said.

"But I like snails," he protested.

Gladys looked at him sadly.

"And anyway," he added hastily, "I don't eat them now that we're always together."

But Gladys had lost the last of her appetite, and was lost in thought. She had an ampule of coramine in her handbag, which was in itself a cardio-accelerator, but she had shaken up a little cocktail with a couple of other drugs, and the mixture was very nasty. As an intramuscular injection, it would work in a matter of seconds. Alec was looking tired, so they went to bed early.

Next morning, Gladys took the hired Mustang from the hotel car park, and picked her way in and out of the traffic jams to Valle Arriba, where the millionaires' mansions and the golf-course made a pleasant change from the chaos of the city below them. It was ten-fifteen when she parked the car. She had taken great pains with her dress that morning, and she was looking Caraqueñan smart. In a city obsessed with fashion, she knew that the well-dressed were a class apart. Two cars raced past her, chasing each other down the precarious slope. She ignored them, and prepared a disposable hypodermic syringe with 3 c.c. of her mixture, It was ten-twenty-two. She put the Cellophane wrapper in her pocket, together with the needle cover, then she put her gloves on, and waited. At ten-thirty she was still waiting, and she was still waiting at ten-forty.

It was only at ten-fifty-two that she heard the click of a woman's heels coming down the hill, strained forward. Gladys was two hundred and fifty yards from the entrance to Maria Perez's home, waiting behind a crag of rock that gave directly on to the road. The first thing to come into her field of vision was a beige chihuahua. Gladys was crouching at the dog's level, and she gave it no more than a scent of Mace. The dog passed out. Behind it came Maria Perez, distraught at her pet's collapse. Gladys had moved back, and now she moved forward.

"Permiso," she said, pushing forward, "I am a vet," and, as she spoke, she plunged her unsheathed needle through the turquoise silk of Maria

Perez's flying suit. Then she stepped back again, bent the needle double, put it in her pocket and walked back to her car. It was ten-fifty-five and Gladys was at the wheel of the Mustang, cruising down past the CADA supermarket, and back to the city itself.

By lunch-time, laden with shopping, Gladys was feeling ready for food. She had decided to eat in a German tea shop known as El Chicken, which was an abbreviation for El Chicken Bar. It had once been a gathering-place for intellectuals, poets, actors, idealists and hangers-on. Now, as she looked around her, she saw no one she knew or even vaguely recognized. But the cakes were still as good, and on the pavement, stretching out from either side of the awnings, the wide avenue of Sabana Grande ranged from official splendor at one end to the heart of gangland crime at the other.

Gladys remembered the gangland Caracas, sewn up into compartments on the four corners of the adjoining streets that met like the tines of a fork at the junction below her. They called the top corner the Bank of Switzerland. Finance, drugs, prostitution and homosexuals each had their own niche. But Gladys's tourist instincts were at a low par. She would rather get back to Alec, who might have finished his meeting and be missing her.

She drove back to the Tamanaco Hotel, to find Alec lying down and upset about something.

"What's up?" she asked him, dropping her shopping at the door of their room.

"I'm terribly sorry, poppet," he said, "something has just cropped up, and I'm going to have to go to a summit in Egypt."

"You poor thing."

"Could you bear to come too?" he asked pathetically, "At such short notice?"

"Of course I will, Alec, you know I always come with you now."

"Egypt is such a ghastly place to do business in, all flies and dark glasses. There will be one day in London between flights, but we may as well stay up."

"I think I'll nip down and see Sally, actually, I don't like to leave her too long," Gladys said.

Back in Norfolk, at the clinic, Gladys sat with her hand on the counterpane of her daughter's bed. In her bag she had a copy of *El Nacional*, which she had bought in the foyer of the Tamanaco on her way out. On the middle pages the obituaries hung, draped in black trails of paper ribbon. Four of them were given over to Maria Perez, "who had died suddenly of a coronary near her home in Valle Arriba". She had been a society figure, a member of what they called "el high." The details were all there. Gladys folded up the newspaper and tucked it into her bag, where it lay beside the file on her next option, a middle-aged American woman who lived on a top-security ranch in Wyoming. She had operated for fifteen years what was coming to be the largest heroin ring in the Western USA. "Research had shown" that she would be in Cairo, supervising the purity of her wares. If only, Gladys thought, this new option had dedicated herself to cancer research with the same fervor that she gave to narcotics, she could probably have found a cure by now. Cynthia had said, "You can't miss her, she has a lavender rinse and fly-away glasses," and Gladys was cheered by these details.

She wished that she had time to go back and see the house. At least she could look forward to it later, tea in the red room, and a walk in the garden. Sally hadn't moved, wouldn't and never could. But Gladys smiled at her. She stayed for half an hour, talking to herself, and then she rose to go. She was wearing the new hat she had bought in Caracas, but she rammed it into her shopping bag before she left. All the way down to the car park she could see the chewed leaves of the flowers. According to Simpson, it was a bad year for slugs.

So, Some Tempestuous Morn

BARBARA PYM

A WET MORNING, thought Anthea sadly, listening to the rain which did not seem to go with the brilliant bird chorus. A wet morning in North Oxford, with its laburnums and flowering shrubs and strange architecture and her great-aunt's gloomy, solidly furnished house . . . If she had opened her eyes for a moment, Anthea closed them again; she was not quite ready to face life yet. People did not always realize that even at nineteen one sometimes had to make an effort.

Anthea was a pretty, gentle-looking girl and her parents were abroad. "My nephew had a very high position in the Colonial Service and is doing brilliantly—how often had she heard Aunt Maude make that remark to the dull people who came to the house. Anthea herself was vaguely "studying English Literature." She was not clever enough to go to one of the women's colleges, but there seemed no harm in her going to a few lectures chosen by her aunt or in her meeting the carefully selected young men, so "suitable" and usually so uninteresting, who were invited to the Sunday afternoon tea parties. Perhaps their grandmothers had known Aunt Maude as a girl, or there was some ecclesiastical connection— Canon Bogle's son, Archdeacon Troup's nephew, or even some distant link with a Bishop or titled person. All were carefully chosen and existed because of their impeccable connections rather than in their own right.

Anthea had never had a young man of her own; sometimes she admired particular undergraduates from a distance, but they never seemed to notice her and they never turned out to be the kind her aunt would ask to tea on Sundays. These might dart frightened glances in her direction through the forests of tables and china ornaments, but Anthea, in her perverseness, felt that she would only despise them more if they appeared to be attracted to her. It was the unattainable ones she pined for—

> The desire of the moth for the star,
> Of the night for the morrow,
> The devotion to something afar
> From the sphere of our sorrow . . .

She did not perhaps appreciate what a comfort English Literature was to her in her lonely state. She saw herself, three months from her twentieth birthday, growing to be like Miss Morrow, her aunt's companion, dim and not very well dressed; the kind of person who had no life of her own and who, in an hour or two, would be tapping at her door to tell her it was time to get up.

Waking at dawn, Miss Morrow heard the rain drumming on the laurels below her window, and no doubt dripping through the branches of the monkey-puzzle too, she thought, imagining it there in the half-light, coming too close to the window.

"This is a *front* bedroom." Miss Doggett had so often reminded her. "It is really one of the best rooms in the house. Not many companions would be given such a room. I happen to know that Lady Victoria Nollard's companion sleeps in an attic on the same floor as the servants."

"She is lucky to have servants as well as a companion," Miss Morrow had said, making one of those unfortunate rejoinders which were so unexpected from one of her meek appearance.

"Lady Victoria Nollard is an Earl's daughter," had been Miss Doggett's simple but magnificent reply.

After five years Miss Morrow had grown used to the room and even liked it. She lay now, listening to the rain, looking at her "things," those objects that make one room a home, without really noticing them. She was so familiar with the faded photographs of her parents—the inevitable clergyman and dim-looking Edwardian lady—the school group, the little souvenirs from a holiday on the Italian Riviera or in the Highlands of Scotland, the prize set of Jane Austen's novels, and the Penguins with their orange covers looking a little garish next to the leather-bound poems of Matthew Arnold.

Matthew Arnold, ah yes, he would be able to describe this morning . . . Miss Morrow raised herself tip on one elbow, imagining the drenched garden at the back of the house.

So, some tempestuous morn in early June,
When the years primal burst of bloom is o'er,
Before the roses and the longest day—
When garden-walks and all the grassy floor
With blossoms red and white of fallen May
And chestnut flowers are strewn . . .

All that heavy rain in the night would have spoilt the flowers she was to pick for decorating the church this morning. She felt almost glad and lay smiling in bed, thinking of the vicar's wife in her silly raffia-embroidered hat and listening to the rain falling among the leaves. So, some tempestuous morn, indeed!

In an hour it was time to get up. Miss Morrow went to the window and, with a daring gesture, Flung aside the net curtain that screened her doings from prying eyes. Opposite, through the dark spiky branches of the monkey-puzzle it was possible to catch a glimpse of the theological college with its architectural extravagances, colored brickwork, pointed Gothic windows and little towers. And inside—Miss Morrow's vivid imagination went rushing boldly in—were the theological students in their narrow cell-like rooms, all behaving in a devout and suitable manner Or indeed, it is to be hoped that they are behaving in such a manner, she said to herself. There was certainly no sign of life now, but after a moment or two a figure on a bicycle appeared in the road and dismounted at the gate of the college. It was a strikingly handsome clergyman, not very young, but certainly not old, perhaps about Miss Morrow's own age which was the late thirties and really quite the prime for a man, though it could be many things for a woman and not all of them quite the prime.

As he stopped to open the gate and push his bicycle in, something must have made him turn and glance at the house opposite and upwards at the figure of Miss Morrow in the window

Going to have breakfast with the principal, she thought. A hearty manly breakfast of mutton chops and beer . . . no, hardly that, manly Oxford breakfasts were not what they were and perhaps men were not either. Tea and cornflakes, more likely . . .

The rain had stopped now and the sun was shining brightly. A sudden impulse made Miss Morrow wave her hand at the clergyman, He raised his hat in reply and smiled; then he was gone through the gate, wheeling his bicycle round the side to the little Gothic bicycle-shed.

Miss Morrow laughed to herself and turned away from the window.

Whatever could she have been thinking of to wave to him like that? Still, no doubt lie had thought it was "one of the servants" and in any case he was probably accustomed to gestures of this kind as a rightful tribute to his good looks. She must hurry down now and help Maggie with the breakfast and call Anthea on the way.

Breakfast was already on the table when Anthea came down. Miss Doggett was pouring out the coffee, the sun was shining and through the french windows the lawn and the drenched herbaceous border could be seen.

"Well, Miss Morrow, I'm afraid the flowers are quite spoilt," said Miss Doggett, almost with satisfaction. "You will find it difficult to pick anything for the decorating. The peonies are all beaten down by the rain."

"Yes, ravaged, aren't they." Miss Morrow glanced indifferently towards the window. "Ravaged, ravished, one might almost say."

"*Ravished?*" repeated Miss Doggett, her voice puzzled as if there was something not quite right about the word, though she was unable to say exactly what.

"Ravished, yes," repeated Miss Morrow firmly.

Anthea giggled.

"Really, Miss Morrow, I hardly think . . ." Miss Doggett's tone was pained but she did not want to have to put what she felt into words. Indeed, she hardly knew how to. The unsuitability . . . and Miss Morrow often had these little lapses. Quite well bred, Archdeacon Troup had given a reference, most glowing, really. It wasn't that she was unsatisfactory, exactly; there was nothing one could put one's finger on. It was these remarks she let fall, these unsuitabilities. Were they perhaps clues to what went on in her thoughts, her mind? Miss Doggett pursed her lips and fingered one of the gold chains which hung on the bosom of her purple dress.

"Anthea, you are late this morning." Her tone was sharp. It was a relief to turn from the darkness of her companion's mind to her niece's unpunctuality. "And what are you going to do this morning? I expect they will want some help with the decorating, you might go along with Miss Morrow. I shall want some cakes from Boffin's, too. Quite a number of people will be coming to tea tomorrow." She smiled, unable to stop herself at the thought of the Honorable Basil Fordyce, a Peer's son and Bishop's nephew, taking tea in her drawing room. She had invited this particular young man on several previous occasions, but his charming replies had always put her off, regretting so much that he had another engagement, nothing would have delighted him more than to take tea with Miss Doggett. And tomorrow, feeling perhaps that he might as well get it over, he was really coming. She did hope that he and Anthea would take to each other, for, to give Miss Doggett her due, she was as anxious as her niece that love should enter her life, though, of course, she would not have put it quite like that. Anthea would marry, naturally, but it must be a suitable marriage. There had already been one or two disappointments, not only in Anthea's failure to impress the young men, but in the young men themselves. Canon Bogle's son had turned out to be a grubby young man in corduroy trousers; Lady Dancy's nephew was too small and apparently interested in nothing but archaeology. That had been a great disappointment; even Miss Doggett could see that there was little future in dry bones and fragments of pottery.

Miss Doggett rose from the table.

"Man goeth forth to his work and to his labor, until the evening," thought Miss Morrow, going up to help Maggie with the beds. She supposed she would have to go into the garden and pick some flowers for the church and then stand by while the vicar's wife arranged them more tastelessly than one would have thought possible.

"I will go for the cakes, Aunt Maude," said Anthea. It was a lovely morning now and she could take a long time over her errand and perhaps walk somewhere by the river, away from the depressing presence of her aunt and her companion. Perhaps it would be better to buy the cakes afterwards; she would not want to carry them into Christchurch meadows.

It was a pity she had not yet reached Matthew Arnold in her studies of English Literature for she would have found much in his poetry to enhance her enjoyment of the beautiful morning and the Oxford scene, but as it was she wandered by the river in a pleasant state of melancholy, wondering if she would have a romantic encounter this morning.

She had been walking for some time before she came upon him, the young man reclining in a punt with a book which he did not appear to be reading. He was anchored round a bend in the river, half hidden by the drooping branches of a willow, so that she came upon him suddenly and was so startled that she stopped involuntarily, for he was—and this seemed right and inevitable on such a morning—one of those she had admired from afar at Professor Lyly's lectures. She must have looked surprised, perhaps she even exclaimed, for he looked up as she approached and smiled.

"An encounter," he said. "What could be more suitable on a June morning. Penelope?"

"My name isn't Penelope," she said stupidly. "And you don't know me anyway, so how could you know my name?"

"But I do know you—sitting in a corner at old Lyly's lectures taking down every platitude that falls from his lips and never raising your eyes from your notebook."

"I don't remember seeing you there," she lied, but their glance had never met. "And what's the use of going to lectures if you don't take notes?" He never did, she had seen him just sitting, looking bored and sometimes drawing on a sheet of paper.

"Of course you are not an undergraduette," he pronounced the word distastefully, "so it may be that you take the study of English Literature seriously. I imagine you living in some Gothic house in North Oxford, a fastness with horrid towers and dark trees, so much more inaccessible than a women's college and so much more intriguing."

She smiled faintly. He was making fun of her, she knew, but how was she expected to respond? She had certainly not imagined their first meeting like this. "I do live in North Oxford." she ventured, "and in a house rather like that, I suppose."

"Why don't you come and sit down and tell me about it?" He held out his hand and she stepped on to the green velvet cushions in the bottom of the punt.

Once there she felt stupid and awkward. Whatever would Aunt Maude say? Why, this young man had just "picked her lip"; she could imagine her aunt's tone and pursed lips as she pronounced the words; it was most unsuitable.

'Tell me about your Gothic house," he said. "Do you live with your parents?"

"No, my parents are abroad. I live with my great-aunt."

"Does she have Sunday afternoon tea parties?"

Why, yes. How did you know?"

"All respectable North Oxford residents do. I have made a study of their habits. I really think I shall have to do some practical field-work and get myself invited to one."

"Oh, dear," Anthea stood up suddenly. "I've got to buy cakes for tomorrow—I'd quite forgotten."

"Surely the guests won't notice what they eat if you are there?"

"I wish you wouldn't say things like that. You're only making fun of me."

"My dear, I assure you I'm not," he said, really looking quite serious. "What is the name or number of your great-aunt's house?"

"It's called Leamington Lodge. There's a monkey-puzzle in the front garden. It's opposite a theological college."

"Perhaps we shall meet again." he said gaily. "You never know." And taking her hand he kissed it lightly. "Now run and buy your cakes."

Anthea hurried away in a turmoil of emotion. It was only when she had got into Boffin's and noticed that the best cakes were gone that she realized that she did not know his name nor he hers and that he had made no serious suggestion about meeting her again. For a moment she felt a little cast down, but she cheered herself up by remembering the lectures. Now perhaps they could smile at each other and speak. He might even sit by her. She did not know how she was going to get through the days until the next lecture. Oh, she thought, carelessly choosing a dozen of any old cakes, it was fine to be young and in love on a fine June morning—not like poor Miss Morrow, grey and in her thirties and decorating the church with the vicar's wife and all the other good ladies who were so patronizing to her.

The peonies, the ravished peonies, thought Miss Morrow, padding about among the wet plants in her goloshes. When she touched one all the petals fell off, but there were other flowers that would do quite well. She cut some syringa and irises. Purple, that was a Lenten color, not really right for Whitsuntide. Still, they were lucky to get anything.

She hurried to the church and into the porch. The mumbling of women's voices with one or two raised in command told her that she was late. The sun was shining brilliantly now and the church seemed all the darker by contrast. The vicar's wife had her back turned as Miss Morrow entered and nobody noticed her come in. On a sudden impulse she laid the flowers down in a corner with the others already there, and tiptoed away. She did not feel like decorating this morning, handing bits of greenery to the vicar's wife up in the pulpit or filling jam jars with water.

She felt very free when she got outside the church—a whole hour of her own, what should she do with it? Morning coffee first, that sinful habit denounced by Miss Doggett as timewasting and self-indulgent. "When one has had a good breakfast and is going to have a good luncheon it is quite unnecessary to eat or drink between meals." Where should she go to waste time and be self-indulgent? Obviously not to one of the places where she might meet one of Miss Doggett's less strong-minded friends. She would go to the fashionable undergraduate haunt of the moment, the café of a large shop, where up to now she had only peered from the cake department into the smoke-laden and vice-infested air. She found a table on the outside edge of the room where she could observe and remain inconspicuous, a dim figure on the fringe of the University melting away into North Oxford, she felt. It was quite alarming the decadence there must be among our youth today, she thought with amusement, noticing how full the tables were. Time-wasting and self-indulgent . . . still, perhaps they had not all had good breakfasts or could not so sure of adequate luncheons. Well, it was not really so very interesting she decided, as she drank her coffee and ate a large sickly cake, and the coffee was not so good as that made by Miss Latimer and Miss Forge, two gentlewomen who ran a dull teashop frequented by Miss Doggett's circle. Still, it was something to have been here, an experience. There would be time to walk through the shop before she need return to Leamington Lodge.

It was here that she really came to grief, fingering a rail of printed summer dresses in gay colors and patterns. Perhaps it was her contact with decadence that made her linger and pick out a dress patterned with green leaves. The girl who helped her to try it on was so kind and encouraging. She said it suited her and it was such a nice day after all that rain early this morning it really made you feel like buying a new dress.

Luncheon was rather an odd meal. Nobody except Miss Doggett seemed to be hungry. Anthea looked quite distracted, but Miss Doggett attributed her strange manner and lack of appetite to the fact that she had given her a severe talking to for having bought such a poor selection of cakes.

"Bishop Fordyce's nephew—he's Lady Mortlake's son, you know—and the new chaplain of Randolph College are coming," she wailed.

"I particularly wanted them to have a nice tea."

"Perhaps clergymen don't notice what they eat," said Miss Morrow demurely. "One feels that they might not."

"And you were a very long time decorating the church this morning, Miss Morrow," said Miss Doggett, turning on her. "I expected you back by half past eleven. Were there a great many flowers to arrange or were there fewer helpers than usual?"

"Oh, there were fewer helpers," said Miss Morrow. "Certainly one less than usual."

Miss Doggett rose from the table. "Well, we shall see tomorrow what the church looks like," she said. "I hope our flowers are in a good position."

"Irises on the pulpit!" said Miss Doggett at luncheon the next day. "Most unsuitable. The color is quite wrong for Whitsuntide. I thought the altar vases were very badly arranged . . . did you do them, Miss Morrow?"

"Oh, no, I did nothing that could be seen," said Miss Morrow quickly.

It was a brilliantly hot day and she had decided to wear her new dress for the tea party.

"We might have tea in the garden, perhaps?" suggested Anthea. "It's such a lovely day." If only she could slip away somewhere by herself and think about *him*, instead of having to sit and make conversation with dull young men in a stuffy North Oxford drawing room.

"Tea in the garden? Oh. no, I'm afraid I should find the sun too much," said Miss Doggett. "Besides, people are not at their best in the open air. Conversation is so difficult and things blow away."

"Wasps get in the food," murmured Miss Morrow

So they sat waiting in the drawing room which faced north and whose windows were obscured by the bottom half of the monkey-puzzle.

The first arrivals were two shy young men who came together. It seemed that they had met on the doorstep and were giving each other mutual support. One of them carried an umbrella which he seemed unwilling to relinquish.

"Ah. Mr. Burden and Mr. Monksmoor," said Miss Doggett, "I knew your aunts. Wouldn't you like to leave that umbrella in the hall? It will be quite safe."

"I have a feeling it is going to thunder," said one of the young men, addressing Anthea in a loud, nervous voice.

But she could not answer him, for at that moment a third guest was announced, the Bishop's nephew and Peer's son, and it was the young man she had met on the river yesterday morning.

"Ah, Mr. Fordyce, at last!" There was a real welcome in Miss Doggett's tone. "I am so much looking forward to having a long talk about your uncle."

So he was the Bishop's nephew, Aunt Maude's young man, not hers. It was a sickening disappointment Anthea could hardly bear to look at him.

"Please try to keep the conversation away from my dear uncle," he whispered.

"Why? It will at least be something to talk about," said Anthea indifferently.

"But he isn't my uncle and I'm not Basil Fordyce. I wanted to find a way of seeing you again and I knew Basil had an invitation to take tea in North Oxford this weekend, so I changed places with him."

Anthea smiled. "But we could have met some other way—at the lectures or in the town. You didn't have to come here."

"No, but I wanted to be accepted by your aunt." He gave her a bright-eyed wicked look that seemed to shut them off from the rest of the room.

"Where is Miss Morrow?" asked Miss Doggett rather sharply. "Here I

am, Miss Doggett" said Miss Morrow, coming in through the door in a
new dress patterned with leaves.

"Miss Morrow and I have been in the garden," said the handsome
clergyman with her. "I somehow missed the front door, and Miss Morrow
found me wandering in the laurels."

Missed the front door . . . wandering in the laurels . . . and Miss
Morrow in that gay unsuitable dress . . . Miss Doggett was bewildered.
She sank down into a chair. This was the new Chaplain of Randolph
College, a very good-looking man, perhaps a little free in his manner for
a clergyman. He and Miss Morrow were actually laughing together. She
was asking him if he had had a good breakfast, had there been mutton
chops and beer . . . what could she mean? Miss Doggett turned away in
despair. She would have a little chat with Mr. Fordyce about his uncle.

"Now, Mr. Fordyce," she began, "how is your uncle?"

"Which one?" he asked brightly.

"Why, Bishop Fordyce, of course."

"Oh, Miss Doggett, I've done a very wicked thing," he burst out.

"Come now, Mr. Fordyce," she had to smile indulgently, he was really
such a very good-looking young man with those brilliant hazel eyes, "I'm
sure you can't have done anything so very bad."

"Oh, but I have. I'm an impostor. I'm not Basil Fordyce at all. I'm
Simon Beddoes."

"Well, really, Mr. Beddoes . . ." Miss Doggett smiled again, but a little
absently. There was a connection somewhere and it was quite a good one,
though she could not remember for the moment exactly what it was.
Something political or diplomatic, she fancied . . . Bishop Fordyce had
not been much of a man really, rather a dull stick, she had never particularly cared for him.

"You see, I wanted to meet your niece, and," he added hastily, "I had
heard of your delightful tea parties."

"Oh, well, I suppose I do manage to collect an interesting circle of
people round me," said Miss Doggett, almost purring. "Do have another
cake, Mr. Beddoes. Now, Mr. Merriman," she turned to the handsome
clergyman, "I do hope my companion has not been boring you?"

"Oh, I am used to being bored by ladies," said Mr. Merriman lightly.
"There is nothing I enjoy more."

"You must see the garden before you go," said Miss Doggett, "though
I'm afraid it is not quite at its best now—that heavy storm yesterday
morning . . ." she paused. Yes, there had been something strange about
yesterday morning. "The peonies were very fine but the rain spoilt them.

They look quite . . ." what was the word Miss Morrow had used, something most unsuitable . . . "quite beaten down," she said rather loudly. "Mr. Beddoes, perhaps you would like to see the garden too? And Mr. Burden and Mr. Monksmoor. I should like to have a chat to you about your aunts. We met in Malvern in 1923."

She rose from her chair and the little procession wound its way through the furniture, out into the dining room and through the french windows on to the lawn.

After they had gone, Miss Morrow picked up a cake and devoured it in two bites Then she too went out through the french windows and followed them solemnly round the garden.

Green Thoughts

John Collier

Annihilating all that's made
To a green thought in a green shade.
—MARVELL

T HE ORCHID HAD BEEN sent among the effects of his friend, who had come by a lonely and mysterious death on the expedition. Or he had bought it among a miscellaneous lot, "unclassified," at the close of the auction. I forget which it was, but it was certainly one or the other of these. Moreover, even in its dry, brown, dormant root state, this orchid had a certain sinister quality; It looked, with its bunched and ragged projections, like a rigid yet a gripping hand, hideously gnarled, or a grotesquely whiskered, threatening face. Would you not have known what sort of an orchid it was?

Mr. Mannering did not know. He read nothing but catalogues and books on fertilizers. He unpacked the new acquisition with a solicitude absurd enough in any case toward any orchid, or primrose either, in the twentieth century, but idiotic, foolhardy, doom-eager, when extended to an orchid thus come by, in appearance thus. And in his traditional obtuseness he at once planted it in what he called the "Observation Ward," a hothouse built against the south wall of his dumpy red dwelling. Here he set always the most interesting additions to his collection, and especially weak and sickly plants, for there was a glass door in his study wall through which he could see into this hothouse, so that the weak and sickly plants could encounter no crisis without his immediate knowledge and his tender care.

This plant, however, proved hardy enough. At the ends of thick and stringy stalks it opened out bunches of darkly shining leaves, and soon it spread in every direction, usurping so much space that first one, then another, then all its neighbors had to be removed to a hothouse at the end of the garden. It was, Cousin Jane said, a regular hop-vine. At the ends of the stalks, just before the leaves began, were set groups of tendrils, which hung idly, serving no apparent purpose. Mr. Mannering thought that very probably these were vestigial organs; a heritage from some period when the plant had been a climber. But when were the vestigial tendrils of an ex-climber half or quarter so thick and strong?

After a long time sets of tiny buds appeared here and there among the extravagant foliage. Soon they opened into small flowers, miserable little things; they looked like flies' heads. One naturally expects a large, garish, sinister bloom, like a sea anemone, or a Chinese lantern, or a hippopotamus yawning, on any important orchid; and should it be an unclassified one as well, I think one has every right to insist on a sickly and overpowering scent into the bargain.

Mr. Mannering did not mind at all. Indeed, apart from his joy and happiness in being the discoverer and godfather of a new sort of orchid, he felt only a mild and scientific interest in the fact that the paltry blossoms were so very much like flies' heads. Could it be to attract other flies for food or as fertilizers? But then, why like their heads?

It was a few days later that Cousin Jane's cat disappeared. This was a great blow to Cousin Jane, but Mr. Mannering was not, in his heart of hearts, greatly sorry. He was not fond of the cat, for he could not open the smallest chink in a glass roof for ventilation but the creature would squeeze through somehow to enjoy the warmth, and in this way it had broken many a tender shoot. But before poor Cousin Jane had lamented two days something happened which so engrossed Mr. Mannering that he had no mind left at all with which to sympathize with her affliction, or to make at breakfast kind and hypocritical inquiries after the lost cat. A strange new bud appeared on the orchid. It was clearly evident that there would be two quite different sorts of bloom on this one plant, as sometimes happens in such fantastic corners of the vegetable world, and that the new flower would be very different in size and structure from the earlier ones. It grew bigger and bigger, till it was as big as one's fist.

And just then—it could never have been more inopportune—an affair of the most unpleasant, the most distressing nature summoned Mr. Mannering to town. It was his wretched nephew, in trouble again, and this time so deeply and so very disgracefully that it took all Mr. Mannering's generosity, and all his influence, too, to extricate the worthless young man. Indeed, as soon as he saw the state of affairs, he told the prodigal that this was the very last time he might expect assistance, that his vices and his ingratitude had long ago canceled all affection between them, and that for this last helping hand he was indebted only to his mother's memory, and to no faith on the part of his uncle either in his repentance or his reformation. He wrote, moreover, to Cousin Jane, to relieve his feelings, telling her of the whole business, and adding that the only thing left to do was to cut the young man off entirely.

When he got back to Torquay, Cousin Jane was nowhere to be found. The situation was extremely annoying. Their only servant was a cook who was very old and very stupid and very deaf. She suffered besides from an obsession, owing to the fact that for many years Mr. Mannering had had no conversation with her in which he had not included an impressive reminder that she must always, no matter what might happen, keep the big kitchen stove up to a certain pitch of activity. For this stove, besides supplying the house with hot water, heated the pipes in the "Observation Ward," to which the daily gardener who had charge of the other hot-houses had no access. By this time she had come to regard her duties as stoker as her chief *raison d'être*, and it was difficult to penetrate her deaf-ness with any question which her stupidity and her obsession did not somehow transmute into an inquiry after the stove, and this, of course, was especially the case when Mr. Mannering spoke to her. All he could disentangle was what she had volunteered on first seeing him, that his cousin had not been seen for three days, that she had left without saying a word. Mr. Mannering was perplexed and annoyed, but, being a man of method, he thought it best to postpone further inquiries until he had refreshed himself a little after his long and tiring journey. A full supply of energy was necessary to extract any information from the old cook; besides, there was probably a note somewhere. It was only natural that before he went to his room Mr. Mannering should peep into the hothouse, just to make sure that the wonderful orchid had come to no harm during the inconsiderate absence of Cousin Jane. As soon as he opened the door his eyes fell upon the bud; it had now changed in shape very considerably, and had increased in size to the bigness of a human head. It is no exag-geration to state that Mr. Mannering remained rooted to the spot, with his eyes fixed upon this wonderful bud, for fully five minutes.

But, you will ask, why did he not see her clothes on the floor? Well, as a matter of fact (it is a delicate point), there were no clothes on the floor. Cousin Jane, though of course she was entirely estimable in every respect, though she was well over forty, too, was given to the practice of the very latest ideas on the dual culture of the soul and body—Swedish, German, neo-Greek and all that. And the orchid house was the warmest place available. I must proceed with the order of events.

Mr. Mannering at length withdrew his eyes from this stupendous bud, and decided that he must devote his attention to the grey exigencies of everyday life. But although his body dutifully ascended the stairs, heart, mind, and soul all remained in adoration of the plant. Although he was philosophical to the point of insensibility over the miserable smallness of the earlier flowers, yet he was now as much gratified by the magnitude of the great new bud as you or I might be. Hence it was not unnatural that Mr. Mannering while, in his bath should be full of the most exalted visions of the blossoming of his heart's darling, his vegetable godchild. It would be by far the largest; known, complex as a dream, or dazzlingly simple. It would open like a dancer, or like the sun rising. Why, it might be opening at this very moment! Mr. Mannering could restrain himself no longer; he rose from the steamy water, and, wrapping his bathrobe about him, hurried down to the hothouse, scarcely staying to dry himself, though he was subject to colds.

The bud had not yet opened; it still reared its unbroken head among the glossy, fleshy foliage, and he now saw, what he had had no eyes for previously, how very exuberant that foliage had grown. Suddenly he realized with astonishment that this huge bud was not the one which had appeared before he went away. That one had been lower down on the plant. Where was it now, then? Why, this new thrust and spread of foliage concealed it from him. He walked across, and discovered it. It had opened into a bloom. And as he looked at this bloom his astonishment grew to stupefaction, one might say to petrification, for it is a fact that Mr. Mannering remained rooted to the spot, with his eyes fixed on the flower, for fully fifteen minutes. The flower was an exact replica of the head of Cousin Jane's lost cat. The similitude was so exact, so life-like, that Mr. Mannering's first movement, after the fifteen minutes, was to seize his bathrobe and draw it about him, for he was a modest man, and the cat, though bought for a Tom, had proved to be quite the reverse. I relate this to show how much character, spirit, *presence*—call it what you will—there was upon this floral cat's face. But although he made to seize his bathrobe, it was too late. He could not move. The new lusty foliage had closed in unperceived; the too lightly dismissed tendrils were everywhere upon him; he gave a few weak cries and sank to the ground, and there, as the Mr. Mannering of ordinary life, he passes out of this story.

Mr. Mannering sank into a coma, into an insensibility so deep that a black eternity passed before the first faint elements of his consciousness reassembled themselves in his brain. For of his brain was the center of a new bud being made. Indeed, it was two or three days before this at first almost shapeless and quite primitive lump of organic matter had become sufficiently mature to be called Mr. Mannering at all. These days, which passed quickly enough, in a certain mild, not unpleasant excitement, in the outer world, seemed to the dimly working mind within the bud to resume the whole history of the development of our species, in a great many epochal parts.

A process analogous to the mutations of the embryo was being enacted here. At last the entity which was thus being rushed down an absurdly foreshortened vista of the ages slowed up and came almost to a stop in the present.. It became recognizable. The Seven Ages of Mr. Mannering were presented, as it were, in a series of close-ups, as in an educational film; his consciousness settled and cleared. The bud was mature, ready to open. At this point, I believe, Mr. Mannering's state of mind was exactly that of a patient who, wakening from under an anesthetic, struggling up from vague dreams, asks plaintively, "Where am I?" Then the bud opened, and he knew.

There was the hothouse, but seen from an unfamiliar angle. There— through the glass door, was his study. There below him was the cat's head, and there—there beside him was Cousin Jane. He could not say a word, but then, neither could she. Perhaps it was as well. At the very least, he would have been forced to own that she had been in the right in an argument of long standing; she had always maintained that in the end no good would come of his preoccupation with "those unnatural flowers."

It must be admitted that Mr. Mannering was not at first greatly upset by this extraordinary upheaval in his daily life. This, I think, was because he was interested, not only in private and personal matters, but in the wider and more general, one might say the biological, aspects of his metamorphosis. For the rest, simply because he *was* now a vegetable, he responded with a vegetable reaction. The impossibility of locomotion, for example, did not trouble him in the least, or even the absence of body and limbs, any more than the cessation of that stream of rashers and tea, biscuits and glasses of milk, luncheon cutlets, and so forth, that had flowed in at his mouth for over fifty years, but which had now been reversed to a gentle, continuous, scarcely noticeable feeding from below. All the powerful influence of the physical upon the mental, therefore, inclined him to tranquillity. But the physical is not all. Although no longer a man, he was still Mr. Mannering. And from this anomaly, as soon as his scientific interest had subsided, issued a host of woes, mainly subjective in origin.

He was fretted, for instance, by the thought that he would now have no opportunity to name his orchid, or to write a paper upon it, and, still worse, there grew up in his mind the abominable conviction that, as soon as his plight was discovered, it was he who would be named and classified, and that he himself would be the subject of a paper, possibly even of comment and criticism in the lay press. Like all orchid collectors, he was excessively shy and sensitive, and in his present situation these qualities were very naturally exaggerated, so that the bare idea of such attentions brought him to the verge of wilting. Worse yet was the fear of being transplanted, thrust into some unfamiliar, draughty, probably public place. Being dug up! Ugh! A violent shudder pulsated through all the heavy foliage that sprang from Mr. Mannering's division of the plant. He became conscious of ghostly and remote sensations in the stem below, and in certain tufts of leaves that sprouted from it; they were somehow reminiscent of spine and heart and limbs. He felt quite a dryad.

In spite of all, however, the sunshine was very pleasant. The rich odor of hot, spicy earth filled the hothouse. From a special fixture on the hot-water pipes a little warm steam oozed into the air. Mr. Mannering began to abandon himself to a feeling of *laissez-aller*. Just then, up in a corner of the glass roof, at the ventilator, he heard a persistent buzzing. Soon the note changed from one of irritation to a more complacent sound; a bee had managed, after some difficulty, to find his way through one of the tiny chinks in the metal work. The visitor came drifting down and down through the still, green air, as if into some subaqueous world, and he came to rest on one of those petals which were Mr. Mannering's eyebrows. Thence he commenced to explore one feature after another, and at last he settled heavily on the lower lip, which drooped under his weight and allowed him to crawl right into Mr. Mannering's mouth. This was quite a considerable shock, of course, but on the whole the sensation was neither as alarming nor as unpleasant as might have been expected. "Indeed," thought the vegetable gentleman, "it seems quite agreeable."

But Mr. Mannering soon ceased the drowsy analysis of his sensations when he saw the departed bee, after one or two lazy circlings, settle directly upon the maiden lip of Cousin Jane. Ominous as lightning, a simple botanical principle flashed across the mind of her wretched relative. Cousin Jane was aware of it also, although, being the product of an earlier age, she might have remained still blessedly ignorant had not her cousin—vain, garrulous, proselytizing fool!—attempted for years past to interest her in the rudiments of botany. How the miserable man upbraided himself now! He saw two bunches of leaves just below the flower tremble and flutter, and rear themselves painfully upwards into the very likeness of two shocked and protesting hands. He saw the soft and orderly petals of his cousin's face ruffle and incarnadine with rage and embarrassment, then turn sickly as a gardenia with horror and dismay. But what was he to do? All the rectitude implanted by his careful training, all the chivalry proper to an orchid-collector, boiled and surged beneath a paralytically calm exterior. He positively travailed in the effort to activate the muscles of his face, to assume an expression of grief, manly contrition, helplessness in the face of fate, willingness to make honorable amends, all suffused with the light of a vague but solacing optimism; but it was in vain. When he had strained till his nerves seemed likely to tear under the tension, the only movement he could achieve was a trivial flutter of the left eyelid—worse than nothing.

This incident completely aroused Mr. Mannering from his vegetable lethargy. He rebelled against the limitations of the form into which he had thus been cast while subjectively he remained all too human. Was he not still at heart a man, with a man's hopes, ideals, aspirations—and capacity for suffering?

When dusk came, and the opulent and sinister shapes of the great plant dimmed to a suggestiveness more powerfully impressive than had been its bright noonday luxuriance, and the atmosphere of a tropical forest filled the orchid-house like an exile's dream or the nostalgia of the saxophone; when the cat's whiskers drooped, and even Cousin Jane's eyes slowly closed, the unhappy man remained wide awake, staring into the gathering darkness. Suddenly the light in the study was switched on. Two men entered the room. One of them was his lawyer, the other was his nephew.

"This is his study, as you know, of course," said the wicked nephew. "There's nothing here. I looked when I came over on Wednesday."

"I've sat in this room many an evening," said the lawyer with an expression of distaste. "I'd sit on this side of the fireplace and he on that. 'Mannering,' I'd think to myself, 'I wonder how you'll end up. Drugs? Sexual perversion? Or murder?' Well, maybe we'll soon know the answer. Until we do, I suppose you, as next of kin, had better take charge here."

Saying this, the lawyer turned, about to go, and Mr. Mannering saw a malicious smile overspread the young man's face. The uneasiness which had overcome him at first sight of his nephew was intensified to fear and trembling at the sight of this smile.

When he had shown the lawyer out, the nephew returned to the study and looked round him with lively and sinister satisfaction. Then he cut a caper on the hearth-rug. Mr. Mannering thought he had never seen anything so diabolical as this solitary expression of the glee of a venomous

nature at the prospect of unchecked sway, here whence he had been out-
cast. How vulgar petty triumph appeared, beheld thus; how disgusting
petty spite, how appalling revengefulness and hardness of heart! He
remembered suddenly that his nephew had been notable, in his repulsive
childhood, for his cruelty to flies, tearing their wings off, and, for his bar-
barity toward cats. A sort of dew might have been noticed upon the good
man's forehead. It seemed to him that his nephew had only to glance that
way, and all would be discovered, although he might have remembered
that it was impossible to see from the lighted room into the darkness of
the hothouse.

On the mantelpiece stood a large unframed photograph of Mr.
Mannering. His nephew soon caught sight of this, and strode across to
confront it with a triumphant and insolent sneer. "What? You old
Pharisee," said he, "taken her off for a trip to Brighton, have you? My
God! How I hope you'll never come back! How I hope you've fallen over
the cliffs, or got swept off by the tide or something! Anyway—I'll make
hay while the sun shines. Ugh! you old skinflint, you!" And he reached forward his hand, and bestowed a contemptuous fillip upon the nose in the
photograph. Then the usurping rascal left the room, leaving all the lights
on, presumably preferring the dining-room with its cellarette to the schol-
arly austerities of the study.

All night long the glare of electric light from the study fell full upon
Mr. Mannering and his Cousin Jane, like the glare of a cheap and artificial
sun. You who have seen at midnight in the park a few insomniac asters
standing stiff and startled under an arc light, all their weak color bleached
out of them by the drenching chemical radiance, neither asleep nor
awake, but held fast in a tense, a neurasthenic trance, you can form an
idea of how the night passed with this unhappy pair.

And toward morning an incident occurred, trivial in itself, no doubt,
but sufficient then and there to add the last drop to poor Cousin Jane's
discomfiture and to her relative's embarrassment and remorse. Along the
edge of the great earthbox in which the orchid was planted, ran a small
black mouse. It had wicked red eyes, a naked, evil snout, and huge, repellent ears, queer as a bat's. This creature ran straight over the lower leaves
of Cousin Jane's part of the plant. It was simply appalling. The stringy
main stem writhed like a hair on a coal-fire, the leaves contracted in an
agonized spasm, like seared mimosa; the terrified lady nearly uprooted
herself in her convulsive horror. I think she would actually have done so,
had not the mouse hurried on past her.

But it had not gone more than a foot or so when it looked up and saw, bending over it, and seeming positively to bristle with life, that, flower which had once been called Tib. There was a breathless pause. The mouse was obviously paralyzed with terror, the cat could only look and long. Suddenly the more human watchers saw a sly frond of foliage curve softly outward and close in behind the hypnotized creature. Cousin Jane, who had been thinking exultantly, "Well, now it'll go away and never, never, never come back," suddenly became aware of hideous possibilities. Summoning all her energy, she achieved a spasmodic flutter, enough to break the trance that held the mouse, so that, like a clock-work toy, it swung round and fled. But already the fell arm of the orchid had cut off its retreat. The mouse leaped straight at it. Like a flash 'five tendrils at the end caught the fugitive and held it fast, and soon its body dwindled and was gone. Now the heart of Cousin Jane was troubled with horrid fears, and slowly and painfully she turned her weary face first to one side, then to the other, in a fever of anxiety as to where the new bud would appear. A sort of sucker, green and sappy, which twisted lightly about her main stem, and reared a blunt head, much like a tip of asparagus, close to her own, suddenly began to swell in the most suspicious manner. She squinted at it, fascinated and appalled. Could it be her imagination? It was not.

Next evening the door opened again, and again the nephew entered the study. This time he was alone, and it was evident that he had come straight from table. He carried in his hand a decanter of whiskey capped by an inverted glass. Under his arm was a siphon. His face was distinctly flushed, and such a smile as is often seen in saloon bars played about his lips. He put down his burdens and, turning to Mr. Mannering's cigar cabinet, produced a bunch of keys, which he proceeded to try upon the lock, muttering vindictively at each abortive attempt, until it opened, when he helped himself from the best of its contents. Annoying as it was to witness this insolent appropriation of his property, and mortifying to see the contempt with which the cigar was smoked, the good gentleman found deeper cause for uneasiness in the thought that, with the possession of the keys, his abominable nephew had access to every private corner that was his.

At present, however, the usurper seemed indisposed to carry on investigations; he splashed a great deal of whiskey into the tumbler and relaxed into an attitude of extravagant comfort. But after a while the young man began to tire of his own company. He had not yet had time to gather any of his pothouse companions into his uncle's home, and repeated recourse to the whiskey bottle only increased his longing for something to relieve the monotony. His eye fell upon the door of the orchid-house. Sooner or later it was bound to have happened. Does this thought greatly console the condemned man when the fatal knock sounds upon the door of his cell? No. Nor were the hearts of the trembling pair in the hothouse at all comforted by the reflection.

As the nephew fumbled with the handle of the glass door, Cousin Jane slowly raised two fronds of leaves that grew on each side, high up on her stem, and sank her troubled head behind them. Mr. Mannering observed, in a sudden rapture of hope, that by this device she was fairly well concealed from any casual glance. Hastily he strove to follow her example. Unfortunately, he had not yet gained sufficient control of his—his *limbs?* —and all his tortured efforts could not raise them beyond an agonized horizontal. The door had opened, the nephew was feeling for the electric light switch just inside. It. was a moment for one of the superlative achievements of panic. Mr. Mannering was well equipped for the occasion. Suddenly, at the cost of indescribable effort, he succeeded in raising the right frond, not straight upwards, it is true, but in a series of painful jerks along a curve outward and backward, and ascending by slow degrees till it attained the position of an arm held over the possessor's head from behind. Then, as the light flashed on, a spray of leaves at the very end of this frond spread out into a fan, rather like a very fleshy horse-chestnut leaf in structure, and covered the anxious face below. What a relief! And now the nephew advanced into the orchid-house, and now the hidden pair simultaneously remembered the fatal presence of the cat. Simultaneously also, their very sap stood still in their veins. The nephew was walking along by the plant. The cat, a sagacious beast, "knew" with the infallible intuition of its kind that this was an idler, a parasite, a sensualist, gross and brutal, disrespectful to age, insolent to weakness, barbarous to cats. Therefore it remained very still, trusting to its low and somewhat retired position on the plant, and to protective mimicry and such things, and to the half-drunken condition of the nephew avoid his notice. But all in vain.

"What?" said the nephew. "What, a cat?" And he raised his hand to offer a blow at the harmless creature. Something in the dignified and unflinching demeanor of his victim must have penetrated into his besotted mind, for the blow never fell, and the bully, a coward at heart, as bullies invariably are, shifted his gaze from side to side escape the steady, contemptuous stare of the courageous cat. Alas! His eye fell on something glimmering whitely behind the dark foliages. He brushed aside the intervening leaves that he might see what it was. It was Cousin Jane.

"Oh! Ah!" said the young man, in great confusion. *"You're* back. But what are you hiding there for ?"

His sheepish stare became fixed, his mouth opened in bewilderment; then the true condition of things dawned upon his mind. Most of us would have at once instituted some attempt at communication, or at assistance of some kind, or at least have knelt down to thank our Creator that we had, by His grace, been spared such a fate, or perhaps have made haste from the orchid-house to ensure against accidents. But alcohol had so inflamed the young man's hardened nature that he felt neither fear, nor awe, nor gratitude. As he grasped the situation a devilish smile over-spread his face.

"Ha! Ha! Ha!" said he. "But where's the old man?"

He peered about the plant, looking eagerly for his uncle. In a moment he had located him and, raising the inadequate visor of leaves, discovered beneath it the face of our hero, troubled with a hundred bitter emotions.

"Hullo, Narcissus!" said the nephew.

A long silence ensued. The spiteful wretch was so pleased that he could not say a word. He rubbed his hands together, and licked his lips, and stared and stared as a child might at a new toy.

"Well, you're properly up a tree," he said. "Yes, the tables are turned now all right, aren't they? Do you remember the last time we met?"

A flicker of emotion passed over the face of the suffering blossom, betraying consciousness.

"'Yes, you can hear what I say," added the tormentor. "Feel, too, I expect. What about that?"

As he spoke, he stretched out his hand and, seizing a delicate frill of fine, silvery filaments that grew as whiskers grow around the lower half of the flower, he administered a sharp tug. Without pausing to note, even in the interests of science, the subtler shades of his uncle's reaction, content with the general effect of that devastating wince, the wretch chuckled with satisfaction and, taking a long pull from the reeking butt of the stolen cigar, puffed the vile fumes straight into his victim's center. The brute!

"How do you like that, John the Baptist?" he asked with a leer. "Good for the blight, you know. Just what you want!"

Something rustled upon his coat sleeve. Looking down, he saw a long stalk, well adorned with the fatal tendrils, groping its way over the arid and unsatisfactory surface. In a moment it had reached his wrist, he felt it fasten, but knocked it off as one would a leech, before had time to estab-lish its hold.

"Ugh!" said he. "So that's how it happens, is it? I think I'll keep out-side till I get the hang of things a bit. I don't want to be made an Aunt Sally of. Though I shouldn't think they could get you with your clothes on." Struck by a sudden thought, he looked from his uncle to Cousin Jane, and from Cousin Jane back to his uncle again. He scanned the floor, and saw a single crumpled bathrobe lying in the shadow.

"Why!" he said. *"Well!*—Haw! Haw! Haw!" And with an odious backward leer, he made his way out of the orchid-house.

Mr. Mannering felt that his suffering was capable of no increase. Yet he dreaded the morrow. His fevered imagination patterned the long night with waking nightmares, utterly fantastic visions of humiliation and torture. Torture! It was absurd, of course, for him to fear cold-blooded atrocities on the part of his nephew, but how he dreaded some outrageous whim that might tickle the youth's sense of humor, and lead him to *any* wanton freak, especially if he were drunk at the time. He thought of slugs and snails, espaliers and topiary. If only the monster would rest content with insulting jests, with wasting his substance, ravaging his cherished possessions before his eyes, with occasional pulling at the whiskers, even! Then it might be possible to turn gradually from all that still remained in him of man, to subdue the passions, no longer to admire or desire, to go native as it were, relapsing into the Nirvana of a vegetable dream. But in the morning he found this was not so easy.

In came the nephew and, pausing only to utter the most perfunctory of jeers at his relatives in the glass house, he sat at the desk and unlocked the top drawer. He was evidently in search of money; his eagerness betrayed that; no doubt he had run through all he had filched from his uncle's pockets, and had not yet worked out a scheme for getting direct control of his bank account. However, the drawer held enough to cause the scoundrel to rub his hands with satisfaction and, summoning the housekeeper, to bellow into her ear a reckless order upon the wine and spirit merchant.

"Get along with you!" he shouted, when he had at last made her understand. "I shall have to get someone a bit more on the spot to wait on me; I can tell you that. Yes," he added to himself as the poor old woman hobbled away, deeply hurt by his bullying manner, "yes, a nice little parlor-maid."

He hunted in the telephone book for the number of the local registry office. That afternoon he interviewed a succession of maidservants in his uncle's study. Those that happened to be plain, or too obviously respectable, he treated curtly and coldly; they soon made way for others. It was only when a girl was, attractive (according to the young man's depraved tastes, that is) and also bore herself in a fast or brazen manner, that the interview was at all prolonged. In these cases the nephew would

conclude in a fashion that left no doubt in the minds of any of his audi-
tors as to his real intentions. Once, for example, leaning forward, he took
the girl by the chin, saying with an odious smirk, "There's no one else but
me, and so you'd be treated just like one of the family, d'you see, my
dear?" To another he would say, slipping his arm round her waist, "Do
you think we shall get on well together?"

After this conduct had sent two or three in confusion from the room,
there entered a young person of the most regrettable description; one
whose character, betrayed as it was in her meretricious finery, her crude
cosmetics, and her tinted hair, showed yet more clearly in florid gesture
and too facile smile. The nephew lost no time in coming to an arrangement with this creature. Indeed, her true nature was so obvious that the
depraved young man only went through the farce of an ordinary interview as a sauce to his anticipations, enjoying the contrast between conventional dialogue and unbridled glances. She was to come next day. Mr.
Mannering feared more for his unhappy cousin than for himself. "What
scenes may she not have to witness," he thought, "that yellow cheek of
hers to incarnadine?" If only he could have said a few words!

But that evening, when the nephew came to take his ease in the study,
it was obvious that he was far more under the influence of liquor than he
had been before. His face, flushed patchily by the action of the spirits,
wore a sullen sneer; an ominous light burned in that bleared eye; he muttered savagely under his breath. Clearly this fiend in human shape was
what is known as "fighting drunk"; clearly some trifle had set his vile tem-
per in a blaze.

It is interesting to note, even at this stage, a sudden change in Mr.
Mannering's reactions. They now seemed entirely egoistical, and were to
be elicited only by stimuli directly associated with physical matters. The
nephew kicked a hole in a screen in his drunken fury, he flung a burning
cigar-end down on the carpet, he scratched matches on the polished table.
His uncle witnessed this with the calm of one whose sense of property
and of dignity has become numbed and paralyzed; he felt neither fury nor
mortification. Had he, by one of those sudden strides by which all such
development takes place, approached much nearer to his goal, complete
vegetation? His concern for the threatened modesty of Cousin Jane,
which had moved him so strongly only a few hours earlier, must have
been the last dying flicker of exhausted altruism; that most human characteristic had faded from him. The change, however, in its present stage,
was not an unmixed blessing. Narrowing in from the wider and more
expressly human regions of his being, his consciousness now left outside

its focus not only pride and altruism, which had been responsible for much of his woe, but fortitude and detachment also, which, with quotations from the Greek, had been his support before the whole battery of his distresses. Moreover, within its constricted circle, his ego was not reduced but concentrated; his serene, flower-like indifference toward the ill-usage of his furniture was balanced by the absorbed, flower-like single-mindedness of his terror at the thought of similar ill-usage directed toward himself.

Inside the study the nephew still fumed and swore. On the mantelpiece stood an envelope, addressed in Mr. Mannering's handwriting to Cousin Jane. In it was the letter he had written from town, describing his nephew's disgraceful conduct. The young man's eye fell upon this and, unscrupulous, impelled by idle curiosity, he took it up and drew out the letter. As he read, his face grew a hundred times blacker than before.

"What," he muttered, "'a mere race-course cad . . . a worthless vulgarian . . . a scoundrel of the sneaking sort' . . . and what's this? '. . . cut him off absolutely . . .' What?" said he, with a horrifying oath. "*Would* you cut me off absolutely? Two can play at that game, you old devil!"

And he snatched up a large pair of scissors that lay on the desk, and burst into the hothouse—

Among fish, the dory, they say, screams when it is seized upon by man; among insects, the caterpillar of the death's-head moth is capable of a still, small shriek of terror; in the vegetable world, only the mandrake could voice its agony—till now.

The Fig Tree

V.S. PRITCHETT

I CHECKED THE GREENHOUSES, saw the hose taps were turned off, fed the Alsatian, and then put the bar on the main gate to the Nursery and left by the side door for my flat. As I changed out of my working clothes I looked down on the rows of labeled fresh green plants. What a pleasure to see such an orderly population of growing things gambling for life—how surprising that twenty years ago the sight of so much husbandry would have bored me.

When I was drying myself in the bathroom I noticed Sally's bathcap hanging there and I took the thing to the closet in the bedroom, and then in half an hour I picked up Mother at her hotel and drove her to Duggie and Sally's house, where we were to have dinner. I supposed Mother must have seen Sally's bathcap, for as we passed the Zoo she said. "I do wish you would get married again and settle down."

"Dutch elm disease," I replied, pointing to the crosses on one of two trees in the Park.

The Zoo is my halfway mark when I go to Duggie and Sally's—what vestiges of embarrassment I feel become irrelevant when I have passed it.

"It worries your father," Mother said.

Mother is not "failing." She is in her late seventies and Father was killed in the war thirty years ago, but he comes to life in a random way, as if time were circular for her. Father seems to be wafted by, and sows the only important guilt I have—I have so little memory of him. Duggie has said once or twice to Sally that though I am in my early forties, there are still signs that I lacked a father's discipline. Duggie, a speculative man, puts the early whiteness of my hair down to this. Obviously, he says, I was a late child, probably low in vitality.

Several times during this week's visit I have taken Mother round the shops she likes in London. She moves fast on her thin legs, and if age has shortened her by giving her a small hump on her shoulders, this adds to her sharp-eyed, foraging appearance. She was rude, as usual, to the shop assistants, who seemed to admire this—perhaps because it reminded them of what they had heard of "the good old days." And she dressed with taste, her makeup was delicate, and if her skin had aged, it was fine as silk; her nose was young, her eyes as neat as violets. The week had been hot, but she was cool and slightly scented.

"Not as hot as we had it in Cairo when your father was alive," she said in her mannish voice.

Time was restored: Father had returned to his grave.

After being gashed by bombs during the war, the corner of early-Victorian London where Duggie and Sally live has "gone up." Once a neighborhood of bed-sitters, now the small houses are expensive and trim; enormous plane trees, fast-growing sycamores, old apple and pear trees bearing uneatable fruit, crowd the large gardens. It was to see the garden and to meet Duggie, who was over from Brussels on one of his monthly trips, that Mother had really come: in the country she is an indefatigable gardener. So is Sally, who opened the door to us. One of the unspoken rules of Sally and myself is that we do not kiss when I go to her house; her eyes were as polite as glass (and without the quiver to the pupils they usually have in them) as she gave her hand to my mother. She had drawn her fair hair severely back.

"Duggie is down in the garden," Sally said to Mother and made a fuss about the steps that lead down from her sitting-room balcony. "These steps my husband put in are shaky—let me help you."

"I got used to companionways going to Egypt," said Mother in her experienced voice. "We always went by sea, of course. What a lovely garden."

"Very wild," said Sally. "There used to be a lawn here. It was no good, so we dug it up."

"No one can afford lawns nowadays," said my mother. "We have three. Much better to let nature take its course."

It is a clever garden of the romantic kind, half of it a green cavern under the large trees where the sun can still flicker in the higher branches. You duck your way under untidy climbing roses; there is a foreground, according to season, of overgrown marguerites, tobacco plants, dahlias, irises, lilies, ferns—a garden of wild, contrived masses. Our progress was slow as Mother paused to botanize until we got to a wide, flagged circle which is shaded by a muscular fig tree. Duggie was standing by the chairs with a drink in his hand, waiting for us. He moved a chair for Mother.

"No, I must see it all first," Mother said. "Nice little magnolia."

I was glad she noticed that.

There was a further tour of plants that "do well in the shade"—"Dear Solomon's-seal," she said politely, as if the plant were a person. A bird or two darted off into other gardens with the news—and then we returned to the chairs set out on the paved circle. Duggie handed drinks to us, with the small bow of a tall man. He is lazily well-made, a bufferish fellow in his late fifties, his drooping grey moustache is affable—"honorable" is how I would describe the broad road of sunburned baldness going over his head. His nose is just a touch bottled, which gives him the gentlemanly air of an old club servant, or rather of being not one man but a whole club, uttering impressions of this and that. Out of this club his private face will appear, a face that puts on a sudden, fishy-eyed stare, in the middle of one of his long sentences. It is the stare of a man in a brief state of shock who has found himself suspended over a hole that has opened at his feet. His job takes him abroad a good deal and his stare is also that of an Englishman abroad who has sighted another Englishman he cannot quite place. Not being able to get a word in while the two women were talking, he turned this stare on me. "I missed you the last time I was home," he said.

Again, it is my rule that I don't go to the house unless he is there.

"How is that chest of yours?"

I gave a small cough and he gave me a dominating look. He likes to worry about my health.

"The best thing your uncle ever did for you was to get you out of the city. You needed an open-air life."

Duggie, who has had to make his own way, rather admires me for having had a rich uncle.

Was he shooting a barb into me? I don't think so. We always have this conversation, he was born to repeat himself—one more sign of his honorableness.

Duggie takes pride in a possessive knowledge of my career. He often says to Sally, "He ought to put on weight—white hair at his age—but what do you expect? Jazz bands in Paris and London, hanging round Chelsea bars, playing at all that literary stuff, going into that bank—all that sort of nonsense." Then he goes on, "Mother's boy—marrying a woman twelve years older than himself. Sad that she died," he adds. "Must have done something to him—that breakdown, a year in the sanatorium, he probably gambled. Still, the Nursery has pulled him together. Characteristic, of course, that most of the staff are girls."

"It's doing well," he said in a loud confidential voice, nodding at the fig tree by the south wall, close to us.

"What a lovely tree," Mother said. "Does it bear? My husband will only eat figs fresh from the tree."

"One or two little ones. But they turn yellow and drop off in June," said Sally.

"What it needs," Duggie said, "is the Mediterranean sun. It ought to be in Turkey, that is where you get the best figs."

"The sun isn't enough. The fig needs good drainage and has to be fertilized," Mother said.

"All fruit needs that," said Duggie.

"The fig needs two flies—the Blastophaga and, let me see, is it the Sycophaga? I think so—anyway, they are Hymenoptera," Mother said.

Duggie gazed with admiration at my mother. He loves experts. He had been begging me for years to bring her over to his house.

"Well, we saved its life, didn't we, Teddy?" he said to me and boasted on his behalf and mine. "We flagged the area. There was nothing but a lake of muddy water here. How many years ago was that?"

"Four or five," I said.

"No!" said Duggie. "Only three."

Was he coming into the open at last and telling me that he knew that this was the time when Sally and I became lovers? I think not. The stare dropped out of his face. His honorable look returned.

Sally and Duggie were what I call "Monday people" at the Nursery. There is a rush of customers on the weekend. They are the instant gardeners who drive in, especially in the spring and autumn, to buy everything, from plants already in bud and flowers, the potted plants, for balconies of flats. The crowd swarms and our girls are busy at the counter we had to install to save costs as the business grew. (The counter was Duggie's idea: he could not resist seeing the Nursery as one of his colonies.) But on Monday the few fanatic gardeners come, and I first became aware of Sally because she was very early, usually alone, a slight woman in her late thirties with her straw-blond hair drawn back from a high forehead in those days, a severe look of polite, silent impatience which would turn into a wide, fastidious grimace like the yawn of a cat if anyone spoke to her. She would take a short step back and consider one's voice. She looked almost reckless and younger when she put on glasses to read what was on the sacks and packets of soil, compost, and fertilizer in the store next to the office, happiest in our warm greenhouses, a woman best seen under glass. Her eyebrows were softer, more downily intimate than anything else about her. They reminded me when I first saw her of the disturbing eyebrows of an aunt of mine which used to make me blush when I was a boy. Hair disturbs me.

One day she brought Duggie to the Nursery when I was unloading boxes of plants that came from the growers and I heard her snap at him, "Wait here. If you see the manager, ask about grass seed and stop following me round. You fuss me."

For the next half-hour she looked round the seedlings or went into the greenhouses while Duggie stood where he was told to stand. I was near him when the lorry drove off.

"Are you being attended to?" I said. "I'll call a girl."

He was in his suspended state. "No, I was thinking," he said in the lazy voice of a man who, home from abroad and with nothing to do, was hoping to find out if there were any fellow thinkers about. "I was thinking, vegetation is a curious thing," he said with the predatory look of a man who had an interesting empire of subjects to offer. "I mean, one notices when one gets back to London there is more vegetation than brick. Trees," he said. "Plants and shrubs, creeper, moss, ivy," he went on, "grass, of course. Why this and not that? Climate, I suppose. You have laurels here, but no oleander, yet it's all over the Mediterranean and Mexico. You get your fig or your castor-oil plant, but no banana, no ginkgo, no datura. The vine used to swarm in Elizabethan times, but rare now, but I hear they're making wine again. It must be thin. The climate changed when the Romans cut down the forests." For a moment he became a Roman and then drifted on, "Or the Normans. We all come down to grass in the end."

He looked at our greenhouses.

"My job takes me away a lot. I spend half the year abroad," he said. "Oil. Kuwait."

He nodded to the distant figure of his wife. She was bending over a bed of tobacco plants.

"We spent our honeymoon in Yucatán," he said with some modest pomp. He was one of those colonizing talkers, talking over new territory.

"But that is not the point," he said. "We can't get the right grass seed. She sows every year, but half of it dies by the time summer comes. Yet look at the Argentina pampas." He was imposing another geography, some personal flora of his own, on my Nursery. Clearly not a gardener: a thinker at large.

I gave him the usual advice. I took him to a shed to show him sacks of chemicals. His wife came back from the flower beds and found us. "I've been looking for you everywhere," she said to him. "I told you to wait where you were." She sounded to be an irritable woman.

He said to me, in an aloof, conspiring way, ignoring her, "I suppose you wouldn't have time to drop round and have a look at our lawn? I mean, in the next week or two—"

"It will be too late by then," she interrupted. "The grass will be dead. Come along," and she made that grimace—a grimace that now struck me as a confidence, an off-hand intimation.

He made an apologetic gesture to me and followed her obediently out of the Nursery.

I often had a word or two with Sally when she came alone: grass seed seemed to be the couple's obsession. She said it was his; he said it was hers. I was a kind of umpire to whom they appealed when we met.

So one afternoon in November when I was delivering laurels to a neighbor of theirs down the street, I dropped in at their house.

A fat young man was sitting sedately on a motorbike outside it, slowly taking off a fine pair of gauntlets. Sitting behind the screen of the machine, he might have been admiring himself at a dressing-table mirror. In his white crash helmet he looked like a doll, but one with a small black moustache.

"Those lads get themselves up, don't they?" I said to Duggie, who came to the door.

"Our tenant," Duggie said. "He has the flat in the basement. He uses the side entrance. Under our agreement he does not use the garden. That is reserved for ourselves. Come through—I had these iron steps put in so that my wife has strictly private access to the garden without our interfering with him or he with us. My wife would have preferred a young married couple, but as I pointed out, there would be children. One has to weigh one thing against another in this life—don't you find?"

We went down to the garden. Their trouble was plain. The trees were bare. Half of the place was lifeless soil, London-black and empty The damp yellow leaves of the fig tree hung down like wretched rags, and the rest had fallen flat as plates into a very large pool of muddy water that stretched from one side of the garden to the other. Overnight, in November a fig collapses like some Victorian heroine. Here—as if she were about to drown herself. I said this to Duggie, who said, "Heroine? I don't follow."

"You'll never grow a lawn here. Too much shade. You could cut the trees down . . ."

At this moment Sally came down and said, "I won't have my trees cut down. It's the water that's killing everything."

I said that whole districts of London were floating on water. Springs everywhere, and the clay held it.

"And also, the old Fleet River runs underground in this district," I said. The only thing you can do is to put paving down."

"The Fleet River? News to me," said Duggie, and he looked about us at other gardens and houses as if eager to call out all his neighbors and tell them. "Pave it, you say? You mean with stones?"

"What else?" said Sally curtly and walked away. The garden was hers.

"But, my dear," he called after her, "the point is—what stones? Portland? Limestone?"

The colonizer of vegetation was also a collector of rock. A load of geology poured out of him. He ran through sandstone, millstone, grit, until we moved on to the whinstone the Romans used on Hadrian's Wall, went on to the marble quarries of Italy and came back to the low brick wall of their garden, which had been damaged during the war.

Presently there was the howling and thumping of jazz music from the basement flat.

"I told you that man has girls down there," Sally said angrily to her husband. "He's just come in. He's turning the place into a discothèque. Tell him to stop—it's intolerable."

And she looked coldly at me as if I too were a trespasser, the sort of man who would kick up a shindy with girls in a quiet house. I left. Not a happy pair.

I sent him an estimate for paving part of the garden. Several months passed: there was no reply and his wife stopped coming to the Nursery. I thought they were abroad. Then in the spring Duggie came to the Nursery with his daughter, a schoolgirl, who went off to make up confidently to a van driver.

Duggie watched her and then said to me, "About those paving stones. My wife has been ill. I had a cable and flew home."

"I hope it was not serious?"

He studied me, considering whether to tell me the details, but evidently —and with that kind of reluctance which suggests all—changed his mind. "The iniquitous Rent Act," he said disparagingly, "was at the bottom of it."

He gave an outline of the Act, with comments on rents in general.

"Our tenant—that boy was impossible, every kind of impertinence. We tried to get rid of him but we couldn't. The fellow took us to court."

"Did you get an order against him?" I asked.

Duggie's voice hurried. "No. Poor fellow was killed. Drove his motor-bike head-on into a lorry, a girl with him too. Both killed. Horrible. Naturally, it upset my wife: she blames herself. Imagination," he apologized. Duggie spoke of the imagination accusingly.

"The man with the little black moustache?" I asked.

"She wouldn't have a married couple there," he said.

"I remember," I said. "You mentioned it."

"Did I?" he said. He was cheered by my remembering that.

"You see," he said. "It was clearly laid down in the agreement that he was not to go into the garden under any pretext, but he did. However, that is not what I came about. We're going to pave that place, as you suggested. It will take her mind off it all." He nodded to the house. "By the way, you won't say anything to her, will you? I'm away so much the garden is everything to her."

Shortly after this I took one of our men over to the house. Duggie was stirred at the end of the first day when he came home from his London office to see we had dug up a lot of brick rubble—chunks of the garden wall which had been knocked down by blast during the war. On the second day he came back early in the afternoon and stood watching. He was longing to get hold of my man's pickaxe. The man put it down and I had turned around when I heard the dead sound of steel on stone and a shout of "Christ!" from Duggie. He had taken the pickaxe and brought it down hard on a large slab of concrete and was doubled up, gripping his wrists between his legs, in agony. Sally came to the balcony and then hurried down the steps. Her appearance had changed. She was plumper han she had been, there was no sign of illness, and she had done her hair in a new way: it was loosened and she often pushed it back from her cheeks.

"You are a fool, Duggie," she said.

The man was shoveling earth clear of the slab of concrete, which tilted down deep into the earth.

"It's all right. It's all right. Go away. I'm all right," said Duggie

"What is it?" he said.

"Bleeding air-raid shelter," my gardener said. "There's one or two left in the gardens round here. A gentleman down the road turned his into a lily pond"

He went on shoveling and dug a hole. The concrete ended in a tangle of wire and stone. It had been smashed. He kneeled down on the ground and said, "The end wall has caved in, full of wet muck." He got up and said, disappointed, "No one in it. Saved some poor bloke's life. If he copped it, he wouldn't have known, anyway."

Sally made a face of horror at the gardener. "Those poor people," she said. "Come indoors. What a fool you are, Duggie."

Duggie refused to go. Pain had put him in a trance: one could almost see bits of his mind traveling out of him as he called triumphantly to her, "Don't you see what we've got, my dearest?" he cried, excitement driving out his pain. He was a man whose mind was stored with a number of exotic words: "We've got a *cenote*."

How often we were to hear that word in the next few days! For months after this he must have continued startling people with it in his office, on buses, men in clubs, whoever was sitting next to him in aircraft on his way to Kuwait.

"What is a cenote?" I said, no doubt as they did.

"It's an underground cistern," he said. "You remember Yucatán, Sally—all those forests, yet no water. No big rivers. You said, 'How did the Mayas survive?' The answer was that the Maya civilization floated on underground cisterns."

Duggie turned to me, calling me Teddy for the first time. "I remember what you said about London floating on underground rivers—it's been on my mind ever since you said it. Something was there at the back of my mind, some memory, I couldn't get it. There it is: a cenote. That's where your fig tree has been drinking, Sally. You plant your fig tree on a tank of water and the rubble drains it.

"Sally and I saw dozens of cenotes, all sizes, some hundred feet deep on our honeymoon," he confided to me.

Sally's eyes went hard.

"The Mayans worshiped them: you can see why. Once a year the priests used to cut out the heart of a virgin and throw it into the water, Propitiation," he said.

"It's an act for tourists at the nightclubs there," said Sally drearily.

"Yes," Duggie explained to us and added to me, "Fake, of course" Sally said, "Those poor people. I shall never go into this garden again."

In the next few days she did not come down while we turned the ruin into a foundation, and the following week Duggie superintended the laying of the stones. His right arm was in a sling.

When the job was finished Duggie was proud of the wide circle of stones we had laid down.

"You've turned my garden into a cemetery. I've seen it from the window," Sally said.

Duggie and I looked at each other: two men agreeing to share the unfair blame. She had been ill; we had done this job for her and it had made things worse.

Imagination, as Duggie had said. Difficult for him. And I had thought of her as a calm, sensible woman.

It happened at this time I had to go to the Town Hall about a contract for replanting one of the neglected squares in the borough, and while I was there and thinking of Duggie and Sally I tried to find out who had lived in their house and whether there was any record of air-raid casualties. I went from office to office and discovered nothing. Probably the wrong place to go to. Old cities are piled on layer after layer of unrecorded human lives and things. Then Duggie sent a check for our work, more promptly too than most of our customers do. I thought of my buried wife and the rot of the grave as I made out a receipt. It occurred to me that it would be decent to do something for Duggie. I was walking around the Nursery one morning when I saw a small strong magnolia, a plant three feet high and already in bud. It was risky to replant it at this time, but I bound it, packed it, and put it in a large tub and drove to their house one Saturday with it, to surprise them. Sally came to the door with a pen in her hand and looked put-out by my sudden call. I told her I had the plant in the van.

"We didn't order anything. My husband is in Kuwait—he would have told me. There must be a mistake."

The pen in her raised hand was like a funny hostile weapon, and seeing me smile at it, she lowered her hand.

"It's not an order. It's a present. In the van," I said. She looked unbelieving at the van and then back at me. In the awkward pause my mind gave an unintended leap. I forgot about Duggie.

"For you," I said. I seemed to sail away, off my feet.

"For me?" she said. "'Why for me?"

I was astonished. Her face went as white as paper and I thought she was going to faint. She stood there, trembling. The pen dropped out of her hand to the floor and she turned round and bent to pick it up and stood up again with a flustered blush as if she had been caught doing something wrong.

"You're the gardener," I said. "Come and look."

She did not move, so I started off down the few steps to the gate. She followed me and I saw her glance, as if calling for protection to the houses on either side of her own.

"Why should you do this?" she said in an unnatural voice. I opened the gate, but she made me go through first.

The swollen rusty-pink and skin-white buds of the plant were as bright as candles in the darkness of the van.

"Advertising," I said with a salesman's laugh. She frowned, reproaching me doubtfully But when she saw the plant she said, "How lovely!"

My tongue raced. I said I had been thinking of the paved circle in the middle of the garden; the magnolia would stand there and flower before the trees shaded the place, and that it could be moved out of the tub wherever she wanted it in the garden later in the year.

"You mean that?" she said.

So I got out a trolley, put up a board, and wheeled the plant down from the van carefully. It was very heavy.

"Be careful," she said. She opened the side entrance to the garden and followed me there.

No muddy puddle now. It's gone," I boasted. It was a struggle getting the heavy tub in place and she helped me.

"You've got a gardener's strong hands," I said.

I looked around and then up at the trees. Her wide mouth opened with delight at the plant.

"How kind you are," she said. "Duggie will love it."

I had never been alone with her in this garden and, I remember, this was privileged ground. She walked around and around the plant as if she were dancing.

"It will be in full bloom in ten days," I said. "It will cheer up the fig tree. It's trying to bud."

"This time of the year," she said, despising it, "that tree looks like a chunk of machinery."

A half-hour passed. We went back to the house and she thanked me again as I pushed the trolley.

"Leave it there," she said. "I must give you some tea or a drink. How lucky I was in. You should have telephoned."

In the sitting-room she laughed as she looked back at the plant from the window. It was, I realized, the first time I had heard her laugh. It was surprising not to hear Duggie's voice. She went off to make tea and I sat in an armchair and remembered not to put my dirty hands on the arms. Then I saw my footmarks coming across the carpet to me. I felt I had started on a journey.

I noticed she frowned at them and the cups skidded on the tray when she came back with the tea.

I said apologetically, "My boots!"

Strange words, now that I think of it, for the beginning of a love affair; even she gaped at them as if they had given me away.

When she had only half filled my cup she banged the teapot down, got up and came across to squeeze my hand.

"Oh, you are so *kind, kind,*" she said and then stepped back to her chair quickly.

"You *are* a friend," she said.

And then I saw tears were dropping down her cheeks. Her happy face had collapsed and was ugly. "I'm sorry to be so silly, Mr. Ormerod," she said, trying to laugh.

Ten shelves of Duggie's books looked down, their titles dumb, but listening with all ears as I sat not knowing what to do, for, trying to laugh, she sobbed even more and she had to get up and turn her back to me and look out of the window.

"It's all right," she said with her back to me. "Don't let your tea get cold. My husband wanted to put an urn there," she said. "I suppose he told you."

Duggie had not been able to control his drifting mind. "This is the first time I've been in the garden since you were here last," she said, turning round.

"By the way," I said, "if you're worrying about the shelter, I can tell you—I've looked up the records at the Town Hall. There were no casualties here. There was no one in the shelter."

I did not tell her no records could be traced. Her tears had made my mind leap again.

"Why on earth did you do that?" she said, and she sat down again

"I had the idea it was worrying you," I said.

"No, not at all," she said, shaking after her cry, and she put on an off-hand manner and did not look at me.

"The shelter? Oh, that didn't worry me," she said. "The war was thirty years ago, wasn't it? One doesn't have to wait for bombs to kill people. They die in hospital, don't they? Things prey on my husband's mind. He's a very emotional man; you mightn't think it. I don't know whether he told you, we had trouble with a young man, a tenant. It made Duggie quite ill. They flew him home from Kuwait."

I was baffled. She had exactly reversed the story Duggie had told me. She said with the firm complacency of a married woman, "He talks himself into things, you know."

After she said this there was a question in her eyes, a movement like a small signal, daring me for a moment. I was silent and she began talking about everyday things, in a nervous way, and intimacy vanished.

She stood at the door and gave a half wave as I left, a scarcely visible wave, like a beckon. It destroyed me. Damn that stupid man, I thought when I got home and stood at the stove getting a meal together. The telephone rang and I turned the stove off. I thought the call was from my mother—it was her hour—but the voice was Sally's, firm but apologetic. "You've left your trolley. I thought you might need it."

O blessed trolley! I said I'd come at once. She said curtly she was going out. That, and the hope that she was not interrupting my dinner, were the only coherent, complete sentences she spoke in one of the longest calls I have ever had. On her side it was a collection of unfinished phrases with long silences between them, so that once or twice she seemed to have gone away—silences in which she appeared to be wrestling with nouns, pronouns, and verbs that circled round an apology and explanation that was no explanation, about making "that silly scene." No sooner was she at the point of explanation than she drifted off it. It struck me that listening to her husband so much, she had lost the power of talking.

There was something which, "sometime in the future," she would like to ask me. but it had gone from her mind. "If there is a future," she added too brightly. Her silences dangled and stirred me. The manner was so like Duggie's: it half exasperated me and I asked her if she would have dinner with me one day. "Dinner?" This puzzled her. She asked if I had had my dinner. The idea died and so did the conversation. What affectation, I thought afterwards. Not on my side: desire had been born.

But on the following day I saw her waiting in one of our greenhouses. She was warmer under glass. I had collected my trolley. That, for some reason, pleased her. She agreed to have dinner with me.

"Where on earth are we going?" she said when we drove off.

"Away from the Nursery," I said. I was determined to amuse her. "To get away from the thieves."

"What thieves?" she said.

"The old ladies," I said.

It is well known, if you run a nursery, that very nice old ladies sometimes nip off a stem for a cutting or slip small plants into their bags. Stealing a little gives them the thrill of flirtation. I said that only this week one of them had come to me when I was alone in a greenhouse and said,

"Can I whisper something to you? I have a *dreadful* confession to make. I have been very naughty. I *stole* a snippet of geranium from you in the summer and it has struck!"

Sally said, "And what about old men? Don't they steal?"

My fancy took a leap. "Yes, we've got one," I said, "but he goes in for big stuff."

There was a myth at our Nursery that when a box of plants was missing or some rare expensive shrub had been dug up and was gone, this was the work of a not altogether imaginary person called Thompson who lived in a big house where the garden abutted on our wall. Three camellias went one day, and because of the price he was somehow promoted by the girls and became known as "Colonel" Thompson. He had been seen standing on a stepladder and looking over our wall. I invented a face for the colonel when I told Sally about this. I gave him a ripe nose, a bald head, a drooping moustache; unconsciously I was describing Duggie. I went further: I had caught the colonel with one leg over the wall, and when I challenged him he said, "Looking for my dog. Have you seen my dog?"

Sally said, "I don't believe you."

This was promising. A deep seriousness settled on us when we got to the restaurant. It was a small place. People were talking loudly, so that bits of their lives seemed to be flying around us, and we soon noticed we were the quietest talkers there, talking about ourselves, but to our plates or the tablecloth, crumbling bread and then looking up with sudden questions. She ate very fast; a hungry woman, I thought. How long, she asked suddenly, raising a fork to her mouth, how long had I known my wife before we were married? Four months, I said. She put her fork down.

"That was a rush," she said "It took Duggie and me seven years."

"Why was that?"

"I didn't want to get married, of course," she said.

"You mean you lived together?" I said.

"Indeed not. We might not even have married *then*," she said, "but his firm was sending him to Mexico for three years. We knew each other very well you know. Actually," she mumbled now, "I was in love with someone else." She now spoke up boldly, "Gratitude is more important than love, isn't it?"

"Is that the question you wanted to ask me," I said, "when you telephoned?"

"I don't think I said that," she said.

I was falling in love with her. I listened but hardly heard what she said. I was listening only to my desire.

"Gratitude? No, I don't," I said. "Not when one is young. Why don't you go with him on his jobs?"

"He likes travel, I don't," she said. "We like each other. I don't mind being alone. I prefer it. You're alone, aren't you?"

Our conversation stopped. A leaden boredom settled on us like a stifling thundercloud. I whispered, looking around first to be sure no one heard me and in a voice I scarcely recognized as my own, "I want you."

"I know," she said. "It's no good," she said, fidgeting in her chair and looking down at the cloth. Her movement encouraged me.

"I've loved you ever since—"

She looked up.

"—since you started coming to the Nursery," I said.

"Thank you, but I can't," she said. "I don't go to bed with people. I gave that up when my daughter was born."

"It's Duggie'" I said.

She was startled and I saw the grimace I knew.

She thought a long time.

"Can't you guess?" she said. And then she leaned across and touched my hand. "Don't look so gloomy. It's no good with me."

I was not gloomy. That half wave of the hand, the boredom, the monotony of our voices, even the fact that the people at the next table had found us so interesting that they too had started whispering, made me certain of how our evening would end.

"Let us go," I said.

I called a waiter and she watched me pay the bill and said, "What an enormous tip." In our heavy state, this practical remark lightened us. And for me it had possessive overtones that were encouraging; she stood outside, waiting for me to bring the ear with that air women have of pretending not to be there. We drove off and when I turned into a shopping street almost empty at this hour I saw our heads and shoulders reflected in the windows of a big shop, mocking us as we glided by: two other people. I turned into a street of villas; we were alone again and I leaned to kiss her on the neck. She did not move, but presently she glanced at me and said, "Are you a friend?"

"No," I said. "I'm not."

"I think I ought to like that," she said. And she gripped my arm violently and did not let it go.

"Not at my house," she said.

We got to my flat and there she walked across the sitting-room straight to the window and looked down at the long greenhouses gleaming in the dark.

"Which is Colonel Thompson's house?" she said.

I came up behind her and put my arms round her and she watched my daring hands play on her breasts with that curiosity and love of themselves that women have, but there was a look of horror on her face when I kissed her on the mouth, a hate that came (I know now) from the years of her marriage. In the next hours it ebbed away, her face emptied, and her wide lips parted with greed.

"I don't do things like this," she said.

The next day she came to me; on the third day she pulled me back as I was getting out of bed and said, "Duggie's coming home. I have something bad to tell you, something shameful." She spoke into my shoulder. "Something I tried to tell you when I telephoned, the day you came with the plant, but I couldn't. Do you remember I telephoned to you?

"I told a lie to Duggie about that young man, I told Duggie he attacked me." She said, "It wasn't true. I saw him and his girl at night from my bedroom window going into the garden with their arms round each other, to the end of it, under the trees. They were there a long time. I imagined what they were doing. I could have killed that girl. I was mad with jealousy—I think I was really mad. I went out into the garden many nights to stop them, and in the afternoons I worked there to provoke him and even peeped into their window. It was terrible. So I told Duggie. I told him the boy had come up behind me and pulled at my clothes and tried to rape me. I tore my blouse to prove it. I sent a cable to Duggie. Poor Duggie, he believed me. He came back. I made Duggie throw the boy out. You know what happened. When the boy was killed I thought I would go out of my mind."

"I thought you said Duggie was ill," I said.

"That is what I'm ashamed of," she said. "But I was mad. You know, I hated you too when Duggie brought you in to do those stones. I really hated anyone being in the garden. That is why I made that scene when you brought the magnolia. When you came to the door I thought for an awful moment it was the boy's father coming for his things; he did come once."

I was less shocked than unnerved. I said, "The real trouble was that you were lying to yourself." I saw myself as the rescuer for a moment.

"Do you think he believed you?" I said.

She put on the distant look she used to have when I first met her, almost a look of polite annoyance at being distracted from her story. Then she said something that was true. "Duggie doesn't allow himself to believe what he doesn't want to believe. He never believes what he sees. One day

I found him in the sitting-room, and he started to pull a book out of the bookcase and closed it with a bang and wiped his eyes. 'Dust,' he said. 'Bad as Mexico.' Afterwards I thought, He's been crying."

"That was because he knew he was to blame," I said.

I went to my window and looked at the sky. In the night he would be coming across it.

"What are we going to do?" I said. "When shall I see you? Are you going to tell him?"

She was very surprised. "Of course not," she said, getting out of bed.

"But we must. If you don't, I shall."

She picked up her dress and half covered herself with it. "If you do," she said, "I'll never see you again, Colonel Thompson."

"He'll find out. I want to marry you."

"I've got a daughter. You forget that. He's my husband."

"He's probably got some girl," I said lightly.

The gentleness went out of our conversation.

"You're not to say that," she said vehemently. We were on the edge of a quarrel.

"I have got to go," she said. "Judy's coming home. I've got to get his suits from the cleaners and there are some of yours."

My suits and Duggie's hanging up on nasty little wire hangers at the cleaners!

We had a crowd of customers at the Nursery and that took my mind off our parting, but when I got back to my flat the air was still and soundless. I walked round my three rooms expecting to see her, but the one or two pictures stared out of my past life. I washed up our empty glasses. Well, there it is, I thought cynically. All over. What do you expect? And I remembered someone saying, "Have an affair with a married woman if you like, but for God's sake don't start wanting to marry her."

It was a help that my secretary was on holiday and I had to do all the paperwork at night. I also had my contract for re-planting the square the council had neglected and did a lot of the digging myself. As I dug I doubted Sally and went over what I knew about her life. How did she and Duggie meet? What did they say? Was Sally flaunting herself before her husband, surprising and enticing him? I was burned by jealousy. Then, at the end of the week, before I left for the square at half past eight, I heard her steps on the stairs to my office. She had a busy smile on her face.

"I've brought your suits," she said. "I'm in a rush." And she went to hang them in their plastic covers on the door, but I had her in my arms and the suits fell to the floor.

"Is it all right?" I said.

"How do you mean?" she said.

"Duggie," I said.

"Of course," she said complacently..

I locked the door. In a few minutes her doubts and mine were gone. Our quarrel was over. She looked at me with surprise as she straightened her skirt.

Happiness! I took one of our girls with me to the square and stood by lazily watching her get on with her work.

After lunch I was back at the Nursery and I was alarmed to see Duggie's bald head among the climbing greenery of our hothouse. He was stooping there, striped by sunlight, like some affable tiger. I hoped to slip by unseen, but he heard me and the tiger skin dropped off as he came out, all normality, calling, "Just the man! I've been away."

I gave what must have been the first of the small coughs, the first of a long series with which I would always greet him and which made him put concern into his voice. I came to call it my "perennial hybrid" —a phrase that struck him and which he added to his vocabulary of phrases and even to his reflections on coughs in general, on Arab spitting and Mexican hawking.

"I came over to thank you for that wonderful magnolia. That was very kind. I missed it in flower but Sally says it was wonderful. You don't know what it did for her. I don't know whether you have noticed, she's completely changed. She looks years younger. All her energy has come back." Then in a louder voice: "She has forgotten all that trouble. You must have seen it. She tells me she has been giving you a hand, your girl's away."

"She was very kind. She took my suits to the cleaners."

He ignored this. We walked together across the Nursery and he waved his hand to the flower beds. Did I say that his daughter was with him? She was then a fat girl of thirteen or fourteen with fair hair like her mother's.

"Fetched them," said the pedantic child, and from that time her gaze was like a judgment. I picked a flower for her as they followed me to the door of my office.

"By the way," he said, "what did you do about that fellow who gets over the wall? Sally told me. Which wall was it?"

Sally seemed to tell him everything.

"He's stopped. That one over there."

He stood still and considered it. "What you need is a wire fence, with a three-inch mesh to it; if it was wider, the fellow could get his toe in. It would be worth the outlay—no need to go in for one of those spiked steel fences we put up round our refineries." He went on to the general question of fences: he had always been against people who put broken glass on walls. "Unfair," he said. He looked lofty—"Cruel, too. Chap who did that ought to be sent off the field.

"Come and have a drink with us this evening," Duggie said.

I could think of no excuse; in fact I felt confident and bold now, but the first person I saw at the house was Duggie wearing a jacket far too small for him. It was my jacket. She had left his suits at my office and taken mine to her own house.

Duggie laughed loudly. "Very fishy, I thought, when I saw this on my bed. Ha-ha! What's going on? It would be funnier still if you'd worn mine."

Sally said demurely she saw nothing funny in that. She had only been trying to help.

"Be careful when Sally tries to help." He was still laughing. The comedy was a bond. And we kept going back to it. Judy, her daughter, enjoyed this so much that she called out, "Why doesn't Mr. Ormerod take our flat?"

Our laughter stopped. Children recklessly bring up past incidents in their parents' lives. Duggie was about to pour wine into Sally's glass and he stopped, holding the bottle in the air. Sally gave that passing grimace of hers and Duggie shrank into instant protective concern and to me he seemed to beg us all for silence. But he recovered quickly and laughed again, noisily—too noisily, I thought.

"He has to live near the Nursery, don't you, Teddy? Colonel Thompson and all that."

"Of course," said Sally easily. "Duggie, don't pour the wine on the carpet, please."

It was a pleasant evening. We moved to the sitting-room and Sally sat on the sofa with the child, who gazed and gazed at me. Sally put her arm round her.

Three years have passed since that evening when Judy spoke out. When I look back, those years seem to be veiled or to sparkle with the mists of an October day. How can one describe happiness? In due time Duggie would leave and once more for months on end Sally and I would be free, and despite our bickerings and jealousies, our arguments about whether Duggie knew or did not know, we fell into a routine and made our rules. The stamp of passion was on us, yet there was always in my mind the picture of her sitting on the sofa with her daughter. I came to swear I would do nothing that would trouble her. And she and I seemed able to forget our bodies when we were all together. Perhaps that first comedy had saved us. My notion was that Duggie invented me, as he had invented her. I spend my time, she says, inventing Duggie. She invented neither of us.

Now I have changed my mind. After that evening when the child Judy said, "Why doesn't Mr. Ormerod take our flat?" I am convinced that Duggie *knew*—because of his care for Sally, even because he knew more than either of us about Sally and that tenant of theirs who was so horribly killed on his motorbike. When he turned us into fictions he perhaps thought the fiction would soon end. It did not. He became like a weary, indulgent, and distant emperor when he was home.

But those words of Judy's were another matter. For Duggie, Judy was not a fiction. She was his daughter, absolutely his, he made her. She was the contradiction of his failure. About her he would not pretend or compromise. I am now sure of this after one or two trivial events that occurred that year. One afternoon the day before he was due home—one of those enameled misleading October days, indeed—Sally was tidying the bedroom at my flat. I was in the sitting-room putting the drinks away and I happened to glance down at the Nursery. I saw a young woman there, with fair hair, just like Sally's, shading her eyes from the sun, and waving. For a moment I thought it was Sally who had secretly slipped away to avoid the sad awkwardness of those business-like partings of ours. Then I saw the woman was a young girl—Judy. I stepped back out of sight. I called Sally and she came with a broom in her hand.

"Don't go near the window like that"—she was not even wearing a bra—"look!"

"It's Judy! What is she up to? How long has she been there?" she said.

"She's watching us," I said. "She knows!"

Sally made that old grimace I now so rarely see.

"The little bitch," she said. "I left her at home with two of her school friends. She can't know I'm here."

"She must do," I said. "She's spying."

Sally said crisply. "Your paranoia is a rotten cover. Do you think I didn't know that girl's got a crush on you, my sweetheart? Try not to be such a cute old man."

"Me? Try?" I said jauntily.

And then, in the practical manner of one secure in the higher air of unruffled love, she said, "Anyway, she can't see my car from there. She can't see through walls. Don't stand there looking at her."

She went back to tidying the flat and my mind drifted into remembering a time when I was a boy throwing pebbles at the window of the girl next door. What a row there was with her mother!

I forgot Judy's waving arm. Duggie came home and I was not surprised to see him wandering about the Nursery two days later like a dog on one of his favorite rounds, circling round me from a distance, for I was busy with a customer, waiting for his chance. He had brought Judy with him. She was solemnly studying the girls, who with their order books and pencils were following undecided customers or directing the lost to our self-service counter inside the building. Judy was murmuring to herself as if imagining the words they said. She was admiring the way one of the girls ordered a youth to wheel a trolley-load of chrysanthemums to the main gate.

When I was free Duggie came quickly to me. "That counter works well," he said. He was congratulating himself, for the counter had been his idea, one item in his dreamy possession of the place. "It has cut down the labor costs. I've been counting. You've got rid of three girls, haven't you?"

"Four," I said. "My secretary left last week to get married."

Judy had stopped watching and came up with him. Yes, she had grown. The child whose face had looked as lumpish as a coffee mug, colorless too, had suddenly got a figure, and her face was rounded. Her eyes were moist with the new light of youth, mingling charmingly with an attempt at the look of important experience. She gazed at me until Duggie stopped talking, and then she said, "I saw you the day before yesterday"— to show she had started to become an old hand—"at your window. I waved to you."

"Did you?" I said.

"You weren't in your office," she said.

Cautiously I said, "I didn't see you."

"You were ironing your shirts."

A relief.

"Not me. I never iron my shirts," I said. "You must have seen the man who lives in the flat below. He's always ironing his shirts, poor fellow. He usually does it at night."

"On the third floor," the girl said.

"I live on the fourth, dear," I said.

"How awful of me," the girl said.

To save her face Duggie said, "I like to see women scrubbing clothes on stone—on a riverbank."

"That's not ironing, Daddy," she said.

There was the usual invitation to come to his house for a drink now that he was back. I did my cough and said I might drop in, though as he could see, we were in a rush. When I got to his house I found a chance to tell Sally. "Clever of her," I said. "It was a scheme to find out which floor I live on."

"It was not what you think," Sally said.

The evening was dull and Sally looked unwell and went to bed early. Duggie and I were left to ourselves and he listened to me in an absent-minded way when I told him again about my secretary leaving. He said grumpily, "You ought leave the girls alone and go in for older women," and went on to say that his sister-in-law was coming to stay, suggesting that married life also had its troubles. Suddenly he woke up, and as if opportunity had been revealed to him in a massive way he said, "Come and have dinner with me at my club tomorrow."

The invitation was half plea, half threat. *He* was being punished Why not myself also?

Duggie's club! Was this to be a showdown? The club was not a bolt-hole for Duggie. It was an imperial institution in his life and almost sacred. One had to understand that, although rarely mentioned, it was head-quarters, the only place in England where he was irrefutably himself and at home with his mysteries. He did not despise me for not having a club myself, but it did explain why I had something of the homeless dog about me. That clubs bored me suggested a moral weakness. I rose slightly in his esteem once when I told him that years ago my uncle used to take me to his club. (He used to give me a lot to drink and lecture me on my feck-less habits and even introduced me to one or two members—I suppose to put stamina in me.) These invitations came after my wife's death, so that clubs came to seem to me places where marriages were casketed and hid-den by the heavy curtains on the high windows.

There was something formidable in Duggie's invitation, and when I got to his club my impression was that he had put on weight or had received a quiet authority from being only among men, among husbands, in mufti. It was a place where the shabby armchairs seemed made of assumptions in leather and questions long ago disposed of. In this natu-ral home Duggie was no longer inventive or garrulous. Nods and grunts to the members showed that he was on his true ground.

We dined at a private table. Duggie sat with his back to an old bro-cade curtain in which I saw some vegetable design that perhaps had allayed or taken over the fantasies of the members.

A couple of drinks in the bar downstairs and a decanter of wine on the table eased Duggie, who said the old chef had had a stroke and that he thought the new chef had not got his hand in yet. The sweetbreads had been runny the last time; maybe it would be better to risk the beef.

Then he became confessional to put me at my ease: he always came here when his sister-in-law came to stay. A difficult woman—he always said to Sally, "Can't you put her off? You'll only get one of your migraines after she has been."

"I thought Sally didn't look too well," I said.

"She's having a worrying time with Judy," he said. "Young girls grow up. She's going through a phase."

"She is very lovely."

He ignored this. "Freedom, you know! Wants to leave school. Doesn't work. Messed up her exams."

"Sex, I suppose," I said.

"Why does everyone talk about sex?" said Duggie, looking stormy. "She wants to get away, get a flat of her own, get a job, earn her living sick of the old folks. But a flat of her own—at sixteen! I ask you."

"Girls have changed."

Duggie studied me and made a decision. I now understood why I had been asked.

"I wondered," said Duggie, "has she ever said anything to you—parents are the last to hear anything."

"To me?"

"Friend of the family—I just wondered."

"I hardly ever see her. Only when Sally or you bring her to the Nursery. I can't see the young confiding in me. Not a word."

Duggie was disappointed. He found it hard to lose one of his favorite fancies: that among all those girls at the Nursery I had sublimated the spent desires of my youth. He said, taking an injured pride in a fate, "That's it. I married into a family of gardeners."

And then he came out with it—the purpose of this dinner: "The girl's mad to get a job in your nursery. I thought she might have been sounding you out—I mean, waving to that fellow ironing his shirt."

"No. Nothing," I said.

"Mad idea. You're turning people away! I told her. By the way, I don't want to embarrass you. I'm not suggesting you should take her on. Girls get these ideas. Actually, we're going to take her away from that school and send her to school in Switzerland. Alps, skiing. Her French and German are a mess. Abroad! That is what she needs."

Abroad! The most responsive string in Duggie's nature had been struck. He meant what he said.

"That will be hard on Sally," I said. "She'd miss her terribly."

"We've got to do the best for the girl. She knows that," said Duggie. And without warning the old stare, but now it was the stare of the interrogator's lamp, turned on my face, and his manner changed from the brisk and business-like to the commandingly off-hand.

"Ironical," he said. "Now, if Sally had wanted a job at your nursery, that would be understandable. After all, you deal with all those Dutch and French, and so on. Her German's perfect. But poor Judy, she can't utter."

"Sally'" I laughed "She'd hate it."

Duggie filled my glass rod then his own very slowly, but as he raised the decanter he kept his eye on me: quite a small feat, indeed like a minor conjuring trick, for a man who more than once had knocked a glass over at home and made Sally rush to the kitchen for a cloth.

"You're quite wrong," he said "I happen to know."

Know what? "You mean *she's* mentioned it," I said.

"No, no, of course not." he said "But if you said the word, I'm certain of it. Not last year, perhaps. But if Judy goes to Switzerland, she'll be alone. She'd jump at it."

Now the wine began to work on him—and on me, too—and Duggie s conversation lost its crisp manner. He moved on to one of his trailing geographical trances: we moved through time and space. The cub became subtropical, giant ferns burst out of the club curtains, liana hung from the white pillars of the dining-room, the other members seemed to be in native dress, and threading through it all was the figure of Sally, notebook in hand. She followed us downstairs to the bar, which became a greenhouse, as we drank our port. No longer wretched because her daughter had gone, no longer fretting about the disastrous mess she had made of her life when she was young, without a mother's experience to guide her. I heard Duggie say, "I know they're moving me to Brussels in a few months and of course I'll be over every weekend—but a woman wants her own life. Frankly," he said with awe in his voice, "we *bore* them."

The club resumed its usual appearance, though with an air of exhaustion. The leather chairs yawned. The carpets died. A lost member rose from the grave and stopped by Duggie and said, "We need a fourth at bridge."

"Sorry, old boy," said Duggie.

The man went off to die elsewhere.

"And no danger," said Duggie, "of her leaving to get married."

And now, drunkish as we were, we brought our momentous peace conference to an end. The interrogator's lamp was switched on again just before we got to our feet and he seemed to be boring his way into my head and to say, "You've taken my wife, but you're bloody well not going to get my daughter into your pokey little fourth-floor flat ironing your shirts."

I saw the passion in his mottled face and the powerful gleam of his honorable head.

After Sally had put up a fight and I had said that sending Judy away was his revenge, Sally came to work for me. Duggie had married us and I became as nervous and obsequious as a groom. There was the awkwardness of a honeymoon. She dressed differently. She became sedate— no strokings and squeezes of love were allowed: she frowned and twisted away like a woman who had been a secretary all her life. She looked as young and cross as a virgin. She went back to her straight-back hair style; I was back in the period when I was disturbed by the soft hair of her eyebrows. Her voice was all telephone calls, invoices, orders, and snapping at things I had forgotten to do. She walked in a stately way to the filing cabinet. Only to that object did she bend: she said what a mess her predecessor or I had left it in. If she went downstairs to the yard when the lorries arrived, she had papers in her hand. The drivers were cocky at first and then were scared of her. And in time she destroyed our legend—the only unpopular thing she did—the legend of Colonel Thompson. Dog or no dog, he had never come over the wall. The thief, she discovered, had been one of our gardeners. So Colonel Thompson retired to our private life.

Before this, our life had been one of beginnings, sudden partings, unexpected renewals. Now it hummed plainly along from day to day. The roles of Duggie and myself were reversed: when Duggie came home once a week now from Brussels, it was he who seemed to be the lover and I the husband. Sally grew very sharp with both of us and Duggie and I stood apart, on our dignity.

I have done one thing for him. I took my mother to dine with him, as I have said.

"What a saintly man," she said as we drove away. "Just like your father. He's coming to see me next time they're at their cottage."

About the Contributors

J. G. Ballard (1930 -   ) has been increasingly acclaimed as one of contemporary literature's most significant voices. His novels include *Crash* (1973), *Empire of the Sun* (1984), *The Kindness of Women* (1991) and *Millennium People* (2003). "The Garden of Time" is an early tale, first published in 1962, that Anthony Burgess called "one of the most beautiful stories of the world canon of short fiction."

Sandra Cisneros (1954 -   ) is an award-winning poet, short story writer and novelist whose works include *Caramelo* (2002), *Woman Hollering Creek and Other Stories* (1992), *My Wicked   Ways* (1992) and a children's   book, *Hairs/Pelitos* (1997). *The House on Mango Street* (1984), from which the following story is taken, presents a series of vignettes about a little girl, Esperanza—her name means "hope"—Cordero, who moves with her family into a house in a decaying section of Chicago. The "monkey garden" she remembers here and so vividly describes, in fact, once housed a real monkey amid its formerly lush, once carefully tended foliage.

Colette (1873-1954) was the pen name of the prolific French writer Sidonie Gabrielle Colette. Her most famous works include the four autobiographical *Claudine* novels (1901-1903), *La Vagabonde* (1910), *Gigi* (1945), *Chérie* (1920), and *My Mother's House* (1922). "Grape Harvest," in its sensuous evocation of the natural world, is typically Colette-like. But it is equally a celebration of artifice, and the sly mingling of the two is what makes it uniquely hers.

John Collier (1901-1980) was a Londoner who moved to Hollywood in 1935 to write screenplays, enjoying a long career there; among the films he worked on are *Elephant Boy* (1937), *The African Queen* (1951), *I Am a Camera* (1955) and *The War Lord* (1965). However, he was also a poet (*Gemini*, 1931) and a novelist (*His Monkey Wife*, 1930; *Defy the Foul Fiend*, 1934) as well as a prolific short story writer specializing in the archly fantastical and the ingeniously macabre. "Green Thoughts," his first published story, takes us to Torquay on the English Channel and behind the scenes in a suddenly sinister suburban greenhouse.

Jane Gardam (1928 -   ) is equally well known in the realms of adult and children's fiction. She published her first book, *A Few Fair Days*, a collection of rural stories for children, in 1971. Among her novels for adults are *Crusoe's*

Daughter (1985), *Faith Fox* (1996), and *The Flight of the Maidens* (2000), while her juvenile titles include the Whitbread Award-winning *The Hollow Land* (1981). "Blue Poppies," from her 1994 collection *Going Into a Dark House*, takes us along for a momentous garden visit to a not-quite stately home.

Robert Graves (1895-1985) was an English poet, novelist and critic whose best-known works today are the historical novels *I, Claudius* and *Claudius the God* (both 1934). Other significant books he wrote over the course of a long career include the memoir *Good-bye to All That* (1929) and the speculative study, *The White Goddess* (1948). In "Earth to Earth," which appeared originally in *The New Statesman*, he considers the question of compost.

David Guterson (1956 -) is best known as the author of *Snow Falling on Cedars*, for which he received the 1995 PEN-Faulkner Award. His other books include the novels *East of the Mountains* (1999) and *Our Lady of the Forest* (2003), and the collection *The Country Ahead of Us, the Country Behind* (1989) in which the preceding tale of a young man and a garden that will forever haunt him first appeared.

William Wymark Jacobs (1863-1943) was an English novelist and short story writer whose legacy is one of the most famous tales of all time, "The Monkey's Paw" (from *The Lady of the Barge*, 1902). His work mainly featured traditional sailors and old-fashioned seafaring adventures; *More Cargoes* (1899), *Castaways* (1916), *Light Freight* (1901), *Cruises and Cargoes* (1934) and *Snug Harbor* (1944) are just a few of his many titles. The story included here, however, is entirely landlocked.

Garrison Keillor (1942 -) created the live radio variety show, "A Prairie Home Companion," in 1974 in St. Paul, Minnesota, and today its audience comprises more than two million listeners. His books include *Lake Wobegon Days* (1985), *The Book of Guys* (1993), *A Prairie Home Home Companion Commonplace Book* (1999), and *Love Me*, 2003. Here, in this tale of a small-town backyard, Keillor looks behind the ordinary, as he regularly does, to reveal the complicated simplicity that is the essence of our lives.

Stephen King (1947 -) is one of contemporary literature's best known—and best-selling—writers. His name has become synonymous with jump-out-of-your-skin horror fiction, and yet his many novels—*Carrie* (1974), *The Shining* (1977), *The Stand* (1978), *Bag of Bones* (1988), *Dolores Claiborne* (1992), *From a Buick 8* (2002), among them—are as much about human relationships, love and redemption, and the unrelenting pressures of modern life as they are about shape-shifting bogeymen. He's also very funny, as can be seen here in the plight of Harold Parkette, who has the misfortune of needing his grass cut.

Doris Lessing (1919 -) is a much-celebrated English writer whose work resists easy categorization. She has produced classics of the colonial experience (*The Grass is Singing*, 1950), of political commitment (the Martha Quest books, 1952-69), feminist fiction (*The Golden Notebook*, 1962), of family dysfunction (*The Fifth Child*,

1988), and of allegorical science fiction (the "Canopus in Argus: Archives" series, 1979-83), with many others, besides. The first installment of her autobiography, *Under My Skin*, was published in 1994, and the second, *Walking in the Shade*, in 1997. A collections of four short novels, *The Grandmothers*, appeared in 2003. In "Flavors of Exile," the ripening of an exotic fruit, growing against all odds in hostile soil, takes on talismanic significance.

Hector Hugh Munro (1870-1916)—or as book lovers know him, the incomparable Saki—was a writer of fictional bonbons, stories that one reads addictedly, savoring their delicious drolleries. Born in Burma to a colonial civil servant, he himself joined the Burmese police as a young man and then switched careers to become a journalist. He was killed in action during World War I, after volunteering for active service at the age of forty-four. But he left behind such classic tales as "The Open Window," "Tobermory," and "Sredni Vashtar," along with the preceding wicked portrait of that person of decidedly dubious character: the gardener-who's-willing-to-take-short-cuts.

Edna O'Brien (1932 -) born in Ireland, moved to London six decades ago, and yet in her work she has returned to her native terrain again and again. Her earliest success came with "The Country Girls Trilogy" (1960-64), of which the middle volume (*The Lonely Girl*, 1962) was adapted into that classic of '60s British cinema, *The Girl with Green Eyes*. Among her recent books are *Lantern Slides* (1990), a collection of stories, the novels *Down by the River* (1997) and *In the Forest* (2002), and a biographical study, *James Joyce* (1999). "Christmas Roses," taken from *A Rose in the Heart* (1979), introduces us to Miss Hawkins, a retired cabaret dancer of a certain age whose spinsterish world revolves safely around the garden she tends.

Rosamunde Pilcher (1924 -) published her first novel in 1949, but it was not until 1987, with *The Shell Seekers*, that she became an internationally known—and beloved—writer. Here, in a story taken from her collection *Flowers in the Rain* (1991), she uses a garden to remind us that there's the possibility for surprise in every relationship.

Sir Victor Sawdon Pritchett (1900-1997), a novelist, short story writer, critic and biographer, was one of the twentieth century's most distinguished men of letters. Among his fiction works are *Marching Spain (1928), Mr. Beluncle (1951), The Camberwell Beauty* (1974), and *A Careless Widow and Other Stories* (1989), while his non-fiction includes *Balzac* (1973); *The Gentle Barbarian* (1977), a life of Turgenev; and two memoirs, *A Cab at the Door* (1968) and *Midnight Oil* (1971). In "The Fig Tree," he has given us a carefully paced, immensely entertaining story of a clandestine affair played out against the backdrop of a thriving London nursery.

English novelist **Barbara Pym**—the pen name of Barbara Mary Pym Crampton (1913-1980)—had a career in two parts. After publishing her first book, *Some Tame Gazelle*, in 1950, she went on to bring out subsequent novels such as

Excellent Women (1952) and *A Glass of Blessings* (1958) to the admiration of a readership ready to appreciate her gently sly send-ups of ordinary English eccentrics. But as the staid postwar 1950s gave way to the volatile 1960s, Pym's work suddenly seeemed out of step with the times. Reinstated by the acclaim of her peers—in a 1977 *Times Literary Supplement* list in which undervalued writers were named by fellow authors, she was cited twice—she published *Quartet in Autumn* in 1978 and *A Few Green Leaves* the year of her death. Though never really a writer of short stories, she did leave behind a few, including the preceding piece, which, like much of Pym's work, presents an orderly world where everyone knows his place—or should—and where floral arrangements are not taken lightly.

When **Anne Rosner**'s "Prize Tomatoes" was accepted by the literary journal *Tri-Quarterly* and published in its Fall 1981 issue, it marked her first appearance in print and gained for her the honor of being included in *Best American Short Stories 1982*. In life, there are many gulfs that need to be bridged, Rosner reminds us, and, sometimes common ground is exactly that, with blue-ribbon vegetables just one aspect of a garden's ability to bestow grace.

Victoria Rothschild (1953 -   ), an associate fellow of medieval literature at London University, has published both poetry and short stories, and is currently researching the life of George Anne Bellamy, an eighteenth-century woman of the theater. In "The Secret Garden," she has given us a cautionary tale of a little man's unexpectedly large influence.

Jane Smiley (1949 -   ) won the Pulitzer Prize in 1992 for *A Thousand Acres*. Her other books include the novels *The Greenlanders* (1988), *Moo* (1995), *The All-True Travels and Adventures of Lidie Newton* (1998), *Horse Heaven* (2000) and *Good Faith* (2003). "August" is taken from *Ordinary Love & Good Will: Two Novellas* (1989): here Bob, *Good Will*'s narrator, while being interviewed for a book on innovative gardening, can't help but reveal his smug pride in the perfectly self-sufficient homestead he's created for his family.

The work of **Lisa St. Aubin de Terán** (1953 -   ) often follows the paths of young women who themselves are following their hearts into exotic landscapes. Among her novels are *Keepers of the House* (1982), *The Long Way Home* (1983), *The Slow Train to Milan* (1984), *The Tiger* (1986) and *The Palace* (2000). She also edited *The Virago Book of Wanderlust and Dreams* (2000) and *Elements of Italy* (2002). In "The Lady Gardener," nothing is what it seems, and certainly not Gladys, the unsentimental gardener as devoted to efficient pest control as she is to her comatose daughter who has lain, unwaking and inanimate, in a London nursing home for half of her short life.

One seizes any opportunity to publish a story by **James Thurber** (1894-1961).With his sophisticated whimsy and neat sense of life's many close calls, he occupies a special niche in the crowded arena of homegrown American humor, and, as an early and longtime contributor to *The New Yorker*, he greatly influenced that magazine's characteristic voice. Among his works are *Is Sex Necessary?* (1929, written with E. B. White), *The Thurber Carnival* (1945), and *Alarms and Diversions* (1957), as well as the classic children's stories, *Many Moons* (1943) and *The Thirteen Clocks* (1950). "See No Weevil" is vintage Thurber, deftly capturing the tone of the exasperated marital spat but in the context of a pedantic disagreement about horticultural nomenclature.

Sylvia Townsend Warner (1893-1978) was an English poet and novelist whose books include *Lolly Willowes* (1926), *Mr. Fortune's Maggot*, *The Corner That Held Them* (1948) and *Kingdoms of Elfin* (1977). In this story, taken from an early collection, *More Joy in Heaven* (1935), she convincingly compresses into just a few pages (and a small bouquet) the idea that even flowers shed their innocence when snobberies cloud the air.

Rose Tremain (1943 -   ) was chosen one of the twenty "Best Young British Novelists" by the literary magazine *Granta* in 1983. Her award-winning books include *The Swimming Pool Season* (1985), *Restoration* (1989), *Music and Silence* (1999), and, most recently, *The Color* (2003). Here, in the title story from a collection of the same name (*The Garden of the Villa Mollini and Other Stories*, 1987), she makes the possibilities of landscape into an embodiment of human caprice and its resultant disharmony.

As one of 20th-century America's most admired writers, **Eudora Welty** (1909-2001) was also one of the most grounded in her native soil, spending virtually the entire of her life in Jackson, Mississippi, the southern state capital where she'd been born. Publishing her first book, the short story collection *A Curtain of Green*, in 1941, she won the 1973 Pulitzer Prize for her novel *The Optimist's Daughter*. But she is equally known for, among other works, *Delta Wedding* (1946), *The Ponder Heart* (1954), and the autobiographical memoir, *One Writer's Beginnings* (1984). In the story "A Curtain of Green," we meet Mrs. Larkin, a self-anesthetized figure of tragedy, and watch, spellbound, as she regains her sense of life in the very place she has obsessively buried it .

Acknowledgments

Careful effort has been made to trace the copyright holders of all stories included in this collection. Therefore, if any error or omission has occurred, it is inadvertent and will be corrected in subsequent editions after written notification has been made to the editor c/o The Overlook Press, 141 Wooster Street, New York, New York 10012.

"The Garden of Time" by J.G. Ballard. Copyright © 1962, 1990 by J.G. Ballard. From the collection *The Voices of Time* by J.G. Ballard. Reprinted by permission of the author and The Robin Straus Agency, Inc., acting in conjunction with Margaret Hanbury, London.

"The Monkey Garden" by Sandra Cisneros. From *The House on Mango Street* by Sandra Cisneros. Copyright © 1984 by Sandra Cisneros. Published by Vintage Books, a division of Random House, Inc., New York, and in hardcover by Alfred A. Knopf in 1994. Reprinted by permission of Susan Bergholz Literary Services, New York. All rights reserved. Additionally: reproduction by kind permission of Bloomsbury Publishing PLC.

"Grape Harvest" by Colette. From *The Collected Stories of Colette*, edited by Robert Phelps, and translated by Matthew Ward. Translation copyright © by Farrar, Straus & Giroux, Inc. Reprinted by permission of Farrar, Straus and Giroux, LLC.

"Green Thoughts" by John Collier. Copyright © 1931, 1938, 1939, 1940, 1941 by John Collier; copyright © renewed by John Collier. Reprinted by permission of the agent.

"Blue Poppies" by Jane Gardam. Taken from *Going Into a Dark House* by Jane Gardam, published by Sinclair Stevenson, 1994. Reprinted by permission of the agent.

"Earth to Earth" by Robert Graves. Copyright © Robert Graves. Reprinted by arrangement with Carcanet Press Limited.

"The Flower Garden" by David Guterson. Copyright © 1989 David Guterson, from *The Country Ahead of Us, The Country Behind* by David Guterson. Reprinted with permission from Georges Borchardt, Inc., for the author. Additionally: reproduction by kind permission of Bloomsbury Publishing, PLC.

"The Garden Plot" by W.W. Jacobs. From Light Freights by W.W. Jacobs, 1901. Reprinted by agreement with the Society of Authors, as the Literary Representative of the estate of W.W. Jacobs.

"How the Crab Apple Grew" by Garrison Keillor. From *Leaving Home* by Garrison Keillor. Copyright © 1987 Garrison Keillor. Used by permission of Viking Penguin, a division of Penguin Group (USA) Inc., and, additionally, by permission of the author.

"The Lawnmower Man" by Stephen King. Reprinted with permission. Copyright © 1976, 1977, 1978 by Stephen King. All other rights expressly reserved.

"Flavors of Exile" by Doris Lessing. From *The Sun Between Their Feet* by Doris Lessing. Copyright © 1957 Doris Lessing. Reprinted by kind permission of Jonathan Clowes Ltd., London, on behalf of Doris Lessing.

"Christmas Roses" by Edna O'Brien. From *A Rose in the Heart* by Edna O'Brien, 1979. Copyright© Edna O'Brien. Reprinted by permission of the author and by arrangement with David Godwin Associates.

"The Tree" by Rosamunde Pilcher. Copyright © 1985 Rosamunde Pilcher. From *The Blue Bedroom and Other Stories* by Rosamunde Pilcher. Reprinted by permission of St. Martin's Press, LLC.

"The Fig Tree" by V.S. Pritchett. From *Collected Stories* by V.S. Pritchett. Copyright © 1947, 1949, 1953, 1956, 1959, 1960, 1961, 1962, 1966, 1967, 1969, 1973, 1974, 1979, 1982 by V.S. Pritchett. Used by permission of Random House, Inc. Additionally: from *Collected Stories* by V.S. Pritchett, published by Chatto & Windus and used by permission of The Random House Group Limited.

"So Some Tempestuous Morn" by Barbara Pym. From *Civil to Strangers* Copyright © 1987 Hilary Walton. Reprinted by arrangement with Hilary Walton.

"August" by Jane Smiley. From *Ordinary Love and Good Will* by Jane Smiley. Copyright © Jane Smiley. Used by permission of Alfred A. Knopf, a division of Random House, Inc., and by additional arrangement with The Aaron Priest Agency.

"The Secret Garden" by Victoria Rothschild. Copyright © 2004 Victoria Rothschild. Published by arrangement with the author.

"The Lady Gardener" by Lisa St. Aubin de Terán. From *The Marble Mountain and Other Stories* by Lisa St. Aubin de Terán. Copyright © 1989 Lisa St. Aubin de Terán. Reprinted by arrangement with Ed Victor Ltd Literary Agency, London.

"See No Weevil" by James Thurber. From *Thurber Country* by James Thurber. Copyright © 1953 James Thurber. Reprinted by arrangement with Rosemary A.Thurber and The Barbara Hogenson Agency, Inc. All rights reserved.

"The Nosegay" by Sylvia Townsend Warner. From *Collected Stories by Sylvia Townsend Warner*, published by Chatto & Windus. Used by permission of The Random House Group Limited.

"The Garden of the Villa Mollini" by Rose Tremain. From *The Garden of the Villa Mollini and Other Stories* by Rose Tremain, published by Chatto & Windus and also by Vintage Books. Copyright © 1987 Rose Tremain. Reprinted by arrangement with Sheil Land Associates Ltd.

"A Curtain of Green" by Eudora Welty. Copyright © 1941 Eudora Welty, renewed in 1969 by Eudora Welty. Reprinted by the permission of Russell & Volkening as agents for the author.